SIGNAL PEAK

DAVID EDWARD WALKER

THOUGHTFUL PUBLISHING COMPANY
SEATTLE

DISCLAIMER: This is a work of fiction.
All of the characters, organizations, and events portrayed in
this novel are products of the author's imagination except
geographical place names, historical events, and public
figures. Any similarity to persons living or dead
is unintentional and coincidental.

www.tessasdance.com
davidwalker@anisahoni.com

Cover Design:
Seth Walker Design
www.sethwalkerdesign.com
seth@setherama.com

GRATITUDE

For Sue, Ben & Seth
ínk átawi mash

In memory of Long Standing Bear Chief (Piikani)
ni kso ko wah

My deep thanks to Levina Wilkins (Yakama), M.Ed.,
Program Manager and Cultural Specialist,
Yakama Nation Language Program, and
Marilyn Goudy (Yakama), M. Ed.,
Special Education Teacher,
Stanley Smartlowit Education Center,
Yakama Nation Tribal School,
for their friendship and counsel over the years.

Certain ceremonies have been purposely obscured or
creatively altered to preserve their cultural integrity.
I apologize for any additional inaccuracies.
This story is a like a song that was given to me
that I wish I could sing more clearly.

ONE

This is the center. I live here.
The red spot is my heart; everybody can see it.
The yellow grass grows everywhere around this place.
The green mountains are far away
All around the world.
There is only water beyond—salt water.
The blue is the sky and the star is the North Star.
That star never changes; it is always in the same place.
I keep my heart on that star—I never change.
–Smohalla, Waashat prophet,
explaining his flag to Major J.W. MacMurray, 1884

Alice Neir leaned on both hands and eyed me suspiciously as I eased a mandarin orange Jarrito across her scarfed-up store counter. Little sequins tipped horn-rimmed glasses much like those of my high school biology teacher, a woman who could make two tardy young women cry simultaneously. Alice's brittle salt and pepper hair was gathered into what I believe is called a bouffant. Her missing teeth showed when she opened her mouth, so she wasn't much on smiling.

"Thought I saw a sex offender come out your place t'other day from the post office mailer," she declared.

Alice chaired the Stand Down local action committee battling what she considered a local Indian uprising. I was a known sympathizer with the Yakama Nation's attempt to tax alcohol sales on tribal land, and beer sales paid her bills. The

Neirs were one of the families referred to as 'Old Settlers,' white families who don't really believe their ancestors discovered the Valley before the Yakama people, but might feel they have as much claim to the reservation land. For Alice, I fit a suspect profile.

I had no other choices when I craved a soda—and her general store was right across the street. Besides, Alice was my landlord.

"I can't really say much about who comes to my business, Alice. Sorry but that's how it is."

Her thick-set, unshaven husband, Warren, sat on a wooden stool, leaned back on the two rear legs, and rested his close-cropped head against a chew tobacco display with thick hands folded across his beer belly. The tattoo on his left arm read "Lost Soul." He sipped Mountain Dew, and his grey eyes met mine with a laugh when he spoke to her.

"Stop nosin' 'round, Alice," he mumbled. "You're embarrassin' yourself.'"

Dog, Bounty Hunter barked from a tiny TV on the side counter. Alice frowned and handed me my change.

"Well, folks ought to be on their knees to their Lord instead of cryin' crocodile tears to some counselor."

"Aw, hush," Warren muttered, concentrating on the screen.

She glared at me malevolently as though I'd said it.

I looked at the ashtray by the register with the misspelled handwritten note, 'Need a penney, take a penney,' and dropped in my dime and two pennies. She scowled more deeply, and Warren chuckled at something *Dog* said.

I stepped out front, screwed off the bottle cap, and savored orange that was more than real. Wind hooked tumbleweed into a wound-up clothes hanger barely holding the muffler to a blue 1989 Gran Fury parked across the street. Wind is always trying to take apart my possessions around here. It had pummeled so much dust against the car exterior over the years that factory primer bled through the surface like a rusty rash.

Harrah, Washington, a town of three hundred souls, had but one recreation spot, Pioneer Park, which happened to be adjacent to my new private office, and I stood watching more activity than usual for a Monday. There must have been a half-day at school; kids were choosing up sides for a pick-up game. A Filipino guy grilled burgers and hot dogs under a blue pavilion tent, but no one was with him. Maybe he was going to eat them by himself. Some local guy was mowing the park. Trimmings and fine dust flew all around me, and I sneezed. The grass was burned brown and dry, and the constant wind aerated dirt from between the blades, pulling topsoil loose.

Thunderheads broke apart overhead; sunlight baked amber foothills. Clouds pregnant with promise got your hopes up, but then came apart and drifted lazily onward toward the Cascades.

I lowered my gaze to catch Emily Miyanashatawit pondering me, standing beside Elisi's immaculate Pontiac Sunfire. I still thought of her as too young to drive, but she was nearly eighteen. I wondered how long she'd been watching.

"How you?" I asked, crossing the street.

"All right," she said, watching a small girl shoot hoops with acrobatic ease. The Rezhogs' rap, "Yakama," distorted out of a ghetto blaster set at the corner of the court.

"She's pretty good," I observed.

"She's a Heslah. She's got a few skills."

"How's Ámashitum?"

"Okay, I guess," she shrugged and watched the play some more.

She was more restrained than Tessa, yet less so in appearance. She wore a tiny rhinestone stud in her right nostril, something her older sister would never do. Thick, black, razor-straight hair grew to traditional length well below her waist, but was mixed with crimson highlights. She kept it held back from her eyes with a sterling barrette.

Ámashitum was Tessa's horse, the spirited animal who saved both our lives five years earlier. Emily likely spent more time riding her these days.

"Don't go overboard now; I don't need too much detail," I teased. She had on worn jeans and packer boots. "Looks like you're ready to ride right now."

"I just come from there, doctor. Tess gives Frank Mathis what she can to buy oats and alfalfa. I bring him a homemade huckleberry pie or whatever now and then for shoveling her stall. But she'll jump fence without more attention. Uncle Edward says he'd take her, but they're all the way to Granger."

I sipped my soda and nodded, meeting the pace of her interaction. She shifted back to watching the court for a few moments.

Tessa was sixteen years old when she gave birth to her daughter, Chase, by deceased boyfriend, Parker Heslah. While she was still pregnant, Emily helped her nurse the skittish Ámashitum, who'd originally been gifted to Tessa by her grandfather Arnold. Prior to the mare's bullet wound, all of us had helped gentle Ámashitum into accepting a rider under the tutelage of her horsechaser uncles, Leon and Edward Kusitway. Emily spent more time than Tessa tending the infected bullet graze across her withers, and for a while, only Emily could ride her. The near-mystical connection between Tessa and Ámashitum now extended to Emily.

Ámashitum would stretch her gait with Tessa's younger sister snuggled low and close to her neck, gripping her mane tightly, legs molded to her girth. Even Elisi would worry and shout, "You're going to break your neck!"

I still had memories from over five years earlier of being flopped over Ámashitum's back bleeding and moaning with Tessa struggling to keep me from falling off, and 'Cowboy' Jack Brie and her uncle and cousin—Tiller and James—chasing us overland in a pickup truck. They'd been intent upon murdering us in the basement of the old Mission Boarding School and nearly succeeded.

Everyone involved, including my wife, Ruthie, and me, still kept tabs on the players. Tiller recently transferred to Monroe Prison and James stayed housed at Coyote Ridge, both convicted of attempted murder, kidnapping, and gun-running. They wouldn't be outside locked gates for a long time.

Elisi said Charlie Whitcomb hoped to make amends with me after his release about two years after the crisis. He'd been released from prison early for good behavior after a stint for aiding and abetting. Whitcomb, the tribal cop Jack Brie corrupted, had pulled a gun and handcuffed me to a drainpipe in the Mission School basement. These days, he had a job as an assistant bondsman not too far from where we lived in the city of Yakima. I didn't want him anywhere near me, but Elisi reminded me he'd shot a rifle right out of Jack Brie's hands just as he was about kill both Tessa and me.

When Whitcomb stopped by our house unannounced one day, Ruthie got nervous, and I stayed pretty unfriendly. He literally held his hat in his hand standing out on the front porch apologizing, his long, neat braid now cropped off. I knew it was a big thing in the Indian way for him to own his shame in front of me. But the image of him handing me over to Brie still stuck. Frankly, I thought he should still be in jail.

Emily's black eyes moved from the pickup game to the jack pines hedging the park. She stroked her hair absently, and glanced back at Elisi's car. She tended to be shy.

"How are things at Leila's?" I asked, trying to fill the lull.

"Fine," she answered, "crowded."

"Uh, do you want to come inside for some coffee or

tea? I don't have a client for another hour. I've got a little spot in the kitchen. . ."

"No thanks, doctor."

The sun broke through, and she cupped her hand along her forehead, watching me for a while more.

"I was hoping you'd talk with Franklin," she finally declared.

"How come?"

"He's not taking his Ritalin."

"I'm not big on making kids take their meds."

"That's not what I mean. I believe he's stashing the pills. I think he pretends to take them. I'm afraid he's pounding and snorting them like Tessa used to do. I don't want to talk to Leila 'bout it until I know more."

"Why not talk to him yourself?"

"He won't sit down with me. He's all running with little gangbangers on Larena Lane ever since . . . I thought maybe you'd talk to him."

"Does he have extra money?"

I'd asked a stupid question.

"Nobody in my family has money, doctor. A couple of those boys he's in with huff gas for sure."

She kicked pea gravel with her foot. A huge combine paced slowly down Harrah Road, followed by several pickups and SUVs longing to pass. It's harder when what's in front of you takes up half the passing lane. The roar drowned out any further conversation for several minutes.

"Emily," I told her, "it doesn't usually work out well for me to chase a kid down because somebody in his family wants me to visit with him. See if you or auntie Leila can talk him into coming into my office to meet, and I might be able to find out more. Who prescribes the Ritalin?"

"Leo Aspen probably, I don't know." Her face brightened slightly. "Oh, yeah—one of your old Indian Health clinic pals."

"I'm not associated with Yakama Indian Health Clinic anymore. Or Leo Aspen."

"You can still look at medical records there," she asserted.

"Not without a good reason. And Dr. Gaillard doesn't like it when I stop by even if I do have a reason."

"Doctor, we've got to know what Franklin's up to with those pills. I keep thinking he's got something going with refills where he has some extra bottle he's filling on the side. He's being all slick ever since. . ."

She pursed her lips, and shook her head slightly.

"I understand," I covered her grief. "But, Emily, last I heard, Leila has legal custody of Franklin and you too until you're of age. She could just ask to look at his record over there."

"Maybe, but I don't want to bring up this pill thing with her unless I know for sure what he's doing. Franklin's all moody and Leila's got so much on her plate now, and it might get her all stressed out. And Tessa don't live with us now, so she don't see what I'm seeing. I'm his big sister, too. Let Dr. Gaillard sort out his ugly feelings about you with his Creator. So what if you cancelled his ticket."

"What's that supposed to mean?"

"Mocassin telegraph," she answered blankly. "He got passed over for promotion to Portland Regional Indian Health some months back and word is it had something to do with you and what you went through."

After having a bullet removed from my left buttock and a rhinoplasty for the broken nose I got from Tiller while held hostage five years back, I was full of piss and vinegar to sue the Indian Health Service. My mind had become flooded with involuntary images of being chased and wounded, and of Jack Brie just missing shooting Tessa with the same pistol I'd bought to protect myself, a Taurus 85. Brie was never found after careening off into the darkened foothills, suffusing blood from wounds opened by Tessa's assault with Parker's fold-out Navaja knife and Arnold's miracle shot from an old Marlin rifle.

Arnold, a skilled hunter, tried to track Brie despite Tessa's vehement protests but never located him. I still held worries that Jack Brie was alive and would find his way back somehow to kill me and Ruthie as he promised after I inadvertently stumbled into his gun-running business out in White Swan looking for Tessa after Parker died.

"Dead and eaten by coyotes," Arnold would reassure me, responding to my thousand-mile-stare when my good friend Trick and I met him at sweatlodge. He knew exactly who was on my mind.

Trick joked with me about "going for a chat to that lady therapist up there in town." He acted like he was teasing, but I knew Ruthie had talked to him.

I finally gave in, and set up time with the woman. She lost her professional cool after I told her that her eye-movement wand-waving technique to 'heal' my traumatic memories seemed like "neo-shamanist ritual á la Carlos Castenada." Her motions had no effect on me whatsoever but made me laugh. She then got very flustered and irritated yet remained willing to verify in writing that I appeared emotionally-disturbed.

I hoped her letter might be enough to mount a tort claim through Francis Munoz, JD, a local attorney who came highly recommended. I felt I'd been psychologically traumatized in the course of performing my duties and a tort claim is the only way to sue the United States government. However, while such an action might net a monetary award, it doesn't hold anybody responsible. You can't sue the federal government and hold anybody responsible. Obtaining redress from the Indian Health Service, Frank explained, was not so different from getting help anywhere else in the federal system. Somebody in authority had to state that either nothing happened to me or nothing that happened could have possibly been traumatic, and then declare that I didn't deserve any assistance in either case. Frank said we needed all that in writing.

He encouraged me to submit a formal request to the national IHS personnel office in Rockford, Maryland for worker's compensation, where they'd certainly never heard of me or my situation. Once they said 'no,' he'd use their response with the therapist's letter attesting to my craziness to try a tort claim. I drove back and forth across Snoqualmie Pass in a single day during the worst blizzard in the Cascade Mountains in fifteen years for Frank's $500 dollar invoice and one hour of advice.

Six weeks after being beaten, shot, chased, and nearly murdered in the course of my various duties as a psychologist, I used a government form to write a formal request for worker's compensation just as Frank specified. I attached a six-page-long, single-spaced description, and named names, including that of medical director, Dr. Bill Gaillard. I also mentioned the slander and bureaucratic interference I'd endured from fledgling IHS psychiatric nurse, Dominia Garcia, and her patronizing mentor, Leo Aspen, in my efforts to work as a therapist for Tessa.

I described how Dr. Gaillard did nothing to stop either of these people from trying to pump Tessa full of medication or from having her involuntarily hospitalized and 'chemically-restrained' in a psychiatric unit under the supervision of Dominia's cousin, biopsychiatrist Dr. Margaret Fitzsimmons. I did say how Dr. Gaillard tried to help me oppose efforts to stop me from burning sage for native clients. He wasn't all bad, I was trying to say—I tried to paint his behavior during events in a balanced way.

After I finished, I second-guessed Frank's entire idea for a good thirty seconds before I pressed 'send.'

Forty minutes later, Bill Gaillard knocked on my office

door, and with a contemptuous expression wordlessly handed me a memo warm off his printer:

"I am directing you to refrain from circulation within or outside the Clinic documents you've written unless I assign you to do so. You must discuss with me first any written documents you may wish to circulate amongst the staff at this Clinic or outside the Clinic. You must adhere to this directive: Violation will lead to immediate disciplinary action."

I was put on the shit list. That's an Indian Health Service manager's default approach to threats: If a soldier 'leaves the fort to join the natives', that is—bears witness to the inadequacy and corruption already totally obvious to the people IHS serves—he or she should be shot down like a feral dog.

I never received any response except Gaillard's initial memo. After that, he arranged sit-down meetings every Friday between himself, Elmira Squibb, the new personnel lady, and me, to review all my clinical notes, emails, and reports. He had no clue about anything related to the practice of psychology, but that didn't stop him from 'managing' my duties in the months following all I'd already been through. Elmira took copious notes as to alleged laxities in my administrative procedures Gaillard dreamed up, and wrote nothing down when I clarified or tried to point out reasons why I did things the way I did.

Across several months, they collected their jaded but detailed catalog of my procedural failures and violations of policy. I was eventually placed on a 'performance plan'—a bureaucratic device for identifying me as a screw-up. In this way, the silver bullet was molded. If I ever pressed a tort claim or attempted to expose the tender underbelly of IHS mismanagement, I would easily be branded a dysfunctional employee. Elmira Squibb and Bill Gaillard made certain I'd never receive another promotion or increase in pay while working at the Indian Health Service.

Elmira Squibb is Alice Neir's niece, by the way.

One day, I saw my IHS mental health 'colleague' Kent hunkering down near a genuine potted plant, jotting notes while I talked to a state worker over coffee at a Toppenish café about the recent suicide epidemic among tribal youth. He was spying on me on behalf of IHS management.

I quit the Yakama Indian Health Service a week later and felt free to mention my misadventures to anybody willing to listen. My disclosures earned me knowing smiles and a tribal contract, much to my former IHS colleagues' dismay.

While Emily was technically correct that I retained some access privileges to patient records at the clinic at the insistence of the Yakama Nation Tribal Council's Health and Fitness Committee, I had never gone there and tried to use them.

"My *tila* would say 'soak yourself in pickle brine,' doctor," she encouraged.

"Franklin's not even requesting my help, Emily; you are. For me, it's better to let sleeping dogs lie over there. I'd rather just talk with you about dealing with Franklin's behavior without stirring up trouble at the clinic."

She didn't blink and didn't say anything more. She didn't have to.

"Oh, all right," I relented. "I'll take a quick look. Only you have to get Leila to fill out a release of records form, whether or not you want her to know what I'm doing. I won't do it unless I have that in place."

"No worries. I can pull that off." She eased into a smile.

"By the way, is she planning on taking guardianship for all the kids?"

She stiffened. "No."

"Who is? Do you know?"

It was an honest question, but instead of answering, Emily peered back at Elisi's car.

"Doctor, there's hurt feelings in my family right now on that subject, so I don't feel good talking on it. You could check with Tessa if you want to know more."

A large, black bird floated down lazily onto the utility line over our heads. The sounds of the park died away, and he cawed portentously, flapping his wings before turning his head sideways to give us the eye. I could tell who he was by the sharp angle of his tail feathers and his deep voice. He was no crow.

"What's up, Raven?" I whispered, awed by his size.

Emily immediately strolled across the narrow street back to Elisi's car, reached in through her open window and into a small bag, and then tossed a quarter of a sandwich out on to the street. He surged off the line and swooped down, grabbing it in his beak all in one motion.

"Got to give him something," she declared. "You never know—people along the coast would say he came by for his own reasons."

I slipped inside my office for a minute and brought back a copy of the release form I needed signed. She nodded at me, didn't say goodbye, and shot gravel down the street as she drove away.

After she left, I sat on my office's newly-built front steps finishing my Jarrito before my next client. I thought about the current predicament of the Miyanashatawit kids. So much had gone to hell since their *tila* (maternal grandfather), Arnold Miyanashatawit, died in a house fire that destroyed their home in White Swan.

Burning scrap wood out in an unscreened, open steel drum invites disaster, explained the Yakima County fire chief under the headline "*Revered Yakama Elder's Tragic Death*" in the *Herald*. Nothing like blaming the victim, I thought at the time. Fires skip from grass to structures too often around White Swan, he said; the public should be careful. In this case, wind tipped the steel drum over and blew sparks through dry grass, eventually feeding flames against the back of Arnold's hand-built, mostly wooden home.

I learned more than I would have ever felt right asking about a week after the fire while having coffee with my friend, Trick, one of Arnold's nephews. Pulling on his ear, his voice shook describing how Arnold and the kids fought the flames themselves at first, delaying their 911 call. Yakima County Fire District No. 5 volunteers pulled in twenty minutes later, but the "whole place went up like kindling."

Arnold got the kids out quickly but stayed inside, throwing furniture and all manner of things out the windows and doorways. Smoke engulfed him as he stood in the doorway and the arriving firefighters scrambled forward. A backdraft beneath the front porch ignited, blocking his path out and theirs in. His granddaughter Eloise had to be wrestled to the ground when they retreated; she was running up right behind them. She just popped back up when somebody tackled her and wouldn't be restrained.

"A few seconds passed," Trick continued, "and there's uncle peering out through smoke funneling out the side attic window above, and everyone's all relieved, you know? They're yelling to jump out to the porch roof or something. Some female firefighter run up with a ladder and started to climb up there but that fascia caved in and the porch roof slid from under her. She fell right in," he smacked one palm onto the other, "and somebody had to jump to pull her out. About then, uncle's head come back in view like he'd try to crawl out, but he couldn't fit through that tiny window frame. So he moved back somewheres, probably downstairs to try and get out from the other side of the house."

"'Back off and protect the kids!'" Trick smiled falsely, and his eyes watered. "'Back off and protect the kids!' That's what he keeps yelling at them. And I could only think, that's how he was. That's how he lived."

After that, the entire house went up in a surge of heat and flame, and the kids screamed in anguish. All of them, down to little Samuel, knew exactly what was happening. Their *tila* wasn't going to make it.

A month or so later, Leila, the kids' aunt and one of Arnold's two daughters, told us about how Tessa shot up the two-track at the very moment the flames exploded, jumped out of Arnold's pickup screaming, and sprinted towards the burning house. She was taken to the ground by a firefighter and gave him a black eye, but he still didn't let her up, and she fainted. Leila said nobody even caught his name.

They eventually found him in the crawlspace below the first floor, curled around a partially-melted box of various papers, clutching his deceased wife Georgina's old jewelry. He probably thought he could make it by staying below the smoke—'stay low and go,' as they say. Fire feeding that wooden structure was so intense, said the coroner, it sucked out all the oxygen. He never had a chance and suffocated before he burned.

From that point almost everything fell on top of Leila, and I never saw her shed a tear in public about Arnold's death, but knew she felt the loss as deeply as anyone. Elisi said Leila went through the box he was holding when he died looking for a will or insurance papers, but she only found an old journal and a stack of hand-scrawled notes from his American Indian Movement days. I wanted to read that journal and notes but didn't feel right asking about it.

Beyond the burned-down house and the land it stood on, he'd left only his truck (on its last legs), about $600 dollars cash, the jewelry, the Lazy Boy, an old TV, several dresser drawers of clothes, and his prized Marlin 30.06 rifle.

By tradition, the Marlin rifle should go to one of the boys—Franklin was considerably older than Samuel—but Leila said he wasn't ready. He hadn't had a first kill in a hunt, which was one way a Yakama young man earned his rifle. I was afraid of what she'd do given what little money Arnold left and talked Ruthie into letting me buy the Marlin for $400 dollars. Arnold used that rifle to save my life, and I felt I should take care of it.

The neophyte newscasters over at KNPP-TV news butchered his last name, but managed to say kind things about him. They even started a fund for the kids and raised about a thousand dollars. Leila still had to hock Georgina's jewelry and take out a personal loan from Yakama Nation Credit to make funeral expenses. Poverty or near-poverty is an insufficient excuse for avoiding the cost of a dignified funeral for an elder so widely-loved as Arnold.

Hundreds of people showed up, and the overflow crowd peered in through open doors or stood outside in the hot sun, holding tarps over their heads. The service combined Seven Drum and Indian Shaker traditions, blending the two most prevalent spiritual paths on the reservation. Arnold would've liked it that way. Although he identified himself as Shaker, he was always careful to mention that his grandfather was a Waashat drummer.

"*Piná' iwaat ku kw'ałáni*," Elisi whispered to Ruthie and me when we had entered. "*Piná' iwaat ku kw'ałáni.*"

Her wrinkly lips trembled, and we nodded, not really understanding.

When I'd first met her years back, she was a mystery to Arnold's grandchildren. Until then, she'd not revealed herself due to the uncomfortable secret of her father's illicit love affair and the shame attached to it. In fact, for nearly fifty years, she'd remained their grandmother Georgina's secret half-sister. But with all the troubles brought on by Leila's sister, Tina, Georgina extracted a vow from Elisi while on her deathbed that she'd look out for Tessa and her sisters and brothers. After Georgina died, Elisi stepped out from the shadows as their new *kała*, first with Tessa—who resisted the idea initially—and then with Leila and the other children of

Tina Miyanashatawit.

Arnold already knew about Elisi's connection and welcomed her presence in the children's lives. By the time of his death, she'd become fully integrated into the family.

I rehearsed her Yakama words in my head, and tried to repeat them for Trick after the service ended when Ruthie and I ran into him.

"You need coffee for that 'k'—it comes from the back of your throat," he explained, "*Piná' iwaat ku kw'aɫáni*. She's saying uncle put everybody before himself. It's a special quality—not everybody's like that, right? He was a leader who did whatever was needed for others and didn't care much about himself. He was a man who'd go without food so others could eat."

He pretended to pinch his nose to mask his tears.

"Yeah—it's not our way to say the name of somebody who's passed on, you know," Trick lowered his voice like Arnold was standing next to us. "I known him all my life. He always looked out for us. I always wanted to be just like him."

He pinched his nose again and turned away.

Tessa walked into the service carrying Chase, now four years old. Her daughter with Parker Heslah (a young man I'd known and tried to help before his death) was a beautiful child with almond-shaped eyes, long lashes, and a built-in expression of defiance garnered from both parents.

Tessa had helped Elisi, Leila, Emily, and some Coastal Salish relatives over the prior night to dress Arnold's unrecognizable body in handmade regalia. This would be his wish, the gruesomeness of the task offset by a certain wisdom regarding actually handling the body of a deceased loved one and facing the truth of severed bonds. When they'd finished, they draped a carefully-crafted splay of eagle feathers across his adorned torso along with two unopened packs of Pall Malls and prayed for his journey until the sun rose.

Only Tessa's bloodshot eyes revealed her vigil. She

turned counterclockwise with her hand over her heart in the proper manner at the entranceway to the longhouse, holding Chase as though she was weightless. Ruthie patted my knee as we sat waiting at a long table in the community kitchen, then got up, entered behind her, and used her hand in the same motion as we'd both been taught. I walked outside and around the building to go sit on the men's side. By then, Ruthie was directly across the longhouse floor from me, sitting next to Tessa with Elisi and the rest of the kids.

After the Shaker songs finished and before the seven drummers began, Ruthie glanced, and I nodded in agreement. She reached in her purse, palmed three hundred dollars, and slid it into Tessa's empty hand. This was all we could afford. Tessa looked at the cash and shook her head, but Ruthie gently closed her open hand over the money. Chase wrapped her arms around her mom's neck and hugged her tightly, looking in my direction with a severe expression, intuiting that we'd somehow made her mother cry.

In the row next to Tessa and Chase were the other daughters of Tina Miyanashatawit, lined up by descending age: Emily and Eloise, the twins, now seventeen years old, sat with their smooth, thin faces subdued, dressed in simple, dark-patterned, cotton dresses cinched with woven, beaded belts, their hair pulled back and beautifully braided.

Ce Ce sat next to them, her cheeks swollen from crying, no longer so little at about ten years old. She was Tina's daughter by 'Cowboy' Jack Brie. When she was only five years old, he'd walked in when no one was home and left a note on Arnold's kitchen table saying simply, "I'm back, baby." Tessa was terrified by the note, sure he intended to violently intimidate her or Arnold or perhaps even kidnap Ce Ce.

I concluded Brie's behavior back then had more to do with Ce Ce than Tessa or anyone else. Still, his cryptic note inaugurated our shared disaster —Tessa already knew about his operation at the old Mission Boarding School—Parker told her. With peculiar teenage reasoning, she decided the note meant she should run away from home and find and kill Brie before he could harm Ce Ce or her family. Brie, Tiller, and James were ready for her and took her captive easily. Elisi helped me figure out where she'd gone, and then Tessa somehow texted me. I fell into the trap of seeking help from Charlie Whitcomb, who it turned out was Brie's illegitimate adult son. Brie manipulated Whitcomb within his undercover role with Yakama Nation Tribal Police, blackmailing him to do his bidding—including taking me hostage rather than rescuing Tessa, and locking me in the basement coal room, where I was beaten by Tiller and then scheduled for a 'fatal accident.'

I watched Ce Ce, unable to avoid thinking about all that happened back then. Next to me sat Samuel, Tina's nine-year-old son by an unknown father, and Franklin, short but stocky and quiet like Emily. Beyond Franklin's very light handshake—a touch of hands, really, as we sat down together—neither he nor Samuel communicated with me. Samuel started to cry for a very brief moment before Franklin nudged him hard, and he stopped. I knew I should remain sitting within my own quiet thoughts and not try to interact with them.

Tina Miyanashatawit, Leila's sister, did not attend her father's funeral. She was entitled by law to petition for a prison guard escort to such an event, but Trick told me she'd declined. Arnold helped get Tina arrested, more than likely in order to save her life. Maybe she blamed him for getting her imprisoned instead of Brie, who'd made sure she took the fall for their shared involvement in drug dealing. Trick told me he'd heard Tina was getting closer to a sentence review at Walla Walla penitentiary.

Tessa had a highly negative but deep connection with Tina, whom she considered to be an utter failure as a person, and this was magnified by the idea that her mom knowingly allowed her and her sisters to be subjected to the perversities of Jack Brie. I knew Tessa worried she shared some inherent flaw with her mother. Unfortunately, this made her somewhat ambivalent in her relationship with Chase.

"Tina Miyanashatawit," I spoke aloud, taking down a last swig of my Jarrito.

The raven was still watching me from the line above my head. I felt sorry I had no food to offer.

TWO

I heard the Shadow Indians;
The *Chat-chi* or ghost people,
Singing and playing with sticks at night,
Gambling noises just as living still.
These old people are long dead,
And that is why I heard the Shadow Indians.
No, I was not scared!
It was only the Spirit People,
Who love to dwell about the ancient home.
—*Salatkin, 1925*

"Will you be disappointed if we have a girl?" she whispered gently into my ear.

"Huh?" I answered sleepily.

"Just tell me, Ret," Ruthie chided. A scented candle burned on my dresser. "First thing that comes to your mind."

"You always ask heavy questions after we make love."

She poked me hard in the side, jolting me out of my doze. "I don't always do anything."

I rolled over, and faced her. "I'm happy we're having a baby. Honest. Boy or girl."

"You're *sure* you're happy?"

"I have a shaky, brand-new private practice and a first baby coming, and I'm already forty-five years old. I'm a little insecure—but I'm happy."

"Well, at least you finally admit it," she declared, laying her head on my shoulder, pulling me closer.

We both passed out immediately.

I am on a long drive in a 1954 two-tone, light-blue and white, Chevy BelAir. How do I know it's a 1954? I just do but have no idea how. I become concerned about how long I've been driving and pull into a small town diner to find out where I am and get something to eat. As I walk inside, I see an alabaster statue in the town square of a figure that looks like Sequoyah. It is inscribed "Buck" at its base. I order a sandwich and ask the cashier where I am. She speaks in an Oklahoma accent and says "You're in Missoura, sir." I ask if I'm anywhere near Neosho. She says "Nawzha? That's about two hours or so west of here, sir." I ask, "What is this place?" and she says "Well, you're in Hunter, sir, Hunter, Missoura."

Ruthie found me at the computer, sitting in the dark.

"It's four o'clock in the morning," she slurred, rubbing her eyes. "Don't you have an 8:00 a.m. client?"

I told her about the dream.

"Ret," she yawned, "can we just pretend your dreams are like everybody else's?"

"I've got to tell Elisi about this . . ."

"Good idea. Hopefully, she's sleeping right now—so why not come back to bed?"

"But this is amazing!" I hurriedly pulled my dog-eared road atlas off the floor and peered into it under the high-intensity lamp. "Hunter is nowhere in the index. I've never heard of it in all the family stuff I've got. There are many different routes for the Trail of Tears. But here it is—tiny Hunter in Carter County. You see, they don't put towns that small in the index! I got the magnifying glass out and found it just from my dream—it's right here!"

I pointed again, trying to get her to share my excitement. She struggled to muster enthusiasm while I continued: "This town wasn't founded yet when Benge's Route crossed onto the old Spanish Road to Arkansas! And 'Buck'—you know who he is? The name on that statue? That's Elias Boudinot's nickname, signer of the Treaty of New Echota. I never even knew who he was until I looked up the nickname. He was one of the major signers of the treaty that led to the Trail of Tears. And Nawzsha? The exact way the woman said it—well, that just happens to be the Osage pronunciation for Neosho, near where all my Barlow and Gibson relatives lived. This dream is a message!"

"Oh no, no, no," she protested, shaking her head, and leaning over my shoulder. "We don't need messages from your dreams around here again. Last time that happened, you got chained in a basement, kicked in the face, and almost killed."

Her eyes were closed and her head was heavy against my neck.

"Okay. I'll come back to bed—even if I can't sleep," I said. "But it wasn't a bad dream, Ruthie; it was just telling me about my family. Elisi said some dreams are like that."

"Cosmic hippy." She yawned widely and loudly. "Maybe some family ghost finally took pity after all the rummaging around you've been doing."

"Yeah, that's what I think too."

"And that way you can get used to the idea of settling in with me to start our own family."

I should've affirmed what she said, but I wasn't very tuned in. I knew I'd missed something when she broke free with a start and shuffled back to bed. I stayed awake for another hour, dozed off, and then jumped out of bed when I realized she'd already gotten up. But she'd left for work. I knew I'd stung her and felt sorry.

I texted her: "ILU and want to have a baby."

About ten minutes later, she texted back "You're not biologically capable," and I knew we were back on track.

I called Elisi on my drive out to Harrah.

"Aren't you feeling hungry, doctor?"

I invited her to breakfast. We went to Mel's in Toppenish, and she ordered an English muffin and fruit, eating slowly and gingerly, pondering each bite. I had the special—a

Swiss cheese omelet, tomatoes, sausage, hash browns well-done, sourdough bread toast, and coffee.

"Don't put your stress to your appetite, doctor," she offered. "You'll get fat and get the diabetes."

I only smiled and chewed. We listened to two older, white fruit farmers talking loudly at the lunch counter.

"I put a sign to stop them from bugging for work," the first said, throwing his hands out loosely to the bar. "I'm writing cherries off. Folks are finding no work south or north. It's a hell of a thing."

"Evelyn Thompson's got some sleeping in her barn," said the other man, "and giving what food she can while they pass through. But you can't subsidize people. She finally kicked out that foreman with the big motorbike—Hector Amezquita. That guy's a low life. She found him playing house with you know who in her son's old bed. Can you imagine, Harry?"

Harry leaned back. "You mean the room where her little boy passed on? Why't were my place, they'd both be sittin' on buckshot. Who knows, they go through her jewelry or God forbid her credit cards." He pointed to his paper, "Whenever crops don't come in, we start getting all this here wetback crime. They're short sixty officers up in Upper Valley."

"Aw, now that ain't got anything to do with the price of wool on Friday, Harry," Fred exclaimed. "That kind of overreaction makes for another police state. Just 'cause little *seniorita* Maritza's whoring with Hector inside Evelyn's house don't mean some sort of Mexican crime wave's started up."

They settled their bills and strolled out to together, lost in debate. I was still eating. Elisi was all finished.

"Now, there's a good example of selective memory," she declared, wiping her mouth daintily with her napkin.

"I never thought I'd hear you use psych jargon."

"Psychologists don't own words, doctor," she laughed. "That man there, I know his name, but I won't say it, his family got rich playing the Yakama families off the Mexican families when they first migrated in, looking for work. You know, we Yakama were always the pickers back then—hops, fruits, and vegetables. I did the back-breaking work in the hops when I was little. It was all our people could find after reservation days and land beneath our feet deeded out by the Dawes Act. But then orchard owners like that man's grandpa saw the Mexicans coming 'round and starving and thought, 'why I can make a bidding war between these *jefas* and these Indian elders, and I'll come out the winner no matter what.' So he built shacks for the Mexicans. We never had any shacks but just slept where we could when we were too tired to walk home."

I nodded, and she sipped her tea.

"Anyway, the Mexican girls were pretty, and some of the Yakama boys took a liking to them. We've tended to have more girl babies than boys, so their presence gradually became a threat to our bloodline."

"Bloodline?"

"Our family connection; it's important to us. Elders have always tried to be sure cousins don't marry blood to blood, you know. We're a closely-related community, so we had strict rules about who could marry who and how courting was supposed to happen. A boy and girl back then couldn't hardly look at each other. *Pina ch'achanwit wawnak'sash* was the expectation—which are words that mean keeping oneself pure and whole in body. It was up to elders what the match would be."

"Arranged, huh?"

"I suppose that's what it's called," she said. "The Mexican people had the same kind of idea too—they just practiced it somewhat differently. Eventually, the cultural traditions on both sides were all broke down."

"I assumed you meant 'blood quantum' when you said 'bloodline' . . ."

"That's a wrong assumption. No, blood quantum was the genocidal idea of the white people, doctor. That was about tearing our families apart, not keeping the bloodline safe. We didn't recognize what they were doing with that idea at first. If you were born white and married Yakama, you were considered part of our family, and so were your children. Federal government made that law, and so it came about as to those who had enough 'blood' would be officially called 'Yakama' and those who didn't were not. From that it came about that we didn't want our children to intermarry with the Mexican kids because their offspring might not be able to enroll with the feds and be entitled to the treaty-guaranteed benefits our ancestors fought for. All this was just one more effort to shrink our people and to limit our numbers."

I wanted to tell her about my dream but sipped my coffee instead, having learned what was expected when an elder's talking.

"I got no ill will toward Mexican people—they come here poor just looking for a way to live. Many of them are *mestizo*, you know, and their ancestors suffered terrible from the Spaniards. Mexican people used to understand the Yakamas in what we go through for our children—not so much anymore. They used to understand how we felt when we'd say we were not so happy about our young getting together with theirs."

"Anyway, those two orchard men are complaining about people they rely on to let them live the way they do—they didn't get up to hominy and beans this morning and then pick twelve or fourteen hours; they spent their time bellyaching about Mexicans and sucking on a jelly donut." She pondered me. "Doctor, you look fit to pop about telling me something. What is it?"

I told her all about my dream and what I'd learned. She

nodded when I finished.

"*Káła*, can you tell me more?"

She watched me for a moment and then chuckled. "Seems you already milked that cow, doctor. I mean, I'm not some spiritual shaman. We don't have such people. It's plain as day *Tamanwilá* sends you a dream like that from time to time. So pay attention's what I say. Your ancestors come to tell you about your own bloodline. I'm glad for you."

That was all she had, and she stood up, our conversation being at an end.

We drove back to her place listening to KYNR, Yakama Nation Radio at 1490. In a weirdly seamless programming mix, "Rainy Night in Georgia" by Gladys Knight was followed by "Come and Get Your Lovin'" by Redbone, and then, "Memorial Song for Nathan Jim, Jr." by Black Lodge Singers. Against her objection, I turned the radio up and cracked the windows.

I jerked and skidded right and then swerved hard onto the soft shoulder, howling and cursing loudly only a foot short of an irrigation canal.

A two-toned, light-blue and white, Chevy Bel Air sped past us after crossing the centerline and heading straight toward me. He revved his engine loudly as he turned right onto Wapato Road.

I peered sharply out the window but couldn't see him. Then, I glanced over at Elisi to see if she was okay.

"What, *káła*??" I demanded.

She just shook her head and didn't answer me. She had her Cheshire cat grin on.

On Wednesday morning, I sat stewing on a bench under the lone sycamore at the Yakama Nation RV Park stress-smoking again and very much not wanting to go inside the Yakama Indian Health Service clinic.

The release for Franklin's chart, signed by Leila, stuck

out of my shirt pocket after being dropped off by Emily that morning. There was nothing anybody could do to stop me—I had a contract allowing me access to such records. It wasn't so much looking at Franklin's chart that made me uncomfortable as seeing former coworkers who thought I'd left my position in disgrace. I'd left due to not being able to take the harassment anymore.

Several birds sang overhead, and I watched someone step out of the rickety door of a Winnebago to hack and spit on the ground. Immediately after this repulsive observation, something wet splattered on the back of my neck, and I reflexively wiped my fingers through a lump of bird shit. A few choice expletives followed before I concluded this was all some kind of perverse provocation to make me walk across the street and into the clinic. It might have all just been coincidental.

On entering, I made my way directly across the lobby to the restroom to wash my hands. Naturally, Leo Aspen opened the door and walked out at the exact moment I put my hand forward to push in. I almost put my soiled hand on his chest and immediately faced a profound moral dilemma.

"Hello, Leo," I said, extending my shat-upon hand with feigned goodwill. Although delayed, my conscience spoke, and I pulled my hand back quickly when he put his out, which made me rude.

"Huh," he grimaced contemptuously and pushed past me.

"Sorry, Leo, you should know I just saved your life," I proclaimed, certain I'd rescued him and his patients from *e coli*. A nursing assistant passing by grinned at my remark. Leo shot past her, clearly unmoved.

I washed up and followed familiar hallways to Medical Records where a former client, Adrienne, was manning the desk. She looked over Leila's release, saw it was all in order, and went to grab the chart.

Dr. Bill Gaillard came around the corner as soon as she went back the other way. Leo must have had to run to get the word to him that fast.

"Hello, Barlow. What brings you out of your hole today? Short on dirt?"

"Nice to see you, Dr. Gaillard. And it's okay to call me Doctor Barlow in a professional setting," I answered. "I have a chart to look over with a proper release and then I'll be out of your hair."

Adrienne walked back around the corner with chart in hand.

"Hold up a moment. Let me see that release," he demanded.

She handed it to him, looking a little worried. Gaillard perused it for a few moments then handed it back to her.

"Still working with the Miyanashatawits?" he said. "Don't you have any other families in your practice, Barlow?"

"Sure do, and thanks for asking, Dr. Gaillard. Plenty, plenty. Doing fine. My practice is doing fine."

"Well, there's no accounting for taste," he muttered and then turned and walked away.

"Woh. That wasn't pleasant," said Adrienne, her eyes widening. "I've never even seen him act like that. Why's he so hostile?"

"He thinks I sabotaged his economic progress through the morass of bureaucratic ineptitude people call the 'Indian Health Service'. . . ."

I had more to say, but her look stopped me.

"And you didn't . . . do whatever you said?"

"Adrienne, I don't mind anybody knowing my relationship with Dr. Bill Gaillard is a collateral casualty of trying to keep kids safe on this rez."

"Only at IHS do we get this kind of drama," she sighed and shook her head, handing me the chart. She thought again, "Well, except for over at the Agency." She gestured me toward the chair and desk where I used to sit and catch up my files. "And, then again, at General Council."

I leafed through Franklin Miyanashatawit's record carefully. There were 'well-child notes' by Dr. Ekk (an unfortunate name for a pediatrician) indicating poor follow-through on inoculations and nutritional counseling during Franklin's early years. There were also notes about chronic otitis media, viruses, etc.

There was nothing at all in the mental health section from my former colleagues Leo Aspen, Dominia Garcia, Kent Williams, or Eileen Scoville.

I finally found Franklin's ADHD diagnosis where I wasn't expecting it. A letter in the pharmacy notes from Dr. Margaret Fitzsimmons at Provincial Medical Center documented a psychiatric diagnosis including Attention Deficit Hyperactivity Disorder, Oppositional Defiant Disorder, and Major Depression, Recurrent.

I'm sure these labels had done a lot for Franklin's reputation with Mt. Adams School District out in White Swan.

She'd placed him on eighty milligrams of methylphenidate, the generic name for Ritalin, QID—meaning 'divided into four doses' of twenty milligrams daily at regular intervals. That's an awful lot of stimulant. Her letter was an update; she'd seen him only about five weeks earlier after several prior meetings. She'd added one hundred milligrams daily of fluoxetine, a selective serotonin reuptake inhibitor (SSRI), exceeding the maximum recommended dose for adults, four milligrams of alprazolam (the generic name for a common tranquilizer often sold on the street), and a half a milligram of respiridone.

I called Emily as I walked out and told her I needed to meet with her. I worked hard to maintain a calm demeanor.

"I recommend you bring Tessa, too, Emily."

"Why?"

"I think she needs to be brought into this picture, too."

"But not Leila?"

"Of course Leila too, but not yet given what you said about her stress level at the moment. Let's get our ducks in a row. I want to talk to you and Tessa first about who's involved in getting these pills for Franklin. Okay?"

They were both standing by the outside door to my Harrah office at about 8:15 a.m. the next morning. The weather had turned, and the early morning was chilly enough to make our breath visible.

Emily was anxious. "I took off school, Dr. Barlow, and have to be back to White Swan in a half hour."

"Freezing, Barlow," Tessa complained. "I thought you got here earlier."

She pushed her hands into her light blue and red Pendleton sweater. I hadn't seen her in a while, and she looked worn down by young motherhood and grief.

"Sorry. Come on in," I responded.

"What is it, Barlow? Why are you so serious?" Tessa asked.

Emily stared at the window tensely, seated on the couch next to her.

"Do either of you know how Franklin got hooked in with Fitzsimmons?"

"Fitzsimmons?" Emily looked uncertainly at Tessa.

I grabbed my notes off the desk and spoke to Tessa. "Do I have permission to talk about our experiences five years ago with your sister here? You can tell me to shut it—and I will, Tessa. What I learned about Franklin has to do with back then."

Tessa nodded slightly. "I don't care what my sis knows. That's all history now."

"Provincial Medical Center," I reminded her, "inpatient psychiatric unit, the lady doctor with the four-point restraints who shot you up with halperdol before you went to the chemical dependency program. That's who's prescribing

Ritalin to Franklin. And she's evidently got him on a bunch of other crap as well."

"Her!?" Tessa turned toward her sister as the nearest culpable party. "What the hell, Emily??"

Emily looked back and forth between us and then thought for a moment.

"Oakley," she announced.

"What?" Tessa demanded.

"That's her name. Ms. Oakley, Tess. Some sort of guardian or something. She come 'round right after *tila* died before we all went to Leila's. She took us up there for check-ups."

"Why would she take you to Provincial Outpatient instead of Indian Health?" I asked. "That doesn't make sense."

"She said she thought it's better care," said Emily. "She works out of the Juvenile Court up in the city."

Tessa glared at her and Emily noticed.

"It was all mixed up after *tila* was gone, sis! You never wanted to know anything!"

Tessa's hopeless expression returned. "Sorry. I don't mean to get all mad."

Emily explained to me: "Family was in chaos and me, Franklin, and all got sent up to stay with cousins for a few nights in Yakima. Leila had to get the funeral planned—and this lady, Ms. Oakley, came and took us to some office in the hospital med center. Franklin was just suspended from school. They said they wouldn't let him come back unless he had an eval with a mental health person. Leila had to work and was glad that this Oakley lady was going to help."

"So she let her take Franklin to *her*!?" Tessa snapped. "We don't need some *shuyápu k'usik k'úsi* pumping psych drugs into our brother, Em. And Franklin actually went along with even seeing her??"

The distinction between *shuyápu* for 'white person' and *pashtin* for 'American white person' is interesting to me.

Of course, *k'usik k'úsi* made Dr. Fitzsimmons a 'white dog,' or more exactly a 'white bitch,' and Tessa's intent was clear there. But the root of *shuyápu*, that is '*shuy*', suggests a 'reformer' or someone who attempts to rehabilitate somebody else.

"You went too, Emily?" I asked.

"Yeah, for some blood draw, or whatever. Ms. Oakley said we were all overdue for seeing a doc. All I remember is Franklin was supposed to see somebody so he could be cleared back to school. He got pissed off and pushed over some desks in class on the Friday before the fire. He was all set to catch it from *tila*."

"Well," I finally said, "you may not like Franklin seeing Fitzsimmons, Tessa, but I think this Oakley woman's a guardian ad litem, and she can make a lot of headaches. She must have used a Medicaid coupon up there at Provincial. It's odd they'd see a native child more than once and not send him back to IHS. She likely had some sort of pull there."

"It was Dominia," Emily observed. "I'm sure. Leila said she got involved from Franklin's school in White Swan because the administrators said he was all mental for busting the chair, and he couldn't come back in unless he was cleared. Dominia does all the IHS phone consults over there at the White Swan health annex."

"Hmm, I thought I might get some business over there, so that's new information for me."

Tessa had fallen silent.

"But I never knew about Franklin going to see that doctor up in Yakima again past the first time," Emily pondered. "I know Leila wouldn't have had time to take him up there. And she never said a thing about it."

I shrugged, "Maybe this Oakley lady gave him a ride? A fourteen-year-old can consent to his own mental health counseling, you know. Other than that, I have no idea."

"Well, I know I got no idea what a guardian ad litem is, and why she'd be messing with our family," Tessa sighed.

"Guardian ad litem works for the juvenile court to figure what's in the best interest of the kids," I explained, "usually having to do with where they should live. The guardian ad litem gets appointed after a Child In Need of Services or CHINS petition gets filed. Do either of you know if that was done for your brothers and sisters?"

"Leila had to go see somebody from Tribal Child Welfare Office not long after *tila* died," said Tessa. "That's all I know."

"And did she meet with Eva?" I asked. "Somebody at the state fills out the CHINS petition and ICWA, the Indian Child Welfare Act, says the tribe has to be involved. So that means Eva to me. Preference is supposed to be given to placing Indian kids with relatives or at least in their home community. She knows this community."

"All Leila ever said was papers were getting put together," Emily declared.

We sat together in thought for a minute.

"Leila is providing a temporary placement for you and your brothers and sisters, Emily," I surmised. "With your *tila* gone, there will have to be a permanent plan in place. And they probably came up to a deadline for when that's supposed to be done by and started putting some pressure on Leila to figure it out."

"Oh, they figured something out all right, Barlow," Tessa remarked bitterly.

"What do you mean?" I asked.

Tessa didn't respond.

"It's the sensitive subject I was mentioning to you before, doctor. I know exactly what she means," Emily said.

"Then shut it, Em," Tessa responded.

Emily rolled her eyes and smirked with embarrassment.

"What?" I challenged. "Will one of you tell me what's going on? Emily, how did you and Leila hear about Ms. Oakley?"

POW!

The window over my couch exploded with a whoosh and glass flew everywhere as a large rock thudded onto the carpet. We all flew out of our seats; Tessa jumped onto the couch, and peered out. Emily shot past me down the hallway.

"Goddamn, Tessa, get out of the window!!" I yelled. "Emily, stay in here with us!"

Neither of them did anything I said. So I ran out the front door after Emily, brushing flecks of glass out of my hair. I heard rather than saw a car tear down Pioneer Street in the opposite direction and glanced up only to see it spouting a fog of dust as I pulled out my cell and started dialing 911. A robot voice announced I was being transferred to the Yakima County Sheriff.

The line rang and rang.

"Shit, pick up!" I whined, trying to peer through the dust.

"Who the hell??" Emily shouted back at Tessa. I caught a light blue blur shooting across an intersection out at the edge of town.

Emily and I stood in the middle of Pioneer Street; Tessa looked out through my obliterated window perched atop the arm of the sofa inside. The park appeared completely empty.

"You OK?" Emily asked her, calmer, and turning to head back inside.

"Fine. Did you get the plate?" asked Tessa.

"Hardly saw—too much dirt and dust." Emily looked questioningly at me, but I couldn't see anything either.

The 911 operator finally answered, and I put my finger in my ear so I could understand her squeaky voice over the breaking cell signal.

"Yeah, it was old!" Tessa told us both when we came back into the office, her cheeks flushed with excitement "I saw two people."

I was assured a deputy would be by shortly. We started picking glass fragments out of our hair before I noticed Tessa had a thin current of blood dripping down her face from the inside of her left eye. She poked at it with a blood-soaked tissue.

"Hey! Let me look at that."

"No way. It's nothing."

"Come on—you're bloody. Let me see what's going on," I moved toward her to look closer.

"No, Barlow, you're just a shrink, thanks anyway," she said and then stood up. I got the message. She turned to Emily. "This man wouldn't know shit about first aid."

"Hah, hah, hah," I laughed sarcastically and made my way to the bathroom.

"You're dripping blood onto his carpet here; no wonder he's worked up," Emily doted roughly, pushing her onto the couch and peering down. "You're crying blood. We got to make sure there's no glass."

I returned triumphant, carrying an overstuffed suitcase.

"First aid." I pointed it toward Tessa as I opened the suitcase. "Disaster mentality. You forgot who bombed the shit out of Jack Brie and Tiller and James with just a little bleach and some tin foil so we'd have a chance to run."

I pulled out a large swathe of prepackaged gauze and handed it to Emily.

"Dab this on and keep pressure. I'm not speaking to her right now."

"Barlow," Tessa perked up slightly. "Never knew you were a fucking Eagle Scout."

"Shush," Emily scolded. "No need for cussing. Be nice."

It was more warmth than I'd had from her in a while.

While Emily tended her, I fetched my reading lamp and put on my magnifying glasses to take out the glass splinters in my palm from running my hand through my hair. I pulled out the little tweezers from my Swiss Army knife.

Five more minutes passed and still no sheriff, no siren, nothing. Tessa poked at her eye—the bleeding was nearly stanched. Emily pulled a brush out to try to get any remaining chips of glass out of her hair.

I let Deputy Sheriff Almont Anderson in a few minutes later. He said he had to keep his flashers on while parked out front. My office was now a beacon for Alice Neir, and she and her husband hobbled out to the porch of their store. I waved; they didn't wave back. Wind blew the door handle from my hand and smacked the door against the opposite wall. Warren guffawed loudly as I reached for it.

Anderson sauntered through my little lobby and into the office, glancing at Tessa and Emily long enough to say hello and then picking the rock up. He was small but wiry with thick-lensed black horn-rimmed glasses—a fashion statement around here, I decided. He looked more like a museum store clerk. His bullet-resistant vest pushed his shirt out like football pads on his shoulders and his pants bunched over his shoes, tugged down low by the weight of his Sam Browne belt.

"'Git out'," he said as he picked up the rock and stared at Emily lazily. "Somebody don't like you?"

"What?" I asked. He sounded almost psychotic to me.

"Well, I don't know," said Emily. "What exactly do you mean by that?"

"What it says right here." He turned the rock around for all to see, revealing a sticky note with hand printing on it, affixed with strapping tape, and held it up toward us. "'Git out.' Bad speller."

"Weird," he said, trying to peel off the note with his fingertips.

"Won't we need that for evidence?" I asked.

"Not likely," he smiled vacantly. "We're not likely to catch 'em, sorry to say, unless one of you knows outright who it was. You say you saw the car?"

Alice Neir strolled right into my office like she owned the place. Of course, she did.

"Some old car from the fifties, but in good shape," she announced, "blue and white. My husband couldn't catch the plate. We were ringing up somebody. Now this is what happens when you got the kind of people coming around to your place as you've been visiting with, doctor."

I gaped before blurting out, "A 1954 Chevy BelAir?!"

"Maybe, but that's not what I'm saying, I'm talking about who's going to pay for fixing this window," she answered, a strange look coming into her eyes. "But it could've been a Chevy, I'm not sure. You saw it?"

Tessa and Emily stared at me. Now I sounded crazy.

I tried to recover. "An old Chevy crossed over the centerline near Harrah and West Wapato the other day and almost knocked Elisi and me into a ditch."

"Okay." Anderson chewed on that for just a moment. He hefted the rock in his hand. "Heavy. This here's andesite. You said you saw two?"

"Two what?" I asked.

"Two people in the car," Tessa clarified.

"Who are you asking, Deputy?" I didn't really understand his mode of interacting. Anderson was a study in cryptic questions. He seemed more focused on the rock.

"That's right," Alice answered. "There was two."

She'd sat down on my couch and started cleaning her glasses with a tissue from the box on my coffee table. She looked fifteen years younger with them off. Emily watched me watch her and tried to keep a straight face.

"Not all at once," Anderson took out a little pad of paper and pen and began jotting notes. "And I'm asking whoever's answering. Did any of you get a closer look at the people in the car to where you might spot them in a picture?" Everybody shook their heads. He closed his pad back up and put it back in his shirt pocket. "Well, then, there's not much to go on. But it's not just vandalism; we could also call it assault with that nick above your eye."

"We got splinters too in our hair from the glass," I mentioned.

"Sure," he said. "That counts. I'll write it up and maybe get us some traction with state cops along 97. Couldn't have been spur of the moment, after all . . ."

"Why do you say that?"

"Andesite's extrusive igneous."

He shifted the rock around in his hand, lifting his glasses to get a better look at it. Tessa and Emily and I glanced at each other, marveling. Alice put her glasses back on, swept a look over my office shelves and desk.

"Forms from cooling lava near the surface, a lot of time mixes with basalt," Anderson concluded.

"Geez," chuckled Alice. "Never met somebody thought so much of rocks."

He glanced up from his studiousness. "Just a hobby. You won't find chunks of andesite big like this around plateau farmland here in the Valley. More likely, find it in the highlands—the cliffs near Columbia Gorge or up around Mt. Hood or Mt. Adams."

He handed it to me, and I turned it over and read the note, written in solid black letters. It could've been written by anybody. He watched me handling it as he spoke.

"What I'm saying is this rock came from some other place. Somebody picked it up and brought it. More of a planned out thing unless they happen to carry around chunks of andesite. Seems unlikely, doesn't it? So somebody got it from a ways away from here before they tossed it through your window, doctor. It wasn't random or for fun. Can you think of anybody'd want to throw rocks at you?"

There were only too many people who might throw a rock at me, and I couldn't single anybody out. Tessa said much the same while Emily couldn't think of anyone who'd want to throw rocks at her.

"Well, this town is going to hell is all I'll say," said Alice, rising reluctantly as she made to leave. "I got to get back. I'll be calling the glass man, but we'll need to charge it back on top of your rent, doctor. I don't got good insurance for this kind of thing. Deductible's too high."

She looked around at everyone and then at me. "Not bad what you done with the paint and furniture in here, I'll give you that. Maybe the Lord's trying to help you help the desperate."

She focused on the broken window before exiting. "Still there's a tithe to pay at that."

Alice never said 'hello' or 'goodbye.'

Anderson took our report and left, promising to let us know if he caught up with the BelAir or heard of a similar incident. Tessa, Emily, and I started picking up chunks of glass from the floor together. I set the rock up on my desk and started vacuuming.

"That cop was certifiable," Tessa laughed after I finished.

"A rock-collector cop," said Emily.

"Couldn't take down a drunk old lady either," said Tessa. "Alice sure wanted to survey what you've done with her little rental here, Barlow."

"David took down Goliath," said Emily.

"Well, Goliath wasn't drunk," Tessa bantered.

Emily checked my clock and shook her head. "I am so totally dead for being late."

"I'll write you a doctor's note, Emily. That's something I can do since your sis doesn't think I'm a real doc."

I think we were all pretty shocked by what happened. I

asked them to bring Leila back to talk about Franklin before I'd be ready to meet up with him.

Emily breathed in deeply. "Works for me . . . so who do you think's trying to scare you, Dr. Barlow?"

"Just call him Barlow, sis."

"No, I'm being respectful."

Emily stared at the rock sitting on my desk.

"No idea," I admitted. "Maybe somebody was trying to scare Tessa here."

"I don't scare too easy," Tessa said. "But I admit it did make me jump. How'd you really guess the car, by the way? I know it was more than what happened with Elisi."

"Well, to be honest, I saw that car in a dream a couple nights ago."

"Oh, uh oh," Tessa's eyebrows rose. "I shouldn't have asked. Not that shit again."

"Just a dream was all."

"We gotta go, Tess," said Emily. "Anything else?"

They started to make their way down the hallway.

"Do you have any idea whether Franklin's taking other pills right now, Emily? It's not just the Ritalin—she's got him on drugs that sedate a person and alter their mood."

"Not that I've seen." Emily looked at Tessa and drew a blank. "I didn't know about any other pills."

"Whatever," Tessa declared. "We just got to get him off that shit. There's nothing that lady doctor does but lock up minds and hearts."

"Let's get you two and Leila together to talk about this Ms. Oakley too."

"And *káta* too," said Emily.

"Better fix your window first," Tessa chided as Emily pushed in front of her and called dibs on the driver's side of Elisi's car.

THREE

A special case in the control of venereal disease
Is the rehabilitation of the prostitute. . .
What reports there are indicate that
Some success may be expected,
Both when the service is offered
For voluntary acceptance or rejection
By the person concerned
And as a condition of probation. . .
The promiscuous woman
Has been discovered as a person,
Not a specter
To be emotionally discarded by all society.
–Paul Lemkau, Mental Hygiene in Public Health, 1949

It was a sultry afternoon on Friday, so it seemed fitting that Maritza Rios would saunter into my office in jean cut-offs, knee-high boots, leather vest, and a low-buttoned red denim blouse. She was nearly seated before she saw the broken window stuffed with cardboard.

"Who done that?" She gazed up at the hole.

"If I knew that, they'd be locked up."

"Just happen?"

"Yesterday. I'm still working on getting it fixed."

"Hmm," she looked at the couch cautiously. "Is it safe to sit?"

"The glass is all vacuumed up, Maritza."

"It was a rock or brick or something?"

"You're right."

She smiled. "I don't want to get hit on the head if

somebody does it again."

"At this point, I don't think I can guarantee that won't happen."

"Maybe you should move, doctor," she proclaimed in a mild accent, sliding over to the far end of the sofa. "It's too dangerous around here. How do you ever get your business going here anyway?"

Maritza worked as a local prostitute. I'd pulled my Swiss army knife out of my pocket while she talked so as to deal with a hangnail plaguing me, using the little scissors. I tugged it more than cut it, and grimaced slightly, licking the blood off my finger. Glancing over, I discovered she'd mistaken all my fidgeting as pangs of desire.

"Something bothering you?" she asked with a well-rehearsed lilt.

"I'm not a john."

"Professional client, doctor," she huffed. "He is no different, maybe worse. For example, you call me a sprack whore last time."

"You called yourself that. I just said it's a sad thing to say about yourself even if it might feel true."

"You imply it is true."

"I said it's sad you call yourself that even if it felt true. I'm not judging you, Maritza."

"That wasn't what you say. You say 'if it's true', like you're saying 'if the shoe fits' or whatever."

"Maritza, maybe I misspoke. I'm sorry. I do not think you're a sprack whore."

"Then, how do you describe what I do?"

"You're a sex worker economically supporting your methamphetamine addiction. How's that?"

She shifted uncomfortably. "*Cualquiera que sea, esta es una mierda que tengo que vivir con.*"

"Fine, let's talk about the shit you live with Maritza."

"I thought you don't speak Spanish. . ." She tugged a

cigarette from a pack in her boot. "Can I smoke here?"

"Not usually," I said, opening a drawer, pulling out a small ashtray, and leaning over hard to hand it to her. "One addiction at a time. I don't speak Spanish, but I understand a little."

"*Gracias . . .*" she murmured.

I bathed in second hand smoke, having quit only two weeks earlier. Thus far, Maritza hadn't used our sessions in any meaningful way at all—I had much more to do to build any approximation of trust with her.

"You know," she puffed away for a second, "I never like this counseling thing. I never know what to talk about."

"I figured. By the way, do you have your court paperwork with you?"

"I'm sorry; I forget again. I bring it next time."

"Well, I can't bill without it. Who's your probation officer?"

"Harold Lettie."

"How's Harold?"

"Not a nice man."

I smiled recollecting Harold's demeanor. "He uses pepper more than salt."

She took a deep drag. "Whatever. He says I got problems with men, and that is why I have to see you."

"Is he right?"

"Sure," she blew a long plume of smoke ending with a smoke ring she watched fade into the air around my head.

"What are they?"

"I'm attracted to stinky white cowboys who don't talk. Also, short Mexican men, very strong but not nice. Guys who like motorcycles."

"Bad boys."

"Okay. But this is expected, what you would say about it."

"What I say doesn't bring anything new to you."

"Hmm," she flicked her smoke into the ashtray. "Oh, I'm sure it all goes way back to my childhood, doctor."

I was trying to read between her jibes.

"I'll try not to behave to type, Maritza. I have no idea how your childhood factors in. So try telling me a story from your life."

"I am to entertain you?"

"After all, I'm letting you smoke."

This seemed to have a facilitative effect on her. She smiled very slightly. "Better than sitting here bored, I guess."

She thought for a moment, squinting like she was facing hard weather.

"Hmm. Here's one: First off, I grew up in a little place not far from Zitácuaro in Michoácan. My real father was Yakama but I never knew him. My mother was Mexican. She got pregnant when she come picking around here. When I got older, she come back north for a time after my step-father run off, and I got adopted by an aunt. Then my mom and sisters go back home and I stay here. Then I got older and my aunt couldn't control me. Maybe she drank a lot. I started running around all over and she gave me up to foster care. I lived in group homes run by the state since I was fourteen. Anyway, then I age out, and I make my way in the world. That's the story."

"Are you enrolled Yakama?"

"I don't know who my Yakama father is. My mother said she was only with him for a short time and he say, 'I don't want no wetback baby.' After that, she went back to Mexico and that's where I got born. That's all I know of who that Yakama guy is. I'm not interested in knowing more. The man I called my father, I never really call him step-father because he never knew all this about me and always thought of me as his flesh and blood. Not that this made any difference to him. It was my mother who told me the truth about my Yakama father after my step-father left us. So when I say

'father', I'm talking about my stepfather. I always looked up
to him before he left us and never knew him as anyone but my
own father.

"I will tell you a story about my father, then, who I call
as such, before he left us. You have to understand that the area
where I was a little girl around Zitácuaro, no offense, but you
never know nothing about this kind of place. Already, the
crank business had taken over. There are gangs all around
there. Headless bodies get found at the side of the roads.
Maybe you hear the news and think this is a recent thing, but
it's been like that there for hundreds of years. Not safe for
women. Growing up, little girls don't get to go places."

"That is why one day I was very glad my dad, he takes
me along with him to sell some vegetables in Zitácuaro. He
favored me, I guess. He was a farmer and did work on other
people's land too. We were so poor! I was getting older and
bigger, and he needed me to help push a cart full to sell to this
market man in town.

"I was so excited to go, and after we get there, I was
very impressed. There are large pole buildings and stand after
stand of people selling all kinds of pretty fruit, vegetables,
crafts and such. The man we're supposed to sell our
vegetables to is not available. So my dad tells me go wander
around. Maybe this was not good of him as a parent, but I
think mostly he wanted to go drink mezcal. He didn't say I
could just go anywhere, only across the square to look at this
big church where a crowd of people were standing around. He
said I need to come back and find him when the next bells on
the church rang.

"So I went over there. I was maybe ten years old but
big-boned, a big girl. What was happening was they were
holding a funeral of some well-known local guy who had been
murdered, which was as common then as now. You have been
to Mexico?"

"Sure, around Rosarito," I decided to answer in order

to keep her talking.

"Ah, for *langosta*. That is where you got your souvenir?" She pointed to a hand-tooled briefcase sitting on the corner shelf that Ruthie had bartered for me. She must have noticed it the first time she came in.

"Tijuana."

"That is pressed leather, you know, not real hand-tooled."

"Right," I responded, considering her subtle need to diminish me. She was testing me out, I concluded—seeing what I could take.

"I am just saying—you have to go elsewhere to get the real thing."

I simply nodded.

"Well, there I was, and all these people are gathered. I am very young, and I am free to explore. I sit down in the back of this church. No one saw me or would have cared what I did. The priest spoke about this man and how special he was. When the priest was all done, thirteen black horses come by out in the front of this beautiful place and pull the dead man's hearse to the cemetery. I watched the men as they lifted his coffin into the hearse, and then I followed for a little way.

"You see, my own grandma died a year before then, and we could never afford a real funeral. At the time she got buried, I didn't know any different, but now I saw a difference for those who got money, you see? This is maybe where I see really rich people for the first time and also where my family fits in all that. We got no money; they got lots of money. I mean I really notice that. Anyway, after a time I hear the bells and remember I have to go back.

"My father is not in the market where I left him, and this got me scared some. I remember I get panicky for a minute and run around there looking for him. But I find him pretty soon in an alley standing in a circle with many men. I ask him what is he doing and he tells me he has sold some jewelry belonging to my grandmother. That is weird to me because I am just thinking of her only moments before. I was very close to her, and I'm thinking of the beautiful funeral she didn't get.

"She was the only person to really love me. There is something in that for your psychology, huh?"

I decided the question was rhetorical. She blew a smoke ring.

"My father, my mother—they do not even speak to each other most times. He's always getting drunk and playing with young women. There's another thing, okay? You like this story?

"But my grandmother, she was one who always cared. So when I'm with my father there, I'm thinking 'what jewelry did he sell?' because I didn't ever know she owned anything worth money. She was as poor as the rest of us as far as I know. I am very surprised. Only many years later, do I learn from my mother this jewelry from my grandmother she had left behind to help her grandchildren—like in the case they want to try to do something important, go to school or something.

"My father was holding all this money in his hand, a big bunch of bills. I want to say it was many thousands of *pesos*, but I was a child and may exaggerate. I am sure it was more money than anybody I knew ever saw. I knew that it must also be from selling our vegetables. I even believe I knew this money was about all the money we had to our name, even though I was still so young. I never saw my father so excited. He smiled at me and says 'we are all set now because I have bought *Tomador de Vida*.'

"I do not understand what he's talking about. Then this man comes forward holding and petting a large rooster. You know, doctor, *pelea de gallos* has always been a part of my culture. Do you know what I'm talking about?"

"Cock fights happen all over this valley." I tried to

appear familiar with something I knew little about. Why was I trying to impress her?

"Well, not all over," she corrected, "but they happen. Anyway, I understood my father was going to buy this famous fighting rooster. And not only that, but he tells me he is going to fight right then and there against the champion of Zitácuaro, a rooster called *Ángel de la Muerte,* the Angel of Death."

She blew a magnificent plume of smoke and a couple of smoke rings and watched them disperse. I inhaled what I could as the cloud floated near me.

"I watched my father hand all that money over, the money he got from my grandmother's old jewelry, the money from our garden where all my sisters and my mom worked every day, to this very ugly man, and then take *Tomador de Vida* up into his arms. My father's petting his new rooster, talking to him in a soft voice I'd never heard him use. All the other men are watching and talking about the roosters, placing bets on who will win the fight.

"The circle opens, and I try to follow him, but he holds up his hand—'no,' he says, 'watch and wait.' He tells me proudly, 'You will soon be the daughter of a very wealthy man.'

"From his pants pocket, he pulls a piece of paper and unfolds it. Inside is a small blade on a string. He turns over *Tomador de Vida* gently, and he gets helped by some men to attach this to his rooster's left foot. The memory is still very vivid to me. More psychology, right? I remember my heart began to pound.

"The fight was really going to happen, and the noise of the men increased to a level that was frightening to a little girl who has hardly ever been anywhere. My father left me alone with all those men. Some got up off the ground and crowded around me. It still makes me shiver, that memory. I am afraid to leave where I am standing, and I am held still by the bodies of these men. A couple of them touched me and pinched me.

There was no one to stop them. My heart was beating like a baby bird. I could do nothing. I was wishing so much for my grandma."

She paused on the verge of tears but suppressed her emotions quickly.

"*Tomador de Vida* was all that was left of her—a kind of symbol, right? You will like this idea, I think. My father, he never thought of anybody but himself all the time I knew him."

"He sounds like a man driven entirely by his own needs and wants," I affirmed.

"You don't realize how right you are. He held *Tomador de Vida* with his head pushed forward and approached a big man on the other side of the circle holding *Ángel de la Muerte.* They poked their roosters forward at each other which makes them very angry, and then they dropped them on the ground. The dust flies up; everyone is shouting. I'm pushed several directions and getting touched again, too. My little fists go up, and I hit out whoever is doing that to me. Some men laugh; one whispers '*guapa*' in my ear, and I kick at him. I am fighting like the roosters are. I am kicking up dust. This man laughs even more. I feel hatred and fear, and start pushing to get away.

"I succeed in getting farther forward, but it is difficult to see which bird is which. Finally, I can see *Ángel de la Muerte* is down on his back, wounded. And this thrills me and scares me so much that I don't even know the difference between these two feelings. I want to get away so bad, but I can't stop myself from looking."

Another drag, another plume of smoke eased toward me.

"A delay is called to tie the blade that's come loose back on my father's rooster's foot. During this moment, the big man facing my father picks up *Ángel de la Muerte* and places his whole head into his mouth. This was so strange to me—I have never seen such a strange thing in all my young life. I still have bad dreams of a man blowing a rooster up like he's blowing a balloon. What he was doing was blowing air into his lungs. This gives the rooster his strength back. Our bird, *Tomador de Vida*, was still walking around and looking all proud much like my father was doing. My father thought he's the big man that day; both he and his new rooster acted like that together. I can see little difference in my mind.

"You see, my father had no experience; he does not know what to do. He does not understand his own bird is low on strength and breath too. So his bird doesn't get this kind of help. Now the judge starts the fight again—and the shouting gets louder again, and the dust becomes a cloud until the cloud slowly clears away. And *Tomador de Vida* is lying on his back this time. There is nothing to be done—his neck has been slashed, and he is dead. It is all over this fast." She snapped her fingers.

"Wow," I said.

She turned her head, and for once really looked at me.

"Yes. That is the very beginning of my family's biggest troubles. After this, me and my father, we pushed the cart home, and our journey was very slow. He carried *Tomador de Vida* in his arms like a baby. I had to do all the work with the cart—he won't even set him in there and help. We had no car or truck. We had no donkey or mule. We could have bought a car and much more with the money my father had in his hands—I knew that then.

"He is not talking at all. Why is he carrying his rooster like a baby? What good is a dead rooster? Just meat. Tears were streaming down my father's face. As for me, I am not crying. I am only thinking about what a fool I have for a father.

"He finally says one thing to me: 'Do not tell your mother about the bad luck you brought me today.' That is all."

She smoked some more but said nothing else.

"I'm sorry that happened to you." I said.

"I am twenty-six years old last month. I have slept with many men and taken their money since I was only fourteen— even while I was living with my auntie before she gave me up to foster care. Before I come to live with her, our mama supported me and my three sisters making money the same way. She was all ashamed but we all knew, and I didn't think bad of her. I am usually careful but admit I got caught by meth; my stupidity I get from my dad, or maybe my Yakama dad, I don't know. I like a risk, an adrenalin rush. For the men, I am another drug, and they get addicted. "

She had a formidable look in her eyes I didn't understand at the time. She stood up, leaned down, made a lithe motion out of tucking her cigarette lighter into her boot, and put a sway into her exit. We were done, never mind we still had twenty minutes left. I got up and followed, not realizing what instincts were being exploited.

"The new girl in our recovery house," she said as we moved down the hall, "she's a trigger for me. I smoke too much around her just like you. I don't really like her. She's trying to fuck with my main man, please excuse my language. Her name is Tina."

"Tina?"

"Her last name is too long to remember. She just got paroled. Her own son helps her get drug money. I know she is maybe a little like me, *sacacuartos*, huh? She needs to have money all the time."

"Her son?" I repeated, lost in thought.

She stopped by the door. "They meet in the alley near the house I stay at—behind the Dairy Queen. Mother and son special time; she buys him a little ice cream, he gives her his psych meds to sell. She tried to sell some to me."

"Ritalin?"

"Yes," she searched my hazy expression. "You pound it and snort it and get a coke rush from it."

She held her hand up, "I don't do that kind of shit anymore, doctor. She's trying to be my friend. I know she wants my man. I am a whore, but I am at least that smart, huh?"

"No doubt of that," I answered.

"About which?" She laughed. "That I'm a whore, or I'm smart or both, doctor?"

I prevaricated with a nod which didn't seem to suffice.

"Never mind." She pulled out her cell phone while she walked over to a gleaming black Harley Davison Road King.

"Nice bike," I noticed.

"Hector lets me borrow it."

"That's kind of him."

"Just another short, strong Mexican man," she answered. "He's not trying to be nice. He wants to get laid."

She straddled the bike and played with her cell some more. "This Tina, she wants me to put her in touch with somebody I used to know from down in Zitácuaro. A bad man who now lives in the Tri-Cities. She has a favor she wants to do for him."

"Yeah?"

"She says she knows where there is money belonging to him. She is. . . I don't know the English—*cauteloso*. All mysterious. Do you know her?" Her voice sounded sing-song like we were kids playing together.

"I can't say who I know and who I don't know in my profession, Maritza."

"Ah." She acted unaffected, lowered her cell and shook it. "Can I get better reception somewhere?"

"At that picnic table behind the cedar tree over there in the park," I pointed. "For some reason, that's the only spot that just about always works."

I wanted to ask her more about her new roommate. I felt sure she was talking about Tina Miyanashatawit.

FOUR

Cat shoved him harder,
And Coyote saw the land on the other side.
He wanted to see still more,
And the Cat swung him far out over the land
Beyond the ocean.
The swing came back empty,
And Coyote was never again heard from.
He is supposed to have grown dizzy
And fallen from the swing.
—William Charley, 1925

Massive billows of orange, blue, purple, and grey-black enveloped the sun through the picture window of our Montgomery Ward kit house, the oldest on the block. Senior water rights to an antiquated, aqueduct-fed irrigation system made our stand of weeds the very greenest. I gazed at the rock garden I'd put in to make less to mow. I had rocks on my mind.

Ruthie and I had avoided the lure of electronic devices lately by actually sitting down for dinners. I was hungry and eating too fast. She was only trying to eat. We were both tired and quiet.

We'd never been in total agreement about my decision to rent an office out in Harrah. She thought I should be in Union Gap, a violent little community situated between the upper and lower Yakima Valleys and closer to the city of Yakima. But I wanted to be nearer to White Swan. The old veterinarian office out in Harrah was spacious, and I knew that the glow in my eyes would force the issue my way even if she said the backroom smelled like goats.

I'd been proved right—professional work was now coming regularly to me from two recent contracts.

Ruthie had been out late at her book club the night prior, and I thought we'd be playing catch up talking about our week so far. But I didn't want to lie about the rock incident, and I also didn't want to tell her about it. The busted window, an angry invitation to 'git out' written on a rock, and some old car skidding away did little to further promote my choice of business locale. I also rationalized that I shouldn't upset her when she wasn't feeling very well.

"You seem preoccupied," she noted.

"Well, I've met with a lady of the evening today. On a professional basis."

"Umm," she murmured, chewing slowly on a mouthful of red lettuce fresh-picked from our back garden. "I'm glad it was your profession and not hers. Attractive?"

"I keep my eyes on you, darlin'."

She held an impaled cherry tomato in mid-air and looked at me questioningly.

"Your picture's on my desk," I clarified.

"And you think 'the blossom is off the rose,'" she sighed and set the tomato down on her plate.

"Not a chance."

She grabbed a piece of bread and pondered it instead.

"The elder mom in sweats and hoodie while my vulnerable husband works with hookers. . ."

Ruthie was quite miserable with morning sickness. Our recent romantic interlude had been an increasingly rare experience for us.

"And why am I so vulnerable?"

"Never mind," she chewed a very tiny bite of bread. "I'm just a little insecure."

"It was just some things she talked about that were on my mind, Ruthie, nothing else."

She   nodded, knowing better than to ask about

whatever a client said. Her face contorted slightly, and she set her bread down.

"By the way, I forgot to mention I saw Emily on Monday," I told her.

"At Mel's?" she asked, stirring her plate.

"No, in Harrah. Why do you say Mel's?"

"You sneak over there Mondays." She tried to grin through emerging nausea.

"Who said that?"

"You like the Monday special. Leila told me sometime back."

"God, I quit IHS for being spied on, you'll remember. *Chorizo con huevos.*"

Her expression paled. "Yeah, well, let's call it 'Mel's special that shall remain unnamed.' You were seen, and so now you're caught. Coincidentally, Dr. Warner's office called. You're supposed to get your cholesterol checked, Ret."

"Probably."

"Is Emily still going out to White Swan to ride Ámashitum?" She reluctantly sipped from a little cup, scrunching her nose.

"Are you drinking miso again? Uck. Yeah, she still rides their *washánł.*"

"Miso's all that ever stays down. And what's that, uh, whatever-you-said said?"

Her face was now white.

"Wild horse."

"Does Tessa go ride too?"

"She can't very easily."

Her look at me seemed to hold another question, but perhaps it was nausea. I decided to try answering anyway.

"You know, Ruthie, she can't do that as easily anymore. Having a kid changes everything."

She got up, clutched her protruding stomach with one hand and her mouth with the other and ran to the bathroom. I listened to the retching which put me off my salad.

"It's hard on me when you say stuff like that," she called out miserably, crouched down on the bathroom floor when I came in. "I'd like to get through all this knowing you *want* to have this baby."

"Oh, I do," I whispered as I kneeled and wiped miso from her cheek with a wet washcloth. "I do. Sorry."

A light blue package of Bugler tobacco stuck out of the pocket of my morning client's red plaid flannel shirt. His grey denims were loaded up with a fine, bright dust you only get from kicking up the plateau dirt. I tried not to care how the dirt might affect my couch's hue. His middle-age waistline was belted with a buckle worked in silver and embedded with large turquoise pebbles that cost more than the rest of his clothes combined. His hair was thinning, but he kept what he could long, usually in a braid. That day, it was a ponytail. Streaks of grey were visible. His boots were steel-toed Caterpillars, a favorite around here, and more cowboy than cowboy boots. He had a wide face cursed with a chronic expression of contempt, even when he felt happy or friendly. He hadn't been very happy lately.

Frank Mathis sighed, removed a beat-up Stetson from his head, and set it down on my office couch. He was mostly disconnected from the community in which he lived. Arnold Miyanashatawit had been his best friend before he died. Frank was always a man of few words, and for him to come talk with someone like me about his inner feelings was extremely difficult.

"Dreams come bad since, you know, our *xáy* there passed on. Fire, you know, all the time they come on about fire. See him in the little window . . ."

"You mean when he couldn't get out. You saw that?"

"Right, yeah, I seen that," he shook his head. "Now I dream it and can't get back to sleep. That one comes over and over. I carry it, especially when I go and tend Ámashitum."

"There's other ways Tessa and Emily could find to have Ámashitum looked after."

"I wouldn't feel right about that. Arn—it's my little way of doing right by him." He paused. "I'm holding him back, I know. Feel like there's, uh," he pulled out an old, washed-out white bandana from his back pocket, "no way for him," he blew his nose and poked his eyes, "to walk on."

"You feel you're holding his spirit back."

He just looked at me as though I'd have some answer for that conundrum.

I'd been socialized in grief as catharsis, as a personal experience to be encountered, worked through, and gradually reconciled. I had no right to impose this view on his culture. It wouldn't work anyway. In the past, I'd felt stymied. Lately, I'd allowed myself to open to a different worldview and sometimes been able to help.

"Do you ever go to the community sweat, Frank?"

The question surprised him.

"Not in many years. Used to go sweat at Joe Huertes' house years back when I was on council, but that was before my wife passed."

"Maybe you could bring out a song or two and pray for *xáy* there with others. At least, I've been around at sweat when that's happened."

"So you think I ought to go?"

"I'm just saying I heard guys bring things out in the sweatlodge when they were carrying a lot of pain. That seems a healing thing for what you're going through."

He hesitated and looked awkward. Frank didn't seem to want to disagree with me.

"I just couldn't go to that community sweat."

"Why's that?"

He picked his hat back up and twirled it slowly through his fingers.

"Mr. Barlow, years ago, I got brought up to ethics charges while I was on council."

The shame in his eyes made him pick and poke at his hat.

"I see . . ."

"Wasn't right, I suppose. People thought I had my hand in the cookie jar. I made some mistakes with a couple grants to fisheries. I got paid to help with surveys and that turned out to be a conflict of interest. I was told pay back the fees. But then Aida got killed by a drunk-driver, and I spent money on her funeral and some debts. I couldn't pay it back. It was five thousand dollars. Some sort of self-sabotage there, I suppose, was that I also started drinking. I hadn't paid up, and it come up at the General Council. That'd be twelve years ago. Don't get me wrong, I haven't touched a drop since it all came down back then."

He stared inside his hat. "I should've just said I didn't have the funds to pay back. I should've just said how things really were. They said I was cookin' the books, and I got booted off council. Word was I was a drunk, just like the person killed Aida. I don't get around here easy since then, if you understand. Folks remember. You're guilty until proven innocent on this reservation, you know."

"And going to sweat?"

"Well, Joe Huertes stopped having his sweat lodge. If I went to that community one, there'd be people I couldn't be around easy."

He looked up at me, hoping I'd have another idea.

"Is that true for your *xáy* there, too?"

"Huh? How do you mean?"

"Are you guilty until proven innocent for not being able to save him from perishing in the fire?"

His involuntary smirk folded and his eyebrows lifted high. Two tears rolled quickly down his cheeks. He gaped at me with broken teeth, broken smile, and broken heart. I'd gone too far.

"Sorry, Frank," I apologized.   "I thought it'd be better for you to be able to bring that out and may have gone too fast."

He nodded and furled his brows. "Could be but, well, what you say's likely true."

We were silent for a long while.

"You spend time in the service, Mr. Barlow?"

"No, I missed the draft lottery by a couple of months."

"You wouldn't know by the looks of me now, but I was Marine transport in 1968 and stationed in Quang Tri province. That was during Tet, the North Vietnamese offensive."

He sat back in his seat and relaxed a little for the first time since we'd started meeting. I'd be kidding myself thinking this had to do with the remark about not being able to save Arnold. No, it was the apology for making a mistake and pushing too hard that allowed him to feel like he could tell me what he wanted to tell me.

"I seen action there, you see. Fire. Always lots of fire everywhere I was around there."

He paused, and I waited for him this time.

"They bring you up close, you know. The military training—they get you so all you care about is getting through and that depends not just on you but on the next guy keeping you safe. There's some cruelty in that, maybe—these guys get like family and then they get killed. Two of my buddies were heroin addicts, you know; one died in my arms of an overdose. As to me, I smoked as much weed as I could get my hands on while I was over there."

He looked right at me. "One night during my second tour, we were in convoy and come under rocket and small arms fire. It got real hot real fast, and two trucks in front of us blew up all at once. When I say blew up, I mean blew up with pieces of people landing on to our truck windshield."

He eyed my clock and then me for another moment, watching, wondering how much I could take just listening to what he'd tell me about being Frank Mathis.

I nodded affirmatively, just once. 'I can take it,' I said with my eyes.

"What I did is I jumped out the truck cab and flew into the jungle screaming bloody murder. That's it. All my training went to hell. Honest to God, I ran like a scared puppy."

Again, his long look right at me. 'I won't run from what you're telling me,' I nodded.

"Well," he picked up his hat, "what nobody knows, except for that good friend, our *xáy*, is there was this other guy in that truck cab with me. His name was Neuter, like you neuter a male cat, you know?"

I nodded.

"That's his nickname. Stupid, really, to call him that. Some good old boy from Alabama. He was always friendly and always talkin' about how cool that I was Indian. Called me 'Filly Jack' because I told him we're a horse people, and I near choked him out when he said it. Other than that, he was a good man; he was okay. He was nice enough in his own way is what I'm saying."

He seemed to flinch at his own memory. "See, I left Neuter inside there. He'd been hit very bad, I guess, but he was still alive. Being a Marine, we don't leave a brother Marine in a spot like that. I could hear him from where I hid, from where I sprawled down low, shaking all over, from where I was shitting my own pants."

His eyes spun off to the memory, and he was there.

"'Frank! Frank! Frank! I'm hit. Don't leave me, Frank!' And I can't get up to get him, Mr. Barlow. 'He's all weak and dying; he'll die soon,' I'm thinking to myself. There's small arms and mortar fire everywhere, and I can't seem to move at all really. I can't make myself get up. 'Frank, Frank, don't leave me. I can't move,' and his voice is softer, but I hear him, and it's a torture to me because I'm stuck. So I just lay and listen to him. Just hear him over and over saying all that."

He closed his mouth hard and his chin trembled. "A few minutes, maybe only a few seconds, they hit our truck. Blam! They blew the shit out of it. You know what I'm trying to say?"

"And Neuter was no more," I concluded. Our eyes met again in affirmation of the agony in that memory.

"What happened then?"

He grimaced beyond his usual expression. "I stood up and got shot in the leg's what happened. And then I pulled two guys out the next truck who got all shot up."

I thought about that for a moment. "It's incredible you did, Frank, considering the circumstances."

"Nothing incredible about it. Truth is I didn't get up from where I was to try to save anybody. I was suicidal, that's what I believe. Neuter was dead, and I didn't do shit. I just couldn't take anymore. Once I stood up and got shot, I wasn't very well going to lie back down. No, I figured, I'll go die with those motherfuckers over there in t'other truck. I didn't give a shit. I walked over there to die with them. I remember every detail of that. I got up and walked over to their burning truck. That was unreal, like being in a dream. I just didn't give a shit no more. They give me the bronze star for that shit. But nobody but you and our *xáy* knew anything about what happened with Neuter."

He stared at me, totally incredulous. "Conspicuous bravery under fire, what a load of bullshit."

"Frank."

"Huh?"

"I feel I need to say something."

"Yeah?"

"I know our *xáy* loved you like a brother. You know, I knew him too, and I know what he'd likely tell you about

Neuter, and what he'd think you'd try to make of his dying in that fire in White Swan. He'd see you blaming yourself all over again. He'd want to tell you he knows you could not come through that fire to save him. If anything you're doing holds his spirit back, it's thinking you could have." His face fell hard. "You knew him longer than I did, so look in your heart. *Xáy* would forgive you for not being able to save him from fire just like that boy way back during Tet who was under fire. But I think they'd both walk on easier knowing you could start working to forgive yourself."

"Oh," was all Frank could muster, pulling up his bandana to his eyes again.

I reached over to the desk for a bundle wrapped in red cloth and pulled out some Northern California sage. I pulled out a lighter and held a few leaves in the air. Flame, fire held in front of us both, just for a few seconds. I blew it all out and set the smoky ember into a large abalone shell in my lap. The smell was pungent, and I wafted smoke over my face and shoulders, stood up, and passed the shell counterclockwise behind my back and around my body. I held the shell out to Frank, still smoldering. He reached for it and went through these same motions.

In this way, we blessed and purified our tears.

I am a LICWAC member and get paid by the tribe to go to a long meeting every week. LICWAC stands for 'Local Indian Child Welfare Act Committee.'

The Indian Child Welfare Act was passed in the 1970s to challenge generations of social welfare workers placing native kids into non-Indian adoptive families rather than with their own extended family members. ICWA says preference is supposed to be given to keeping kids with their home communities. At LICWAC, we mull over how kids are doing in their placements.

Social workers come in and out and detail cases to the

committee. I'm just one voice among many and usually spend my time trying to avoid arguing because there are never enough relative placements. Placing kids from chaotic backgrounds in good homes can be difficult.

That afternoon, a woman I hadn't seen before brought in photos of a boy in placement who had bruises on both knees. That was all she had, and she wanted him out of the home he was in. She was "deeply concerned" about his safety. It just so happened I'd interviewed him too. His foster parents, who'd been caring for kids for almost ten years, brought him to see me over some school issues.

So I mentioned to her that local native kids are like many other rural children in their play habits—they often run wild and free. I tried to be as sensitive as anybody else to child abuse, I told her and the committee, but I didn't think photos of bruised knees should be enough to pull him from a placement he shared with his sister and brother. His foster parents had already told me he'd taken a tumble.

All I could figure out was this woman had taken the photos because she couldn't get the boy to talk to her. He knew what was at stake; he'd already been in sixteen placements in five years. To my mind, he was finally starting to trust this family after living with them for the last eight months. Truthfully, pulling kids out of good placements and putting them into bad placements happens all the time. I thought pulling this boy would do more harm than good. I suppose I didn't mince words. The worker left the meeting pissed off.

Analise Bordeaux, the LICWAC chair, watched her exit and sighed.

"Dr. Barlow, please go easier on Brenda; she's new to LICWAC procedure."

"Who is she?" I asked.

"Guardian ad litem from Yakima Juvenile Court. She's around more since state cuts came down our way."

"She doesn't seem to know what she's doing . . ."

"Dr. Barlow . . ." Analise sighed again. "Be nice."

After the meeting finally broke up, I cut over on Wishpoosh Street to Fort Road to head back to Harrah. Three big native guys moved out into the middle of the road and flagged me down. I tried to steer around them, but they held their ground, and I had to stop. For a moment, I worried they might be connected to some LICWAC situation and angry about a decision I'd been involved in.

One guy wrapped his fingers over the frame of my open window. The other guy stood directly in front. The third guy walked around to my passenger door. Door frame man spit tobacco juice on the ground, and the third guy unlatched my passenger door. I got a little nervous.

"Culled from fisheries early this morning," door frame man proclaimed with a toothless smile as the third guy lifted a black garbage bag filled with fresh salmon onto the seat next to me. It must have weighed fifty pounds.

"Wow, that's an amazing amount of salmon," I responded, my heart still pounding. "Thank you. I'm not sure what I do with this many fish."

Door frame man watched the sky for a moment, smiling, and reveling in my discomfort.

"Native people like to eat them," he answered lazily. "Grilled or baked. You can smoke 'em too, but be sure you don't inhale. Japanese folks slice 'em up real thin, roll 'em with a bit of rice, and eat 'em raw. Can't think of too much else but talk to your Creator, doc. Maybe He'll have some more ideas."

The guy in front of the car doubled over with laughter as I pulled away. My car already smelled like fish.

I decided to drive out to Elisi's, but she was at the clinic; Chase was at Head Start. Tessa was the only one home.

"Nice!" she grinned broadly while I wrestled the bag through the front door. "How many do you want?"

I watched while she expertly cleaned and wrapped four very large fillets.

"*Kála* wants to know if you'll come out to White Swan on Sunday for a family meeting to talk about Franklin." Her knife flew through two more fish and she ripped and stacked their guts. "Leila and Emily and me too. I got to bring Chase along, of course."

"Tell her I'd love to show her my new office. Why don't you all come by there?"

"Barlow, it's nothing personal—she don't want to have the meeting there. She told me she wanted it at *tila*'s place. It's just an invite. If you and Ruthie got plans, it could be another day."

"Probably Ruthie can't really come if you all want to talk about Franklin's situation. That's family work and a professional boundary."

"Well, we'll miss her. She's always welcome. *Kála* hoped you'd come. That's all I got."

She wiped her hands on a towel and handed me several perfectly trimmed salmon fillets wrapped in butcher paper.

"Thanks for the salmon, Barlow; that's nice of you. Tell Ruthie thanks, too."

The trees at Yvette's still held plenty of fruit. At noon on Saturday, I stood precariously near the top of a picking step-ladder which has only a single pole stabilizing the front.

The sun beat down hard on me while Ruthie chatted with our French friend below.

"Don't tug stems off or you'll hurt the branches, Ret," Ruthie called up.

I reached up and shifted my weight while the sun baked me to a crisp. It was one hundred and three degrees, and my sweat dried quickly in the dry heat which made it easier to get dehydrated without knowing it. I thought of the big bags of Rainier cherries I'd bought at Costco and the delusion I'd been under that they'd been picked by some kind of machine or technology other than human hands.

After plucking a small handful and dropping them in successfully, I tied the plastic grocery bag on to a rung so I could take a big swig of water from the jug slung on a hook at the hinge. How people did this all day, I didn't know. I'd been at it for only twenty-five minutes, and my shoulder muscles were beginning to spasm.

"Kep moving there, *s'il vous plait*!" Yvette called up playfully. "Zis tree must be complet'ly clare of God's good fruit, *docteur*. I've put a *petite* crate down *pour vous* so you may take home all you weesh!"

Rainier cherries are the best in the world, hands down. They're colored bright red and white—only blue is missing to make them into a patriotic statement about the Pacific Northwest of the United States. Yvette was a master of anything green and could've made two weeks of Ruthie's salary from this one tree selling to gourmet mail-order houses. Instead, she gave her cherries away. We weren't the only people aware she was a soft touch for letting you pick her trees.

I managed to get about eight pounds of cherries into the crate after an hour or so, and I was all finished picking for the day. Yvette thought we needed more sweets and ladled in two Mason jars of homemade strawberry-rhubarb jam and a fresh-baked pear tart. So much for the rigors of dinner salads, I smiled to myself. You can't say no, after all, I told Ruthie.

After goodbyes, we made our way down to the end of her long drive, noticing blueberry pickers taking a break at the farm across the street, huddled in small groups beneath what shade they could find. Large plats of hefty crates filled with fruit were stacked up by their trucks.

"Doctor Barlow!" A familiar voice shouted as I was unlocking the door for Ruthie.

Maritza Rios strolled across the street in our direction,

wearing tight shorts, a sun hat, and a t-shirt.

Encountering clients out in public is a common feature of working as a psychologist out in rural areas. I knew instantly I'd said too much to Ruthie a few nights earlier, and she could potentially figure out who Maritza was. A worker sitting beside one of the trucks and eating an apple nudged his companion as she sashayed over. At the same moment, a muscular Hispanic man rose from a lawn chair with an umbrella above it and followed her.

"What are you doing here?!" she asked with affected delight. "Let me introduce you to my man, Hector, doctor," she gestured without even looking back. "He is *jefa* here."

Hector wore a light-colored, short-sleeved shirt, woven straw hat, and wrap-around shades. He had a carefully groomed mustache and a tight, insincere smile. I don't know why I felt like that about it, but I did. His handshake communicated he could squeeze much harder, and his arms were not quite as big as my thighs.

"*Buenas dias,* doctor . . . *senora,*" he tipped his hat to Ruthie, who was now sitting inside the car with her window lowered. "I have heard good things about you talking with my girl here."

Confidentiality constraints forced formality into my response: "Good to meet you."

I thought the better of complimenting him on his Harley parked alone beneath the old oak tree at the edge of the road. It had much more shade than any of the workers.

"And so who is this?" chattered Maritza, moving around the front hood, around Hector, and bending down to stare at Ruthie over through the open window.

"Ah," I answered. "This is my wife, Ruthie."

I couldn't even offer Maritza's name under such circumstances. She floated closer toward Ruthie's window and stretched out her hand fervently.

"I am Maritza," she announced. "Your husband is a

beautiful man for trying to help somebody like me with his counseling."

Her flattery surprised me, of course, given her manner behind closed doors. Hector raised his clipboard and stared down at it, seemingly disengaged by the work at hand.

"Well, it's very nice to meet you," Ruthie answered slowly. "I do hope he continues to be helpful."

"Oh," said Maritza. "You must be proud to have such a husband. He is very professional. But is he okay in that tiny office out there with all the crime around there?"

I became anxious she was going to tip Ruthie off about the broken window she'd seen.

"I do worry about his new locale a little, but he's always been close to the people living there. And I am proud of him. We've been together a long time."

Even I didn't miss that subtext.

"You were doing some picking?" Maritza asked Ruthie, spotting the partially-filled crate of cherries on the back seat.

"No, that was my doing," I said.

"Well, good." She spied Ruthie's belly. "You cannot let your wife work on those kinds of things, can you? When are you due?"

"Not until mid-October," said Ruthie.

"I wish to have a family someday," Maritza declared.

Hector glanced from his clipboard for a fraction of a second with no facial expression at all.

"Good to meet you both," he said quietly, turning and walking away. He didn't wait for our response. Maritza watched him, shrugged, and with a silent, little wave, followed him back across the street.

"Of course," I answered belatedly, ". . . goodbye."

I hopped in and started driving.

"Well, that was really weird . . .," Ruthie began. "That's her, isn't it? The lady of the evening."

"You know I can't say."

"Well, she's got little to hide and a lot to show. Funny how she used you to play her man."

"What do you mean?"

"Single women don't comment on the wonders of a married woman's husband, especially in front of their own boyfriends. I would think that might be even more true in Hispanic culture. And why was she asking whether you were 'okay' in your office location?"

"I can't imagine."

"Do you have to work with her, Ret?'

"You know I can't comment. Why do you ask?"

"There's something about her. I don't trust her or like her."

"Ruthie. In general, I have certain clients who are court-mandated under my Access to Recovery contract. Also, we need the money."

"There's just something I don't like about her. And I wouldn't trust her."

"Geez, why are you reacting to her like this? You know I've worked with women from the wrong side of the street before. I've never known you to worry about my professionalism."

"Calm down. That's not it at all, Ret," she shook her head. "No, it's not the sexy act. It's something else. There was something menacing about both of them."

"I think you're overreacting. They're just folks from the hard side of life. And I can't really keep talking about this anyway."

"You do realize he never wrote anything on his clipboard."

I gaped at her perspicacity.

"Hey, eyes on the road! People usually click a ballpoint before they write something, don't they? Ink usually appears on the page, right?"

"Well. . ."

"Well, what? Can you explain why he did that? No. I don't like the idea of you having anything to do with her."

She looked out the passenger window, watching sage and scrub sweep by. "She's just not right. Neither is he."

FIVE

The Greedy Ones have torn deep gashes in the Mother Earth,
Making her bleed. Our hearts also bleed,
And the water of life still flows onto the land.
Cities will grow there, but none of us will be here
To see them get very large. That is coming . . .
There is nothing we can do about it, nothing.
Perhaps there is nothing we should want to do.
Perhaps the Watcher wants it that way,
Because the earth freely offers her gifts
To be shared by everyone.
We are so few. . .
Let us pray that the Creator will give us a home
Beside our river forever
Where we can hear the drum when it speaks.
—Puck Hyah Toot, quoted by Now Tow Look (Click Relander)

I drove out to meet Elisi, Tessa, Leila, and Chase at Arnold's old place while Ruthie stayed home to grade essays, happy to have me gone. I hadn't been anywhere near Arnold's home in four months.

As I turned onto the familiar two-track, the colors around me seemed washed out—like some tired artist hurried to finish the visible terrain with what remained of straw greens and various tints of grey before accidentally spilling dirty white and walking away. The scrub was brittle from the constant swing of hard sun, cool nights, and gusts of winds coming out of nowhere. Rain on a summery day would be very rare at this time of year, but the weather was in a mood to defy the odds.

I got out of my car noting the silence of no dogs

barking at me. Charred spires of two-by-four protruding upwards from half a porch and a scorched square of meadow formed a partial echo of the home of a contentious but loving Yakama elder. His absence hit me acutely when I saw the dented all-metal lawn chair he always sat in with its paint mostly burnt away, metal rusting, and seat covered with a thin coat of black soot.

I wondered if he knew how much I liked him.

Passing Elisi's pristine Sunfire, a western kingbird swooped out of the broken window of the carcass of a Dodge Dart, settling onto the arm of his chair. The yellow on her chest could be seen for miles, and I stopped midstride to look her over. She did the same with me, and I had the odd sense she wanted me to state my business.

I heard angry voices, but when I came on Leila and Elisi sitting in lawn chairs, they were both quiet. Tessa stood solitary while Chase, next to her, peered through the corral fence at a stocky mare fifteen hands at the withers with a rusty black coat nibbling lazily at a broken bale of alfalfa. The mare lifted her head and that was as much greeting as I got.

"All *this* land's in *your* last name, kála—going all the way back to Treaty days," Elisi said. "We're a people stayed out here—never left, never went to the cities for work, never gave up our land. Do you know there are Indian people stuck in the big city who long for the land their family once had?"

She caught up a handful of dirt from the ground and held it toward Tessa so tightly you could see dust bursting from clumps between her ancient fingers. Tessa didn't look at her.

"It's got to mean something to you! *Our* language, *our* freedom, *our* ways, they tried to take it all, but we have held this land for our children. It has to be lived on by *only* our people! *That's* our sovereignty, kála, that's what it means, not some piece of paper."

Tessa watched the hills with both hands halfway into

her jeans pockets. Leila gestured me into an empty lawn chair while Elisi continued.

"If you won't live here, there's nobody can. I got my place; Leila's got hers. When your *tila* left his share to you, he trusted you. This deed runs ninety-nine years, and time's near up. He knew that deed can only be renewed through occupancy of a family shareholder, and that's you and your family living in a new built house. If that don't happen, your brothers and sisters get separated. Don't look to us to qualify to take them in—I'm too old, and Leila's place is too small. They'll go off to foster care, *káɬa*, to live with who knows who, probably Seattle or Tacoma. Their connection to this land will die. And along with that, this family begins to die.

"Think on your sisters and brothers," Elisi said more softly. "You spent time in foster care with your sisters when things went bad with your mother and before your *ála* and *tila* took you all in. We're not talking about living out here forever, only 'til someone else can take it on."

"Please quit trying to make me feel all guilty and ashamed! My brothers and sisters are not my children. . . *and this land is my tila's!*"

Tears popped from the corners of Tessa's eyes, and she turned away.

"*This is his land!!*" she shouted out to the hills. Chase trotted over toward her mother.

"What's wrong, Momma?" Chase asked, staring at me. Once again, I seemed to be around when her mother cried.

"Hi there, little bunny."

"I'm not a bunny," Chase glared at me.

Tessa ignored her and spun toward Elisi and Leila to speak.

"This allotment will stay mine no matter what I do. You both just want to wash your hands and make me into some single welfare mom taking care of Chase and all my sibs. So thanks for that! I'm to keep them from foster care. Do you think about what kind of future that leaves for Chase and me? I'm *going* to finish school, so you need to get used to that!"

"Tessa, you can still do that living out here without leaving behind your very own child," Leila answered. "You don't have to go off. You can help keep your sibs out of the system."

"Huh?" I asked, perplexed and confused.

Tessa crossed her arms tightly and responded to Leila instead. "Three months between Basic and AIT total. Then I'm all back home and can do what's needed. I just need your help to take her for only that long—why is that so much to ask given what you're asking of me?"

"Well, you didn't bother to ask, *káła*; you just went ahead and did it."

Elisi acknowledged me with a nod before clarifying. "Tessa's joined up the National Guard."

"What?!" I almost fell from my lawn chair.

"Soon after her *tila* died; she signed herself up. Didn't tell anybody until she found out she had to ask me or Leila to take temporary custody of Chase. That's when she tipped her hand—after the fact. She didn't want to bother herself with details."

"You didn't want to mention any of this to me. . ." I said to Tessa, who was holding Ámashitum's halter while we spoke.

"Nothing personal, Barlow. If I wanted to talk with you about it, I would have."

"She don't want to hear your disapproval," Elisi suggested.

"Bullshit," Tessa whispered to Ámashitum's ear as she moved up and hovered over her shoulder . . . but we all heard it.

"Do not talk to me that way!" Elisi sputtered. "Do not speak with such ugliness!"

Tessa ignored her, tugged Ámashitum in, and feigned checking her teeth.

"I am at my rope's end!" Elisi spoke to her back. "I done everything I could! I honor my sister's request and keep you safe, and now you do this!

"Look at the beauty of this land that's here for you to live on with your little girl! Instead you'd leave her behind without even thinking who's to care for her. If we do have to look after her for you, maybe we ought to report you to the child protection worker because you had no thought but to yourself when you brought all this situation about, *kála.*"

"I brought this situation about?!" Tessa faced her with fury, letting go of Ámashitum who started backwards. "You and auntie Leila brought it about!"

Leila shook her head and looked at me, "We been trying to sort this through for weeks, Dr. Barlow. We want to try to get her out of what she's done, but she won't listen. We thought you might come out here today and help us to bring these things out in a better way."

The grief and care of the last few years had weakened Leila's cheeks and etched crow's feet around her eyes. Her face looked twenty-five years past cheerleading at Wapato High School.

"*Shíx páchway*, Frank," Elisi said.

I hadn't noticed him walk up and reached up from my seat to shake his gnarly hand lightly. We each acted as though we hadn't seen each other only a couple days ago. Chase watched him expectantly.

"You want your lasso back, cowgirl?"

"Yeah!" she shouted.

"Come on, then."

For a few minutes, we watched them play near the barn as Chase struggled to spin the tight-wound rope over her head and throw it at a broken post about ten feet away. Frank quietly coached her, standing by the barn door, fashioning a cigarette from his bag of Bugler tobacco.

"They pressured me hard only two days after *tila* was laid to rest," Tessa told me, "and kept it up. Everybody's eating commodity food, they complained, like that's my fault. Nobody's bringing fish or venison or elk now he's gone. So Hamburger Helper instead, Kraft macaroni in a box, cheesy potatoes, the USDA poison, government giveaway junk food. They know if me and my brothers and sisters live out here together in a rebuilt house, the state would kick in, and all of us won't cost more money that nobody has. So that's why they want me tied down out here."

"Oh, you know that's not it at all, Tessa," Leila snapped.

"*Náktkwanin ttáwaxt,*" Elisi said. "There's the words for you which means being responsible for your family, *káła,* but they mean more than that because there's no real words in English for how our language expresses love for family. What you should say is Leila and I made you a very good offer. Care for these little ones for a time of a few years on this land out here, and you'll own the new home gets built on it."

"By the by, Tessa, what is it you think I been doing for your mom?" Leila exclaimed, suddenly angry. "How long do you think I looked out for you and your brothers and sisters anyway? How come I care for five kids living in my tiny place right now? You just go behind everybody's back and decide to leave your own little girl behind, and we're supposed to just deal with that, right? I just don't understand you on that, not at all. When do you really want to grow into being a mother, Tess?"

Tessa clamped her jaw. "Yeah, auntie, maybe you forgot I cared for my sibs all by myself 'til I was eleven years old. Maybe you don't know I cleaned Samuel pissing his pants while your sis shotgunned beer and swung her fat ass for Jack Brie. Maybe you don't know I was bumming milk while she smoked crystal. *I been their mother already*! And while *tila* was alive, what did I do out here, *káła,* auntie?" Her voice caught momentarily. "What do you think? Who do you think was mother to them then? Who?? You think you can tell me I don't know nothing about being a mom and being responsible?? That's *all* I been!"

Tessa stomped away to lean against the rails and stew. Ámashitum's ears perked as she came near, and she snorted playfully, trotting over to nibble at a nearby alfalfa bale. Chase laughed uproariously at tangling her foot in her rope, and Frank chuckled quietly.

The conflict seemed to pull everyone present in different directions, each of which had its own kind of sense. What could I say to help fix this? I pulled a single cigarette from my shirt pocket and lit up.

"Thought you quit, doctor." Elisi crinkled her nose. "Maybe you want to die a Marlboro man."

"I don't do it that often, *kála,*" I responded defensively, pulling in a big, defiant drag.

Her rheumy eyes took me and my manner in for a moment.

"How's your wife? I saw her for a few minutes at the market last week."

"Sick of feeling sick, *kála.*"

"Morning sickness?" she grimaced. "That's hard on the woman. If we dig around here for a while we might find you a root to boil up for her. What we call *tíi.*"

"Tea?"

"Pretty much the same thing," she chuckled. She looked at Tessa over by the corral.

"Our girl here, she's pretty *kw'shɨm.* Reminds me of my sister who passed on."

She noticed my confusion. "Kind of stubborn. You tend to be *kw'shɨm* too, doctor."

I moved over to the railing to try to reach out toward Tessa in the least threatening way I could. "So what's AIT?"

"Advanced Individual Training," she answered, watching Ámashitum. "MP school. After I'm done with Basic and that, I'm back home on reserve with drill pay and education benefits."

Tessa turned and faced me. "Mel said he's cutting my hours when they raise minimum wage. Right now with work, Chase, and classes, I can't get my GPA at Heritage College strong enough for the MS in Law and Justice program at Consortia."

"Ah, Consortia," I responded without enthusiasm.

The school she mentioned constructed their own sleek building in downtown Yakima in only two months and were now dropping slick brochures at every vet gathering within a hundred miles. They wanted that GI Bill dime. You could look up their parent company on the New York Stock Exchange. Consortia College was sucking hard on the taxpayer's breast in secondary cities all over the country.

"I get fifteen thousand dollars my first year in the Guard and a free ride to Consortia with my reserve status. I can do school full-time and be a better mom."

There was no way I was going to debate with her over the hazards of a school like Consortia, so I didn't say anything.

"You're already a good mom," Leila reassured, overhearing what she said.

"Come on; you all know I suck as a mom."

It was clear everyone was trying to cool down.

Chase tossed her lasso on the ground in front of Frank and walked towards her mother, stopping uncertainly in front of her. I sat back down with Elisi.

"Somebody looks tired," she observed before whispering to me: "Part of what you see here is what boarding schools and BIA campaigns attacking native moms in those years past has left to us. Tessa learned her lack of confidence likely from her own mom's problems, and that come down through Georgina's time in boarding school. So we got to help Tessa unlearn all that."

"Come here," said Tessa, and Chase jumped up into her arms.

"What do you mean?" I whispered back to Elisi.

Elisi gave me a somewhat scathing glance. "I mean Bureau of Indian Affairs 'Save the Babies' campaigns five generations ago. You must know about those, doctor."

I tried to look contrite.

"Take the long view, doctor. That's what native people do. Look up Emmerich's paper on your computer; I don't have time to explain."

"Seems like your elder here has got a point, Tessa," said Frank, strolling up behind Chase, "and then again you may have one too."

We all looked at him, surprised he'd been able to hear what we'd been discussing.

"Oh, I heard you all dickering and the doctor trying to make some peace between quarreling *áyat*."

He threw the butt of his cigarette onto the ground

"Let's face facts." He looked at the lasso he held. "Kids here get roped in. The tribe don't offer much of what they really need."

His flinty eyes spied Tessa. "I'm one seen this young woman flash a knife and jump right on top of a grown man to protect her family. Talk about responsibility. *Yáych'unal* with her—so I think she'd make a fine tribal officer, and the military's a good road for that."

Elisi's sad eyes and wizened face didn't change, framed by thin, tight braids, streaked with white. Frank kept his eyes on Tessa. Elders don't always agree.

"But, Tessa, your *tila* meant you to respect your *káła*. You walk away from the gift he left you—his allotment, what he regarded as sacred land here—and there could come a day you'd not forgive yourself. You may believe you needed to go your own way behind your *kála*'s and auntie's back, but there's too much at stake for you to do that and feel right about it."

Tessa only stared at the ground. He looked at the hills beyond which his own property lay and said no more. Tessa finally spoke haltingly to Elisi and Leila.

"Well, I don't have him no more, and I didn't know what to do. I figured this way out and thought you two'd back me up."

She pondered her hands. "I know he would've backed me; I know it. And so I thought you two would and didn't think further. I didn't mean to do wrong. It's just I never had anybody I trust except *tila* and *ála*, you know that. Okay, maybe Barlow some," she pointed lazily at me, "but he wasn't raised here, and he doesn't always know what he's talking about. I didn't want to talk to him about the military."

Leila watched her as she spoke. Elisi peered off toward the hills.

Tessa's eyes filled. "I need to follow my dreams. I got pregnant so young. I know that's my doing; I'm trying to make my life better now. You said you'd be a best friend to my dreams, *kála*, do you even remember saying that?"

She couldn't speak anything else for a second.

"Nobody ever said anything like that to me. I still believe it in my heart, even though you're all angry. I didn't mean to take advantage. I only need to get away for a short while to learn about police work, so I can make a good life and be a better mom."

She turned her head away from us.

"Please, please," she muttered. "Try to understand."

It was very quiet for a minute or so.

"With all respect to you both," Frank said to Elisi and Leila, "I'm okay with watching over this land. You don't have to set it in my name, although a temporary deed might keep it safer from getting disputed. What I mean is I'm not going anywhere. I owe a lot to the man built out here. After my wife got killed, I got all twisted up. He didn't judge me but kept creeping 'round and putting home-canned salmon on my porch. Christ, I even shot one of his dogs, and he didn't hold that against me. Least I could do is look after what he wanted left for family."

"Thank you, Frank," Elisi finally responded slowly, "thanks from our hearts. Tessa here knows full well I'm eighty years old next summer. Most people around here don't live so long."

Tessa watched her.

"I hear your words, *káɫa*, and understand how you been thinking. You weren't so sure about who loves you. I can't agree with what you did, but I understand it. I'm too old to raise a little girl for three months, no matter how much I love her or you."

"Well," said Leila, "what's done is done. I'll just have to kick in and help, I guess."

Tessa turned toward her auntie, perhaps realizing more deeply what she'd brought to bear on others.

"Look," said Leila, "yes, I feel you've done wrong, Tess; I made mistakes when I was young too. Yes, you should have talked all this through with us. Now you're all signed up and there's no turning back. We'll have to make do.

"*Náktkwanin ttáwaxt*," Leila repeated, "like our elder says. We'll show you what that means. That way you don't have to doubt. Do you understand what I'm saying?"

"Yes, auntie," Tessa answered. "I won't be gone long. The recruiter said deployments are declining. He said I won't have to worry about that."

"Bullshit, *káɫa*," Elisi enunciated, and we looked at her in amazement, never having heard her talk that way.

"Hunh," she stared back, "like I don't know how to cuss."

"*Káɫa*, you told me not to say that!" Chase shouted

crossly. "I want to go home!"

Ámashitum whinnied.

"You'll need to wait a minute, little one. What about Ámashitum, your 'Owl Child' here?" Elisi asked Tessa. "She's been good to you."

"I'll get back to her," Tessa responded, rising to leave.

"I'll keep an eye on her," Frank answered. "Ámashitum's as much a part of this land as anything out here."

Frank said a quick farewell and walked back into the hills toward his place. I helped Leila lower Elisi through the passenger door opening of her Sunfire while Tessa loaded Chase into a car seat. Leila and I waved them off, and she started toward her truck.

"Hey Leila, I thought we were all getting together out here today to talk about Franklin," I told her. "Was I wrong?"

"Oh, Tessa and Emily mentioned some worries you had about the medication. You know, I never wanted that Oakley lady in their lives, doctor, but that's the state system. By the time she brought all the kids over to me from their cousins, she had his pills all set up. She's pretty pushy; she told me he had to be on them, or I'd get reported to CPS for medical neglect."

"Hmm, I don't think Ms. Oakley has a right to push you or him around on that."

"You may say that, but I wouldn't cross her. I've got too much on my plate without having the state breathing down my neck. I was curious what you had to say about him taking that methyl . . . methyl . . ."

"Methylphenidate."

She laughed. "What you said. That's a kind of speed, isn't it? What do you think of him taking those pills combined with all the others? You know with the, uh, resperi—"

"Resperidone? Well, I understand that has side effects on the liver. And I'm told he's got fluoxetine and diazepam in his little cocktail too. Who really knows? All I can say is I don't believe it's good for him or helps his situation. You could ask Dr. Fitzsimmons, but she has strong beliefs about the pills. Does Franklin really take all those pills every day?"

"Oh, no. He doesn't," she said sheepishly. "Franklin's a boy who don't do anything very regular. I remind him, he forgets, you know. He's been runnin' wild all over Larena Lane."

"Well, better for him to not take them, Leila, than take them every now and again. Saying that doesn't mean I agree with taking them at all, by the way. You should tell Dr. Fitzsimmons he's not following through on what she set up. That alone means she should get him off them as soon as possible. Nobody really knows what all those pills do together anyway. Not her or anybody else. Your nieces say they're worried he might be selling them."

She climbed into her truck and gripped the wheel tightly before remembering to get her keys out of her pocket.

"Oops. I'm so distracted right now. I don't know when I'll talk to that pill doctor, but I'll try. I'd like you to meet up with Franklin for some counseling, doctor. I can't handle him—he won't respect anything I say. Lately, I've had to put in double shifts if Mel will let me. The state don't give a person enough money to take care of all these children, and I got to bank some money up for us. We're always coming up short."

I agreed to call her to try to set a session up for Franklin when I could get back to my calendar.

SIX

The first Americans—the Indians—
are the most deprived
And most isolated minority group in our nation . . .
The time has come to break decisively with the past
And to create the conditions for a new era
In which the Indian future
Is determined by Indian acts
And Indian decisions.
—*President Richard Nixon, 1970*

On Monday in the early afternoon, I was parked and sleeping off a large plate of Korean bi bim bap along Fruitvale Boulevard in the city of Yakima. Business was slow for me that day, and I'd grown tired of salads. I awoke to my cell vibrating in my shirt pocket, and I answered quickly.

"Dr. Barlow, this is Brenda Oakley."

"Ah. Hello there," I slurred from a deep nod.

"I'm calling about Franklin Miyanashatawit. I'd like to talk to you about him before you meet with him this week."

How she knew, I wasn't sure. But asking how she knew would be confirming what I couldn't confirm.

"You may already know I'm guardian ad litem for those kids," she added.

"Ah. Ms. Oakley, it's my professional policy not to talk with anybody about anything associated with my clinical practice."

"You mean without a signed release."

"Sure, provided it's stipulated properly."

"Then I'll let you know, doctor, that all that's required for you to talk with me is for me to provide you with a copy of the court order appointing me guardian ad litem. I spoke with Leila yesterday after she made her inquiry to Dr. Fitzsimmons' office about your views on the medications Franklin's taking for his mental illness. Her nurse called me to ask what this was all about, and so now I'm calling you. We've already met. I was at the last LICWAC meeting."

"Oh," I sat up in my seat, putting two and two together. "You're Brenda. You're Brenda Oakley."

"Yes, Brenda Oakley. Now a copy of the court order releases you from liability in talking to me. I'm happy to fax it over."

"Actually, I don't have a fax handy." I picked my teeth with a semi-used toothpick. "And, uh, I'll need to get you one of my own release forms to use so I know the release you mention is fully-informed."

Her voice tone lowered. "The court order appointing me guardian ad litem should be sufficient. It's a legal document. It's a violation of law if you don't cooperate, doctor."

"Are we talking about Washington state law, Ms. Oakley?"

"Yes."

"And will you have me arrested if I don't do things right?"

Her voice hardened. "I'm not appreciating your attitude, doctor. That's beside the point. I've been a guardian ad litem for twenty-seven years, and I can tell you it's a violation of state law for a mental health provider to refuse cooperation when I have a court order entrusting me with a child's best interests."

"You see my office in Harrah happens to be situated on the sovereign land of Yakama Indian Nation, Ms. Oakley."

"I fail to see why that matters."

"I've got a business license in my office issued by the Fourteen Confederated Tribes and Bands of the Yakama

Nation, and I don't want to endanger it. It cost me twenty dollars, and I've only had it a couple of months. That's why I need a signed copy of my own release form to talk to you about anybody associated with my practice."

"Dr. Barlow, I'm quite sure Yakama Nation is not sophisticated enough to have policies governing free-standing professions like yours."

"I know they have unwritten laws going back thousands of years, even predating our own forms of Western jurisprudence, which I think's pretty interesting. I think it'd be a bad idea for us to argue about the sophistication of Yakama people."

"So let's not do so, doctor."

At that moment, I'd made up my mind about her.

"Okay, let's not. I think making Washington state law binding on me in relation to sovereign native people who've always lived on the land where my business is licensed wouldn't sit well with them. They have a treaty recognized by the feds, you know? And federal law trumps state law and all that."

"You're going to run into trouble trying to interpret the law to me, doctor."

"What you're trying to get me to do here is a kind of *shuyápu* idea, do you see? It's not native law we're discussing. The bulk of my practice income comes from my relationship with the Yakama people. So the question here is do the unwritten laws of the Yakama Nation allow me to talk with somebody outside their community about their private lives and their children without being sure they're fully informed. I really don't know the answer there, and I'd rather stay on the side of 'no' until I know more."

The line got quiet, and I thought I heard her breathing a little heavier.

"You're not going to cooperate with a copy of the court order."

"I'd feel much safer with a signed informed release in my own format. I've already had it approved by the Yakama Nation Tribal Court."

"Dr. Barlow, I'm going to bring your behavior to the attention of Judge Martin."

"Okay."

"It's your funeral."

"Uh oh," I responded. My cell screen read 'call ended'.

"You're in trouble, aren't you?" Ruthie asked while we sat at the kitchen table eating homemade tortilla soup and bread.

"Why say that?"

"You put about a pound of butter on your bread. You're sighing over and over. Huh, ahh, huh, ahh. You keep smiling at me in that weird way. And you smell like cigarettes—yuck, Ret, I thought you quit? You were making fists and pacing all around the kitchen before dinner."

"Goddamn, you'd make a good shrink."

"I only have one client. Clue me in."

"I can't, darlin'. It's all confidential. All I'll say is I had to go out on the proverbial limb today."

She grabbed a piece of bread off the little cutting board sitting on the table.

"Not for that little sex pot you're working with, I hope." I shook my head 'no.' "Well, good, you'll tell me that much."

She chewed a little more and kept her eye on me. "By the way, I read somewhere that if you eat bread this way and chew for longer, you won't consume as much."

I sighed.

"Look, I don't mean anything, Ret; I just wish you'd get your blood pressure checked."

"My blood pressure's fine."

"You're absorbed into some social justice issue, I can

tell. You've got your back up about something along those lines."

She was hoping I'd confirm or deny the idea and then grimaced when I only slurped my soup.

"Okay, I'll talk about my day. Did you know the KKK held an induction meeting at Yakima Fair Grounds in 1924 with 40,000 people in attendance?"

"I did not."

"The Neirs' ancestors, you know, your landlords, were on the organizing committee. Their name comes up again on the local defense committee that enforced FDR's order for the Lower Valley Issei and Nisei to get onto trains and leave after Pearl Harbor. People like that stole their farms."

"Ruthie, it doesn't mean their kids turned out like that—those were very different times. I'm not excusing it, I'm just saying. Alice Neir stopped by my office unannounced the other day and declared God Himself may be helping me shepherd the local flock."

"Weird. Isn't a landlord supposed to give you notice before they stop by?"

"I guess she just wanted to see what my place looked like," I said.

"Doesn't she already know? Is she part of your worrying and sighing?"

"Honest to God, Ruthie, I'm fine. Don't worry. You know I can't tell you things about what I do professionally."

"Okay, yes. I'm a little stressed too. This morning we had a real lockdown, Ret—somebody shot bullets across the baseball diamond at Garfield School."

"Goddamn, Ruthie! Are you all right?"

"As good as can be expected. After the lockdown, the bug man came into my class and sprayed which made it smell bad. Then, at lunch, Helen told me the kids over at Burgis Elementary in West Valley are going to Seattle Art Museum on a field trip today."

"Hmm, inequities in public education front and center in Yakima Valley—your day was not so great."

"We'll be talking about racism in the new eighth grade history unit I'm prepping. I worked on it between eating a sandwich and getting ready for parent conferences."

"I know you work hard."

She rested her chin on her palm. "Thank you for that, Sigh Man. My question is—do you think I should include this local KKK angle in the racism unit? I assume you would."

"Uh, that's a tough call."

"Yakima is a small place, and I'll hear from parents whatever I do, right?" I wasn't sure whether her question was rhetorical. "A teacher has to be careful. We're not supposed to offend with the truth. The Texas Board of Education determines the textbooks for public schools in this country, did you know that? They influence the national publishers. There are certain folks on the school board here who want their kids to learn that version of pseudo-truth and *nothing more*. Do you see what I mean?"

"Not exactly."

"I'm telling you I wouldn't want to lose my job right now by talking truth to power regarding the crappy history textbooks we use. That's not a battle I'm going to win, if you know what I mean. History belongs to the people who publish it."

"I can see your point. That's less so with oral history, however."

She chewed her bread some more for another moment with an even more intense expression.

"I have to think about what I do and say in my job every single day, Ret. I love you and your sense of justice. I'm just hoping you'll remember not everyone needs to know your opinion about everything."

I slurped my soup again, and her eyes went wide. She leaned over, and poked buttered bread into my nose. Then she got up and darted backward.

"Are you even *listening* to me?"

I chased her into the kitchen where she tore another chunk of bread from the half-loaf on the counter and threw it right at me. She hit me right in the center of my forehead.

"Our lives shall not be sweated from birth until life closes!" she sang with a semi-crazed expression. "'Hearts starve as well as bodies; give us bread, but give us roses!' That's the old communist Wobblie song, have you ever heard it? Do you think I should include that in the unit, Ret?"

"Probably not a great idea."

She took a firm bite of bread and chewed hard. I didn't understand her.

"Goddamn, you're moody tonight," I snapped. "Is this about the lockdown or educational inequities? What the hell, Ruthie? Hormones? I can't tell what you're up to."

She chewed her bread mockingly, swallowing in a big gulp. "I guess you can't!"

I got mad, threw my own buttered bread on the floor, and walked out of the kitchen.

"Hey, who cleans this up, huh, buster?!"

She followed me into the bedroom where I lay brooding.

"I wonder if you'll remember nearly getting yourself killed by Jack Brie last time you acted all jumpy like this. And I was just wondering, Ret Barlow—if you aren't going to tell me what the hell's going on—could you just lie low so we can start a family together like we've been trying to do *for the last nine years*?"

"Me, I *have* to lie low; why don't you try it? Please don't get on some big crusade—I can tell you're fighting about some issue. I can't stop you—I'm not even sure I want to—but remember we're in a *much* more vulnerable place than five years ago when you were fighting with those nasty people at the clinic and almost got yourself killed chasing Tessa around.

"Also," she exclaimed in complete finality as she stomped away, "clean up after your own tantrums!!"

I was certain it must be hormones.

Maritza pulled up early for her appointment on Hector's Harley, settling it down to a simmer. I'd just come back from lunch and stood by the door waiting for her. She took her helmet off and shook her black hair loose, revealing lighter highlights she'd dyed in for show. She reached up and pulled it together into a loose bun, fixing it with the hairstick she drew out of her back pocket. Then she rummaged in her front pocket before applying some ruby red lipstick. I tried not to watch, but there wasn't much else to look at. She got off the bike, walked up, and smiled with luminous white teeth.

"I am now all put together, doctor. Today I have no stories to tell."

She dropped into the furthest corner of the couch clear on the other side of the room from me. I had no idea why.

"You have a pretty wife."

"Thanks."

"She seems like a good kind of woman."

"Thanks for that too."

"This kind of woman is hard to find, you know. You should keep her happy."

"Okay—I agree. Our sessions are about you, not me."

"Does she know you got rocks coming through your window and rocks in your head trying to keep an office out in this tiny piece-of-shit town?"

"You're not feeling supportive of my practice out here, I guess."

She waved her hand. "I don't think it will work out for you. I never see a counselor put his office in such a faraway place."

"Well, thanks, Maritza. I want to try to make it work.

By the way, do you have your court paperwork today?"

She snapped her fingers expertly. "I forget again!"

"I need to bill for services, and I can't keep working with you without those materials. Now I'm going to have to call up Harold Lettie, and he's going to ask me why you didn't bring it yourself."

"Doctor, I'm sorry; I don't want to get on that man Lettie's bad side. Please—I will get it for you after our session and drop it by for you."

The implications were serious for her. A probation officer like Harold could interpret her laxity on giving me the paperwork I needed as a failure to comply with the terms of her probation.

"Well, I'd rather not do that, Maritza, but I need to get paid. Slide it through my mail chute by 3 p.m. today, or I'll have to call him."

"Okay. I'll do it. I promise."

"Thanks."

I waited for her to bring up a topic. I decided against trying to help her do so, even though she looked at me expectantly for a few moments.

"So," she began, "this woman, Tina, I will talk to you about her, I guess. She is spending way too much time with my man, Hector."

She saw me noticing the scratches on her left cheek and the bruise on her right temple.

"Hector gets a little provoked sometimes, doctor."

"And did that happen over you and him getting in trouble over at the Thompson place?"

She sat back, surprised, and smiled. "Well . . . you hear some gossip around town maybe."

I saw relapse to addiction right in front of me, and sat up to let her know I really meant what I was about to say.

"We've got to start working to help you get your shit together, Maritza. You're in a bad place, and you don't want to talk about that, I understand. But we've got some work to do. You may be clean now, but you're dancing around a big hole you're about to fall into with this guy. You should stay away from anybody who thinks they have a right to hit you, especially if you find yourself putting up with it. I know a domestic violence safe house up in Yakima. I can help arrange a safe place for you to go."

"Hector would love to hear you say this, doctor. Will you protect me from him then?" She batted her eyelashes unsubtly.

"Maritza, come on; I'm seriously trying to help you."

She shrugged. "That is very nice of you. Okay, yes, he was pissed at me about Evelyn Thompson and all that. I don't like having sex in a barn like some pig. Other people come in and out from there. I say let's go inside. Then we get caught by the lady, and he gets the boot. After that, I call him out about Tina. You see, I am sincerely worried. This Tina is trying to get him involved in illegal activities, and he already did time for such things. I don't know if I can say much more to you."

"Whatever you talk about stays in here. The only exceptions are if you say something about a serious threat to yourself, somebody else, or about abusing a child or a vulnerable adult. Other than that, it stays with me."

She just watched me and said nothing more, so I continued.

"If you talk about Hector's illegal activities, I keep it to myself unless it has to do with the things I just mentioned. I hear about illegal activities fairly often."

"But what about Mr. Lettie?"

"I need to get paid is all. Other than that, I say fuck him and the horse he rode in on."

Her eyes went wide. "This is not talk I ever hear from a counselor."

She stroked the fabric on my couch with her fingertips,

contemplating.

"We all go to the same addiction recovery group together and go out and smoke together on the break. I take a break from a talking group, I don't like to talk, you know? Tina and Hector are, you see, very similar people. They started scheming about her little plans. That's what started us fighting."

"Ah. Whatever you argue about, Maritza, he has no right to get physical."

She shook her head slightly. "I can handle him. But I don't like her. I tell him, 'you should stay away from her,' and he takes it like I want to control him. She's going to get him put back behind prison walls. And what's to like about somebody uses her own kid, right? My own ma done that.

"But I do not see Tina with her young man so much lately. She's doing something new. She's—uh— trying to hustle where you don't want to hustle. She's promising him lots of money if he helps her. She wants his protection and is trying to seduce him. I say 'keep your hands off him, if you know what is good for you.' These people she's trying to mess with down there in Tri-Cities are Black Hand. Hector knows them already."

"So Hector must be F-13," I guessed.

She twisted her hair. "Hmm, you know a little about that, doctor. But no, he's not; Hector's Norteno. But he wasn't always Norteno. Before he went to prison he had some distinction with Surenos. Do you know what I'm saying in that? They kept him off their list. They do not want to know him because he helps them out in certain ways. Anyways, they would kill him if they knew he changed his stripes when he's inside prison.

"Tina, I don't know, she has some information. She talked to Hector about this *Florencia* gangster man we both used to know. How she knows him too, I don't know. She says she wants to do right and get this man some lost money but he might misunderstand her if she tried to return it. She wants to get a fee from him for getting it for him. I know who he is, he's an MI, a *mano izquierda*, doctor. He's dangerous. This man's name is Christophe Ruzga."

I shook my head, not comprehending.

She lit a cigarette. "A left hand man to the boss is what that means. Christophe used to buy guns around here. His operation got busted up by DEA or ATF or some such years back. Hector did business with some young Indian boy who was talking too much. He made it look like something else; he's good at that kind of thing. Kids take their lives on the rez all the time, I'm sure you know. This all happened a long time ago before Hector got locked up for possession with intent to deliver."

A cold finger moved up and down the back of my neck. I had to know more, but didn't want to listen. I tried to focus on appearing calm.

"You're telling me Hector murdered somebody."

Her close-lipped smile held no real feeling. "No, I didn't, doctor. What I say is he took care of business. I didn't say what I mean. Yes, Hector's a scary man. I only know he said this boy died, not what happened."

Tessa's boyfriend, Parker Heslah, who fathered Chase, helped run guns for the youth gang, East Side Pirus, along with Jack Brie, Tiller, and James who worked on modifications in the basement of the old Mission Boarding school. He got in too deep and was trying to break free when he met with me in at an office at the Tribal Court. At that time five years earlier, I knew he was in danger and tried to reach out to him, but he walked out on me.

Parker's death had been ruled a suicide by the Yakima County Coroner, but none of us involved really believed that was what happened. I'd always thought Jack Brie, or Tiller and James, killed Parker.

Throughout our entire abduction and escape, I'd never

heard of anybody named Ruzga. I'd also never heard anything in the news media about any follow-up arrests. I had heard Jack Brie mention he had customers in Tri-Cities.

"Anyways," she continued, "Tina told Hector she knows where some big money belonging to Ruzga is hidden. I think she said more than she meant to in front of me. She talks too much—when I wasn't around, she told Hector she knows Ruzga and me were together. That may be true, and Hector already knew that, but that is not something I like her knowing. I was very angry with him for telling her that is true."

"You see, Ruzga was very bad to me, doctor. Hector, he helped me get away from him. Tina knows some other players we never knew. Hector and I both know Ruzga. Christophe's reward for finding what already belongs to him and bringing it back might be he don't skin you alive before he kills you."

"He sounds like somebody to stay very far away from. Actually, Hector does too, Maritza."

"You have no idea. I went to Tina, and I told her she's very full of shit and to leave Hector out of her plans. I told her what Ruzga might do if he knew she knows about some lost money of his. She got all scared and stopped talking to Hector in front of me but she talk with him behind my back instead. I hate her.

"She sees his tattoos and right away knows he's connected. Now she wants to be all Norteno and get Hector up in Ruzga's face. Tina wants to put these two roosters in a box and see what she gets. Maybe she gets all the money because they kill each other off. Hector, he's always thinking he's tougher than Ruzga."

She kept her eyes on me, waiting for me to say something.

"That's quite a story," I allowed, wishing I'd never heard it.

"Yes, very interesting to you in particular, doctor?"

"Why would you ask that?"

"I don't know. I guess a counselor like you might hear many things he don't like too much. That's all I'm saying."

"Ah," I uttered uncertainly.

"I do ask that you don't write down any of what I've told you about all these things."

"Write what down?"

"I don't want you to write about these things in your little notes because I don't want Mr. Lettie to read about it. You said it's confidential here. I don't want you to tell him what I've mentioned or have him be able to read it anywhere."

"You're court-ordered so I do have to keep certain notes, Maritza. I can extend confidentiality to not keeping notes in certain situations in the state of Washington, but not when a third party is involved. But that doesn't mean Mr. Lettie has an open window into what you and I talk about. I'm not his appointee or officer or anything."

She looked as though she was having misgivings. "These kind of secrets maybe I can talk to you about because they are very hard on me but I don't want them written down is what I'm saying."

"Certainly, what you've told me is confidential. As to me writing it down or not, that's kind of my business, Maritza." Her eyes flashed at this remark. "I do keep any notes I make locked and secure here and I don't tend to write much detail, if that's what you're worried about."

"Uh, maybe I say too much then. I think I want to go now anyway. I got something else I need to do before I come back to drop those papers for you. What I need to know is does it count with probation as meeting with you if I have to leave the session early?"

"I'd have to see what the court order says specifically." Something was wrong and I felt the need to reassure her. "I do mean what I say about the confidentiality of my files, so don't worry, Maritza."

"And I understand what you say," she answered too brightly and got up to leave, pausing by the office door. "I am riding out to a place called Signal Peak. Do you know where I find it?"

"Would that be where this money you're talking about is?"

The joke fell flat; her expression became serious. "I don't know a thing about this money Tina talks about. If I had lots of money like that, you would never see me again . . . No, Hector's been all mushy and sorry. He said it's a good ride out there."

"I'm not sure how he'd know. You should stay away from him and maybe get a bike of your own. I believe that's up in the closed area, and you can't go back there without an enrolled Yakama member or a special permit. I don't see how Hector would know anything about riding back there."

"I take care of myself. Today is the first time I ever get his bike to ride all day, and this is something I really love to do."

The breeze pushed the cardboard out of the hole in the window as she pulled out and I peered through the quivering blinds trying to see what direction she took. I could hear her thundering toward White Swan.

Maritza's boyfriend, Hector, knew something about the death of Parker Heslah five years ago. Christophe Ruzga, her old flame, was likely a customer of Jack Brie's gun-running operation. And Tina was playing a new game on an old chessboard since her release from prison.

I was learning much more than I really wanted to know from Maritza Rios.

Four clients later, I was crossing the street from *La Guadalupana* salivating with three fresh-made pork tacos in a little white bag as Deputy Almont Anderson hopped out of his

Yakima County Sheriff's cruiser by my office.

"Hi, deputy. Did you find something out?"

"Huh? Oh, the rock. No. Sorry, not here for that. I haven't seen any classic cars around lately either. I didn't forget, see? I just came by to deliver something."

He handed me a letter in a sealed envelope with the official logo for the Yakima County Superior Court, Juvenile Justice Division. He was back inside his cruiser already by the time I'd skimmed it.

"What's this?" I asked when he rolled down his window.

"Summons. It's not a subpoena. Somebody's filed a court complaint against you. Maybe your rock thrower for spraining his palm?"

He rolled his window up, waved, and started to pull away. Then he rolled it back down.

"Have a nice afternoon!"

"Thanks," I muttered, reading more carefully through 'therebys' and 'heretofores,' sitting on the picnic table in Pioneer Park where I had cell reception.

"It's a little intimidating," I spoke. "It has the guardian ad litem's name, Brenda Oakley, as a complainant and some wording about violating Rule 4-f regarding access to records."

"Meaningless." Frank Munoz declared over the line. "And this is pro bono rather than free, Ret. I'll be sending you an invoice. She likely wrote it herself, and got the family court judge to sign. Not binding on Indian land, especially with the Indian Child Welfare Act and the LICWAC overseeing placement of kids. You'll also notice the phrase 'except as limited by law or unless good cause to the court.' Write the judge a letter saying you'd be violating ICWA and the Revised Code of Washington talking with Oakley without a signed informed release. Explain you're working your profession on Indian land, and you have a form approved by the Tribal Court there. Nothing to worry about—a misuse of public resources."

"Can I ignore it?"

"I can't really say that because total lack of cooperation might bite you in the ass if something comes up later about those kids. But there's no way she can force your cooperation; the law doesn't stipulate enforcement."

I was relieved, thanked him, hung up, and checked the clock.

It was 3:30 p.m., and nothing had been slid under my door. Maritza hadn't returned so I made good on my vow and called Harold Lettie.

Harold had never heard of Maritza Rios. He had no one by that name on his case roster.

He'd never heard of Hector Amezquita either.

Ruthie and I spent an unpleasant evening together. I did a lot of sighing and not talking about what was on my mind.

SEVEN

Sometimes there is an old man
Who has lost all his people.
He feels lonely; he is sad.
He goes up on the mountain somewhere.
He builds up stones.
He sits there and cries,
For he is alone in the world.
In this way were many of those stone-heaps made.
The white man should not tear them down.
—*Tom Hill, Nez Perce, 1911*

The first thing I noticed when I walked into the office the following morning was the smell of burnt coffee and the pot on its side on the floor, a big puddle of brown seeping into my new light beige carpet.

"Shit," I said, wondering if I forgot to turn the coffeemaker off again, and then how the pot managed to fall onto the floor. I came around the corner.

My sofa was turned over. The pieces of cardboard I'd temporarily stuffed into the broken window were scattered. My big desk was pushed on its side and the drawers were lying on the floor next to my locked file cabinet, which had been jimmied. The old typewriter was on its end in the corner. File folders lay strewn about everywhere.

"Goddamn it!" I shouted involuntarily.

The wind outside kicked hard, and the hanging blinds shook loudly. I became certain somebody was inside with me, and froze in place in the back hallway. Then I heard the front door open and close. I spun and ran forward but had a thought about what Ruthie had said to me and stopped in my tracks.

What the hell was I doing? There was a lot at stake. I pulled my cell out to call 911 and held myself up near the front door, cracking it open very slightly.

He looked directly back at me from about a hundred yards away and then started to run. As soon as he got around the corner by Neir's, I swallowed hard and ran outside to get a better look. I held the cell to my ear, running hard, totally out of breath at the corner.

I saw the BelAir.

Hector grabbed the right rear door handle and jumped in as the driver patched out. A flash of light tan in his hands; he was holding folders, but I couldn't tell how many. I squinted but having not been willing to admit to Ruthie I needed glasses, I couldn't catch the plate. So I sprinted to the middle of the street to try to keep my reception clear, watching the car fade into the distance along Harrah Road.

"Fucking 9-11!" I exclaimed.

"Don't expect those fuckers to help you once they put you on hold!" Warren Neir called out, standing erect on the front porch of his store pointing a pump action shotgun up to the sky. "That son a bitch sure could run.

"Sorry," he added, noticing the gun in his hands. "I couldn't exactly justify shooting him for B & E. By the by, Alice already called 911."

"Well, thanks," I said, hanging up.

"Don't mention it."

He spit tobacco juice, brought the shotgun into a lean against his shoulder, and walked back inside without another word.

I wasn't thrilled about sitting and waiting for the Sheriff with Alice and Warren and decided the best place for me was back in the office. I paced around inside, circling the disaster that had been my work space, and finally settled onto the couch. I admit I sat trembling there for ten minutes or so.

Deputy Anderson took a long while to arrive.

"Barlow?" He called back from near my front door.

"Well, it sure as hell took you a while!" I shouted at him. "Back here!"

He didn't show, so I peered around the corner. The barrel of a pistol pointed into my face, and I stumbled backwards onto the floor.

"Jesus, don't shoot me, Deputy!"

"Well, calm down. I got to make sure it's all secure in here, after all," he said harshly. "I wasn't going to shoot you, you know. I saw it was you!"

I thought I might be having a panic attack and tried to control my breathing. He poked and then spoke staccato to a shoulder-mounted transceiver, "Baker-5, dispatch, I'm with complainant at 7 Pioneer Street, the old vet office in Harrah. We're secure. We're going to need Detective Jacinto."

He struggled to re-holster his gun.

"Do you still need backup, Baker-5?" a female voice crackled back.

"Uh, negative dispatch, cancel backup. We've got a mess, and I'd like Daisy to take a look."

"Don't let her hear that name on chatter, Baker-5."

He whistled softly. "Oops. Uh, apologies, Detective Jacinto." Then, he glanced at me. "Did a number on you this time, doc. Gang job, looks like."

"The BelAir. I saw him," I said, still trying to calm my breath. "He calls himself Hector, but it's not his real name; I checked. Evelyn Thompson knows him. . . I met him. He must've hid in the bathroom. What the hell took you so long? Some asshole's walking around . . ."

He sniffed the air.

"Easy there, doc. There's me and troopers along Highway 97. Don't expect nobody else. City police in Toppenish and Wapato got their perimeter, and we contract with them to help in town, not the other way around. Harrah don't have a police department, in case you didn't notice. I was in Zillah. Tell me what the guy looked like."

"Hispanic, stocky, muscular, neat mustache. Baggy jean shorts, below the knees, banger style. Black t-shirt, white shoes. About six feet tall."

"That's pretty good," he responded approvingly. "Not used to such a good description."

"I've met him. Calls himself Hector—but that's not his real name."

He called out a description on his shoulder radio.

"Anything missing?"

"Yeah. He had some of my files."

"Anything important in them?"

"Absolutely. It's protected information. And I'm the one who's supposed to protect it."

"Let's back out of here and sit in your lobby. I want to leave all this mess alone." I looked at him questioningly. "You're getting harassed. I got Detective Jacinto coming to talk with you."

"Jacinto?"

"Sheriff's Detective Dolynda Jacinto. Sometimes we call her Daisy. But don't you. She's been with us a thousand years. She should be along in about ten minutes."

I pointed out I didn't see the rock I'd left on my bookshelf lying anywhere.

"Well, we won't like it if it doesn't turn up somewheres," he noted.

Detective Jacinto was so quiet I didn't hear her open the front door. She was an older Latina, slightly plump, with a solemn expression, soft-spoken, and dressed too professionally for little Harrah. Deputy Anderson and I followed her back to the office area and watched her survey the scene.

"Looking for something," she said, picking up various things.

"I'm not sure what you mean," I said. "I know the guy

who did this—he calls himself Hector. He's a migrant foreman. But that's not his real name."

"How would you know that?"

"I talk to Harold Lettie in probation up in Yakima. He's not on his case roster."

"Why do you talk to Harold?" she asked while handling my books, bric-a-brac, and even my files lying on the floor.

"Uh, I'd appreciate it if you don't tamper with those. I talk to Harold because what he does is sometimes criss-crossed with my line of work."

"You're a shrink, right?"

"Yeah. Listen, Detective, he took some files of mine. That's not a good thing in my business."

"Oh," she affirmed while moving about, touching, lifting, peering, squinting, as though what I said didn't seem to mean much to her. "Too bad. Lots of Hectors out there. It's a good fake name—like who would choose that name? Maybe we'll get you over to the sheriff's office, and you can look at some pictures. It's not a typical pattern."

"How do you mean?"

"The old typewriter and the phone are good for thirty bucks, and this little stereo next to your bookshelf isn't bad, maybe another ten." She turned to face me. "So what files did you say he took?"

"I didn't. I'd have to go through them to be sure."

I told her about Maritza Rios, and how she wasn't on Harold's list. Oddly, I felt a sudden surge of rage realizing I wasn't going to get paid for seeing her.

"Hmm," she observed, moving files around with her foot. "Once you go through these, let me know what you notice missing. I've heard of a Maritza Rios around here. Working girl, isn't she?"

She suddenly grinned to herself and saw me noticing. "Oh, sorry, I was just thinking—I bet a girl like Maritza'd play somebody in your line of work like a violin."

I decided I didn't like her manner. She took out a small digital camera from her purse.

"Question is, why does she want to play somebody like you?" she whispered, paying no attention to me, absorbed, and clicking away.

When she was done looking over the place, she interviewed me—going through who I was, where I lived, what time of day I arrived, who was Maritza again, how do I get referrals, when had she first come around, etc. Detective Jacinto was very methodical, even mechanical.

She finally asked about the rock incident and the blue and white BelAir, disproving the idea that she hadn't been listening. After that, she asked me more about Maritza and Hector as a couple.

"They were out there at the blueberry farm, you say. Sounds like this whole idea they were in recovery together and going to groups up in Yakima somewhere won't turn out to be accurate."

"Harold Lettie never heard of them and didn't have either of their names on any of the rosters in his system. But it's pretty loose with those recovery groups as to who actually shows up."

"Doctor, let's consider the idea that Maritza may have had reason for getting involved professionally with you and may have even 'accidentally' run into you and your wife at that farm. Any idea what her motives might be?"

This hadn't occurred to me to that point, and the idea made me nervous. "I don't know."

"Do you have any readily accessible valuables here or at your home? For example, do you invest in gold or silver or stamps and coins, that sort of thing, or does your wife have any valuable jewelry?"

"We have a savings account and keep a little cash around, but not much else."

"What did this woman called 'Maritza Rios' talk about in her counseling sessions with you?"

I told her about the rooster story and began talking about the session after that.

"Wait," she held up her hand. "The rock through the window came before or after the next session?"

"Before."

"And you saw her for an intake session before then?"

"That was only a half hour and pretty straightforward. I usually go through a semi-structured interview when somebody comes to see me for the first time."

"The intake session, another session, the rock, and the most recent session yesterday. That's the order."

"The rock was nothing to look at," Anderson chimed in. He'd been standing around looking bored, shifting between polishing his glasses and playing with his cell phone. "Andesite. Not a special rock at all."

"Ah, andesite," she responded, looking at me instead of him. "I guess I'd find a lot of that around here, Deputy?"

"Actually, no . . ." he began. "Well, like I said it's common, but andesite is more something you'd see . . ."

Her unhappy gaze at him might have melted butter.

"It had a sticky note taped on it," I added, "It said 'Git out'."

"Okay, thanks about the rock. Maritza, whatever her name is, saw that broken window when she came in. Did she say anything about it?"

"Sure. She asked if she should sit somewhere else, if I thought another rock would come through the window. And she said maybe I should rethink my business locale."

"That's kind of interesting," said Anderson, raising his eyebrows.

"Um," Detective Jacinto seemed to bite her lip. "Please don't talk right now, Deputy. Did Maritza say anything else significant during your sessions with her?"

"Uh. . ."

I wasn't sure how much more I should say. I thought for a moment about Maritza's complaints about Tina. I'd never met Tina. All the Miyanashatawit kids marched before my mind, and I considered the repercussions of mentioning her. I didn't know how far I should go in revealing privileged information, really. My palms began sweating profusely, and I automatically wiped them on my pants. Detective Jacinto watched me do that. She didn't seem to miss much.

"Uh, she talked a lot about her boyfriend Hector, and the bike he let her ride."

"Okay, what else?"

Yeah, I thought as I looked at her, what else? Two roosters in a box. Ruzga and Hector. Do I tell Detective Jacinto about Maritza's stories about them?

"Doctor?"

"Hmm."

I was five years back, and Tessa was telling me we'd never escape alive from the basement, we'd never get past Charlie Whitcomb and—many other bad people. What did she say? I saw her young face within painful images mouthing the words: 'Mexican Mafia', Tri-Cities, 'Black Hand, Surenos.'

Ruzga was Surenos. Ruzga was in Tri-Cities. Ruzga, according to Maritza, dealt in guns and had connections local to Yakima Valley. I sighed loudly like I did when I was stressed out around Ruthie.

"Are you okay, doctor?"

I wiped my sweaty hands on my pants again.

"Deputy, go out to the kitchen and get the doctor a glass of water, will you please?"

Anderson strolled out of the lobby. The blueberry farm, Maritza acting as a fake client. What about the rock and the note that said 'git out'? I couldn't put it all together, but one thing seemed certain: she had *wanted* to tell me about Tina, Hector, Ruzga—what she'd said during our last two sessions fit seamlessly with events Tessa and I'd gone through five years earlier.

I began thinking Maritza hadn't uttered a word that wasn't rehearsed. Detective Jacinto was looking me over, waiting for me to say more.

"I'm a little shook up," I confided, sweat breaking across my hairline.

"A lot of people get that way when somebody violates their space. Do you recall this Maritza saying anything related to the harassment you've had out here?"

"Well, she wanted to know where Signal Peak was," I noted.

"Signal Peak?"

"Yeah, she was going to ride her boyfriend's bike out there."

My reluctance must have begun to appear to be more than just nerves. The truth is I hadn't the slightest confidence in Sheriff's Detective Daisy or Deputy Almont Anderson protecting the Miyanashatawits or me.

Or Ruthie! For God's sake, they'd both met Ruthie!

"Well," I added, "the rock is gone. We figured that out, Detective, before you arrived."

"And that's not good." Deputy Anderson handed me my glass of water.

"Deputy, do be quiet, please." And she watched me for a while longer. I tried to look natural while I sweated.

"Okay," she said with finality while I sipped. "Let's talk again soon. I don't like all this. We've got a lot of gang tension going on around the Lower Valley right now. And somebody doesn't like you. This is a new place of business for you?"

"Yeah," I answered flatly. "Yeah, it's new."

She said she'd put together a report with Hector's description and patterns of the break-in that would go into a county database. She'd talk to Evelyn Thompson and to Alice

Neir. She'd talk to Tessa because she was there during the rock incident and had also seen the blue and white car.

Before she left, I organized all the files on the floor and went through them. I confirmed to her that the file I'd made on Maritza Rios was definitely missing.

I was missing other files, but I didn't tell her about them.

Every single file I had on the Miyanashatawits from over the last seven years was gone, including Tessa's, Franklin's, and also files I had on Ce Ce, and Samuel, both of whom I'd seen for school issues. Even notes on Arnold, Emily, and Eloise from family work we'd done was missing.

I recognized immediately how somebody could string all that information together and get a pretty accurate picture of the Miyanashatawit family's proclivities, worries, and dynamics.

I couldn't tell Ruthie about any of this and felt very ashamed. She'd already had the instinct that Maritza would turn out to be trouble. I anticipated she'd insist I shut my office down and get the hell out, and I wasn't about to leave. We had a family to start, and I had no other place to work. If I told her, and then still insisted on staying, she'd fret through the rest of the pregnancy.

To assuage my guilt, I took her to see a movie called *Secret Window,* a bad choice, especially for me under the circumstances. We slept fitfully the rest of the weekend. After listening to me toss and turn, I gave in to her demands that I go see Dr. Warner the following Monday.

"You have high blood pressure," he said with an edge of blame, gazing at his old beat-up sphygmomanometer hanging on the wall. He unwrapped my arm, picked up an ipad, and set it on his knee.

"BP 145 over 95," he proclaimed loud enough for anyone within thirty yards to hear.

"Wow."

"Sorry, just using a voice program to dictate."

"Ah," I said.

"Are you exercising?"

"Yeah, I run."

"How far?" He interviewed me and watched his screen.

"Huh?"

"How far do you run?" he looked up at me.

"Oh, couple miles, couple times a week."

"Might hurt your feet lugging an extra forty pounds. I'm going to get you started on medication."

He held his ipad to his face.

"Patient is obese. Reports participating in regular mild exercise," he enunciated authoritatively. "Candidate for Lipitron."

"Great," I responded. "What's that?"

"Low-dose beta blocker."

"How long do you want me on it?" I asked as he put his freezing stethoscope on my bare chest.

"Long as needed. You could afford to lose some weight. Cough."

I did so, and he reached down and tinkered with me in mildly painful ways.

"Recommend increased exercise regimen to four times weekly with Lipitron combo," he shouted, tapping his ipad screen.

I found his manner confusing. "Are you yelling at me?"

"Sorry, I have to do this this way, and it's goddamn distracting. I get crossed up sometimes trying to ask questions and dictate at the same time."

"Oh."

He made brief eye contact with me.

"Stop the bacon cheeseburgers."

"Okay," I responded, amazed. "How'd you know?"

"Big Macs, gyros, or subs. Bacon cheeseburgers are the biggie all around here because they're on the restaurant menus. Guys your age want to eat like they're nineteen. You under stress?"

"Always."

"Make my job harder, Barlow," he sighed, poking at my testicles.

He stared at the ipad screen before raising his voice again, "Testicles are round and firm. Penis is unremarkable."

"That's what she said," I offered with a smile.

"Hah," was as much as I got in return. "Problems with impotence?"

"Uh . . ."

He became impatient. "Erection issues? Premature ejaculation?"

"No, not really. Stress gets in the way sometimes, I suppose."

"What times? How often?"

"Uh, maybe once a month or so."

"Once a month for which?"

"Which what?" I started getting a little embarrassed.

"Poor erection or premature ejaculation?"

"For sex. I mean, my wife's pregnant, and she's been losing sleep. We don't get as much chance and . . ."

He held up his hand. "No problems with erection?"

"Well, like I said, not lately, worked just a few days ago, but stress or whatever, every now and then. . ."

He shifted to the ipad and again spoke loudly.

"Some evidence of early erectile dysfunction. No evidence of chronic sexual dysfunction. Recommend medical counseling and medication provision as needed."

"Do you want a script for Levitart?"

"Honestly, it's not a big deal."

"Let me know if you change your mind."

He gelled the index finger of the latex glove he'd been poking my groin with.

"Bend over and lower your shorts."

"Oww, okay. Yeah."

"Mild benign prostate hyperplasia!" he yelled into his ipad. "You get up to pee a lot at night?!"

"Once or twice!" I shouted back.

"Calm down. We'll live with that. If it gets worse, let me know."

I don't know how he thought he was the one who'd be living with it along with me.

"You're the shrink," he said. "What do you do to cool down stress?"

"Go to sweatlodge with native friends."

"It'd be against my medical advice. If you're used to it, do what you want. It's your funeral."

"I wish people would quit saying so."

He didn't see the humor in that and only raised his eyebrows while he wrote notes in my chart. He started toward the door and turned around.

"I'll see you in four weeks. You can set it up on your way out. The nurse will be back with scripts. Fill 'em, and start 'em today."

I checked my cell phone as I had when he entered the room. He'd checked me out for seven minutes total.

EIGHT

An illusion is a misinterpretation
Of something real.
For example . . .
A person hearing the wind blow through the trees
And believing it is the sound of a child crying . . .
Illusions come from a misinterpretation of a physical reality.
—*Trainee Manual, Community Health Representative,
Indian Health Service, 1985*

I rushed over to the day-long conference in downtown Yakima. The marquee spun its letters, dilated, and expanded while I impatiently waited for an elderly lady to back out of her parking space—'Welcome! Access to Recovery Providers: Addiction, Recovery & Relapse Prevention.' I worked to bolster my mood for schmoozing, struggling to open the mirror glass doors of the garish building and took a spot in the long registration line. I didn't see a soul I knew.

"How are you doing today?" said a guy behind me.

"Fine, thanks, how about you?"

He didn't respond.

"What brings you to the conference?" I tried again, challenging my inhibitions and peering congenially back toward him. The guy nodded slightly before continuing to speak into the wireless hanging from his ear.

A petite elderly lady with coiffed silver hair and a narrow expression frowned as I pointed out that my name tag read 'Rhett Barlow, MD.'

"I can make you a new one, sir, if you pick it up on the break in an hour or so."

Several bodies ambled closer like we were stacking up to get on an airplane.

"Don't you have any blank ones I can just write on? I'm a Ph.D. psychologist, not a psychiatrist."

"Psychologist, Ph.D; psychiatrist, MD; people get them mixed up. Sorry, no blank tags right now."

"Won't you be making a new one for me by using a blank one?"

"I suppose, but I don't make them. Margaret does, and she's still setting up tables."

The guy behind me said to his wireless, "I'm trying to get through the line, but there's a hold-up. Fitzsimmons is keynote."

I didn't know that.

After using my ballpoint to cross out 'MD' and illegibly squeeze in 'PhD', I browsed through the brochure they provided and entered the grand ballroom. Tables circled a podium; there were maybe a hundred-fifty people on hand. I found a place at the rear for ease of escape and sat down with an older gentleman and two young women. A familiar voice caught me from behind as I pulled out my chair.

"Ret, how are you?"

Well forward into my personal space, Dr. Margaret Fitzsimmons held her plastic smile high and extended her hand. She had a firm grip. I'd shaken many Indian hands of late, where the appropriate etiquette is a loose grip and light touch.

She frowned at my flaccidity.

"I've heard you have some odd views about psychiatric medication and children. I didn't know about your expertise in that area."

"Margaret, I can't comfortably discuss cases from the small community I work with without a release, even if

HIPAA says it's alright."

"Hmm," she frowned. "Did you notice Dominia's here?"

"How nice."

Dominia Garcia, now a full-fledged Indian Health Service psychiatric nurse, and I had crossed swords on many occasions.

"Ret," she spoke very quietly and pulled in too close, "to be frank, you're delving into things way over your head. I must caution you about making recommendations to the Miyanashatawit family outside your range of competence. This state doesn't license prescribing privileges to psychologists."

I watched the front of the hall and feigned ignoring her. "I really can't say a word one way or another, Margaret. Whenever you'd like a public debate about the psychiatric drugging of children, I'm there. My practice, by the way, is independent of your authority."

"Oh my," she smiled sardonically. "I've struck a nerve. Did you know I'm now the lead consultant to the county administrator for the Access to Recovery Grant? In fact, I need to move up front. I'm on in a moment."

I actually didn't know that and should have. Five minutes later, she was being introduced by the Yakima County executive as "our foremost child mental health expert, deeply concerned with the future of children here in Yakima Valley."

I felt my own version of morning sickness coming on. As it was, however, I was curious about what she'd say. She brought out the usual smoke and mirrors of brain scan images at the start of her presentation, along with descriptions of complex human behavior digested into gross collections of allegedly aberrant neural firing. The huge variation within the brain scans was thereby obscured, reduced to a deceptively simple master image supposedly demonstrating how some hypothetical child's brain 'had' ADHD or 'had' bipolar disorder. I was well aware of research showing that lay people will believe doctors much more when they use the word 'brain' and 'neuro' when they talk.

I bit my tongue listening to her hawk her snake oil with chummy but authoritative vernacular. When she started talking about a so-called genetic susceptibility to addiction and chemical imbalances and 'emotional problems among ethnic minority populations,' I rose from my chair to go to the bathroom, out for a smoke, a coffee and a Danish, anywhere but there. But I heard my name.

"Now Dr. Ret Barlow has joined us today," all eyes jerked back to follow her finger pointing at me. "And we're so glad to have a psychologist with us who enjoys a good rapport with the community out around White Swan. Dr. Barlow and I are apparently not of the same mind. He's appropriately drawn our attention to the critical psychosocial and cultural factors we should be considering. And Ret, I'm pleased to report that neural science is sophisticated enough these days that we can now study the effects of psychosocial trauma at a brain level. Thus, what we used to study sociologically back in Ret's training days, we now recognize as permanently disrupting brain chemistry, even tissue development. Fortunately, there are new psychopharmacological solutions emerging for these kinds of troubles every day."

"Utter bullshit," I said under my breath, and the two young women sitting with me raised their eyebrows in unison. The old guy laughed out loud. Several nearby heads spun around, aghast. I didn't realize I'd said it so loud. At least Margaret didn't hear.

". . . and along with it, we can trace, via fMRI and PET, an inability to regulate emotions and behaviors. So the old, antiquated approach of talking, counseling, and family intervention has been gradually dying away so as to make room for the careful application of psychopharmacology. Time and time again we see bipolar children in crisis stabilized through the careful application of polymedication. Only when we've fully stabilized such children through medication can behavioral methods be of any use at all."

She nodded toward the front row of tables, and I spotted Dominia.

"That's why I'm recommending to Access to Recovery providers like Dr. Barlow that we exercise more caution about therapy without medication, a perspective which really dates back prior to the mid-1970s before the point when psychiatric neural science had achieved its entirely new level of sophistication and evidence."

I noticed Trick, and we made eye-to-eye contact from where he was, kitty-corner to me on the far side of the ballroom. He gazed at me with mock disapproval as Fitzsimmons continued the hyperbole.

I somehow waited it all out. At the break, Trick met me at the door.

"That *áyat* psychologist doesn't go for you," he said, lighting up a smoke as we stepped outside. "She told everybody there you're basically no good."

"Psychiatrist, Trick, and no, she doesn't like me. She's slandered me."

"You're the Lone Ranger around here—friend to the Indians. You're the mixed-blood white guy who goes to sweat—maybe you'd be better off going to key her car, *kemosabe*."

He couldn't get over his own humor.

"What I'm going to do is leave."

He noticed I was genuinely upset.

"Don't let it mess with you, doc. She's just one of your secret admirers."

"And how do you figure that is?"

"She's so jealous; she's making you her subject, that's all I'm saying. You never call somebody out like that in front of people in our way. We got a whole crew come out from the

drug and alcohol program. They all heard her. You ever do
what she's doing in a General Council meeting on the rez, and
there's going to be fists flying. There's not an Indian
counselor here don't know what you were up against over at
the IHS clinic. Some of the native people been shaking their
heads. Don't worry; she's not going over."

"Thanks, Trick. You're a good man." I said, hugging
him. "I don't care what everybody else says."

His expression became serious until I said, "aaaaaaaz,"
and we both laughed.

"'Kay, _xáy_," he whispered.

He warmed my heart a bit before I left, and I
appreciated it too, considering a whole conference load of
people had just heard I was a piece of shit.

"Oooh! You should sue her!" Ruthie blurted out while
we laid in the dark. "I can't stand having you taken down like
that."

"I thought you fell asleep."

"I can't sleep, Ret," she said. "I'm busy having
homicidal fantasies."

"I shouldn't have ever told you. Let it go, Ruthie."

She sat upright. "There's some things you don't let go.
Why won't you talk to Frank Munoz about it?"

"She was careful about how she said what she said.
There's not much I can do about it. And he's already taken
enough of our money. Just let it go. Go to sleep."

She rolled back and forth several times, went quiet,
and then her breath started to become longer. Soon, she was
snoring. Then she shot back up again.

"Ret, didn't I read in the _Herald_ that Margaret
Fitzsimmons leads the local Access to Recovery grant
provision?"

"Ruthie, I thought you were asleep." I'd almost
dropped off too.

"You need to talk to Munoz again."

"I already milked him for some free advice."

"About what?"

"Can't say."

"Tell me."

"No."

"God!" she exclaimed in frustration. "At least tell me why you won't go after her!"

"Only kill the king when you can do it with one blow."

"Uh," she responded, "that's very Byzantine. But what the heck do you mean?"

"I mean now's not the time."

"God! It's like living with some CIA agent," she huffed and started snoring again almost immediately.

Someone is after me. I'm not sure I'm Indian but I seem to be dressed like a Cherokee, like Sequoyah, with a green long shirt, a turban, and feather. A woman stands very near me. I can't make her face out, but I'm certain I know her well. She suddenly shouts "Run!!" A horseman gallops down the trail, and I spring behind a tree. The woman is captured and screams. The horseman has an English accent, and I hear him say, "I can certainly find the other" to someone I can't see. I know that he is a colonist, a plantation owner, and he intends to capture and enslave me. I dash off into the woods, jumping over large tree roots and weaving back and forth. I hear the sound of galloping hooves close behind me.

My eyes shot open, and I wasn't sure where I was at first.

She'd formed herself all along my side, and I could feel a slight plump in her belly. The sun streamed in through the old lead-filled windows of our bedroom. I tried to clear my head. Dust floated across the rays. I watched and considered how remarkable it was that bits of light could contain the recipe for human life.

The alarm buzzed softly. That's what it does if you

don't pull the stem on its back plate out all the way. It seemed to have been buzzing like that for quite a while. I turned my head gently, not really wanting to check the time.

"Ruthie . . ."

"Hmmm."

"It's 7:30."

"Shit!" She pushed off me, reached across, and smacked the alarm clock.

In response, the switch kicked in, and the alarm belted out very loud and clear. I couldn't get it to turn off and finally had to get up to unplug it.

"Tina is back," Elisi announced, standing outside my office front door when I pulled in. She never wasted time with platitudes. "She got out three weeks early.

"I really didn't know and should have," she fretted. "No one expected it this early. She's in a halfway house up to Yakima. Did you know?"

"Come on in, *kála*," I parried her question and helped her up my front steps. "Do you want some tea?"

"Herbal, if you have it."

I brought it to her, and she eased herself down, grimacing with arthritic pain. She had no beadwork. She just sipped her tea, and I waited. She set her mug down and played with neatening her homemade dark blue dress, gently smoothing it so the interspersed tiny yellow flowers looked more uniform. She looked younger than seventy-nine years, but older than I'd ever noticed. She stared at the wall in front of her. I knew she was gathering her thoughts.

"This changes everything," she began slowly. "She's already called Eva over to social services, and said she wants her kids back. She told her she wants to take in Ce Ce and Samuel as soon as possible. Oh, if Arnold were only here with us. I keep praying, asking Creator, 'what do we do'? The permanency planning hearing is this Thursday."

"That soon?!"

"You know how state services can be—reunite the family—their version. No rhyme or reason to it. It don't make no difference she hasn't parented in seven years, and she was never much of a parent anyway. They know Leila's space don't work out. Oh, I wanted Tessa to take those kids in a new home out to White Swan before Tina ever got out of prison. Now, they'll say Tina's all rehabilitated. They'll want to keep those kids out of the foster care system and try to put them with her! Eva said this Brenda Oakley lady has the authority. She thinks the court's going to listen to her."

She looked directly at me and then at the wall. "I want to know if you will go there and speak for us."

"Uh, Brenda Oakley doesn't like me too much, *káła*. I never answered her juvenile court summons. Besides, I haven't done any sort of evaluation with Tina."

"This is a friend's work," she shot sternly at me. "It's on the frontier, this kind of talking, this kind of court business with kids; it's one way a mixed-blood white man like you can help us. Now, I'll ask again, *will you go* and speak for us?"

"*Káła,* Oakley already tried to push me around. You know I don't respond to that well. She's already angry with me. She's also allied with Dr. Fitzsimmons in all that's going on with Franklin. It might not be good to have me speak there."

She stood up all in one motion, defying the weakness of age, ready to walk out. "Are you saying you *won't*??"

I moved my eyes toward the floor.

"I got to ask you—what does our family mean to you anyway? You've been all through what's happened to these kids! You seen it! We need a professional voice speaking across these racial lines here. How can you say you won't speak for us?"

I knew that in her beliefs to not speak on an important matter when you might have something significant to say was something akin to a spiritual and moral failure.

"Okay," I eventually gave in. "I'll talk if I'm called upon. But I can't come as a professional, *káła.*"

I told her about my dream. I couldn't give her any clue of what I'd learned about Tina as a result of recent events.

"Many people have to live life being chased. I guess it's your turn, doctor. Your ancestors are giving you counsel to be on the watch and to take care," she cautioned. "They're saying 'run, dodge, watch out.' So listen to them."

She sat back, and closed her eyes, which became awkward after a few minutes passed by. I thought she'd fallen asleep.

"*Káła.*"

"Shush. I'm praying."

"For what?" I blurted.

"You."

After several more minutes, my cell rang. The caller ID said 'private caller.' I knew from experience that meant someone official.

"Go ahead," she muttered from her contemplation.

Eva Alexander from Child Welfare sounded rushed. "Your name's included as an interested party for a permanency hearing at Tribal Court this Thursday morning for Ce Ce and Samuel Miyanashatawit. Do you know about that?"

Leila and Elisi had apparently already counted me in.

"I'm just a friend of this family, Eva. I haven't done any sort of professional evaluation or anything."

"Whatever, I don't care. We need your input. Tina Miyanashatawit is back in the picture."

"You can't possibly think those kids should go live with her again."

"What I think on this don't necessarily matter much, doctor. Those two kids aren't even enrolled. As you know, an Indian child welfare program doesn't always work for Indian children's welfare."

"You're preaching to the choir on that, Eva."

"There's lots of negative gossip floating around about that family; some of our staff members even think the Miyanashatawits are just 'bad blooded' and should stay with their own so they don't pollute the rest of us."

"Yeah, there's a kind of bullshit getting internalized by folks that originates in academic pseudoscientific bio-reductionist hyperbole."

"Uh. . . that's very interesting, doctor, but please don't talk that way in front of Judge Waldrup. What's at stake here is the state generally favors kids living with their mothers and won't look at other options. That's what we need you to comment on. I'm just glad she'll hear this in tribal court after Brenda Oakley tried to get it on the Yakima County Family Court docket instead."

"For these kids to go back to Tina right now would be a disaster. Eva, you need to stop this train."

"It's already left the station. With everything up in the air, Tina has an opportunity. She's claiming she's reformed and competent to parent. She went through parenting classes in prison. She has full rights to petition for regaining her parent role."

I jotted down the time on a sticky pad. As I hung up, Elisi's eyes opened.

"Tina's got a chance for custody of Ce Ce and Samuel," I told her.

A tear had already etched its way onto her face, which otherwise held no expression.

I had a new vinyl window Warren had installed, although not quite level. I got up, slid it open, and listened to little kids scream in delight across the street.

"Do you know the Fitzsimmons family?" she asked me out of the blue.

"*Káła*, I know this thing with Tina is hurting your heart now. We don't need to focus on Fitzsimmons and my problems."

"Pay attention," she chided. "All that happens is for a reason. You are a mixed-blood man, but you were raised white. You don't realize. Try to understand how events go together, how they coincide. Watch your life play out before you, and see connections. Now, I'm asking if you really know this person, this professional person who don't like you much, Dr. Margaret Fitzsimmons."

"Huh. Well, no. I don't. I'm not holding a lot of interest or compassion for Margaret Fitzsimmons right now."

She waved her hand. "That's like a bug in your eye, really, because you're anger makes you unable to see. The Fitzsimmons, they're old settlers—they had a big place near Granger and got wealthy in real estate. They bought land from Maude Bolin to make the city of Toppenish back in the 1920s. Maude was the first American Indian woman pilot—did you know that?"

I shook my head.

"Well, she was. There wasn't ever an old-time Western town around here back then—they just wanted to build some hot spot with stores and saloons in the 1920s to soak up the car tourists' cash. But Toppenish was too far off the beaten track. Ray Fitzsimmons was a big investor in all that; grabbed the land for practically nothing from Maude. Lucullus McWhorter done battle with him over the Jones Bill."

"Lucullus McWhorter? What's the Jones Bill?"

"Yes, yes," she waved her hand impatiently. "Don't you pay any attention to what I give you? The old pamphlet I passed on from that Blackfoot Piikani friend of mine who got himself fired over to the *Herald*. Didn't you ever read it??" I shook my head. "You might have at least read it. He was a real Indian man, through and through. He wanted you in particular to have that pamphlet, doctor."

"I do have it. I just got busy. '*The Crime Against the Yakimas*,' right?"

"By Lucullus Virgil McWhorter, 1912."

"I leafed through it, *káła*. I didn't really understand why he wanted me to have a copy."

"As I try to tell you, things happen for a reason. That pamphlet's not just about Yakama people way back when. It's about a white man from that time who helped our people living around here. That's who Lucullus Virgil McWhorter was. He was no hero, but he tried his best. That's who the Piikani man there was telling you to look toward in thinking about what you do around here."

I sat back down. She sipped her tea and thought for a moment before continuing.

"Land owners like Ray Fitzsimmons from up in Yakima wanted to charge the Yakama people for the aqueduct and canal system they built here without our permission across our own valley and reservation. Our people couldn't pay up; we didn't have any money. And so the white folks kindly offered to take some more of our land instead. That was the Jones Bill."

"Now Lucullus Virgil McWhorter hadn't one drop of Indian blood. But he taught himself to speak our language and explained this bill to our elders—see, most of them didn't speak or read the borrowed language of English. And Mr. McWhorter faced off with Dr. Ray Fitzsimmons before the Indian Affairs committee in Washington, DC. He went out there using his own money and helped to beat that bill down. This got him labeled an 'Indian lover,' and that was a very bad thing to be as it isn't so good for an outsider even now."

She looked at me very intensely, holding one finger up. "Now listen here, doctor—Ray Fitzsimmons, that's Margaret Fitzsimmon's grandpa, do you understand? And he was Mr. McWhorter's biggest opponent on that Jones Bill situation after he and his family moved out here from leaving his big job in Canton, South Dakota. I know all that story from my own uncle."

"Canton, South Dakota." I repeated, glancing at the clock and sipping my tea.

"It's not necessary to repeat what I say. It's also rude of you to run the clock on me when I'm teaching you. Do you know this town I'm speaking of?"

"No, I don't, *kála.*"

"It should be famous to an Indian shrink like you. That's where the Hiawatha Asylum for Insane Indians was located."

I laughed.

"That's funny?" I could see it wasn't to her.

"In a ridiculous way, *kála*, it's funny to me to hear of such a place at this particular moment."

"What I'm wondering is how come they don't teach you nothing in your degree? Look it up—it was a real place of torture for many native people. It got closed before I was born. If you resisted having your kids sent off to boarding school or you fought the powers that be, if you took issue with white folks wanting you to stay off their clean sidewalks in town, if you got all hopeless and turned to alcohol or maybe morphine, well, you must be some kind of crazy Indian, do you understand? That's how things were done—they'd lock you up!"

I shot a glance at the clock again, and she caught me.

"Hmph. In my college days, I read to where there were riots in some French towns when the clock was introduced to the market square. Do you see how such contraptions divide your attention?"

"*Kála*, I'm sorry; I have a client coming up very soon."

"Well, they're going to have to wait. Must be some European aristocrat in your past generations. Margaret Fitzsimmons' grandfather, Raymond, was the head psychiatrist at the Hiawatha Asylum for Insane Indians."

This astonished me greatly. "*Kála*, how can you even know that?"

"Unlike some folks, I studied when I was in school up in British Columbia.   Also, my great uncle spent three years inside there after the Great War. That's the First World War in case you forgot that too. He had the shell shock, what gets called the PTSD now."

"In those times, many native men gone off to fight. My uncle got buried in a trench near a place called Verdun—and still couldn't walk right when I knew him. Nothing wrong with his balance, the war wounded his spirit. He used to scare us, talking about that asylum—chains and shackles, screaming, people being beaten and dying.

"You think I'm kidding, don't you? I got his own medical papers back home."

"No, I'm amazed you know so much about this. I'd like to see those papers."

"Well, I'll tug 'em out from somewhere, and you can look 'em over. My uncle fought for this country and couldn't even vote. After he come home, they sent him to rot in that place. My grandma told us they had to cut the chains and leggings off him when they finally shut it down; they'd carved right into his skin."

"Dr. Fitzsimmons wasn't the last superintendent, but he got pushed out somewhere along the way. So he left with his family and come out here to settle. My uncle was finally allowed to come home and eventually recognized him. He'd tell us kids, 'old Doc Fitzsimmons will chain you up someday.' Hearing all that, eventually none of the native people would let Fitzsimmons doctor them."

I heard the front entrance open with the arrival of my next client. "Does Margaret Fitzsimmons know all this about her grandfather?"

Elisi pursed her lips at my obtuseness. "Well, of course she does, doctor. She lived with her grandpa for years after her mother shot her father and then herself for his philandering."

"What?!"

"Yes, yes, that's the wound she carries. That's the wound you should know about. Her grandfather was very old by then, of course. That murder-suicide all happened around '67 when she was no bigger than Chase. The story even made the Seattle papers. Everybody knew about it."

She rose from her seat slowly, and I helped her, still amazed. Her eyes riveted into mine.

"*Ínk átawi mash, kála*. What I'm saying is 'I love you dearly', doctor. But Margaret Fitzsimmons witnesses how you carry yourself—working with our people around here and making friends and all—and thinks on her grandpa who died here, a broken man. There wasn't a soul among us would let him touch us because of the life my uncle described being locked in that place. You know, that asylum was eventually closed in the nineteen-thirties. White people saw what they were doing and shut it down. Ray Fitzsimmons' name came out in the investigation. That may be why he moved his family out here. He thought he could hide. But his days at the Indian asylum come into the news reports about the murder-suicide of Margaret's mom and dad. Such things meant you likely had insanity in your bloodline. He couldn't doctor and became a kind of recluse, developed an addiction to his own medications. Margaret spent her childhood years without her folks and watching him decline to his death.

"Her life has been about staying numb, doctor. Think on that. She's shut off from her own spirit. She's got layers and layers of scars. I really shouldn't be talking on her this way; it's opposed to our unwritten law. But I felt you need to understand her for who she is and what she's lived through."

She looked down at the floor where she stood. "I may not be able to help you much with all that's coming about."

"What do you mean, *kála*?"

I hadn't noticed the light sheen on her face. She stopped and breathed softly by the door.

"I got the pancreatic."

I heard voices out in the waiting area, but they meant nothing to me.

"Cancer, *kála*?" She gave a single nod and a tight smile.

"Don't look so disheartened. Everybody's got an expiration date," she chuckled softly. "They got me on gemcitabine to buy me time, but of course, maybe you understand now why I don't like watching clocks as much as you do."

"What about Tessa and all her military plans?"

"*Náktkwanin ttáwaxt.* That's what Leila and I agreed we need to teach her and all these children. I'm fine for now and who knows how long. Leila's got Chase if I happen to get sicker."

"Does Tessa know?"

"No, and I don't expect you or Leila will tell her or anybody either, if you know what's good for you."

"*Kála . . .*"

My eyes filled.

"Now stop," she said. "I'm making good on my word to Georgina to do all I can for these kids before I walk on."

"This situation has to meet the definition of family hardship for Tessa, *kála.*"

"You're not to say a word, doctor. Not one word. *Náktkwanin ttáwaxt.* That's what this is about. Life only matters in loving and helping others toward their dreams. Tessa was right about that."

"Ah," I said, momentarily unable to fathom love's stupendousness.

NINE

Never again
Will we attack your religions,
Your languages, your rituals,
Or any of your tribal ways.
Never again
Will we seize your children,
Nor teach them to be ashamed
Of who they are.
Never again.
—Kevin Gover, Assistant Secretery-Indian Affairs,
Department of the Interior, 2000

Yakama Nation Children's Court Judge Leonora Waldrup was more than grumpy.

"This CHINS petition got brought up at Yakima County Superior Court, but this situation clearly falls under the Indian Child Welfare Act," she snapped, gazing at a seemingly unruffled Brenda Oakley and tribal social worker, Eva Alexander, who appeared nervous. "I don't understand why the matter would ever even make it onto the docket at Superior."

"Yes, your honor," said Eva, rising slightly from her chair. "I apologize. Ce Ce and Samuel were born to different fathers, both white, and they are not on the rolls at Yakama Nation."

The Judge eased her glasses and pointed at Eva. "Do we have paternity verified? I don't see anything but 'unknown' about their fathers on their birth certificates here."

"You know," her tone became more irritated, "these children are recognized members of our community, whether or not they're enrolled. ICWA covers them—says so in black and white in the legal language of that law. Are you all stuck on blood quantum like the white man over there at Child Welfare? Get them enrolled. We know their lineage. Their grandfather's death and the plight of these children are well known. I could put in an ethics grievance in for this lapse."

Eva looked terribly embarrassed. Brenda Oakley remained unreadable. The Judge turned to Emily, who sat bolt upright on the witness stand.

"Ms. Emily Miyanashatawit, I wanted to talk to you in chambers, but you insisted you had to talk in open court. I'll grant you that, but it's not usually appropriate in family matters like this. I hope you'll be careful in what you say, and be truthful. What are your views on your younger sister and brother going to live with your mother?"

A thin, muscular, native woman with short-cropped hair watched her daughter on the stand carefully. I could only see her from behind and changed seats out of curiosity. A scar below her right eye and a frown mixed with hardness marred her otherwise pretty features. Tina Miyanashatawit's tattoos covered her neck and left arm. They were not the artsy kind. She came from the rough side of life.

Emily paused, glanced around, and then looked for a long moment at her sister, Tessa, sitting in the rear of the courtroom. I was next to Leon and Edward Kusitway. Elisi and Leila sat with the rest of the kids on the other side of the room.

Emily focused an emboldened stare at the wood railing in front of her. I thought Judge Waldrup would become impatient but she waited.

"I . . . was almost eleven years old when my mom gone to prison. I can't really describe how hard life was in my childhood years before then."

She took a sip of water from a paper cup she'd poured at the judge's suggestion.

"I visited my ma regularly. My *tila* took us there when he was alive. I heard my ma say she was making changes. The proof is in the pudding, my *ála* would say."

Tina's eyes riveted her daughter as she spoke.

"When we lived with my ma before she got arrested, the Child Protection people came, and we got sent off to foster care. She was making those same kind of promises to change back then when she stayed in her room days and nights getting stoned with Jack Brie. Or she'd go off drinking on her own and leave us dealing with him."

Her speech took on a kind of staccato. "Then she'd come back around after being gone for days on end. Jack Brie didn't do nothing for us so us kids, we'd whine for food or love. She'd be doped up so much, she'd act like a robot. Maybe she'd get each of us a bag of chips, a Mountain Dew, maybe not even that.

"When my ma went out to party, Jack Brie, he would hurt my sisters and me, especially Tessa. I believe she knew all that happened to us."

"I didn't," Tina grunted under her breath.

"Hush and let your daughter speak," Judge Waldrup cautioned.

Emily stared directly into her mother's glaring eyes.

"She didn't do a thing to stop Jack Brie. Never. She didn't protect us, and she sure never made him leave. She'd say she was lost in her addiction; I know that's how she would explain it. As far as I'm concerned, she had a choice; she wasn't always loaded. I don't think that's an excuse, more like an explanation. I remember her promises to take better care of us, just like I remember going out to steal Hostess Pies from the party store on Olden Way Road.

"I remember believing her so many times," her voice caught but she regained composure. "My ma lied all the time about everything. Now she wants to take my sis, Ce Ce, and my brother, Samuel. She wants for us to believe she'll be a good mom to them."

Emily paused and sipped her water.

"She says she's all changed now. Well, truth is, I never seen my mom be a good mom. It's hard to have to say it, but I have to get that off my heart right here and now."

Tina's face showed no expression at all.

"To me, she still has a lot to prove before she's allowed to take care of kids. I understand my older sister and my auntie can't take care of us—I'll be eighteen in two months. If Leila can take care of us all 'til my birthday, I'll move to *tila*'s land and see our house get rebuilt. I'll take care of my brothers and sisters, including Eloise." Eloise smiled. "I'll be old enough and don't mind—I don't have big plans like Tessa."

Emily turned her head toward Judge Waldrup. "I wanted to tell you, my spirit is strong, your honor! *Tamanwiłá*, my Creator, will heal our hurt when we open up to Him! I done that, and I'm just as strong as my big sister. That's to tell you, your honor, with my sisters and brothers, we *always* got each others' backs, and that's how we got through, sis, 'idn't it?"

Tessa smiled back at Emily as she spoke. "So I want to step up now and say *at'aw pina shuukt*! And what I'm saying is although I'm young, I know who I am to speak this way from what my elders have taught me—and I don't want my mom involved with these little ones—this is *my* little brother and sister I'm speaking about, your honor, and I'm their big sister, here in the world to look out for them. We need more time before my ma comes back into their lives. So that's all I have to say."

Emily stopped, and the judge looked back at her for a moment.

"Aaaiii." Judge Waldrup enunciated, raising her right hand next to her shoulder and then touching her heart in traditional acknowledgement that someone has spoken from a heartfelt and spiritual place. "The court will consider your words carefully, Emily. You may step down."

Emily looked uncertain for a moment and then rose and quietly walked back and sat down next to Tessa. Elisi watched her, radiant with pride.

Judge Waldrup peered down at several papers. "Let's hear from Mr. Leon Kusitway, please."

As he came to the front and took his seat, Leon retained the slightly comical and awkward expression I remembered when Ruthie and I worked with him when we all helped Tessa gentle Ámashitum.

"Now, Mr. Kusitway, you're listed as an interested party. That tells me you've stepped forward rather than being sought out. I assume that's so?"

"Yes, your honor," said Leon. "We read the posting in *Yakama Nation Review*. We don't know much about these children's mother, but we got to know the kids while they were with their *tila* and felt we should speak. My bro here says I can speak for him too. Well, we got a place down to Granger where there's plenty of room. And my point being, we could take these children in. Neither of us ever had kids, but we get along with them. Edward was married once, but I never been lucky at love."

Judge Waldrup smiled at him.

"Don't get me wrong," he continued, tripping a bit on his words, "we figure their big sisters and us could work together to make a home. We felt bad about what happened, you know, to their grandpa, and want to help. We also aren't judging their mom, having been in trouble ourselves in our younger days."

Edward shot a quick negative nod at Leon.

"Uh, these kids had a good home with their grandpa. We thought maybe we could help keep them all together until the officials decide what they want to do in planning their future. Heck, they could stay with us until they're full grown.

That's about all."

Leon didn't wait for the judge's okay but just got up and ambled gingerly back to his seat.

"Thank you, Mr. Kusitway. We'll think carefully about your kind offer in considering what to do. We have an elder here who's requested to speak."

Elisi got up slowly and made her way forward. Judge Waldrup showed rare deference, muttering "thank you" as she sat down. There was no preliminary on the judge's part as with the others. We all just waited.

"I don't know these children's mother," Elisi nodded toward Tina, who held a spiteful look on her face. "In our way, we don't judge other people. Only in a place like this would we go along with that because it's a court of law, and the lives of children are at stake. Back when I was young, we'd have a council between elders and talk it over. This way we're doing is an invention of the Europeans who brought their ways to force us to use. That's the history is all I'm saying, but I'll go along with it."

She seemed to gaze at each person individually in the court before continuing.

"In our ways, the children are sacred. That's the unwritten law. Most of these kids, those who can remember, say that life was bad with their mother, and all of the findings from what's written down says so too. There's no denying this mother here hurt her children. We only have to think about a man like Jack Brie and his trying to kill Tessa and that man there," she pointed to me, "to know the kind of man their mother brought into her home."

Tina's eyes squinted with hatred at Elisi.

"I'm not here of my own count. I'm from a medicine family, and there's nothing in your bad wishes that can touch or harm me," she spoke to Tina. "I am the sister of your mother, and I'm responsible to speak for the future of these children. Even though you never knew me, that don't mean much to me. You don't have to know me. Your own mother, my sister, asked me to look after your children when she passed on and you were locked up, and I fully intend to do what she asked.

"You may not know but some hard changes come for your kids over the last few months. I don't know your own ability to reform yourself. I can't say whether you have been healed up. I don't really know to your being ready to care for children in a more positive way. So I'm saying I'm not going to speak to that because I don't know."

She looked up at the judge. "My real reason for speaking here is to say to you, your honor—please do not separate these little ones. They need to stay with their older brothers and sisters. What's being decided here to putting the littlest of these kids in their mother's care—I'm saying don't do that now, not at this point."

She eyed Tina, just as Emily had. "Your own mother and father wouldn't have any part in this idea at all because it's not right. That's all I have to say."

Elisi was helped by the bailiff to make her way back to her seat.

"Thank you," said Judge Waldrup. "We will consider your words before making a decision." She turned to me. "Dr. Barlow, I understand you're an interested party."

I came to the front and took the stand. I waited for a moment in the quiet space before beginning. I'd learned to take it slow in such situations.

"I didn't undertake an evaluation with these children, your honor. Over the last seven years, I've become a friend of the family. I've done my best to behave in accord with the ethics governing my profession about friendships developing like this, but it sometimes moves me into grey areas. At this point, I'm back under the constraints of confidentiality professionally for a variety of reasons.

"I'm not a tribal member. I was asked by family

members to speak only a few days ago. This is why I couldn't talk directly to the guardian ad litem when she called me. To have done so would have blurred boundaries I've tried to manage carefully."

"What are you recommending about how I listen to what you say today, doctor?" asked the judge.

"As a personal opinion."

"Okay," she said, "then I'll ask you: what's your personal opinion of Ce Ce and Samuel going to live with their mom?"

"Your honor," Brenda Oakley rose. "I realize this is family court, but I object to you asking this sort of question of a non-family member. I'm asking that you insist Dr. Barlow provide me with access to his documentation on Ce Ce, Samuel, and Franklin Miyanashatawit and back up whatever remarks he decides to make here today."

I had the sense Judge Waldrup didn't like Brenda Oakley. I also knew she was being pushed into a corner.

"Dr. Barlow—Ms. Oakley does have certain legal rights under the laws of Washington State that Yakama Nation also recognizes. I have to ask you to supply her with what she requests."

"With all due respect, your honor, I don't have the documentation she's asking for."

Tina cocked her head back and smirked. Brenda Oakley shook her head.

"And why is that, doctor?" asked Judge Waldrup.

"That documentation has been stolen."

"Stolen??"

"Yes."

"And have you reported this to the police? It's not just lost or something?"

"Yes, your honor—I reported it to the police. My office was broken into and those materials were definitely stolen."

"I see. Well . . ." the judge pondered. "I guess there's not much to be done about that for now. I'd still like to hear your opinion about this matter of returning Ce Ce and Samuel to their mother."

"Your honor, I strenuously object," said Brenda Oakley, jumping up from her seat. "You shouldn't be listening to his opinion as an expert when he has no notes or anything to back up what he says."

"I'll listen to him as a family friend, then. Or for that matter, anyway I like, Ms. Oakley. Objection overruled," Judge Waldrup gave her a scathing look. "Please sit back down."

It was my turn.

"I would like it in the record that I never saw Tina Miyanashatawit before today. Even so, I think the idea of Ce Ce and Samuel going to live with her is a bad idea. My reasoning has nothing to do with her or her past. It has to do with what I know of the lack of thoughtfulness and deliberation that usually goes into most of these kinds of decisions."

Eva Alexander set her pencil down, leaned back, and peered down her nose. Brenda Oakley's expression became even more unfriendly.

"The state child welfare system is broken. The tribal agency here works under this state's mandates and funding. So it's broken too. Over years now, I've watched child welfare social workers send brothers and sisters in different directions, sometimes with only a few hours to say goodbye. These sibling relationships are often all the kids have left. I respect they have a hard job. I respect the guardian ad litem role Ms. Oakley has, although I consider that job to be under-trained and under-credentialed.

"My point is all these people are hog-tied—they don't have sufficient resources or placement choices available. They have to choose from a list of bad choices for these kids. Native and non-native children are regularly subjected to abusive, neglectful circumstances under the name of 'child welfare system'. For the native kids in particular, generations of violence continue to disrupt their lives and hurt them. I've witnessed native teenagers with no placement options at all being housed over at the tribal jail. Throwaway kids, that's what they conclude about themselves. And I'm the one working with the emotional fall-out of those kinds of placement decisions.

"The Miyanashatawit kids had a good home with their *tila*. They had the key ingredients of love and positive influence. They healed up from terrible experiences they had living with their mother. He took good care of them. The youngest was also cared for and nurtured by the oldest, and that's an Indian way I've come to know here. Now their *tila* is gone, and their mother has reentered their lives. They've already lost him and their home. Just about everyone here knows their *tila* was estranged from their mother, Tina, his daughter. I know he wouldn't want any of them going back to her. It's my opinion that his desires should be honored. That's all I can think of."

I started to get up.

"Your honor," Brenda Oakley spoke. "I'd like to ask Dr. Barlow some questions."

Judge Waldrup thought this over reluctantly. "I'll permit it."

Oakley got up and walked over to where I was sitting on the stand. She put both hands on the front rail and leaned in.

"Dr. Barlow, have you seen successful placements and family reunifications developed by state social workers?"

"Of course."

"And, doctor, what do you know of the ratio of placements and reunifications that succeed to those that don't?"

"Not much."

"You didn't evaluate this woman. You couldn't do so if you'd been asked to because you know the kids personally already, and it would be unethical.   Why? Because your opinion would be viewed as biased rather than objective. You don't have your own files on them available for perusal. So where does that leave you?"

"Are you asking or grand-standing?"

"My question is—should this court consider your opinion unbiased and objective—when you haven't done any evaluation and don't even have your files?"

Judge Waldrup sighed.

"Dr. Barlow? Please answer."

"I don't think my personal opinion can be viewed in the same light as a professional opinion. I've already said that."

Brenda Oakley smiled slightly. "Your honor, I have a letter here from Dr. Margaret Fitzsimmons, a psychiatric expert who is lead consultant with the Yakima County Access to Recovery Grant. She feels nothing in state records pertaining to these children and sent for her review justifies a preplacement evaluation regarding living with their mother. She only recommends a home study by the social worker."

Oakley placed the letter on the judge's desk while I stumbled back to my seat. My face surged with rage and urgency. Edward looked at me with concern.

Tina Miyanashatawit was next up. Facing her head on, she appeared stocky and rough, but also pretty. I noticed Franklin sitting alone and away from everyone else in the back of the courtroom. He was on the opposite side from Tessa, watching his mom.

"I don't know either of you," Tina began, gazing at Elisi and then at me. "I never met you before. You're not family or friends to me. You say you're not going to judge me, well, that's good—'cause I don't know why you'd think me or my children are even your business."

"I've heard what my daughter, Emily, said today, and it hurts me. I feel what she said in my own heart. I know I have let my kids down—first, by not caring for them and loving them enough, second, by my addiction and, last, by ending up in prison. I had a lot of time to think, you know. I'm finally out of a cell after seven years and ready and excited to make a clean start if only I'm allowed to. I took parenting classes three times while I was locked up. I wrote my kids letters the whole time and told 'em I loved them. I told 'em I loved them when my dad brought them to visit. I'm always going to be their mother and love them, no matter what.

"My first little girl back there, Tessa; she's got the most call for anger toward me. I understand that. And maybe my own sister, too." Leila reached forward to tap Samuel on the shoulder and mouth "hush." "She's stepped in for me since our dad passed on. I can only say how I appreciate her."

Leila's expression held little reciprocity.

"It's been a long time I waited. Now I'm these kids' mom, and I do love them. I done wrong and neglected my children. I know I failed them. I don't know how many times I have to admit it. I have paid a terrible price, and my life speaks to that. I have made many mistakes while lost in addiction."

"But I earned my second chance. I'm asking you, your honor, and everyone here not to punish me or my children more by keeping me away any longer from being their mother. I need a chance to prove I can be their mom and a good one."

She got up slowly, looking at Judge Waldrup, and then making her way to her seat.

"Thank you for your statement, Ms. Miyanashatawit. Let's hear the final recommendations."

Eva stood up.

"Your honor, Tribal Child Welfare has no sound reason to keep Ce Ce and Samuel Miyanashatawit from being returned to Tina Miyanashatawit, their mother, under a supervised reunification plan. Abuse in the past occurred at the hands of Mr. Brie, a known criminal. According to law enforcement, he's deceased. Back at that time, Ms. Miyanashatawit's parental rights were terminated under founded complaints of neglect but not abuse. Mr. Arnold Miyanashatawit took responsibility for his grandchildren's care and became permanent guardian after she became incarcerated. He is now also deceased, leaving a void in these children's lives.

"Ms. Leila Miyanashatawit has cared for them well, and we appreciate all she's done. However, the understanding was always that their placement in her home would be temporary. Her home is not big enough, and they shouldn't stay there for any prolonged period. It is always my intention and the state's intention to keep native children in particular out of foster care and in relative placements whenever we can, just as ICWA stipulates.

"Tina Miyanashatawit's neglectful parenting occurred while she was suffering from addiction. She is currently in recovery and has been sober based on random urinalysis throughout her seven-year incarceration and also in the month since her release. We've interviewed prison officers at Walla Walla, probation officers, an apartment manager, and other parties who speak highly of her efforts to reform herself."

Brenda Oakley now stood up and spoke. "Dr. Fitzsimmons advised me that the loss of the grandfather has deepened Franklin's depression. He needs a dedicated parent figure in his life. Placing Ce Ce and Samuel with Tina allows us to avoid foster care and start working toward a family reunification plan in which *all* the children can eventually go back to live with their mother, possibly when their grandfather's house is rebuilt."

"No!" Tessa shot forward, bounding over benches as if they were hurdles. "NO! She can't walk on *tila*'s land!"

She struggled to make it past Leila's reaching arms, and Leon and Edward rushed in with the bailiff.

"You bitch!!" she screamed at her mother, swinging at her. Tina covered her head with her hands. "Stay away from them!!"

Tessa managed to club the back of her mother's head with a fist before she was taken to the ground and handcuffed. I don't think anyone else did, but I saw the flames shoot up in Tina's eyes.

"Take her out of here!!" yelled Judge Waldrup. "She's barred from coming back inside. Do you hear that, bailiff?"

"Yes, your honor," and he took her outside, removed her handcuffs, and posted himself by the doorway. I could see Tessa pacing back and forth in front of him through the window.

The judge caught her breath and then appeared pensive.

"Is anyone hurt?" She scanned the courtroom.

"No one appears to have been injured. I could throw the book at Tessa, but I'm going to overlook this. This is a very emotional and contentious situation."

Several chairs were put back in place, and we sat back down.

"Resume your statement, Ms. Oakley."

Brenda Oakley, visibly shaken, stood up again. "It's in the children's best interests to be returned to their mother's care under controlled and supervised conditions which Tribal Child Welfare can provide. The first step is to return Ce Ce and Samuel. After monitoring and a successful transition, housing of some sort will be sought for the entire family, and all the children can be returned."

"Do you concur, Ms. Alexander?" asked the judge.

"Provided the plan includes supervised visitation for several weeks before Ce Ce and Samuel actually go live with their mom, this is a permanency plan we can support."

"I need a break," said the judge. "I'm calling a half-hour recess."

I walked down to grab a coffee at the Yakamart. Tessa stood in the parking lot, holding Chase who was brought out to her by Elisi after getting very upset over her mother's outburst and ejection.

"Don't talk to me now, Barlow."

"I wasn't going to try," I said, lighting a smoke.

"She's getting what she wants," she said, unable to keep herself from talking.

"I know."

"You understand how this feels."

"Can't really know because I'm not you. But I do know you've been through a lot, Tessa."

"I leave for basic training in a week and couldn't go at a worse time. Please don't tell Elisi or Leila that I did check into getting out of going."

"I've heard the military's not too interested in helping you get out once you sign up."

"I can't use family hardship because they only look at Chase's needs, and I already said Elisi has temporary custody of her. Ce Ce, Samuel, they aren't considered my responsibility. If I went AWOL for any reason having to do with this shit here, the sergeant said I'd be court-martialed, end up in military prison, and never be a cop."

"Can you defer going off to basic?"

"Under really strict guidelines, Barlow, and if I even meet them, that would set me back from starting Advanced Infantry Training for MP for six months, totally screw up my schooling, my financing, everything."

"Sorry."

"So I'm leaving for training next week. Will you let me know what happens?"

"Where are we going, Momma?" asked Chase, holding her mom's hand.

"Home, *tiskáy.*"

"Sure," I said. "I'll keep you posted."

I walked back inside just in time; Judge Waldrup returned five minutes early. She looked unhappy, and her shoulders were hunched as though carrying a dead weight.

"I've listened carefully this morning. I want to commend you children for sitting quietly through all this talking. You are very special to me, and I feel you deserve a good life. I'm sorry about your loss of your elder and your home out there.

"We're going to look out for you. We can't continue to have you living with your auntie Leila because her place is too small. You might like to go back to your *tila*'s land instead, but that can't happen now. Emily's a good sister to want to care for you, but I feel it's too big a responsibility for somebody her age. I also heard what your cousins Leon and Edward said. They are good men, and you can learn a lot from them. You must always look to elders like these to guide you. But they're only distantly related to you. I'm not allowed to consider having you live with them while disregarding the efforts your mother has made to have her children back with her. This court has a history of trying to keep mothers and their children together. Although there are many wonderful foster parents in the system, I wish to avoid having you enter that system as so many native children have experienced in their lives growing up. It is almost always better to live with family, in my opinion, provided the environment is safe and nurturing."

She looked at Tina Miyanashatawit.

"Tina, I listened carefully to what you said. I want to support you in resuming the important responsibility of parenting." A quiet smile emerged on Tina's face. "I'm going to accept the Child Welfare Program and Guardian Ad Litem recommendation that these children be returned to you—gradually—as a part of a careful reunification and permanency plan. I'm not entirely persuaded by all that's been brought before me. It's your actions from this day which will decide whether I am being wise."

"I won't disappoint you, Judge," chimed Tina.

"If I learn I've made an error, and you somehow compromise my reasoning, I'll have your kids removed to temporary placement by sundown that same day. You can count on it."

The severity of Judge Waldrup's gaze commanded response.

"I understand," Tina answered.

"'I understand, your honor.' Very well. The court accepts the recommendations and orders the proposed permanency plan be instituted. I'd like bi-weekly updates on progress."

She rose immediately and rapped her gavel quickly.

"Court adjourned."

She exited the courtroom rapidly, despite Elisi's efforts to get her attention.

TEN

I saw my people, and I knew them.
I tried to go to them, but a man stopped me.
He held an Indian flute in his left hand,
A flute made from a bloody gun.
His arms were blood to the elbow.
I attempted to pass him, but he held me back,
Barred my way with the gun.
He said: "You cannot come here now.
See my hands?
They are yours, all blood and bad.
Go back to where you came from!
Clean the blood from your hands and arms.
Do good for your people!"
—*Yakama twáti,*
death vision reported to L.V. McWhorter, 1925

After the hearing, I dropped in at Yakamart to pick up a soda. Franklin was standing by my car when I walked back out, wearing oversized jeans slung low, holding both hands in his pockets. His thick black hair, cropped short on the top and sides where it bristled, flowed long down onto his back. He squinted hard at the horizon and didn't look at me at all when I walked up.

"'S'up, Franklin?" I aimed my outmoded teen vernacular.

"Hey, Barlow," he answered acceptingly.

"Haven't seen you around. Your sis and auntie and *kála* are all upset and worried about you."

"I'm chill," he answered softly, staring at traffic sailing along on Fort Road. "Just 'cause I been runnin', they think I'm all mental."

"They're just worried. They want you and me to maybe sit down and talk about what's been going on."

"No way out at your place, Barlow. I'll talk now. Just to tell you my ma shouldn't have nothing doing about Ce Ce and Samuel."

"Maybe you needed a chance to speak to the court too."

"I'm telling you—that's all who I'm telling. I ain't no snitch, especially with family. She's still clicked in, Barlow. Always, since we were real little."

"What's all that mean?"

He was not very articulate yet had a great deal to say: "She's bangin'. She's got a new man and going all Nortena; she thinks she's Mexican."

"What new man?"

"Hector. He says he knows you."

His black eyes surveyed my demeanor. The chipped incisor was new and showed when he grinned slightly. To me, he looked forty instead of fourteen.

"Hunh, well, just so you know, that's not his real name, Franklin. I don't like that guy, and you should stay away from him too. I'd also like to know his whereabouts."

"I couldn't say, Barlow."

"Ah. Will you tell me what happened to your tooth?"

"Nothin'."

"Not nothin'."

"Shit, Barlow, nothin'. Jumped to TNKs. So what?"

He tugged his hair back, and I noticed four little dots tattooed on his right hand.

"True Native Kings? Your *tila* wouldn't like that too much."

"Larena Lane, Barlow; that's how it is 'round there. That's why I can't hang at my auntie's too long—'cause of ESLs."

"Uh . . ."

"East Side Longos. Surenos. 13 pack."

"TNK claims blue?"

"Thought you'd know. TNK, Nortenos, we all run together. ESLs don't like us. We don't like them. I try to stay away from home so's my family don't catch it."

"Catch what?"

"There was squab along south Camas Road maybe three weeks ago," He leaned back against the fender of my car. "Me and Jamison flew colors and a busta called BK came with a carload, yelling out 'red nigger crabs'. We thought he's fluff so we yelled back. Turned out he had a gat, so we booked over to Track Road. They all came 'round after us and popped cap for reals."

I watched him from the other side of our language barrier.

He fingered a pistol shot at me.

"They missed, Barlow. Yeah. You could hear bullets whizzin'. Pop, pop! But they missed. Now ESL's tagging about me and Jamie everywhere."

"And what's your mom got to do with it?"

"She's the reason."

"How?"

He turned his hard squint stare toward me again.

"Ma told Hector about some money got ripped years back. She's playing him and he's too stupid; he don't know he's her scam-bro. It's all connected. ESLs, the money, I don't know. What I'm saying is she's nobody for my sis and bro to be around."

"You know, Franklin, I heard somewhere you've been helping her get money."

I risked putting it out there. I had to know if what Maritza was feeding me about Tina held any truth. He tried to look like he didn't comprehend.

"Selling your meds, Franklin. What you do with them

doesn't matter to me."

Two Washington state police cars pulled into the Yakamart parking lot as I said it, which was very inconvenient. They parallel parked with one another, each on the driver's side, shooting the breeze. They were too near for him.

"Hop in," I said hurriedly, getting into my car and lifting the passenger door lock. He only held the door open and stood there.

"Nah," he said, leaning his head inside. "I gotta roll, doc. It's not what you think: I told that lady doctor I don't need no pills, but I could use the money. She thought I was shittin' and wanted to get me back in school. I knew my ma was out of jail 'cause she had my cell number and called me. I caught a lift up to town and brought my script along and asked her if she'd get pocket cash for me and my crew. So it was all the other way around."

"And she took her cut."

He shrugged, pulled his head out, and looked over the top of my car at the nearby state cruisers.

"Gotta go, Barlow."

"Will you come out to my office and meet with me if your auntie brings you?"

He laughed a little. "That's all right, Barlow. I'll stay away from your place."

"And why's that?"

"You're being played, Barlow, if you don't know yet. Ma and Hector asked me all about you. She thinks you stick your nose in and almost got my sister killed back when. She wants Hector to scare you away."

I pondered that for a moment. "With a rock through my window, maybe? Does he own an old blue and white old car?"

"Well, if you got a rock through your window, I just tipped you who sent it. There's some other bitch they're trying to play. So who knows who's gamin' who right now? I'm just saying I don't want my brother and sister around my ma. She's a bullshitter. She wants Ce Ce to herself, and I don't know why. She don't ever say one word about little Samuel. But she's all about Ce Ce, she's all she talks about."

"Why'd you decide to tell me this?"

One of the cruisers flipped his flashers on and off. I don't know why; maybe it was an accident.

"I'm out of here, Barlow. You helped my sis and *tila* always said you ain't bad. That and Jamison knows Hector from way back when he was little and told me he's a blood killer. I been staying with my boys 'cause I don't want ESLs coming around and shootin' auntie's windows. You need to stay away from around here too—it's getting all hot these days between different crews. You're up for family soon. Better move north, Barlow. Word."

He pulled his cell out, clicked it, and stared at it.

"Get out of where you're doing business and help keep my little sis Ce Ce and bro Samuel from going to live with ma."

I raised my hands in a helpless gesture. "Franklin, the court's got a placement order going. I can't do much."

"You'll think of something."

One of the cops started to get out of his cruiser to head into Yakamart. Franklin closed the car door and started walking the Fort Road shoulder without saying goodbye.

What choice did I have? I worked the rest of the week out in Harrah. Nothing happened. What did I tell Ruthie if I stopped going down to work? I had no other way to make money. That Saturday afternoon, I decided to go sweat to ease myself down a little. Trick had remarked I should maybe sweat twice that day from the look on my face, but I headed back home feeling more relaxed.

Track Road, which is all gravel, rises up a small hill to

connect with the smooth asphalt of Yakima Valley Highway. I was accustomed to powering my way up there in my jalopy and making a quick right into traffic.

My surge of gas and motion fell off completely when I reached the rise. A young man's head rested on his chest. He seemed to be kneeling on the ground. His face was turned away from me. He wasn't moving. I saw him first before I saw all the cruisers and people. My throat closed in revulsion.

I couldn't see who he was and had to know. I pulled onto the shoulder and strolled across the street.

"Crime scene! Stay back please!" said a Wapato city cop when I closed in on the yellow tape.

"I have information for Daisy." I knew she was my ticket.

He eyed me skeptically and thought about that. "She's standing over to the left. Do not, I repeat, do not go through the tape."

Detective Dolynda Jacinto and several other officers were on the other side of the wide circle made by the tape. The corpse of the brown-skinned teenage boy sat in the middle, his knees pulled up beneath him and his face on his chest, arms limp, as though he'd crumpled downward to pray before oblivion. A wide pool of blood eased out of head and neck wounds and soaked the asphalt around him.

I'd never seen someone murdered before. His eyes were still open; they were hollow and void. I didn't recognize him.

"It's gang-related with a Yakima city connection," Detective Jacinto said to a *Yakima Herald* reporter, a thin man with bright pimples on both cheeks tapping an oversized cell phone. "We're combining investigation with Wapato city and state police.

"We need help from the public," she handed him her card, "please squeeze my contact info in."

The reporter shoved it in his pocket, fingered in a few

more notes, thanked her, and meandered away.

". . . maybe that'll happen," she muttered to a state trooper wearing shades and wide-brimmed hat. The trooper eyed me disapprovingly from where I stood. I didn't have a hall pass. Jacinto raised her eyebrows in recognition. The trooper began to step forward to send me on my way.

"It's okay, Williams. Hello, doctor. What brings you to our little horror show?"

"I might have information about this."

"Ah, being helpful," she answered sarcastically. "Thanks for that. It'd be nice to have information beforehand, however, don't you agree?"

"Look, I think I know who this kid is. I think his name's Jamison. Jamie Jamison."

"And how do you know him?"

"I don't. But I'm guessing he's a friend of Franklin Miyanashatawit, and I know Franklin."

"Well, I'd like to know more about Franklin, then." She squinted at me darkly.

I told her about Jamie and Franklin's involvement with TNKs and the apparent war with ESLs. I said nothing about what Franklin mentioned regarding Hector and Tina or Maritza.

I didn't want to put him in that story. I was trying to protect him.

"There is a gang war on, doctor, make no mistake about it. It's my job to stop it and for that I need any information that pertains. I mention it because I get the sense you're not saying all you could."

"No, no, that's all I've got, Detective," I lied, trying to not blink.

Daisy put her hand lightly on my shoulder and steered my attention to the young corpse at the center of the big circle before us.

"I get to sit with another mother in an hour or so and

tell her the worst news she can ever hear. The way I see it, you hold back from me, you hold back from her, do you understand me?"

She smiled artificially. "An ESL boy got shot through the back of the head on the south side of Yakima two days ago. Same age too, stuffed in a dumpster along Fair Avenue." She pointed graffiti out to me on a nearby fence. "Those boys are going to be after somebody, and I'll bet it's your boy."

She pointed absently toward a plainclothes officer whose attention perked up.

"I've got other things to do here. Clarence? Take this guy's statement. Explain to him about obstruction of justice."

She spun back with an expression of restrained fury. "On the rez, we call in the FBI for all felony and capital crimes. If you impede a murder investigation, I'll come for you. I'll lock you up as a material witness without a second thought."

"Okay, Detective . . . Daisy," I stammered. "I get it."

She glanced at Clarence and then leaned up to my ear. I could smell thick, musky perfume as she whispered.

"You ever call me Daisy again, I'll put your nuts in a vice or make you wish I would. And don't leave Yakima Valley without telling me. I won't like it."

Her eyes bored into mine. Then, she shook my hand with an expression that was almost friendly. There was muscle in her grip.

"He's a bullshitter, Clarence. But he wants to give us a little sugar . . ." He nodded at her. "If you catch him lying, I'll want to know. Right away."

Clarence's questions were direct and repetitive. He wrote down my responses verbatim on a tiny pocket pad and didn't respond to chumminess. The Sheriff's department forensics crew pulled in while he interviewed me. I watched Detective Jacinto stroll over as they climbed out, a man and woman. They took her directions and got right to work.

She was all business, and everyone working with her did exactly what they were told.

That might have been a lesson to me.

Three days later, after the band played, Tessa had exactly ten minutes to say goodbye before catching the bus to Joint Base Lewis-McChord for a flight out to Fort Benning, Georgia and basic training with the Guard. Ruthie and I arrived late and frustrated, hurrying up to the scene out of breath.

What was particularly hard was that Chase wouldn't say 'goodbye' to her mom, no matter what her mom or anyone said. She ignored Tessa when she tried to come close. She leaned back hard, rolled her eyes, and pushed back and feigned disgust when Tessa tried to hug her.

"Don't give up," I encouraged Tessa.

"He's right," Elisi echoed.

"I'm a shit mom," Tessa said.

"You're not," Leila responded weakly.

"You're a brave woman," Ruthie stepped in. 'She's likely just tired and maybe a little scared."

The clock was ticking and Tessa's eyes filled. With no more than a couple of minutes left, she stooped, unzipped her duffle bag, and pulled out a worn-out stuffed puppy. I recognized it; she'd brought it to one of our sessions at some point—she'd had it since she was Chase's age. She'd clearly planned on taking it along. Instead, she leaned over, and nuzzled 'Pup' into Chase's neck. Chase pulled back, eyed the toy resentfully, and peered up at her mother.

"Look after Pup for me, *tiskáy*, 'til I come back home."

"I *told* you I'm not a skunk, Momma," Chase answered harshly.

She did take hold of Pup. Tessa reached down and picked her up and this time Chase let her while gripping Pup but then grabbing her mom's neck tightly. It was then that

Tessa finally kissed her and hugged her with all she had. This lasted only a few seconds before the call came to 'mount up'. Tessa lowered her gently, looked into her eyes, flecked with brown, black and grey, and promised to Skype her in two days.

"See?" Ruthie whispered to me. "That's a real mom. She already thought of that ahead of time."

Unlike Leila, Tessa seemed able to bite back the emotion around her brother's absence. He'd run off, and no one had heard from him since Jamie's murder. Tessa, Leila, Elisi, Trick, Ruthie and I drove in various cars all over Lower Valley and stopped by every housing project, street corner gathering, and pick-up game. His friends—those we knew or could find out about—acknowledged the importance of saying goodbye when your sister joined the military. But the code of silence prevailed, and Trick agreed with me that the kids were "closed as a Pike Street clam stand after midnight."

Just before Tessa cued up with her cohort of soldiers-to-be, Leila rested her hands on her shoulders with her lips quivering. Tessa only shook her head. She didn't want anything more to be said. Leila's head dropped in response.

I watched Tessa glance up at the windows of the fancy hydrocell shuttle, thinking about the long fight she'd already been through and the kind of fight that might lie ahead of her. Ruthie leaned half-hip against me, her face tightening while she watched a mother leave behind her only daughter based solely upon some recruiter's assurances.

Tessa turned back around and looked right at me just before she arrived at the door of the bus, nodding upwards slightly, signaling for me to come over closer.

"Time's up, sir," said one of the sergeants as I tried to move forward.

"Just a sec," I answered, trying to get through.

He placed a hand on my chest. "All done, dad, sorry."

"I'm not your dad, son," I answered. "I'm trying to

catch a message here."

"Can't let you through, sorry."

"Barlow!" Tessa yelled over at me.

"What?"

"Back up please," said the sergeant.

"Get Trick and Frank Mathis!"

"What for?"

"Sir, this is the very last time I'm going to ask you to back up before I call military security. Move back with the families now."

"Get Trick and Frank Mathis! Go find Franklin!"

I looked down at the sergeant's hand, loose on my shoulder.

"All right, she's all yours," I said.

Everyone waved furiously at Tessa until the bus turned onto the entrance ramp to the freeway. Leila turned to Ruthie and me with tears on her cheeks.

"I wish I could've found Franklin for her and got him back here," she blurted out. Ruthie reached to hug her. "I been so worried. I know he wouldn't miss her leaving. And she still had to go off like this."

She laid hard sobs into Ruthie's shoulder, and Elisi leaned quietly into them both.

I watched ten-year-old Ce Ce walk over to Chase after the bus left and put her arm around her. "You're being a sad bird, niece, aren't you?"

Chase nodded toward her.

"That's because you have to be so patient and wait for your mom. That's hard to do, but I'm very proud of you."

And she squeezed her close into her, hugging her shoulders. We adults were now watching them.

"Mourning Dove," Ce Ce said. "Do you hear her?"

Chase listened over the departing crowd, and we all did so too. With all the activity, I hadn't noticed the soft coo-coo, but now I did.

"There's a reason she cries that way . . . did you know that?" said Ce Ce. "Sit down right here with me."

They both sat on the grass, and Ce Ce began talking to her little niece in earnest.

"I gave this old story to Ce Ce," Elisi whispered to Ruthie and me. "Just so something like this might happen."

Ce Ce kept her arm around Chase while they sat together on the ground cross-legged.

"I'm your auntie, so I'll look out for you while your mom's gone. Do you want to hear an old story from our *káła*?"

She looked up at Elisi who winked at her.

"I heard it already, auntie. . ." said Chase, reluctantly.

"Oh, okay," Ce Ce answered.

Everyone was standing about, not talking, just eavesdropping.

"But I want to hear it again," said Chase.

"Well, okay. I'll tell it. See, it was the early spring and Mourning Dove and her children were all starving, weren't they? Remember?"

A coo-coo sounded above us where we stood. Ce Ce looked up before continuing.

"And she'd sent her husband off to search for food, but he hadn't returned. There was so little food. Human beings, we love the spring but early spring is very hard on the animals, especially their children. All the food they stored up or hid for winter was gone. Nothing had bloomed yet. There was nothing to dig, nothing to eat, and they were very, very hungry."

Chase nodded. The mourning dove was still nearby. I could see her in a tree near us. Hoo-hoo, she sounded again.

"Mother Mourning Dove worried for her husband, 'where is he?' she cried, 'where is he?' or 'why is he taking so long?' or 'I'm so, so tired of waiting.' Maybe she spoke to Creator, 'we are starving, please send him back home now.'"

Ce Ce's voice took on a cooing prosody similar to the

dove's.

"Listen, do you hear? She got panicky, scared, so worried, she finally thought to herself—'we'll all die here or I'll die and then my children will die' and she worried, 'what if I die and my children have no mother or father to care for them??' And this last thought worried her more than anything else.

"And so to feed herself and survive so at least someone lived on to meet her husband and continue the family, she ate her two children up."

Chase lifted her head inquisitively. "Auntie, did she really eat her own children??"

"Oh yes, she did," said Ce Ce. "And that's why she is now so very sad, you see. Because after she'd done this terrible thing, Sparrow came by the very next morning. He always came at the start of the spring to tell the animal people when the Fish were coming back. *Núsux*, the salmon, were returning, he told them. Sparrow was always the first to know. He could see them. And when the Fish had all returned, all the animals could feel hope again and would celebrate because that meant that there would be lots of food, and soon it would blossom everywhere."

"But it was too late for Mourning Dove," said Chase.

"Yes, you're right. You remember. When the Fish People saw what Mourning Dove had done, they were very sad for her. Their leader said, 'if you had just waited a little longer through hard times and worry, if you had held on when things got bad and not done this, we would have arrived, and you all would have been fed and survived. Now, you've eaten your children, and that's a terrible violation—for children are sacred and must never be hurt or harmed.

"For what you've done, Mother Dove, said the Fish, your voice must remain sad forever so that everyone who hears you call will remember to be patient when life gets too hard.

"And that's why we must try to be patient, niece, even when we have to wait very long. That's why I'm proud of you because you'll try to do that."

Above us, the mourning dove cooed once more before flying off. Ce Ce helped Chase stand up.

"Come on. Let's get back home, and we can play."

"Okay!"

In the middle of that same night, our home phone rang. Ruthie woke first but handed it to me without speaking.

"Barlow," said Franklin.

I sat up on the bed and flicked the light on. "Where are you, Franklin?"

"Nowhere. Gone Rambo for Jamie. Looking for Hector."

"No, Franklin. Leave Hector to the cops. Your sis and family. . ."

"Felt real bad not saying goodbye. Never mind, doc. Hector knocked Jamie. If I don't make it, then you know."

"Franklin, don't hang up."

But he did. And Ruthie was wide awake.

"I need to make a call," I told her.

"About Franklin? Ret, what's going on?"

"He's in big trouble. He's trying to go after somebody."

"Who? God, Ret, I hope you're calling the cops."

"I am," I declared lurching up and pulling my pants on.

I dialed the Yakima County Sheriff first and just missed Daisy. Clarence told me they were pushing nights investigating the murders of Jamie and the boy on Fair Avenue. She'd gone home to get some sleep. I told him that Franklin called, and it was important for me to talk to her.

"Why?" Clarence asked bluntly.

"Franklin says he's going after that Hector guy I told you and Detective Jacinto about. He believes he killed Jamie

Jamison."

"Hold on a minute . . ." I heard him shuffle papers. "Hector Amezquita. Is that the guy?"

"Yeah."

"Enrico Astorgia from Michoacán. That's his real name."

"Ah. Did you find a real name for Maritza Rios?"

"We're still working on her. Your man Enrico AKA Hector was *jefa* at an orchard down near Sunnyside last week. Maybe your boy Franklin won't be able to find him."

"Can you trace the call that just came into my home phone from Franklin, find out where he is, and stop him?"

He sighed. "We'd have to trisect towers to even get the general vicinity. These little gangsters run all over the place, doctor. We'll be back in touch."

I dialed Leila and filled her in. While I was calling, Ruthie got out of bed and stood right in front of me.

"You're talking about that Hector guy and your hooker client we met in front of Yvette's place . . ."

"Yeah," I nodded as Leila's line started ringing.

"Your client, Maritza—her man," she then observed. The proverbial cat was slowly creeping out of the bag.

"Right again," I confirmed.

"Hello?" Leila answered sleepily.

"Little Franklin's out trying to kill that guy!?" Ruthie suddenly exclaimed as she put two and two together.

"Ruthie, please . . . !" I placed my hand tightly over the phone. She sat down on the bed abruptly.

I explained to Leila what the police could and wouldn't do to find Franklin and what his intentions appeared to be. There was nothing I could bring up to be calm about, but I eventually managed to get her to agree to call Detective Jacinto on her own with whatever additional information she might have about Franklin's hangouts.

When I got off the phone, Ruthie glared at me.

"Tell me what's going on." Her entire face darkened. "Now, Ret. I mean the death of this friend of Franklin's, him calling you in the middle of the night, and accusing this guy Hector—whom you'll remember I've also met—and that woman, Maritza."

"You have the gist of it. This guy, Hector, he's a bad guy and Maritza, well, I don't meet with her anymore. Hector's likely gang-involved, and he may or may not have been involved in the killing of Franklin's friend, Jamie."

"And what else?"

"I called Detective Dolynda Jacinto to report that Franklin's putting himself in danger pursuing this guy. I talked to her partner, Clarence. The ethics of 'imminent danger' pertain. I've been trying to work with Franklin, but he's now threatened somebody's life. I have to suspend confidentiality and take steps. I'm just doing work, Ruthie."

"Oh," she nodded. "So is Tina involved?"

"You know I can't comment on other family members. You know that, and I wish you wouldn't ask me."

"This Maritza woman, I knew from the moment I laid eyes on her, she was trouble. It can't be good that Franklin would know Hector."

I didn't answer. We finally went back to bed and both had a tough time getting back to sleep. She tossed and turned, and I lay awake, feeling terribly guilty.

Detective Dolynda Jacinto stood outside my office in Harrah the next morning holding a Starbuck's in one hand, fishing in her purse with the other.

"Hello, Detective," I announced myself, reaching up past her to get my key into the door.

"Just a minute," she clicked off the loud ring of her cell. She looked like she'd been up all night. "I stopped by to tell you, doctor, that the person you call Hector Amizquito was found dead in a canal out in White Swan early this morning. As Clarence told you, his real name is Enrico Astorgia."

I didn't move. "How'd he die?"

"Particulars to a police investigation and not public yet."

I waved my hand dismissively. "God, detective, do you think Franklin did it?"

"Hector was stabbed in the neck."

"Franklin couldn't pull that off easily with a man of Hector's, I mean, Enrico's build."

"You'd be surprised what a gang of young guys can do."

A text came on her cell, and she checked it.

"I'm requesting a felony warrant from the juvenile court judge. We're still looking for the knife."

"For Franklin? What about questioning Maritza?"

"She's a person of interest, of course. Franklin disappeared, called you alleging Hector killed Jamie, and next thing we know, Hector's dead. A knife's been used, and all the little bangers who don't have a pistol have a knife. So we have probable cause, doctor. I came by because I want to have a look at Franklin's file."

"You'd need a subpoena to do so."

We just looked bitterly at each other.

"You know the murder scenario you're alleging would have to be blue on blue," I pleaded. "That doesn't make any sense. Hector's Norteno and TNKs are Norteno-affiliates. Franklin claims blue."

"Well, well. And how can you be so certain Enrico's Norteno-affiliated?"

"Franklin told me."

She wagged an index finger slowly in my face.

"That's a problem, isn't it? And let's quit calling him 'Hector.' The gang war we're dealing with may not factor at all with this Astorgia guy's murder. Let's just assume Franklin hated him for Jamie's death because that's certain. Maybe the murder is sanctioned by some vendetta that benefits some TNK agenda. Who knows? I don't really care. Nortenos may have even sanctioned it. They're all over Tri-Cities."

She pushed her finger up in my face, and I didn't like it. "Don't do anything to help this kid, doctor. Turn him in if he shows up. Encourage him to turn himself in if he calls. I'm giving you and his auntie Leila the word on all that. I'll only say it once."

She adjusted a side holster beneath her light jacket. "We're going to stop this, doctor. Do not get in our way."

ELEVEN

This was the way the Great Maker
Sent White Eagle to be the head of *Pah'to*,
A Law standing high for the world . . .
White Eagle declared,
"Whatever the Great Maker has done, I know.
Women will bear children.
There shall be death;
There shall be sorrow everywhere . . .
The center of power, the head of the Law
Is in me.
I will send my children all over the world
To take up and report to me what is going on.
My power, my Law is stronger
Than all the people who shall ever live."
—*William Charley, 1917*

The little bell sensor tripped when I walked into Neir's for my daily Jarrito. That day, I wanted watermelon flavor. I was surprised while I searched the cooler to overhear Elisi talking to Alice.

"I heard you got fresh pig hocks," she said as I walked up. "I'm making up menudo."

"Sure thing," said Alice, walking to the back of the store. Warren stood up off his position against the chew tobacco display and rang me up with a genuinely pleasant expression.

"I see you're getting some business from your new tenant, Warren," Elisi remarked.

"The doctor?" he seemed practically demure, "Sure. He's getting plenty of business too. I chased some guy who busted into his place. Had to talk Alice out of evicting him for the kind of folks he's attracting. Be easier if he paid his rent on time."

"Uh, well, thanks for that, Warren," I said and then explained, "Warren helped me spot the car Hector jumped into."

"The Mexican man the police think Franklin killed. . ." Elisi nodded.

"Well, he ought to get a medal if he did," Warren reassured.

"Don't need a county jail with the work doctor's doing in our little town," Alice grumbled as she returned, packing up pig hocks for Elisi. "Cop cars and criminals always running up and down the street over there now. Why, I should get my loving husband here to install some bars and a lockup in his office for him."

I followed Elisi out, and she stopped next to me, speaking to the horizon. "You must know, doctor, you have to know—Franklin didn't kill that man Hector."

"I hope you're right, *káła*. I also hope you know why I felt I had to I call the police after he called me. I was trying to stop him from doing anything we'd all regret."

Deep grief emerged on her face.

"I do believe you in what you're saying. But I wish we might've talked with him first. I give it all to *Tamanwiłá*, my Creator, to protect that boy. I happen to have something for you, doctor. Something I said I'd get to you."

We walked into the parking lot, and Chase climbed out of her car window, lowering herself onto broken asphalt.

"I need to go now!"

"To what, little one? To potty?" Elisi responded in an exhausted tone.

"No, home. I'm tired of sitting around here!"

"Well, that's no way to be getting what you need. Creator's watching and knows when you're being pushy; think on that. Just wait a minute 'til I give the doctor something from my trunk."

She rummaged through a pile of items—an axe, sledge hammer, gas can, coils of rope, knick-knacks, old newspaper, several split logs, all mixed in with various books and papers.

"I set it in here so I'd have it. Where?"

She finally dragged out an ancient, dog-eared envelope wedged into the spare wheel well.

"These papers belonged to my uncle. He left them for me so please be kind to them. You said you were interested."

"Yes, I guess I did," I answered, gripping the beat-up envelope she handed me. She looked bemused that I wasn't showing more energy about it.

"And what are you hoping I'll do, kałá?" I asked suspiciously.

She eyed me carefully and then laughed aloud. "Some twáti in you maybe, doctor, trying to stare into my heart. You asked—I give it to you for a time. That's all there is to that. Everything happens for a reason, no matter how little. That's the path I follow."

"Well, kałá, thank you, but I was really asking more about what you're hoping I'll do in loaning this to me."

"All I know is Franklin didn't kill this Hector man. But somebody else did. There's evil walking all around. I really don't know. Something inside just tells me to loan these papers to you for a time."

"Kałá, I don't want any trouble."

"Trouble comes anyways whether we want it or not, don't it?"

She wordlessly herded Chase back into the car and lowered herself agonizingly into the driver's seat, Chase sighing in relief.

"Okay, young one, let's finish up making menudo and then we'll make our drive out to cousin's house at Neah Bay."

"I'm too tired of riding around and that's too far

away," Chase complained. "I want to go home and see my Mom."

"You already know your mom isn't home," Elisi answered, looking up at me. "Ámashitum jumped her pen, by the way. Leon heard from Frank. I didn't have the heart to tell Tessa. She run off the morning after she got on the bus."

She put her seatbelt on and pointed to the envelope in my hand before pulling away, staring ahead, and nodding just once with that Cheshire grin that sometimes makes me nervous.

I found Ruthie crying on the couch, rushed over, and put my arm around her.

She whispered to me. "He's been found. He turned up."

"Franklin?"

Horror crossed her face. "Ret—he's been hurt!"

"Goddamn . . ."

"Leila called again just a few minutes ago. Why do you have to have that office space way out there? It's so hard to reach you when you're away from your landline! She said she can't reach Elisi."

"She went to the coast to visit her cousin with Chase, Ruthie."

"You have to call Leila, Ret. Get hold of her. She's all alone dealing with this. Go help her."

Leila's voice sounded like she was coatless in the middle of a blizzard.

"He's . . . they sedated him. I wanted to get him there fast. . . he just walked in and fell . . . there was blood. I'm sorry. . ."

"Leila, I'm heading to Provincial right now. Elisi's off to the coast with Chase."

"I forgot. Tina's coming here too."

"You called her?!"

"No. No. The police called that Oakley lady, and she just did what she felt like."

I hopped into my car while Leila told the story in one long rattle. Two hours had already passed since a text came on her cell from Franklin that read simply, "lockup now." She got scared, called Samuel and Ce Ce back from playing outside, and told Emily to close the curtains and bolt the front door. Everybody sat on the floor in the bedroom hallway.

A scratching noise emerged and scared the crap out of everyone. Emily couldn't take it any longer and jumped up. Leila tried to grab her foot before she fought her way to the front door, undid the bolt, and cracked it open slightly. Franklin fell unconscious onto the floor, his face covered with blood. Eloise and Ce Ce screamed, Leila shouted for towels, and Samuel scrambled to the kitchen.

Emily and Leila turned him over and tried to determine his wound. When they discovered it was his eye, Emily called 911, but after ten minutes passed, they decided to load him onto the front seat of Leila's truck. She raced north to Provincial Medical Center's ER in Yakima but it took her forty minutes, and she couldn't do much about the blood. She'd heard somewhere you shouldn't apply any pressure to an eye wound.

"God, I just hope he's not in shock," Ruthie said after I recounted the situation to her through the cell sitting in my lap as I drove. "What about the rest of the kids?"

"Emily's with them."

"Well, I'm going down there."

"No, Ruthie."

"Yes. I'm going down there. I'm sure, Ret! She and they all must be scared to death."

"Shit, no, Ruthie! You're pregnant! Franklin just got shot up right near their place!"

"Tessa, Leila, and Elisi—none of them are around, Ret! I'm *not* going to leave them alone after all that's happened!'"

I was immersed in fear but went mute. Hector Amezquita, that is, Enrico Astorgia, had been murdered, but not before he'd burgled my office and stolen all I'd ever written about the Miyanashatawit family. He'd stolen Maritza's file too right after she'd conned me, feeding me stories about Tina using Franklin to sell his psych drugs, and about trying to coax first her and then Hector into helping retrieve money belonging to a gang leader once in business with Jack Brie.

The rock through the window, the blue and white car, and Franklin telling me I'd better get out of Lower Valley. Jamie dead, Hector dead, and Franklin now shot, coming off the run and suspected of killing Hector.

Now my pregnant wife insisted on entering this spiraling mayhem for sake of the Miyanashatawit kids. To stop her, I'd have had to tell her all I'd withheld, and shame paralyzed me.

I'd have willingly quit my office in Harrah; I'd have willingly moved up to Union Gap that day if she'd just stay put. But I couldn't bring myself to tell her all the reasons why I didn't want her to go down there. Cold fear welded both my hands to the steering wheel.

"Ret? Are you there? Are you okay?" she asked over my cellphone speaker.

I struggled to keep my voice even. "Just be careful, Ruthie. Be very careful. Promise me you'll call me the moment you're inside Leila's and with the kids."

"Okay. . ."

I wasn't willing to answer the questioning edge in her voice. I was glad she didn't ask about whatever else she wanted to know.

I couldn't get into the Intensive Care Unit initially, not being a relative. So I called Leila who told the nurses I was her cousin. Camille, an ICU nurse, escorted me through the door with open skepticism.

"Blue-eyed Indian, huh?" she said skeptically. "I've seen a few of those in my time. Second room to the left."

"And now you're here," I heard as I rounded the corner.

I thought Leila was talking to me until I saw she and Tina were facing off with each other.

"Not one word when he's missing. He's runnin' wild but not a worry or a care from you, right, sis? But you come 'round after that *pashtin* lady's set you up with Ce Ce and Samuel so you can still smell sweet to her on all that. Now Franklin matters to you all the sudden. Well, your little boy's all found now, 'idn't he? Go on in and try being a mother for once!"

Leila was small-framed, but rage shook her entire body. With one hand, she gathered her heavier sister's windbreaker collar and flung her through the door into Franklin's darkened critical care room.

"Hey!" Camille warned, walking inside. "Do I call security? Honest to God!"

Franklin's right eye was taped over carefully with a shield and metal disc in the middle having tiny ventilated holes. His gurney was raised; they didn't want him flat on his back. A thin tube line wrapped around his ears and under his nostrils, feeding him oxygen. There was an IV pushing saline and antibiotics, a pulse oximeter pinching his left index finger, and several other sensors and wires running up his opposite arm. He held a button apparatus for self-dosing pain medication loosely in his right hand.

He was definitely conscious.

"Fuckin' shit!" he croaked hoarsely, lifting his hand towards his eye, trying to roll himself into a different position.

"Sit still!" Camille's hand shot out, grabbing his shoulder. "Press that little button, and let your meds kick in,

Franklin."

"This button don't do shit!"

"Every five minutes, it will work. Push it, and then don't move. Do exactly as I say. You *have* to stay very still, Franklin—please. I'll see if Dr. A. can give you more numb drops in a minute."

She turned around toward us. "I think you all need to move to the family waiting room three doors down. I can't have more than one person in here right now. Sally?" She spoke to the nurse at the station. "We have to get him prepped. He's going to Children's; I'm not sure when."

Tina shook her head as Camille tried to sweep us all toward the door.

"I'm here, baby." Tina stepped around her and tried to come in closer.

"Fuckin' leave me alone, *norteña!*"

Tina stopped cold as he caught sight of me with his good eye.

"ESLs, Barlow—blue and white. Your rock people."

"What the hell?" Tina demanded. Leila watched us both closely.

"Come on," Camille gestured. "Everyone out for now."

"The BelAir, Franklin?" I asked, ignoring her. He raised his hand slightly while I backed out the door which I took to mean 'yes.'

Alarm crossed Tina's face, and she sneered, "You don't belong in here."

"But I'm not leaving."

Leila, Tina, and I found the family waiting room. Leila and I sat down; Tina stayed standing. A physician entered the room, a pretty East Indian woman wearing light blue hospital garb.

She shook each of our hands and spoke with a British lilt.

"People have a hard time pronouncing my last name, which is Arundhati, so they call me Dr. A. Who is the parent here?"

"I am," Tina asserted immediately.

"No," responded Leila. "Not yet. I'm his legal guardian."

Dr. Arundhati looked between them and then at me.

"It's complicated," I said.

"Hmm," said Dr. A.. "I will talk to you both but," she looked at me, "if you're not a close relative, please give us a few minutes of privacy."

I had to walk several halls to the outer edge of the hospital to get Ruthie on my cell.

"Nobody's really gone to sleep here," she said. "Emily's overwhelmed. She keeps saying, 'I'm to blame'. I'm having a hard time getting her out of that loop."

"How could she be to blame?"

"She's being a Yakama sister—Franklin's her little brother. You know."

"What about the other kids?"

"They saw it all—Franklin passing out, there's blood still all over the porch. Eloise is wringing her hands. Emily and I put Ce Ce and Samuel in front of cartoons. I can't believe they're supposed to go visit their mother. Ce Ce told me all about it."

"Yeah, there's that. I couldn't say anything. Are you going back home soon?"

I was frankly terrified having her sitting over there.

"I'm sure, Ret!" she exclaimed. "I can't leave! I wouldn't sleep anyway. Emily needs help."

We said goodbye, and I walked back to the waiting room. A tense silence dominated us all until Dr. A. returned to talk with us again.

"Your ruse is up, Dr. Barlow. You are no cousin. I saw you speak at the breast cancer awareness conference in the

Yakama Culture Center two years ago."

"He's a friend of the family," Leila explained.

"He ain't nobody," Tina declared.

Dr. A. looked slightly embarrassed.

"I'm the legal guardian," Leila countered. "You've got the paperwork on that, Dr. A. And so I'm giving permission that you can talk about Franklin in front of Dr. Barlow."

She nodded at Leila. "I will tell you what I can be sure of. Franklin's now sedated and finally asleep. I believe he will lose his eye. Such a thing is hard for anyone, let alone a young man, and you will all need to circle around him for support. We are monitoring the pressure in his wound for the time being . . ."

We were interrupted by Frank Mathis' appearance in the doorway.

"Why's he here?" Tina spat.

"Because I called him!" Leila shouted.

"Well, he ain't family either!"

"*Ítút* called him *xáy*," Leila said, citing Frank as the brother and friend of Arnold without mentioning him by name, "and I call him *átaw mixa*, best uncle. Get used to it or get out."

Frank shook hands lightly with Dr. A. and focused his attention on her while he sat down on one of the upholstered benches, crossed his legs, and wove his hands over his knee. I couldn't guess what he made of the situation.

"This is a dangerous injury," she continued. "The pellet is still inside his eye."

"It's not a bullet?" asked Frank.

"It's a metal pellet from a gas-fired air pistol. I have seen wounds from such weapons before, although not to the eye. If it had been a bullet from a firearm, Franklin would no longer be with us. This kind of wound is called an open ocular injury. We have to do all we can to keep the fluid inside the eye from leaking. The vitreous fluid—"

Leila and I grimaced; Tina's lip curled. Frank's expression did not waver.

"Sorry," said Dr. A, observing our faces. "My point is he is very swollen. Edema places pressure in the wrong places. He'll need surgery; however, we cannot do such specialized procedures here. I want him to go to Seattle Children's to see an ophthalmology surgical specialist. I've spoken with him and he's standing by. It is faster and smoother to fly Franklin there. There is, unfortunately, a motor car accident in the mountains which is slowing medvac, so it'll be a few hours."

"Doctor," asked Frank. "Is there the possibility he could go blind in his good eye? I'd heard that if you lose one eye, you can lose sight in another."

"I don't think that's true. It'd be best to talk to the doctor at Children's about that."

"Could moving him make things worse?" asked Leila.

"Yes," Dr. A. answered evenly. "Whenever we move someone, there is always greater stress on the immune system and risk of infection. But we cannot provide what Franklin needs here."

"You can't move him!" Tina barked at Leila. "It'll kill him."

"That is very doubtful," Dr. A. responded. "He needs to be moved to get the help required."

"I want this man out of here," Tina pointed at me. "He's not family, and he don't belong!"

"Doctor Barlow," said Dr. A., "I need to talk to you alone for a moment." We moved out into the hallway.

"I understand Leila wants you here, but this is getting too complicated right now. Under the circumstances, I have to ask you to leave."

"All right, fine, I'll go."

"Just a moment, please." She hesitated. "This young man is clearly gang-involved, and our admissions office called to tell me he's wanted by the police. A Detective Jacinto from

Yakima County Sheriff is on her way over. Dr. Barlow, are you his mental health counselor? He already has a health record with us and there are numerous psychiatric drugs listed."

"Yeah, I'm working with him. Dr. Fitzsimmons is prescribing the drugs to him with the guardian ad litem Brenda Oakley's support. I don't think he's been taking them correctly. In fact, I don't think he should be taking them at all. Dr. Fitzsimmons and I don't see eye-to-eye, Dr. A."

"One wonders about akisthesia-provoked violence . . ." she speculated.

"Yes, well, I've probably said too much. It's good to hear you mention the idea."

She smiled slightly. "At post-doc in Strasbourg after I left Bangladesh, there was growing recognition of antidepressant-induced violence. I mentioned this idea during a grand rounds luncheon, and Dr. Fitzsimmons became quite irritated."

"She would. Franklin's best friend, Jamie, who was also gang-involved, got shot dead just a few days ago, and the police are interested in Franklin as a suspect for the murder of the man who may have killed Jamie. Even if there is some chemistry related to the medications involved in his actions, this situation has more to do with a street war."

"Yes, but it's so hard to really know what is what, isn't it?" she responded. "There's so much medicating of kids going on, I've wondered at times if we treat in the ER what we induce in outpatient psychiatry. I notice his chart says he's on twice the adult dose of fluoxetine. It's not my specialty, Dr. Barlow. But that seems wrong to me."

"To me too," I said.

"Well, thank you for being willing to leave."

I said a quick goodbye to Leila, who didn't want me to go. Tina ignored me. Frank only nodded at the wall when I said goodbye to him and walked out.

TWELVE

First of all: It is smooth!
Real cool!
It looks like a car ought to look
That's loaded with youngsters
Who love the feel of
A spirited pick-up
And the power of
Broad-shouldered brakes.
—*Magazine advertisement for 1954 Chevrolet BelAir*

Ruthie and I were outside Leila's duplex on Larena Lane, hugging for a moment, trying to mitigate the horror of Franklin's wound. At some point, she broke off and headed home to get some sleep. I was very glad she left because I was feeling paranoid. I didn't like that she decided to go into work, but she's her own person, and she's let me know many times I'm not in charge.

"Life goes on, Ret."

The younger Miyanashatawit kids, Ce Ce and Samuel, were sleeping when I went inside. Emily and Eloise were still awake. Elisi sat between them, having turned right back around on US 410 on route to her cousin's when Leila's voicemail popped up on her cell. She dozed silently, her arms looped around their shoulders. Chase lay on her back on the floor, playing with two plastic trucks, and nodding off. I could only hear her humming and their breathing and closed my eyes.

My cell was set on 'loud,' and everyone jumped when it went off.

"Frank and her had words," Leila's voice crackled over

our bad connection. "Tina left. You know how he is—sat there and didn't say anything for a full twenty minutes. Then he just all the sudden spoke up—'maybe you ought to finally grow up.' Well, he's known her years and years, and he can get to her like that. She went off like a firecracker and started screaming at him, and security got called."

Leila mentioned Dr. A. said I could come back over. I ended the call and stood up, uncertain whether I should leave.

"Go, doctor. Thanks for supporting Leila," Elisi muttered sleepily, not opening her eyes.

She seemed to already know how things were.

A uniformed police officer sat outside Franklin's room. Leila, Frank, and Detective Jacinto stood in the family waiting room as I walked in. It was 5 a.m.

"Using leg irons don't seem right, detective," Frank complained. "Not for a boy."

"Sorry," the detective answered. "It's department policy; I don't have a choice."

"Are the police going to be in the helicopter with me and him?" Leila asked.

"No, but he'll have to keep the irons on. King County will have a police guard meeting you when you land at Children's Hospital."

"Don't you think that's all a bit overboard?" I asked as I walked up.

Detective Jacinto surveyed the three of us.

"I don't think any of this is 'overboard.' I'm not sure any of you quite understand what's happening here. Franklin is currently under arrest for felony murder. I won't lock him up until he's been medically cleared. After that, he'll be incarcerated pending a hearing.

"We have a gang war currently underway. Franklin's gang-involved, a felony suspect, and a flight risk. He'll be under guard and in irons and cuffs the whole way through his medical care for the safety of officers and the public until we complete our investigation and the DA determines what charges are going to be filed."

She walked over and spoke to the officer briefly; I couldn't make out what she said. Then she told us we were free to interact with Franklin as long as medical staff permitted us in the room and we checked in with the officer at the door.

Frank whispered to both Leila and me after Jacinto walked away that we should be aware we were under police surveillance.

I was impressed that three Indian Shakers would climb out of bed in the middle of the night to drive over and pray for a wounded Yakama Indian gangbanger.

"*Nami Piyap, Tamánwiłá, xni xtuyt ku Tamánwash, Nami Piyap, Tamánwit*," they chanted in whispers and quiet song by 6:00 a.m. outside Franklin's ICU door, swaying slightly, one person putting a hand on the shoulder of another, offering strength.

The chanting prayer tapered into a silence that startled me awake and I got up, walked over, and thanked them. The police guard sitting nearby looked bored with everything.

"We prayed that the Creator bring down the Holy Spirit, enter Franklin's body, and heal his eye and his spirit," Andrea, the Indian Shaker minister, explained to me and Dr. A, who stood nearby. "And we do welcome the spiritual ways of everyone."

Leila was curled into an oversize chair next to his bed, fast asleep.

"I am very glad you prayed for him," said Dr. A. "His eye pressure remains stable so perhaps it's helping. The helicopter is on its way and should be here by 6:30 a.m.—not too much longer."

The Shakers nodded politely, and Dr. A. set down her ipad on a nearby chair, looking slightly embarrassed.

"Go ahead. It's good for you to open your heart, doctor," Andrea encouraged.

The police guard's ears perked up, and he leaned slightly towards the doorway, listening.

"Yes, thank you," responded Dr. A. "I thank you for allowing me to pray with you. I really need to do so I think. I have been up almost twenty-six hours now with no break."

"We're all Indians here," Andrea answered. The other Shakers looked long at her, and then everyone burst out laughing, which awoke Leila.

"I know nothing of the Yakama people," said Dr. A, "but I respect the indigenous people everywhere because they are more peaceful and hold onto the best ways of living as a real human being—that is, until they are interfered with, which has happened in my homeland too.

"I am very tired not just in my body but of all the violence hurting all the youth around here. This Yakama boy here is so young. Notice how he sleeps so peacefully. I have known so many children like him all over the world—still a child but acting tough.

"You know," she looked at all of us, "I have tended four gunshot victims near his age just in the last week and one was much younger than him." She sighed. "This hospital is Christian, but I am not. Yet they do not seem to mind a praying Hindu doctor. In Bangladesh, doctors pray along with families all the time."

Andrea watched Franklin sleep, pondering what Dr. A. said. "Jesus says 'In my Father's house are many mansions: if it were not so, I would have told you.' Not all the Shakers use the Bible or agree as to what it means. But I like those words and take them to say we must honor all expressions of the Holy Spirit. I don't know much about your Hindu path, Dr. A., but please do go ahead with your prayers. We'll bear witness to your words."

"Ah, okay," she answered. "I'll sing a verse I learned

from my grandmother many years ago."

The officer looked in through the doorway with a questioning look on his face.

"Is everything okay?" I asked him.

"Sure, sure," he answered. "I just wanted to listen in a little closer. I don't know anything about Hindus."

The sun crept gently toward the horizon through slightly parted curtains, hitting the surface of the empty bed next to Franklin. Dr. A.'s voice rose in repetition from below a whisper, gradually opening up wide, pure and beautiful:

"Tát savitúr váreṇyaṃ bhárgo devásya dhīmahi dhíyo yó naḥ pracodáyāt . . ."

Leila crawled out of her chair, hovered over Franklin's bed, and watched for any movement on his swollen face. Emerging light from the rising sun coincided with Dr. A.'s repetitive chant, rays easing slowly forward until they rested on the gang-banger's chained ankles.

I was so very tired; I slipped around behind her, sat down in the chair Leila had left, and immediately fell into a lull.

Leila roused me hard, and I stumbled up and out of the room, following her and everyone else trying to keep up with Franklin's exit. The police guard had his hand on the gurney as it was pushed into the elevator. Franklin's bare ankle peeked out beneath the sheet with the chain locked to the gurney railing.

"I thought the officer wasn't going to go in the chopper," I said to Dr. A.

"He has to watch them load him in," she answered.

She told me I would normally never be allowed up on the roof but since I was now listed in his chart as her 'consultant,' she'd permit it.

The wind from the blades astounded me. Leila squinted wordlessly at us while being helped uncertainly to climb inside with the air medic and nurse. I knew she'd likely never flown anywhere before in her entire life. Strands of hair shot out of her high pony tail and into her mouth and eyes. The noise was deafening. She watched me from inside the cabin with a strange expression. I think she wanted me to say something wise but I couldn't think of anything.

"*Namaste!*" Dr. A. called out from next to me, reaching to slide the chopper door shut.

"What?!" Leila yelled back, looking at her.

Dr. A. stretched forward and touched her cheek lightly before giving the door a final push shut. Leila gazed through the porthole and shook her head, still not comprehending.

"*Namaste,*" Dr. A. mouthed and then pushed her palms together, first in front of her chest, before raising them high over the top of her head and bowing slightly toward Leila and Franklin.

As the chopper lifted off, she still held her hands like that and bowed several times. She turned to me as the craft throttled up and thundered forward into the sky.

"'I see God in you'," she spoke loudly into my ear. "Tell her that's what the word means and what I wanted to say to her, Indian to Indian, when you see her, okay? She reminds me of a young auntie who watched over me when I went through a hard time when I was very little. She is a very good person to care for all these nieces and nephews when she is so poor."

After saying goodbye, I grabbed coffee at the hospital cafeteria and charged out the front door. I wanted to get back out to brief Elisi and the kids on how things were as soon as I could.

One of four guys waiting for a ride down to the Columbia River to fish sat huddled in the back of a half-ton pickup and glanced at me as he pulled his cap low when I shot past him down Larena Lane. Nobody else appeared up and about yet.

Several of the HUD ranch duplexes I drove by had plywood board covering the windows—rocks being an easy item to throw around there too. 'ESL' was scrawled in angular black letters on a plywood slab.

I slowed down when I saw 'TNK' crossed out with '187', understanding what it meant: War, an invisible war about which the majority of people cared little as long as it didn't touch them; a blood struggle between involuntarily drafted soldiers serving various small-time kings and bishops in places no one else would ever fight over. Corpses piled up, got removed, junior players aged into the game, inking tattoos between thumb and forefinger or maybe blue tears onto their cheeks if they passed the test of snuffing out another human life.

Rez dogs picked at garbage behind Apuṣ Goudy housing project's rear gates while white-tailed hawks hovered overhead, prey and predators vying for position. There'd been six completed youth suicides on Larena Lane over the past year, and no one knew how many more attempts. Desperation and hopelessness formed a wall around this battleground. A little Indian girl in t-shirt, undies, and bare feet stood on the cracked asphalt's extreme edge. I slowed down. She sucked on a dried-out hunk of fry bread.

Further on, I made out the shape of a stooped, elderly woman standing on Leila's duplex porch. Elisi. Ruthie stood directly behind her. Elisi was holding a baseball bat. I got out of my car in a hurry.

"What??"

"They'll be coming back 'round any minute, I expect, doctor," Elisi observed evenly.

I climbed up on the porch and spoke to Ruthie.

"Why'd you come back? Please go inside, darlin'. I thought you said you were going to work."

"I couldn't go," she said. "I just couldn't, Ret. This family's been hurt enough. Nobody ever does anything to help them. I don't want anybody else to touch these kids. I told Zelda just write me down as sick."

A familiar car pulled around the curve onto Larena Lane. The blue and white Chevy BelAir moved toward us in slow motion—not really restored, just repainted in spots with spray gloss, and not very well. The fenders shook and the frame lurched over an ancient suspension.

Inside were a bunch of boys, some older, some younger than Franklin. The driver skitched his tires slightly pulling up before us, revving the engine, trying to score a few points.

"Cut that shit," snarled a wiry, brown kid with Latin features, maybe sixteen years old, who reached through the window and opened the passenger door from the outside. "Maritza don't like you messing with Mr. R's ride."

My eyes scanned them over quickly. As I made eye contact with the kid stepping out, I spotted a pistol stuffed conspicuously into his waistband in front of a spotless white t-shirt.

Two native guys came out of the duplex across the street, stopping to watch the action. The kid strolled forward toward us.

"Ruthie, get inside now!" I hissed.

"No," she answered.

"Far enough, young one," said Elisi, pulling the bat from behind her back and tapping it across her palm.

I couldn't decide if she looked ludicrous or serious. She certainly looked like she'd held one before.

"Ho!" he laughed loudly, glancing back at the car. "Grandma's got stones. Wassup, grandma?"

"Leave this family here alone."

He cocked his head slightly where he stood, raised his eyebrows, pursed his lips, and nodded.

"*Madre dura,* huh?" Another boy in the car chuckled. "Not to worry, grandma. We're not here to party. We just got word to bring. 'Sup, doc?"

I was surprised he spoke to me. Some maniacal rage spoke through me.

"Spit it. Then get out of here," I answered.

"Ret," Ruthie whispered in my ear vehemently. "You stay right here with me."

"Chill, doc." He seemed to hear her. "We got word for you and yours is all—what business's not yours, stay out. Let the po-po do what they do, leave it all alone. Your boy there got too loose; he's lucky to be breathin'. Word is—leave Harrah to the Indians, doc, head back up north!"

"No," I responded.

"Stop, Ret," Ruthie cautioned.

"Hey, doc, maybe you're pussy-whipped." All the boys cracked up. "You're seriously out the numbers to say 'no' to anybody."

"Maybe not," came a voice from the other side of the street.

The two native guys moved down to the end of their driveway, holding shovels they'd pulled off their truck.

"Move on, asshole," said the taller of the two.

"Uh," the kid looked less certain; the driver fired up the old BelAir, which seemed to grunt in its efforts to start.

"Okay. Word, doc; Maritza says it's not safe for you and yours. She said back up from it all. Your boy got hurt; that's just a warning. She's said she's being good to you and said to tell you move on. So listen up."

They sped off back down Larena Lane in the opposite direction and tribal cops roared by twenty seconds later with their flashers on.

I knew they'd never catch them. Kids lucky enough to have access to a car had the two-track paths thoroughly mapped out and were seldom apprehended.

I was out of breath although I hadn't done anything physical.

"Who were they?" Elisi asked.

"ESLs," the shorter native guy said.

"There's something you need to tell me about this, isn't there, Ret??" Ruthie demanded.

The kid had used Maritza's name, and she'd heard that loud and clear. The entire circumstance confused me: Franklin's admitted involvement with TNKs, an affiliate of Nortenos, a gang he insisted Hector and Tina were themselves involved in; these ESLs, supposed to be Surenos affiliates, yet driving the same car Hector climbed into when he ran from my office.

Why does Hector, an alleged Norteno, escape in a car I now see driven by Surenos?

These kids were invoking Maritza's name as an authority who wanted to send me a warning. Maritza and whoever she was involved with were somehow straddling both sides of this gang war.

Ruthie eyed me very hard while I tried to think all this through. Elisi looked at me questioningly like I'd been caught in some sort of lie. I didn't say anything, and Ruthie didn't like it. We went inside the duplex and sat down. Sirens sounded faintly off in the distance.

Ce Ce, Chase, and Samuel were curled together on the floor, not playing, not sleeping, all hiding under a blanket together. I got up and lifted it a little and peered underneath at them. They were hugging each other.

"What are you guys doing?" I asked. "Are you okay?"

"We're pretending we're safe," Ce Ce answered succinctly.

"Why'd you make me stay inside?!" Emily blurted out toward Elisi with uncharacteristic force. "I want my baseball bat back, kála!!"

"Let me hold onto it still for a while more," came the answer. Elisi's face was ashen, and she used the bat like a cane to lower herself down onto a rickety, kitchen table chair.

"I just didn't want you getting hurt."

"But it's okay if you get beat up, *kála*," Emily countered bitterly. "God, I wish my sister was home."

"Well, I'm very glad she's not," said Elisi.

"Who were those kids?!" Eloise cried angrily from where she sat across from her.

"Shh, shh," said Elisi. "Just a bunch of troublemakers. They're gone now."

She turned toward Ruthie and me. "So who is this Maritza woman?"

"I really can't say," I answered.

"I have to respect my husband's ethics," Ruthie clarified, biting back her anger with me. "What he really needs to do right now is talk to the police."

I was still sitting with my wife's glaring looks, trying to ignore her when Leila called us from Seattle to say the doctors had to remove Franklin's right eye. The surgeon said the metal of the pellet would have become a pathogen, and once it was removed, too much damage remained for Franklin to ever see through that eye again. He'd still require more surgery later for muscles around the eye orbit, and eventually could be fitted with a prosthetic. He'd retain vision through his other eye; sympathetic blindness in the unwounded eye was a myth.

Frank Mathis soon meandered into the duplex while we all sat bleakly pondering the expected but tragic news. Leila had called him. After saying hello, he sat down at the table with us, and no one said a thing except Ce Ce, Samuel, and Chase, who had a card game going on the floor.

"Go fish!" punctuated the air.

I pondered the loss of depth of field vision incumbent on seeing with only one eye.

"Go fish!" echoed through me.

"Better go north!" I heard inside me. I had been drawn

in unwittingly and now threatened if I didn't back up.

"Go fish!" shouted Ce Ce at Chase.

"I guess be glad the boy's not dead," said Frank after a few minutes.

"Sister?" Ce Ce gazed at Emily, shielding her cards carefully. "Is my father alive or dead?"

She was referring to Cowboy Jack Brie. Ruthie sipped her tea, and looked hard at me.

"Go now and talk to the cops, Ret," she said.

"I'll get to it," I responded.

She had no idea about all that was on my mind, but she knew more than I intended her to know.

"I don't understand you," Ruthie said irritably, and I didn't respond.

"No, baby," Emily answered Ce Ce. "That man is dead. And he was never your real father anyway."

Emily shifted her gaze questioningly toward Frank Mathis, seeking affirmation of some sort. Yet he immediately looked away, concentrating on tearing open and pouring two packets of sugar into a carry-out cup of coffee. He focused on stirring in his sugar, and didn't look at her or anyone else.

"Yes," Elisi echoed Frank from her position on the couch. "Franklin's alive. So we should thank the Creator."

The taller guy from across the street appeared at the front door. He didn't knock or anything.

"Holy shit!" I exclaimed. Ruthie jumped and then glared at me.

He and his brother were heading to the store, he announced apologetically, and wondered if we might need anything. Elisi coaxed him inside. His eyes widened when he spotted Frank.

"Frank Mathis."

"Delford Smith," Frank answered amicably.

"Haven't seen you in way too long."

"Been around," Frank responded. "Out to White Swan

for quite a while now."

"It's real good to see you, Frank."

"Thanks. Good to see you too."

"Are you doing all right?"

Delford pulled up a chair in front of Frank who was unaccustomed to such direct attention.

"Doing fine."

That was pretty much where the conversation stopped.

Emily got up and returned from the kitchen with a cup of instant coffee for Delford. Frank sipped his own cup; Delford started his. Awkward nods passed intermittently.

Frank tried to muster as much as he knew about a smile.

"Ever think of runnin' again for council, Frank?" Delford asked.

"Oh no, my council days are long done." Frank shook his head.

"Well," Delford responded, "you'd be a good 'un if you change your mind."

Elisi chuckled. Delford seemed to harbor considerable respect for Frank Mathis, despite whatever ethics charges he'd been through.

Nothing else happened from there; we simply sat around for a while.

Ruthie and I left at sunset, life having quieted on Larena Lane. I couldn't help feeling like we were in the eye of a storm.

The two of us were silent all the way home. Once in the living room, we started talking loudly in staccato bursts.

"You need to call the cops! Tell them about the gang mentioning Maritza. You're not going into Harrah to work, Ret! There's no reason to."

"Ruthie, I need you to trust me. I have to do my job. We have to pay our bills."

She threw her hands up. "Ugh! Then I'm going to call the cops. I'm going to do what you won't!"

"I'm asking you not to do that."

"Why?"

"Those kids meant business, Ruthie; they already hurt Franklin. I don't think the police can protect us."

"They threatened you! Directly! You're sure not protected out in Harrah. Please do not go to work, Ret."

After the rock and the break-in and now the gang threat, you'd think I'd have had the sense to listen to my wife.

"I still have a few clients who count on me. I've already let them down with all the cancellations. I'm not going to be intimidated by Maritza Rios or anybody else."

She stormed out of the room and slammed the bedroom door. By default, I was expected to sleep on the couch. When I tried to kiss her before I left the next morning, she wouldn't let me anywhere near her.

She did throw a magazine she was reading at my head and only just missed, which I assumed meant she still cared.

Out in Harrah, I tried to calm myself and sat on my knees with a couch cushion beneath my butt, practicing *vippassana*, moving my mind between the breeze and my breath.

I visualized myself dying. I saw myself dead but nothing could move me. I stayed seated in my posture— not unlike Jamie Jamison, only I wasn't crumpled forward. Perhaps it seems morbid—but it's a Buddhist exercise I'd been taught that was supposed to bolster one's courage.

I saw the wind and rain pummeling me, but I didn't move; I kept sitting. I was upright but dead. My body began to decay; I maintained my concentration and vigilance and never shifted. I kept my posture and focused on my breath.

The stars came out, and I still sat. Small nocturnal animals and bugs picked my flesh. Soon, I was cleansed down to the bone. Still the wind blew, and I didn't move. Little holes formed in my bones, and the wind, rain, and sun weakened them.

I crumpled into dust. I watched from overhead as the dust of my collapsed bones swirled, moved around by the same wind. A gust rose, my body was gone.

Only then did my spirit decide to walk on.

My landline rang, and I popped back into the room. I knew it must be Ruthie. I felt very sorry about how I'd acted toward her.

"I'm sorry," I said as I picked it up. I knew she was right—I should have stayed home. I was in no place emotionally to work anyway.

Margaret Fitzsimmons' voice sparked and sputtered. "You better be. I am the chief of psychiatry in Provincial Medical, Dr. Barlow. I saw Dr. Arundhati's chart note listing you as some sort of consultant. You may have tried that shit with Dominia and Leo Aspen, but it's a completely different matter with me."

"Ah. I'm pretty busy right now, Margaret."

"You're incompetent. I'm filing an ethics complaint against you with the psychology licensing board."

"What for?"

"Interfering in the psychiatric regimen I've prescribed. Professional incompetence."

"Uh, wow, after where I've been lately, Margaret, that gives me an idea about your failure to monitor akisthesic symptoms in a fourteen-year-old native boy struggling with his grandfather's death."

"You don't have the intellectual wherewithal to debate me!"

"I'm a bit slow on the uptake, I guess. Maybe I need stimulant therapy. Or maybe I need electro-shock therapy to forget my troubles."

I slammed the phone down, and then I picked it up and

slammed it down again. I sat back down on my cushion but couldn't get my eyes to close. The phone rang a few minutes later, and I almost didn't answer.

"Hi," said Ruthie, sounding sad.

"I'm sorry," I answered. "You were right; I shouldn't be down here. Did you call the police yet?"

"No, Ret. I decided the police didn't protect Franklin or his friend. I thought back over time, and I decided they've never really come through when we've needed them."

"Are you all right?"

"Ret, I'm spotting. I'm bleeding a little."

I pulled the phone cradle off the desk. "And what does that mean?"

"Dr. Welch wants me to lie on the couch and drink lots of water until she knows what it means. She wants me in tomorrow for tests."

"Goddamn, Ruthie. I'm so sorry. I have a client in a second."

"Ret," she started crying. "I'm afraid we're going to lose the baby!! Can you come home now?

"Cancel! Ret, please!"

THIRTEEN

It is also a question with some people
Whether or not enforced education
And civilization of the Indian
May be a cause of insanity among them.
There can be no grounds for such supposition . . .
I am confident that a great many cases of insanity
Among full-blood Indians exist,
But are unknown to the agency or school officers.
–Oscar Gifford, Superintendent,
Hiawatha Asylum for Insane Indians, Canton, SD, 1905

I'd managed to reach everyone else to tell them I had a 'family emergency.' My income for the month was thus far cut in half by all we'd been going through. One client quit on me right over the phone.

Ruthie lay flat on her back on the couch, trying to sleep, and I sat on the floor. I couldn't sustain my position and quietly stretched to grab the envelope Elisi had loaned me off the coffee table.

"What are you doing?" she mumbled incoherently.

"A little reading—I'm not going anywhere. I'm just binding anxiety."

"Umm, well, do you have any tips on how I bind my anxiety?"

I reached for her.

"Don't," she responded. "You haven't been truthful with me, and I don't feel like being comforted by you right now. At least just stop working. Sit there, Ret. You have to not do anything like I have to not do anything."

"Okay." I sat back and set the envelope back down.

She tried to roll, and I nudged her with my elbow. "Don't roll. You're supposed to stay flat."

"God, I'm so uncomfortable. I can't rest!"

"It's for safety."

"I hate needing you right now. . ."

"And I'm sorry about that."

"No, you're not. You like it."

She drifted into a doze. I made as little noise as possible reopening the envelope. The papers were mostly legal size and folded. There were several loose notes, all yellowed and worn. They smelled musty. I started to sift through, reading several letters.

The first was from a cousin objecting to "the efforts by John Smedley to place Mr. Hiram Kusitway under the care of Dr. Raymond Fitzsimmons at the Hiawatha Asylum for Insane Indians, solely for the reasons of no longer wishing to care for him, after squandering all his money even to the point of selling Mr. Kusitway's artifacts collected during the Great War."

Another letter was from an Army pharmacist named Michaels at Fort Leavenworth, Kansas recommending bromide salts "aid in subduing Mr. Kusitway's passionate outbursts. They also has [sic] the effect of reducing the affected features of his highly disturbed gait."

There were some legal documents, including an affidavit assessing various aspects of Hiram Kusitway's behavior, stating he was "not typically violent but prone to fits, likely the result of shell shock, and a weak constitution." They were all signed by Dr. Roy Fitzsimmons.

A small note fell out from several of the larger documents. The front of it was in handwritten phonetics that I recognized as Yakama—for which there was no written format at the time. On the back side was different handwriting which read: "Making sick people work. We are starving. Get this to the Indian commissioners. This very bad place. We need help." Another script was written along the edge of the back of the note: "H.B. Kusitway, found inside mattress, 9/12/19. Rough translated from Yakima by S. Stillwater." I held up the scrawl along the edge next to Dr. Roy Fitzsimmons' handwritten affidavit and could see it was the same person.

I'm sure after Fitzsimmons had Uncle Hiram's desperate note translated by whoever the Stillwater individual happened to be, he never let the note leave the asylum but stuck it into his medical file instead. Reading it while I sat there, I realized that Elisi's Uncle Hiram had succeeded in letting somebody outside the building know how things were going for him and other patients in the Hiawatha Asylum for Insane Indians after nearly ninety years.

I tried to stand up, but my legs were both asleep.

"What?" Ruthie tried to roll out of her nap.

"Don't roll," I reached out and grabbed her arm.

"*Stop* manhandling me!!" She shook my grip off with a grumpy vehemence. "Look at all that's happening to us! I can't even sleep! Why are you always raising hell?!"

"The stress I've created made this spotting thing happen," I proclaimed guiltily.

"Yes, Ret. Yes, it's all your fault. Absolutely. . . that's exactly why I'm spotting now."

She grabbed a pillow and pulled it over her face and then lifted it slightly to observe my guilt-ridden expression.

"Oh my God, will you stop feeling sorry for yourself? Fine! I don't think it's your fault I'm spotting. There, are you happier now??"

"I wouldn't go that far."

"Oh God, now the pity party. Do you honestly believe I'm going to lie here and reassure *you* not to feel guilty?"

"No."

"Men are so unbelievably self-centered . . ."

She tried to sit up. "Don't, Ruthie; stay still . . ."

". . . narcissistic, self-involved bastards."

Five minutes of silent rage from Ruthie is enough to bring me to my knees.

"All right," she finally said.

"All right what?"

"I said all right, and it's self-obvious what it means. We're going to move on. Now you *will* tell me what the *hell* you're doing that's so important that you can't just sit still like I have to do. Is it something that's going to get us assaulted or killed?"

"Ruthie, I'm only going through some old papers Elisi gave me that her uncle had from when he got sent to the Hiawatha Asylum for Insane Indians."

"Indian asylum?! Hah!! That is such total irony given what's been going on."

"Yeah, well, it was a real place. It closed in 1933."

"Let me see what this is. Hand over what you're looking at, please."

She held up the clump of papers I wedged into her outstretched palm over her head.

"Ugh! I am so tired! I can't even see."

She lowered and plopped them back into my hand. I thought she'd drifted off and started to study them again, but she popped back awake.

"Ret?! You should research this place and do a talk on it. That's an idea. I'll bet nobody else ever heard of it. It'd help your credibility. Maybe you'd get some referrals."

"Nah. There's too much going on right now."

"Oh. Fine. Never mind. It was a stupid idea."

"No, that's not what I'm saying, Ruthie."

"I try to help; you lock me out."

"With all that's happened, how could I begin to think about some talk?"

"Uh, well, Ret, you never want to look at our expenses or your business approach. I'm the one to keep an eye on that and it can be stressful. We haven't been doing very well out of the Harrah venture even when you were getting referrals."

"I guess I know that much."

"Please, Ret. Listen to me for once. Close the Harrah office and open up one up here in Upper Valley. Do a talk; get back on track. You can recover. I'm sorry, Ret, the Harrah thing isn't working."

"I'm not moving."

"Ugh! So stubborn!"

She finally dozed off again. I tried hard to sit still and study while she started snoring loudly. I was also foggy with exhaustion. I leaned my head back on her thigh and went out like a light.

"God, at least do a talk, Ret!!"

"Wha . . .?" I started awake.

"There's a regional APA conference coming up in Ellensburg. The flyer just came in the mail yesterday. So do a talk on this Indian asylum there even—no, especially—if you're going to insist on keeping this stupid office in Harrah."

"Getting a flyer means everything's already all planned. You have to get your proposal in months in advance, Ruthie. Besides, I've quit and rejoined APA six times in twenty years. My relationship with them's not good."

"Don't be a snob." I twisted around toward her irritating critique. "And don't look at me like that! You just get insecure. Quit acting like you're too good for everybody there. You can do this."

"I'm not a joiner."

"I'll help you," she tried to sit up again and fell back. "Ret, we've got to make an investment in your reputation, or it's all over. You haven't had a referral in a month!" She was right. "This regional thing comes up soon, right? I could get coverage at school. You should call Richard Shneider at CWU—he's in the psych department, isn't he?"

"God, Ruthie, I haven't spoken to him in fifteen years."

"But I remember he was a psych history buff too." Ruthie has an exceptional memory. "Don't you remember him boring us to tears about phenomenalism versus materialism in philosophies of science?"

"Wasn't that boring to me."

"Which is the point I'm trying to make. You give a talk to him and his cronies and it ups your reputation here. Wasn't he president of APA at some point?"

"Secretary—he was never president."

"Ret," she started to roll again, and I pushed her back.

"Hey, *hands off*! Violence against a pregnant mother, the lowest of the low!"

"Sorry."

"Listen." She was getting excited. "This is a good idea. You talk to Richard, Ret; he'll help you research about this place, and then present a talk at this APA event. Maybe we can get the *Daily Record* up in Ellensburg and the *Herald* to do a story on it. We need to make it clear *you* know what you're talking about better than . . . that woman."

"How does it work that you come with me, Ruthie? I'm not going anywhere. You lying here on your back—I don't want to leave you alone for five minutes, let alone go sleep in some dorm room and hang with a bunch of psych nerds."

She sighed. "I'm not sure if Dr. Welch will let me travel. But you have to go. That's our terms. That's the deal I'm making if you insist on staying open out in Harrah."

"Ruthie."

"You can't say no. I know what I'm talking about. You have no business sense whatsoever. Give up arguing about it."

When she gets like that, there's nothing I can do.

Dr. Welch didn't mince words.

"Short-term travel only, sorry. No stairs, no marching around, going on hiking trails, or TV aerobics. When you get up, I want you to move slowly and take it easy."

Ruthie had a terribly worried look on her face.

"Look," said Dr. Welch consolingly, "you're not going

to lose your baby, so stop." She sat down at the exam table next to her. "I've seen this kind of situation dozens of times over twenty years and haven't lost one yet."

"But what about my job?" she asked.

"Do you have short-term disability?"

Ruthie nodded affirmatively.

"I'll draft the letter. It's Family Medical Leave Act territory but you should be able to use your disability insurance."

On the drive home, I told her I'd concluded the APA presentation idea was hare-brained, and I didn't want to leave her side.

"Ret, we have a deal. And I already talked to Dr. Welch while she was, uh, you know, you were out of the room. I have plenty of friends at school who want to dote on me. She even wrote me a script for a part-time home health nurse to drop by." She pulled a folded-up piece of paper from her blouse pocket. "See? Insurance covers it! So my situation is no excuse for you to change our deal. There's no excuse for you not to call Richard."

"Ruthie, APA isn't going to just let me come talk. I haven't presented anything in years. And I don't even want to go! Respect me about that."

"No," she answered, staring at the road ahead. "You respect me. I'm pregnant and I have to go through hard times flat on my back—for months! You have to try to get back on your feet professionally and counter Fitzsimmons and her little games—for our family—especially if you want me to go along with you keeping that office that smells like goat cheese."

A few minutes passed, and I knew she was fiddling with her phone but didn't see what was coming.

"Talk, Ret!"

"To who?? What??! What the hell are you doing?"

"Richard! She just connected you. Say 'hello'!"

There are dynamics that happen between us sometimes when times get rough. She had dialed the department secretary before I even knew what she was doing, and pushed the cell up to my ear while I was driving.

I pulled my head away and glared at her. "*Hello? Hello?*" The tinny voice came through my cell.

"God, all right!" I exclaimed and put my ear closer.

"All right, what? Who's this?" Richard didn't miss a beat.

"Hey, Richard, it's Ret."

"Well, I'll be damned!"

I was now in a conversation not of my choosing. Ruthie held a tight smile of satisfaction as she put the phone up to my ear while I stammered through an explanation.

"Hiram Kusitway, huh? Interesting name. So are the papers legit?"

"God, probably; I've never looked at papers from a federal asylum closed in 1933, Richard."

I spotted a radar cop. Ruthie tugged the phone down, lifted it, tugged it down again. She wasn't certain whether it was okay for her to hold it to my ear.

". . . aren't many original case files of that era in existence . . . six APA presidents involved in the eugenics movement, you know."

She pushed it back into my ear.

"Let me hold it, will you??" I whispered vehemently. She shook her head 'no'.

"Hold what?" Richard asked. I just barely heard him as she hoisted the phone back up to my ear."The conference is up here in the Lombard Room, Ret. I mean, we could talk about some sort of break out session down your way . . ."

"Sorry, Richard, bad reception. I hear you now. I was just saying something to my wife here."

He continued to hold forth academically. "As I was saying . . . folks who've written about that history don't seem to realize early IQ tests were often applied to Indian kids in the boarding schools. Yerkes, Otis . . . doing the same thing to soldiers using the Army Alpha Beta tests . . . a small number of American Indians actually served during World War One."

"Yeah," I responded affirmatively, not processing all his chatter.

"So it's all a big, big skeleton in our closet. Do you get me, Ret?"

I remembered him as often brilliant but obscure. "Not really. I learned from an elder here about an early psychologist named Thomas Barth."

"Oh, Barth," he said. ". . . yeah, researching Indian IQ in the 30s."

"All the papers I have here pertain to a psychiatrist at the Indian Asylum named Fitzsimmons."

Ruthie pulled the phone away in surprise, recognizing whose family I was mentioning. She shook her arm out, and I glared at her in frustration. She pressed a couple of buttons and had him on speaker.

"There," she mouthed. "Forgot how to do that."

". . . psychologists, psychiatrists, social workers, there were bunches of mental hygiene folks coming into Indian Country . . . deep into all that eugenics shit. Take what you got with Barth and link it in with those old papers you've got— that's a good topic. For God's sake, Indian boys grew up in boarding schools, experimented on by Sir Frances Galton's protégés, trying to prove they were racially inferior. Going off to fight for a country that didn't even count them as citizens. How did they even bring themselves to even do that? Well, this Kusitway fella would've been one of them. All those soldiers were tested by psychologists using the Alpha-Beta tests which said the Indian kids weren't bright enough to be officers. Put 'em in the front lines, goddamnit! They came back traumatized, and then we locked them up in the asylum. That's growing up Indian 1910-version!"

A deer stumbled out of a cornfield and onto the road ahead. I hit the brakes hard and the phone flew onto the floor. The doe pranced across and off into the woods.

"Totally fucking amazing!" Richard soliloquized in

perfect synchronicity with the deer as we both watched. Ruthie laughed and tried to bend forward to pick the phone back up, but given her pregnancy situation, she stopped herself. I shook my head at her and kept driving.

"Just let him talk . . ." I mouthed at her.

I had forgotten what a maniac he was and why I never called him. His sense of social justice was always spot on, however, although like many academics, he acted like he got paid by the word.

"Richard, can you still hear me okay?" I shouted.

"There's a whiny noise but I hear you fine! Yeah, we screwed them going and coming, didn't we, Ret? That's a part of psych history nobody wants to know. That's your multicultural diversity shit, isn't it?"

"Shell shock back then, by the way," he sputtered— and Ruthie covered her mouth at his vociferousness, trying not to giggle out loud, "was a sign of weakness—they came home, physically and emotionally wounded, unable to walk right, like great uncle Hiram there, unable to sleep. What happens?"

I tried to reach down to the passenger side floor, lowering my line of sight below the dashboard, and Ruthie pulled my shoulder back hard and shook her head disapprovingly.

"We sent 'em up the river," Richard continued, practically spitting through the little speaker. "Indian lunacy hearings—they're in the archives, Barlow! U.S. won't sign the United Nations definition of genocide, will they? No, no. That'd make us perpetrators—we—the shrinks; that'd make us the Josef Mengeles for the native people of this country."

The traffic slowed for construction on I-82, and I managed to reach and get the cell off the floor and into my lap.

"Truly fascinating and important to you and me what we've done to all people of color throughout our professional history," he finally paused for an audible intake of breath, "but I expect nobody at APA will give two shits."

"Hah!" I howled, and Ruthie looked disappointed. "For a second, you had me going, Richard."

"You don't call me for fifteen years, and then you want me to sneak you into a regional APA convention to talk to psychologists about their own oppressive history? 'Don't squish our noses in the grapefruit of the past,' that's what the conference committee is going to say. They're going to squawk 'we don't do that shit no more; it's not relevant.' Worried old hens; they have to have a code of ethics while they're searching for a moral compass."

He guffawed at his own rambling tirade.

I tried to get a word in edgewise.

"Speaking of birds," I said, "we still have school psych using intelligence tests all over the Valley here and pigeon-holing native kids into special education classrooms, Richard. And we've got a local psychiatrist sedating grief and hopelessness with SSRIs, respiradone, methylphenidate, whatever she can push, instead of the old bromide salts like way back when. Different day, different drugs."

"Great, Ret, great stuff," he cackled. "Goddamn I forgot what a good student you were. Too bad you always pissed people off. You want me to put somebody like you in a highly publicized public forum? Well, you're amazingly providential. There's going to be a joint gathering of Division 26, Society for the History of Psychology, my group, with Division 53, Society of Clinical Child and Adolescent Psychology. A truly bizarre collaboration. It's a promo device for 26 because they have such a hard time getting clinicians involved. Amos Welcome is leading. Bring your paper to that."

"Bring what?"

"Your paper, you idiot."

"I thought you said . . ."

"Nobody will give a shit. That's what I said. Plenty of papers get presented at a regional APA conference about which nobody gives a shit."

"But I never applied or submitted an abstract," I protested. Ruthie slapped my arm and held her finger to her lips to try to shush me.

"You're not some newbie post-doc begging a spot in the poster session, Ret. Amos is an old friend. He just called yesterday saying he still has open slots in the afternoon and wanted me to be a discussant. I'd rather schmooze."

"I'm not sure how much what I've got here has to do with the topic you're describing."

"What topic? Did I mention a topic? The history of child and adolescent psych. Do you want me to twist your arm? What you've got will ruffle feathers and that's fun as hell. I'll tell you what—I'll even call and clear it with Amos."

"Richard, that's nice of you."

"I know. Hey! How is your much-brighter-than-you wife?"

"I'm good, Richard! Nice to hear your voice," Ruthie yelled at him.

"Hi Ruthie! Goddamn, and you're both still together. Lyla and I divorced eight years ago. Wow, talk about beating odds. This kind of shit talk takes me back, Barlow. So screw you. Some of us have to work. I'll call you back with details."

"I knew it!" Ruthie exclaimed with delight when he hung up. "You never call on friends to help. You'd rather suffer alone. I knew Richard would help."

I had to admit she was pretty brilliant.

We pulled into the driveway and got out, and I picked the mail up off the floor and shuffled through it. The letter from the Board of Psychology, State of Washington, was not coming at a time of year for my license renewal. I tore it open and lifted the letter into the light. It was from the ethics committee.

Margaret Fitzsimmons had followed through with her ethics complaint.

Franklin was released from Children's Hospital in Seattle about a week later and locked into a cell by himself at the Yakima County Juvenile Detention facility on 16th Avenue. He was under arrest pending further investigation. His time in the hospital, however, did not count as 'being detained,' and Detective Daisy and her crew had seventy-two more hours from his transfer to finish their inquiry and convince the prosecutor to charge him with the murder of Hector Amizquita, also known as Enrico Astorgia. After encouragement from Ruthie, I decided to tag along with Frank and visit Franklin.

We were brought to a small visitor's room with a vinyl couch and a couple of plastic chairs. According to the staff nurse, Franklin was "no trouble at all" in the infirmary. He didn't do anything, wouldn't even watch TV or look at magazines and just stared at the wall or ceiling.

When the guard brought him to us, he was still shackled. There was a large white bandage over his right eye with a metal shield over the orbit. He looked like he'd been wounded in combat, and indeed he had. I began asking a stream of innocuous questions, really just to try to spark conversation, and he responded monosyllabically.

I was beginning to feel it was a mistake that Frank was there. We were only allowed fifteen minutes. He didn't ask Franklin any questions or even offer a word of condolence or sympathy about his predicament. I quickly exhausted all I could think to say or ask about.

"Well, guess it's time for us to head out," I told Franklin when the guard signaled that three minutes remained.

"There's one more thing," Frank spoke.

We both stood up. He pushed his worn-out Stetson down firmly onto his head.

Franklin struggled to his feet against shackles and

cuffs, his short-cropped hair on top slightly matted, and his long hair in back tangled by the bandage. It was as though he'd been ignoring me and waiting the whole time for Frank to say something. Any words of encouragement and counsel I'd shelled out meant nothing.

Franklin wanted to know what Frank had to say.

"I been in a place like this," Frank said. "What I remember from my young days. I don't judge you. I am sorry 'bout your eye. In here, you got time to think about all the trouble you got into and the people you got mixed up with. I believe Creator put you here so as to save your life. I know you lost your *tila*, and now maybe you need to think on what would he really want for you, son. Wouldn't be this. Your *tila*, he was my best friend. I know you lost a young friend, too. So we got that in common.

"Your *tila*, he'd want me to step up and say something to you 'bout now. All I can think is what can we do now for your good eye 'fore you end up in so much trouble you're left blind. What will we do for that good eye you still got left?"

Franklin cocked his head slightly under the weight of the cumbersome bandage. His face was still swollen.

"You see, t'other's gone, and even so fly's still eat shit, if you understand my, meaning," said Frank. "I'll come 'round once and a time to visit and know you a bit. I'd like to talk to you more about what you figure you're doing with that good eye."

Franklin had no response. But he nodded very slightly before the guard escorted him back behind locked doors.

FOURTEEN

The fact that one meets this type
(feebleminded individuals)
With such frequency among
Indians,
Mexicans,
And Negroes
Suggests quite forcibly that the whole question
Of racial differences in mental traits
Will have to be taken up anew and by experimental methods.
Children of this group should be segregated
In special classes and be given instruction
Which is concrete and practical. . .
They should not be allowed to reproduce,
Although from a eugenic point of view
They constitute a grave problem
Because of the unusually prolific breeding . . .
—Dr. Lewis Terman, 1916, future president,
American Psychological Association
and creator of the Stanford-Binet Intelligence Test

The annual regional conference of the American Psychological Association attracts up to twenty percent of the 1,000-plus member psychologists across the Pacific Northwest, I read in my conference brochure. No dorm space was available, so I roomed just off the Central Washington University campus in Ellensburg at a Motel Six and paid for it out of our shrinking savings. We were bleeding money. Even so, I got the only room available for ten miles as the result of a cancellation. I'd brought along a loaf of bread, crunchy peanut butter, and a jar of honey to further defer expenses.

Encountering many psychologists in one place is daunting for a professional malcontent. The first evening, Richard and I literally bumped into each other getting into a crowded elevator. He immediately pulled me along to dinner "with friends from Division 26." I wasn't permitted to say no. About thirteen of us sat around a noisy table at a too-expensive hotel restaurant, and he introduced me to Amos Welcome, a small, pensive man with a psychoanalytic pedigree, who smiled very tightly.

"You're most welcome, Ret," Welcome said, predictably. "We're glad to have you with us, and your subject matter sounds intriguing."

I stayed where I often seemed to end up at such moments—on the outer fringes. The stars, Amos and Richard, held down the center of the combined tables. Everybody got drunk, and this was very boring. They all found themselves enormously amusing and kept trying to pour me glasses of wine. I finally turned my glass over and loudly proclaimed I didn't drink. Everyone thought I was drunk anyway.

The next morning, I discovered that the honey jar cracked in my bag and leaked all over my underwear and socks. I soaked them in hot water and shampoo in the tub, rinsed as best I could, and used the hairdryer to blow them dry, which made them stiff. Thereafter, I sat in quiet agony through keynote addresses and workshops, sipping coffee endlessly. My feet and ankles developed a rash that itched throughout the next three days. I was constantly trying to find an unobtrusive moment to bend down and scratch my ankles.

I talked to Ruthie every day, and she thought the whole situation amusing. She reported that she was being looked in on by friends and a part-time nurse, usually twice a day.

"I'm fine," she reassured. "But Ret, Elisi's in the hospital. Leila's taking care of Chase."

"Oh no."

"Do you know what's wrong with her?" Ruthie asked.

"I don't," and, of course, I did, but I respected Elisi's wishes.

"She hasn't been well lately," she said. "She's so private about her health. I wish we could get by to visit her."

"I do too."

"Leila said Ce Ce and Samuel's supervised visit with Tina is coming up. Do you think the stress of all that is what's got Elisi so sick?"

"She's just getting old, Ruthie. That, and so much else has happened in the last year—Arnold's death, Tessa gone, Franklin hurt, and Tina coming back around—it's been a year of suffering."

Day four and my big talk finally came; I wasn't so much nervous as preoccupied with events back home. I felt confident; I'd worked hard using online library access Richard arranged for me and procured all that could be readily found on Hiawatha Asylum for Insane Indians.

It was Elisi who had really come through for me. A few days earlier, she labored up the front steps of our house carrying her master's thesis from University of British Columbia entitled *The Mental Colonization Strategies of Western Social Science*.

She looked awful, and I was beginning to fully realize the truth of how sick she was. Ruthie saw her too, and Elisi was on both our minds.

I was last on the hit parade, and the guy in front of me went on and on, describing some clever community intervention program he'd dusted off and resurrected. He kept asking me at various spots for "just a couple more minutes." Nobody seemed to be orchestrating things, including Amos Welcome. I should've thought more carefully about being so agreeable.

Richard introduced me with vague, gushing comments I could've done without like "really a remarkable guy." I went so far as to twirl my finger with a 'wind-it-up' motion, which caused him to laugh and remark further about my "directness and candor."

When I hit the podium, I had only twenty-five minutes left for a forty-minute talk. I'd allowed for a half-hour presentation and then ten minutes for questions. I skipped several slides and jumped around, losing my train of thought a couple of times. A couple of students who appeared native sat up front, very attentive and nodding at me. Most of the crowd became restless; they'd been sitting all day.

I mapped out Barth's IQ work in boarding schools, and then showed a nice graphic of the Hiawatha Asylum for Insane Indians in Canton, South Dakota. This drew a murmur and a couple of 'oohs.' I then traced generations of applied psychology from its beginnings in eugenics-based racist policy to contemporary times, current practices, and how they related especially to the overrepresentation of native children in special education classrooms. I mentioned repetition of trauma across generations in families and how that might manifest in kids behaviorally. There were interested looks but a couple folks in the front got up and left. I tried not to take it personally.

Amos Welcome stepped up while I was still talking.

"We're out of time."

"I'm almost done," I whispered back.

He shrugged apologetically. "Sorry, Ret—your presentation was added late. It's a union house, and it's 5 p.m."

"Why didn't you limit the other guy? If this talk was given in Indian Country, I'd be permitted to finish no matter what time it is."

The remaining crowd seemed more interested in the emerging tension between us. People leaned forward to try to hear what we were debating. Amos noticed.

"Calm down, Dr. Barlow," he hissed. "And finish up!"

"Sorry," said the maintenance guy messing with the curtain and projection screen behind me. "We got to shut it down."

"Can't you give me five minutes?"

"Sorry, contract rules." Several folks got up to leave.

"I came here at my own expense, and I'm going to try to finish what I have to say!" I boomed.

Amos Welcome shook his head, eyeing Richard forlornly, who stood by a pillar at the rear. Richard appeared disappointed too; I'd clearly gone off the deep end. I began feeling as though I wasn't really there. The entire event began to seem very unreal to me.

The presentation space continued to be dismantled by several guys. It felt as though they were dismantling what I had to say as well. The maintenance guy reached over next to me and unplugged my computer from the projector after switching it off. I moved out of the way as my slide of Hiawatha Asylum disappeared and began trying to field questions.

"As a member of the perpetrating class, Dr. Barlow," one of the native graduate students, a guy with a Southwestern bolo, spoke as he stood up. "How do you respond to the idea you've been set up as an apologist?"

He surveyed the near empty room. "You're being literally taken apart as you speak."

"Maybe I'm a Buffalo nickel," I answered resignedly. "I came here at my own expense. I do admit I'm feeling somewhat snookered."

He raised his eyebrows and nodded in agreement. I walked across the room and shook hands with him, like a prizefighter who'd been roundly defeated.

I couldn't find Richard or Amos.

Nobody thanked me; I gathered my materials together and left alone.

I had the Harrah office landline forwarded to my cell. Maritza Rios called me while I flew down through the military area between Ellensburg and Yakima.

"I have to meet with you right away."

"Tell me your real name first."

"That makes no difference, doctor. I have to talk to you."

"Then talk to me on the phone."

The line went quiet while I thought more about her demand.

"Are you there?" she asked.

"Okay. In Harrah and in twenty minutes or not at all."

I had an idea to try to trap her in her own urgency.

"Okay."

As soon as she disconnected, I pressed my emergency speed dial function.

"911, state your emergency."

"This is Dr. Ret Barlow on route to Harrah. I need to speak to Yakima Sheriff's Detective Dolynda Jacinto regarding a person of interest she's seeking in a murder investigation. Her name is Maritza Rios, and she's agreed to meet me in my office on East Pioneer in Harrah in twenty minutes."

"Hold on, doctor. 102—holding a call for Detective Jacinto, badge 51."

I heard a voice crackle back to the dispatcher across the radio. A call waiting appeared on my cell, and it was her.

"Maritza Rios is on the way to my office as I speak, Detective," I announced as I answered. "I'm heading there now."

"I'm out in Naches," she said. "Forty-five minutes away. Clarence and Deputy Anderson are in Sunnyside at a hostage call. I'm going to try to get state troopers out your way. See if you can delay Ms. Rios or whoever she is until we can get there."

As soon as I arrived, I began loading my remaining files and other small items into my trunk, deciding to use the time to pull all my sensitive materials away from where they were still vulnerable. Maritza pulled up in an old Mazda a few minutes after I started.

"What are you doing, doctor?" she asked as she walked up to my car.

"Oh, hello, Maritza or whoever. Your deceased boyfriend, Hector, I mean Enrico, made a mess for me. I haven't been able to get it all cleaned up yet."

She raised her chin and smiled slightly. "Ah, you learned some things. I am still very sad about Hector's death. His mother will be devastated. He always would play with the wrong kind of people."

"Yeah, it's all tragic, Maritza," I answered. "I assume that's not why you needed to see me so urgently."

She lit a smoke and stood about five feet from me. For some reason, I noticed her proximity.

"I need my counseling file, doctor. I need to have that from you. Anything you have with my name on it."

"We co-own whatever I have. I can make copies for you. I need to get paid first. I'll need your real name, address, and date of birth to do anything at all for you."

"None of that's important, you see," she said lazily. "I'm sorry but I don't think you'll get paid for seeing me. Now I want my file. I don't want copies. I don't want you to have anything written down about me. Just find my file and give it to me. Then I'll be on my way."

Her eyes held no light as she spoke, and I suddenly didn't like her.

"Yeah. Your file's not here, and I'm all done with being fucked with today, Maritza, whoever. What do you care what I wrote down anyway? Enrico, aka Hector, took your file with him when he busted in here."

A slight look of shock crossed her face for only a moment, but I noticed. She followed me as I walked back inside my office lobby.

"Sure. I see, doctor. Yes, you say Hector stole my file. Did you happen to write down anything in there I said about Christophe Ruzga?"

"I write down what I write down. Whether I wrote about what you said about him, I don't really recall."

I knew I had kept my notes on her to a bare minimum, but I wanted to stall her long enough for the cops.

She drew on her smoke, her eyes beginning to smolder.

"You see, Christophe Ruzga, would kill me if I spoke of past business with somebody like you. Anything you write could go to court. He don't like that sort of thing. He's a very paranoid man as you might guess. I guess Hector or somebody stole my file so I'd get all worried. Who knows? The person who set all this up might even want you worried, too."

"And who's this somebody, this person?" I asked, listening for approaching cars but hearing nothing.

"One of Christophe's friends. A guy double-dealing poor Hector. A guy who wanted Hector on Tina's little treasure hunt so he can keep an eye on her. If only Hector would've listened to me and left all this alone."

"Left what alone?"

Her gaze shot around the room.

"I'm suddenly not liking talking with you, doctor. I'm going to leave now but not before you tell me what you wrote down about Christophe before Hector stole my file. And you are lying if you say you don't remember."

"No dice, Maritza. I haven't been paid a dime. Tell me first who is this friend of Christophe's who set up Hector."

Terror and rage crossed her face.

"Tell me what you wrote!" she spat, coming towards me.

"Who is it?!"

"A man called Jack Brie!"

I didn't even see her pull the knife. The arc and speed of her swing missed the fleshy underside of my jaw by no more than an inch. I fell back and tripped over a kitchen chair, and she lunged again at me. My right hand hit the floor, and I immediately felt the sprain which hurt like hell, but I was on my way down anyway so decided to control my fall and roll right.

She stood over me, holding the blade in an underhand position. It was clear to me she knew how to use it. I was like a man trying to jump a fence topped with razor wire from a prone position. She was the razor wire. I couldn't very well sink further into the floor, and she was poised to pounce. I had no place to go.

I was so frightened, before I knew it my right foot shot out heel first and into her left shin with the energy of a two-hundred-forty-pound man who runs only a couple miles a few times a month, maybe less.

I let loose a scream that would have made my old Kwang Do Kwan instructor proud. She twisted in agony, fell to the floor, and the knife shot across the floor.

It became no more than a fancy potato peeler after that. Maritza writhed around while I stood over her examining it. The knife was Tessa's Navaja. There was none other like it, the very same knife Tessa had used on Jack Brie, given to her by Parker Heslah before his death, the only possession he had from his father who'd picked it up in Spain.

"Where the hell did you get this?"

"AHH! You broke my ankle!" Her face contorted, and she pulled her knee into her chest.

"Not sure I'm capable," I said. "I'm not in very good shape. You shouldn't have pulled it. That's a hard bone to break. Tell me where you got this. I know it's not yours."

"Ahhh! He gave it to me."

"Who?"

"Jack Brie. He gave it to me."

"And how in the world would he get hold of it? At the count of three before cops, Maritza. One . . . two . . ."

She scrawled up to her feet and then staggered toward the door. Then she swung around, spitting words.

"He stole it from your favorite little niece when she wasn't looking."

I vaguely remembered Tessa bitterly informing Ruthie

and me that she'd lost Parker's knife. That must have been over two years ago.

"How long has he been back around?!"

She didn't answer but stumbled out the front door, slamming it behind her.

She'd been gone five minutes when Jacinto and Anderson finally sailed in. Anderson put out a quick call on his radio and patched out quickly through the gravel in the direction I pointed. A state cop drove up about two minutes after that, and Daisy sent him after Anderson.

"Day late and a dollar short, detective," I said. I didn't care that she didn't like what I said. "That's why I don't count on you guys."

She took down a few quick notes. I told her about Maritza mentioning Ruzga and Brie. I thought this would all be a big deal.

"We pulled up the file on what you and Tessa went through quite a while back, doctor. Yes, we've had information that Jack Brie might still be alive. And, yes, the connection between him and Ruzga appears to go back to those years as you're now aware."

"Great that you do your research, detective," I said, seething inside. "I'm heading home."

She didn't let me leave before deciding to admonish me about not getting Maritza's license plate number.

"Stop a knife attack but don't forget to get the license plate, huh? Kiss my ass, Daisy."

Her lips trembled. "Don't call me that. I'm trying to solve three murders in the last week, Barlow."

"Then quit trying to push me around. I'm not your patsy; fuck off for trying to make me one. I'm not your bait either. If you were a decent cop, you would've stopped me from heading out here in the first place. You knew all this shit already. You knew Jack Brie was alive and back around, and you sent me to nearly get my throat slit on a chance he'd turn up."

She walked back to her car so pissed off she forgot about the knife I took from Maritza. I held onto it to give back to Tessa.

I didn't catch a single light all the way home. I was now very late coming back from Ellensburg, and knew Ruthie would be worried.

The house was completely dark, and this really got to me. I hurriedly popped through the front door.

"Ruthie?!"

I called out several times. No answer. I flipped the lights, but they didn't work. My heart rate elevated. She hadn't just left and forgotten to leave the front hall light on like we usually do. She didn't do things that way.

In the darkness, I lurched into the bedroom and felt beneath the nightstand for my flashlight and fishing club, inscribed along the edge with the words, "beat 'em before you eat 'em." Then I inched my way down the hall and checked the other bedrooms, pointing the little light into nooks and crannies, swinging it around, seeing only shadows and shapes.

I descended the staircase to check for a tripped circuit breaker. Our basement is partially finished with musty old carpet put in by former owners, tightly wrapped over the stairs. This made my steps quiet, but that didn't calm me at all. The little flash flickered, and I smacked it, cursing myself for buying batteries at the dollar store. It went out completely thanks to this intervention, and I set it down on the floor.

Without the flash, the moonless night dimmed the windows to such a degree that I couldn't make out anything at all and had to keep my hand on the wall just to guide myself.

I held the club up before me in my other hand while easing forward. I stopped, stepped, and listened closely as I did so. Very soft footfalls duplicated my own rhythm, nearly perfectly but not quite. I pulled Tessa's Navaja from my pocket and struggled to open it. It's a weird knife and hard to open. I finally had it extended in one hand and held the fishing club in the other.

Another very subtle noise squeaked behind me and I turned, swung, and struck out in the dark. I felt the barrel of a gun push into the back of my neck.

"Move one inch, you bastard, and I will blow your brains out!" a voice shrieked, and another flash flipped on. "Oh Ret!!"

She was gripping the stock with the flash wedged into her palm, a very pregnant woman with her stance held wide, eyes like saucers, and a stare I'd never seen. The brightness blinded me but not so much that I couldn't stare down the barrel of a cocked and loaded Marlin 30 odd 6.

"Goddamn, Ruthie!!" I shouted, leaning hard backwards involuntarily. "What the hell!?"

She lowered the rifle and burst into tears.

"Ret!" she sobbed. "A man came! He had a mask! Just a couple of hours ago; he left! I thought you were him!"

She dropped the rifle onto the floor, and I grabbed her before she fell faint. "He told me he wanted some file! He said he'd come back for it!"

"What he wants got stolen. Why is the power out?"

"I flipped the mains. Then I hid, Ret. He can't see in the dark, can he? Oh, I've never been so scared! He was some sort of gangster!"

"Let's get the mains back on and look around."

"No! No! Don't touch them, Ret! He might be watching! No!" She convulsed with fear.

"Okay. Okay. We'll just sit here. We'll just stay in the dark. We've got to sit and figure all this out."

There wasn't much furniture downstairs, but we pulled our old mattress from the floor of the storage room, and I helped her down onto her back. We remained in the pitch dark; I held her, and she held me. An hour, maybe more went by, and she fell into a fitful rest.

I kept the Marlin near and listened. Psychologists are trained to listen, but not like I did then. The noises of the old house emerged. Every sound surged adrenalin through me, and I'd get up with her flashlight to poke around. Ruthie would wake up, and I'd calm her back down; she'd doze; I'd hear another sound, we'd both pop awake.

I checked out the rifle at some point, realizing she'd actually pulled the ammunition off our closet shelf and succeeded in loading it. She might have blown my brains out. I passed out as first light crept through the basement windows, but she woke me right up, wanting to try going upstairs. I helped her over to the couch, insisting she lie down. I wanted to know more about what the hell happened.

She looked haggard and terrified. I hurriedly made instant coffee and chamomile tea in the microwave, filled her in on my Harrah encounter with Maritza, and showed her Tessa's knife.

"I don't want to, but I better call Daisy up, Ruthie . . ."

"No, you aren't going to call her," she declared when I returned.

"Why?"

"Because we already know the police won't do anything. That guy said he'd be watching us, and he meant business. We have to get out of here, Ret! I don't know how, but we have to!"

"One thing at a time," I said. "Tell me more."

"He just appeared right next to me on the lawn about four hours before you got here. I was watering the Impatiens. I didn't hear anything. He was big, taller than you, built like a weightlifter. He had a black ski mask, a Tommy Hilfiger black polo shirt, Canali black pants . . ."

"Jesus, Ruthie, how do you know all this shit?"

"Fashion TV shows; listen!! Shiny black shoes. He was black on black, that's what I'm saying. Not like a gangbanger—like a gangster! It was the middle of the afternoon, and you know nobody's around. He came right up and pushed me into the wall by the front porch, out of view from the street. Honest to God, he pushes a pregnant woman! I almost passed out. He put his fingers around my throat and said 'your husband has a file I want.' He said 'Tell him to give up that office. Let him know I want that file and I got to you. He's been warned.'" She looked at me. "Ret, who is he??"

I thought the question was rhetorical.

"Tell me, Ret! Do not keep any more secrets from me!"

I tried to put them in terms of 'incidents'. Somebody threw a rock through my window; I thought it was probably kids. Tessa was there at the time; the cops got called; they thought it wasn't a big deal. I had the window fixed. Yes, there was a note on it that said 'git out,' but I didn't know what to make of it.

"And this all happened before the gangbangers came by Leila's and threatened you . . ."

"Correct. But the rock could've been for Tessa."

"Right," she said doubtfully.

I mentioned that the car that threw the rock was a '54 Chevy BelAir. Her face hardened.

"You're saying you'd already seen that gangbanger car before. Go on. . ."

I told her about the break-in, the BelAir, and Hector being the guy I chased. After the files were stolen was when I'd first met up with Detective Daisy Jacinto.

"And you didn't tell me any of this stuff because . . ."

"Well," and I felt very badly. "Well, Ruthie, I didn't want to stress you out during the pregnancy."

She cocked her head. "And that's exactly how you would think about it. That's how stupidly you would think about it and how you got us to this point."

"Ruthie, there's also my professional role and confidentiality. I can't tell you all that's going on in my day."

"Right. Sure," she nodded, sarcasm intact. "There's that. Yes, of course, we need to remember your professional role. So then . . . we now have the violent gang who came to Leila's threatening us in our own home. And that's who this guy belongs to, right? He's from them."

"I don't really know that for certain."

"Yes, we're dealing with probabilities, sure. And you didn't tell me all this stuff because . . . you've been protecting me. And if you'd told me this shit in the first place, I might've traveled up to Ellensburg with you despite what Dr. Welch said. But you chose not to tell me, so I didn't get a vote."

"Well, I had no idea somebody like this would actually come here, Ruthie."

Her piercing look cut into me, and I knew I'd been very wrong. And I didn't want to tell her about Jack Brie at that point, believe me.

"So shall we call Jacinto now?" I asked meekly.

"No!" She tried to get up from the couch, and I tried to get her to lie back down. "Damn it, leave me alone! I'm taking care of myself now—and if you call your Daisy friend, I'll never speak to you again. Do you hear that *five by five*, Ret Barlow, psychology policeman?? You've not trusted me; why should I trust you?"

"Ruthie, this is all way beyond us now! We should call the cops."

"You know, I almost shot and killed my own husband last night because he's such an idiot."

"Ruthie, you've never even shot a gun, let alone Arnold's Marlin."

"That's not even what I'm talking about! And I have—my grandpa used to take me to shoot tin cans. I figured out how to load your rifle."

"Well, thank God I have a wife as smart as you. I know I was dumb for not telling you more."

"I'm totally disinterested in your self-esteem issues. We're not going to call the cops or Daisy. This man or his associates are probably watching us."

She peered at me sharply and resolutely.

"I'm not some 'yes, hubby' wife you may think you want, Ret. Maybe that's the real reason you didn't tell me what I deserved to know. We're going to get the hell out of here without being seen. We're going to do it my way."

"Got it," was all I was allowed to say about the matter.

We packed a suitcase. We decided to leave at dusk when visibility was poor. Daylight dimmed, and I crept out and pulled the car forward, easing it right onto the lawn by the back door. We could see most of our lot from there. Ruthie slid the Marlin through the door and onto the passenger side floor of the car and handed me the suitcase. I set that on the passenger seat. I came back inside and helped her to crawl into the backseat and lie down on her back.

I crept to the driver's side, slid in, and pulled myself down so low I could barely see over the steering wheel. Using no car lights, I backed down the driveway slowly, maneuvering via the side view mirror.

Neither of us spoke as we moved north along our street for about three minutes.

"I have a question," she said.

"What?"

"Is Jack Brie in this?"

"I think so, Ruthie."

"I want you to stop treating me like I can't figure things out. Do you see anyone at all?"

"No."

I was halfway down the third block toward Tieton Road when I saw the BelAir parked at the next cross street.

"There!" I whispered harshly and grabbed for the Marlin on the floor. "Stay down!"

I pulled over to the right behind a parked car. The BelAir was maybe a hundred yards away. I could make out two people sitting inside.

"Ret!" Ruthie said harshly. "Get us away from here!"

"What do you suggest I do?"

"Back up! Don't go past them."

"Fast or slow? I have to turn around somehow."

One of the heads bobbed up inside the BelAir, and the

lights came alive as he cranked the engine.

"Fast!" Ruthie yelled.

I slammed into gear and shot back up the nearby driveway in reverse, running over our neighbor's front garden.

"Go!" Ruthie yelled.

Bright halogen motion lights shot out from the house behind that one as we came bouncing in an old, dilapidated Gran Fury through the backyard. I heard the BelAir's engine growl and roar onto the driveway and onto the next street. He'd anticipated where I was going, peeled around the corner, and raced towards us. I put my foot to the floor, but they were nearly on top of us.

There's an alley that's hard to see behind these properties —I made the turn without even knowing; my body took over, my mind was shut off by fear. The frontal lobe curls around toward the hypothalamus; the pituitary tells the adrenal glands to spurt adrenalin.

They saw what I did but not quick enough; I watched him fly past the entrance in my rear view mirror, and could hear him jam his brakes, squealing into reverse. But I had time to pitch a hard left into another driveway which ran all the way to the next street over.

"You okay?!"

"Go, Ret! Fly!!" she shouted.

I crossed through and saw him again in my side view mirror, kicking up dust and gravel but now perpendicular to me, and charging down the alley in the opposite direction.

It must've seemed to him like we disappeared.

We snaked through residential streets behind Franklin Park. My mouth was so dry, I could only grunt when Ruthie demanded I narrate to her exactly what was happening. I was finally able to make clear that nobody was in sight. We decided to aim toward the police station. We figured that'd be the best place to end up dead.

We drove, parked, drove a little more, parked.

Somehow we pulled along 2nd Avenue by the Yakima

police station.

There's a long enclosure for trash bins inside the parking lot at the glass business across the street. We sat behind that spot for a good three minutes arguing over whether we should go inside. After all I'd done to get us there, Ruthie wanted to get out of town. She pulled herself up, got out, and climbed in next to me up front.

"This baby's going to have nerves of steel if I don't end up losing it," she said. "You already agreed we're doing this my way."

She proved a superb navigator for the odd route we took toward Canyon Road, keeping an eye for cars sitting at blind spots and bouncing off each other's surveillance. I told her if these guys were that smart, they'd have already caught us. There was the bold fact that she knew something about surveillance tactics, and I didn't. She's a constant surprise to me.

We actually made it to Canyon Road.

By 9 p.m., we'd checked into a Super 8 in Ellensburg. We parked at a different spot up the street, and I lugged our suitcase down a rear alley. We were very careful.

I ate nearly an entire greasy delivery pizza; she gulped down a fast-food chicken sandwich, and together we emptied an entire liter of caffeine-free soda. We watched a rerun of 'Little House on the Prairie' and held onto each other very tightly.

We simply couldn't speak. We slept like the dead for nine hours and woke up feeling considerably safer.

FIFTEEN

I do not like trouble with my white friends;
Nor do I interfere with them in any way.
I always want to do right by them if I can.
If the whites would be friendly with the Indians,
Do everything friendly and right by them,
We might get along better.
If both Indians and whites would follow this up,
Be friendly and not interfere with each other in any way,
The Creator would know this,
And by doing right,
Nothing bad would happen to us.
—*Nah-schoot*

We were lying on the hotel bed together with the TV on. My cell vibrated, and she handed it to me wordlessly. I held the cell up to my ear and said "hello" hoarsely.

"Doctor, this is Leila. *Káła*'s out of the hospital, and we were hoping you might come by."

Ruthie could hear her voice. "Ret, click the speaker so I can listen." I did so.

"Leila—Ruthie and I aren't at home right now," I said. "Somebody came by and threatened her and me. I don't think I can come by. I don't want to leave."

"Oh, stay where you are then, doctor, stay safe. But Franklin wants to talk with you. He's home and sitting with us right now."

"He's released?!" Ruthie exclaimed aloud.

"Hi, Ruthie," said Leila. "Insufficient evidence. He's all sprung. They couldn't place him at the crime scene or find anything to tie him to the murder. He made those threats after Jamie got killed, and that was really all they had on him. Lots of kids talk tough, but that Detective Jacinto couldn't prove a thing. So he's come home, and he can finally heal up from all that's happened. Frank's picked him up."

"The other thing is *káła*'s come out the hospital against her doctor's advice. We're not too happy with her about that, but she has her own mind. She's insisting I call you because of what's going on."

"What's going on, Leila?" Ruthie asked.

"I thought you might already remember. Today's the supervised visit for Ce Ce and Samuel with Tina. Brenda Oakley come by about an hour ago and picked them both up."

"Well, we're both very sorry about that," I said. "How are you all doing having to sit with that?"

"Emily found something out, and we're all together here trying to understand it. It's a strange thing, and it's got us all worried."

"Something about Tina?" Ruthie asked.

"No, about Ce Ce," she answered.

Ruthie and I looked at each other, confused.

"There's marks on her heel, you see," she said. "They always been there, ever since she's born."

"What marks? Have you seen them?" I asked.

"A thousand times. I always just thought they were some sort of birthmark. But Emily found something her *tila* wrote in that old journal he left us. I couldn't read his writing no matter how I tried; it's way too scribbly. She sorts it out somehow."

"And what did he say?"

"*Túta* was all convinced those marks on Ce Ce's heel mean something real important. He felt they were the reason why Jack Brie tried to take her back when you and Tessa went through being kidnapped and all. You remember how Brie come into the house out in White Swan and nosed around?"

"Too well, Leila," I answered.

"Emily figured out what he was writing in that journal about. *Túta* was pretty sure Brie was going to come try to take Ce Ce because of something to do with those marks."

"You said Franklin's got something to tell," said Ruthie.

"He says how he don't believe anything his mom says about wanting the two little ones back. After Emily said what she learned, Franklin says he figures Tina knows about the marks on Ce Ce's heel , and wants to see them up close so she can figure what they mean. Franklin's been trying to rush on out of here to go after his little sister. We've had to keep him cooled down."

"I wish we could help, Leila," I said.

"Totally understand, doctor. *Túta* copied the marks out in his old book. We got them here. We just can't understand them and thought you might.

"Hold on."

I looked at Ruthie and muted the cell. She nodded back at me.

"Go and try to help, Ret."

"God, I don't want to."

"The police can't help. I'm okay. This thing about Ce Ce is too important."

I hung up from Leila and got dressed quickly. The Marlin lay on the hotel bed within reach, wrapped in the bedspread. I wanted it to stay with her. It was fully loaded with a shell in the chamber.

"Safety off, point and shoot," she said to me reassuringly. "Ret. . ."

"Yeah."

"Don't go anywhere near our house. Take I-82 into Wapato, and the back roads from there . . . they'll know your car! There's none like it."

I held up my hand. "I'll be very careful."

I pulled the hotel room door closed and glanced back inside to tell her I'd call every hour or so.

Dogs barked in the cool down of the evening as I walked up to the front door. A rusty stain could be seen on the concrete beneath Franklin's feet as he met me there.

"That's my blood," he said, pointing.

"I'm sorry for all you've been through, Franklin," I said. "I never believed it was you."

"Wish it was. For sure Hector capped Jamie."

The Miyanashatawit family except for Tessa, Ce Ce, and Samuel sat inside Leila's duplex on kitchen and other chairs. Ce Ce and Samuel had been picked up by Brenda Oakley only two hours earlier.

Emily handed over Arnold's old journal. There were dates and notes, even a few drawings. Leila was right, however; his handwriting was atrocious, and I couldn't decipher it.

"Here . . ." Emily opened it to the middle and pointed.

Arnold had copied the marks from Ce Ce's heel in pen. Leila said they were red and in a tight circle that made them look like a birthmark. I studied them for a few moments:

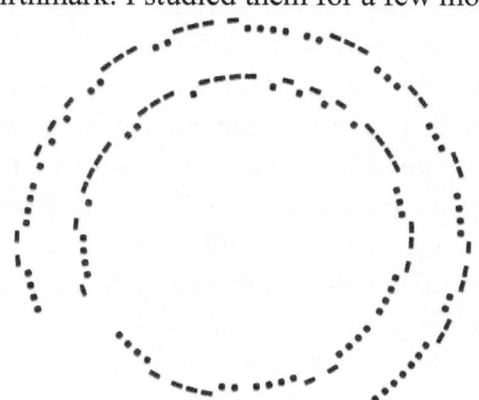

"Any thoughts?" I asked, showing it to Frank, who pulled in when I did.

"Morse," Frank answered, and I agreed with him.

"What it says, I don't know," he added.

"Can you read it, doctor?" Leila asked.

"Not me," I answered.

"We need to figure it," said Emily. "Right away."

"Franklin, you should tell the doctor what Ce Ce asked you," said Frank.

Franklin looked at him and then at me. "Uh, Ce Ce whispered to me, 'what is Signal Peak?' over that little visitor's phone at the detention center. Auntie here," he looked at Leila, "didn't notice Ce Ce doing that. She only asked me once."

"What'd you tell her?" I asked.

"I said I didn't know and why'd she ask me. She said she had some bad dream about she can't get home. Ce Ce and I talked a lot before I got up to some things after *tila* died, but she never said anything about that place before. I checked with everybody I could. She never asked anybody besides me that question—'what is Signal Peak?' It was strange."

"I don't think she's ever been out that way," said Leila. "Why in the world would Ce Ce talk about Signal Peak?"

"Signal Peak is way out on the rez, right?" I asked.

"Closed area," Frank answered.

"*Kluní*, the bald head," said Elisi, "the first mountain of four where the *Páchi'analá*, the giant monster bird, set down the boundaries where our people have wandered and gathered since time immemorial. We don't own land as you know, doctor, we only borrow it from *Tamanwiłá*. A young warrior guarding our people from intruders got kidnapped from his post up on that peak and was taken to a strange, faraway place and then had to make a very long journey home. I always thought that old story was somebody's dream or vision. I won't go into it all." She looked at Franklin. "But a dream that's what Ce Ce was talking to you from, I'm sure of it. We pay attention to any child from a medicine family talking about their dreams."

"Did you tell anybody else about all this, Franklin?" asked Leila.

"That Hispanic detective. I told her I was worried

about my sis, and she should stop Ce Ce and Samuel from visiting my ma. She didn't think there was anything to what I said. She only kept telling me to stop lying about Hector."

We all paused for a moment, trying to understand.

I glanced over and found Elisi was watching me closely. "Doctor, do you know anything about Signal Peak?"

"No—I've never been out to the closed area. Do you mean my own dreams or something? No . . ." Elisi stared hard at me. "I've heard of it, if that's what you're wondering. A woman I've worked with who's been going under a false name and claims she's seen Jack Brie mentioned Signal Peak to me. She tried to kill me before she ran off. I took this away from her."

I pulled the Navaja knife out of my pocket.

"Oh my God! Where'd you get that?!" Emily exclaimed. "Tessa's been looking for that forever!!"

"I promise I'll get it back to her next time I see her. I'd like to hold onto it until then."

I told them all about Maritza—her connection to Hector and past connection to Christophe Ruzga, a likely customer of Jack Brie's gun-running business, her story that Tina was trying to find Ruzga's hidden money, and how this might fit with Hector's demise. Franklin mentioned parallels in the conversation he overheard between Tina and Hector about going to get this hidden money when the time was right.

"So Ce Ce and doctor and Franklin are all getting signs as to Jack Brie and Signal Peak," Elisi observed anxiously.

She struggled out of her chair, looking like death warmed over, stretched slowly upright, and drew out a pistol out of her sweater pocket.

Frank's eyes widened. "Now what the *hell* are you doing, Elisi??"

"I've had a listen to all's been said. I'm going to go get back those children off their visit, and I don't care what that Oakley lady from the court says."

"Put that away, Elisi!" Leila shouted at her. "I don't

want nobody else getting hurt!"

She looked at the patch over Franklin's eye.

Elisi stopped inside Leila's front door. "Desperate times; desperate measures. *Nápayu 'nash ttáwaxt.* Before I was heartsick about Tina getting these kids; now I'm sick with fear to get them back. *Now!* They're coming home."

"She thinks she's going up there to shoot somebody," said Frank, shaking his head.

"I only know I got to go get them. Tina's on to something besides being a mother—she only wants her little girl so to study those marks. You all do whatever you think your Creator tells you."

Frank and I got up to follow. Franklin pushed hard to join us, but we insisted he guard the kids and Leila. He didn't object—he was still recovering from a terrible wound.

Emily pried back the door from my hands as I tried to shut it and slid into the back seat of Frank's extended pickup truck.

"Tessa's not here. I'm looking out for the little ones. Don't try to stop me," she proclaimed.

Given her expression, we would've had to drag her out of the backseat physically. Frank just looked at me and shrugged, watching Elisi back out of Leila's driveway in her Sunrise.

"Goddamn, she's still a fast woman at near eighty years," Frank said as we jolted down Larena Lane. "Hyperactive. Isn't that the saying in your profession?"

"I try not to judge, Frank."

We tried to stay behind her. "Leon and Edward been messing around with that little engine she's got," Frank added. "Who knows what they've done?"

"I do," said Emily. "They found a used turbocharger that fits that little car."

I somehow got Elisi to answer her cell phone. We could see her holding it to her ear while she raced.

"Where is Tina's place, *káła*?" I asked.

"Osborne House. Halfway house for ex-con moms."

"*Káła*, you need to give me back my pistol! Don't do anything crazy!" Emily yelled, leaning over the front seat.

The image of the pistol Elisi pulled from her sweater suddenly came back to me, and I realized it was the same Taurus 85 I'd bought off pawn years ago, the one Jack Brie took from me, and used to try to execute Tessa.

"What do you mean *your* pistol?" I demanded.

"I was all set to go up there two hours ago to get the kids myself. She made me give it to her."

"Damn, Emily! That's not your pistol; it's mine! How'd you get hold of it?"

"My *tila* give it to me. Picked it off the ground where Brie dropped it, and you left it. He said you abandoned it, doctor, and I could keep it."

Elisi ran a light at the intersection of Wapato Road, turning on State Route 97 before flying past two semi-trucks; Frank couldn't seem to keep up with her. She was at least a half mile ahead of us.

In my pants pocket, I had Tessa's Navaja knife; Elisi had my Taurus 85 in her sweater pocket. Both Maritza and Ce Ce had questions about Signal Peak. Ce Ce had telling dreams, and I did too. Andesite, ESLs, Nortenos, an old BelAir, a lost eye, two murders, death threats, a close escape: 'Cowboy' Jack Brie was clearly present in our lives again.

Elisi pulled onto the little service road running in front of the Wolf Den Restaurant and stopped. The road bifurcates off 97 back to Wapato or forward onto the highway up to Yakima. Her silhouette fiddled with her cell.

"I needed to get my little speaker going on this stupid phone," she said. "Now listen. Two of our children been pulled over the line. People 'round this sovereign land are always saying 'our children are sacred, our children are sacred.' That's just words—right here, right now is when you make it mean something. Make 'em safe or die trying. I don't want any extra baggage! Don't follow unless you back me up."

She put the pedal to the metal, patched out back onto 97, and Frank shook his head, slammed on his accelerator, and hugged closely along behind her.

"Good, uncle," Emily declared. "Good."

At the same moment, Deputy Almont Anderson's cruiser pulled up next to us with his flashers on. Then he pulled further up and even with Elisi. I saw her glance over at him and then wave. His panicky wave back said 'pull over'.

"S*hix pawchway, walak'ikláama!*" we heard her say over the cell speaker.

Emily began laughing uncontrollably.

"Goddamn right!" Frank shouted.

Anderson slowed slightly so he was next to us again and made the same gesture. Frank waved, and the deputy looked outraged.

"*Shix pawchway, walak'ikláama!*" Frank shouted gleefully.

"*Holy shit, uncle!*" Emily shouted when Frank surged forward. "We're on the run!"

To be honest, I don't know if I ever felt that degree of exhilaration in my life before.

"Goddamn!" I shouted. "*Run*, Frank!!"

Anderson pulled up near our rear bumper.

"He's trying for a pit maneuver!" shouted Emily.

"Hold on!" Frank shouted.

He floored it, and we jumped ahead again. We heard the cruiser's outside speaker come on.

"Pull over now!" Anderson's mantra came. For some reason, his speaker made his voice sound like he'd inhaled helium. Emily was unable to speak and kept grabbing her gut.

"Nissan Tundra FFE with a 5.7 supercharged, doctor!" Frank shouted. "Can't keep up, and he's getting frustrated!"

Elisi's Sunrise and Frank's truck picked up speed but Anderson's Yakima County Sheriff's cruiser hung close behind.

"Look!" Emily shouted and pointed.

Two state police cars raced out from underneath a viaduct until they were even with Anderson, and we all flew through the Union Gap junction and onto the on ramp for I-82. One trooper moved abreast of Anderson's car, pulling up next to Elisi's pristine Sunrise on the right side. The other trooper drove up on her left. Next, Anderson shot ahead, trying to get in front of her.

"They're trying a running road block, *káła*!" Emily leaned over from the back and shouted at my cell phone.

Elisi's Sunrise wove sharply in front of the trooper on the left and all the way over toward the shoulder, cutting off the trooper on the right. When she veered back all the way across the lanes, she nearly struck the cement-blocked median.

Frank slammed on his brakes. "Watch out!!"

"*Káła!*" Emily yelled.

"Doctor, call Leila!" Elisi shouted over the speaker.

"What for??" I yelled back.

I looked back to see the cop cars breaking through the traffic and sailing forward towards us.

Frank licked his lips, wild-eyed. "They're still coming!"

Elisi shouted again. "Tell her meet us near 16th and Gilbert Road! Tell her 'same place as always.' Fifteen minutes, no more. Franklin has to stay with the kids! Do you got it? Hang up and call right now, doctor!!"

I hurriedly dialed Leila, reporting verbatim what she said.

"I know the place!" I heard Leila respond and then disconnect.

Frank struggled to maintain position. Elisi wove through a red light, honking her horn onto Ahtanum Road. Anderson closed in behind Frank's truck again. A Union Gap city cop car with a female officer zipped up even with us, facing oncoming traffic. I could see troopers catching up behind Anderson, further back. Elisi lit into overdrive.

"I think they must've bored the pistons out on her. . ." said Frank.

He and the female cop were playing chicken with oncoming traffic. I looked back as Emily covered her eyes and screamed. Two horns echoed before they skidded onto the opposite shoulder, but the Tundra pickup and city cop cruiser raced by them holding side-by-side.

"This woman cop is crazy!!" Frank stammered, his gnarly brown hands gripping the steering wheel like a pinned-down calf.

I counted six cop cars behind us. Frank accelerated even more; the Union Gap cop backed off when more cars came into view on the rise ahead. We gained a quarter mile on her making the top of the hill. In front of us, Elisi made a sharp left onto Goodman Road and back onto the reservation, past Lil' Brown Smoke Shack, veering right until it became Meadowbrook Road. I turned back, and Emily and I watched Anderson's cruiser spin out and into a deep ditch, poking its rear end back out into the road. The troopers and Union Gap cop couldn't get around him.

"Uncle Frank!" Emily announced expectantly.

"Huh?"

"We are going to jail *forever*!"

Just past Meadowcrest Lane, veering sharp to the right, Elisi suddenly skidded, and I thought this was the end. Instead, she made a hard left onto an orchard two-track. Somehow, she kept control, pumped her brakes, and brought her speed down quickly. Frank, Emily, and I bumped along behind, jolting up and down, smacking against branches, hearing the thump of falling fruit, and only barely squeezing past small trees.

So this is how it's done, I observed; this is how to disappear on these two-tracks.

Elisi pulled up near an indent in the ground, parked, and shut her car off. When we came up next to her, Frank, Emily, and I could barely breathe.

She rolled down her window, and I rolled down mine.

"What are . . . you people . . . doing??" She shouted, trying to catch her breath. "Get out the car!!"

Emily and I tumbled out onto the ground; Frank ran around the other side and helped us both up. I heard her trunk pop open.

"Oh, oh," she moaned and grabbed her chest as we helped to get her out of her seat. "That hospital doctor was right . . . must be very near my death." She looked us all over. "If I die . . . I'm ready! None of you look very good either . . . Maybe I don't feel so bad.

"Now *túktu!* Hurry! . . . Reach in, *kála*," she instructed Emily. ". . . you'll see what we need . . . pull it out quick . . . they'll be coming!"

Emily rummaged around in the trunk and found a huge camouflage vinyl tarp, folded neatly. She tugged it out, looking at her adopted *kála* with astonishment. We all watched with deep concern as she struggled to catch her breath, holding her chest. She regained control and gave us a look of indignation.

"You need to stop . . . like I'm going to keel . . . over dead right now!! . . . That hive of buzzing yellow jackets . . . we stirred up is coming for us . . . and you're all gapin' at me!"

Emily jumped up, shook the tarp loose, and we spread it over both the car and the truck, weighting it down quickly with rotten apples fallen beneath the trees, and throwing piles of loose brush on top to complete the picture.

"There," Elisi beamed. The morass we'd made looked like any large pile of brush and debris you see in any tended orchard locally. "No time to waste . . . you all got to carry me . . . down to the road."

"Well, not me," said Frank, covered in sweat. "I'll put my back out again."

He nodded toward me.

"Come on, doctor! . . . I can't run . . . if I'm about to die . . . I don't even got my cane. . . pick me up. . . *kála,* carry my purse."

"Well, I'm no superman," I grumbled, struggling to lift her anyway.

She must have weighed about one hundred fifty pounds. It became clear I couldn't carry her like a baby. She started getting angry, and I got angry back at her, and somehow the energy allowed me to lift her into a fireman's carry. I used both my arms to clamp her left arm and left knee together like a necklace and hobbled moving forward.

It was pure hell.

Emily gripped Elisi's bag, while ineffectively pushing Elisi higher onto my back. This didn't help me at all.

"Left, left," Elisi snapped at us. "*Túktu*! Faster!"

We mashed up between two trees.

"Ouch! Ho! . . . Keep quiet . . . we're getting close to the road."

We came up to the last row of trees by the T-intersection at West Gilbert and 16th Avenue. I set her down, and we all peered out through the orchard leaves.

I was completely out of air and nearly collapsed.

"See that fireworks stand?" Elisi asked us in a hushed voice. "We'll need . . . your special whistle, Frank."

"Aw, *nána*," he protested. "I ain't done that since you and I were kids."

The Union Gap police car appeared, easing around the corner from South 11th Avenue onto West Gilbert and then entered the orchard two-track.

"Hush!" Elisi snapped in a breathy whisper. "Watch! Pick a tree . . . stand close!"

She eased under the limbs of a close apple tree and then stood upright until her torso was flush against the trunk. Then, she reached out her arms and meshed them in with the branches. Frank, Emily, and I quickly chose trees and did the same.

"Pray hard," I heard Elisi whisper. "Pray very hard."

The Union Gap cop car crept through the tight space

alongside a row of trees right next to ours.

I glanced at Emily; she had panic on her face. We didn't dare breathe.

The Union Gap female cop drove past our camouflaged cars and saw nothing but a pile of debris. To be fair, she must have had a lot of adrenalin pumping still. She was looking for threat more than detail. She was so close, we could hear her radio and see her head moving right and left.

She looked at the form of a tree and her eyes told her 'that's a tree.' The branches and leaves where Frank stood were all very tangled. Most of us would have to look several times and focus on a particular tree that small to notice a person standing flush with it. I think if we had stood behind the trees, rather than close in among the branches, the effect wouldn't have worked.

She pulled forward gradually, looking and listening carefully. Then she was out on the other side and back onto 16th. Her radio crackled and she accelerated, speeding past an empty fireworks stand and back toward Ahtanum Road.

We stayed where we were a few moments longer. A loud bird startled me—a white-throated sparrow. Although I'm not a birder, Ruthie and I woke to that sound at 5 a.m. for almost a year until I figured out where she'd built her nest. By that time, there were babies, and Ruthie wouldn't let me do anything about it.

An engine started, and a pickup truck pulled out from a dense stand of trees back behind the fireworks stand. It jumped the shoulder, came onto the road, and pulled up in front of us.

Leila leaned out, popped the broken door handle from the outside, and shouted: "Well, we don't got all day!"

We piled in tightly together, and she drove carefully, taking us onto 3rd Avenue and through downtown Yakima first. There were cops on several corners, but nobody paid attention to us.

"I know . . . we're being helped," said Elisi

reassuringly. "Thank you, *Tamanwilá*. We are . . . sustained by You."

It had been three hours since I left Ruthie. I hurriedly called her while we rode and apologized, explaining how things were. She'd been beside herself with worry but still felt safe. I did too for some strange reason. We agreed an hour check-in was too fast, and I'd try again in a couple of hours.

Leila pulled into the driveway of a large brownstone home converted into small apartments. A small sign hanging outside read "Osborne House."

"Let me go in first." Leila was only gone a minute.

"Well, Ms. Brenda Oakley doesn't want us here, that's for certain," she said upon returning.

"Get me inside there," said Elisi.

We helped her take the lead up a steep flight of stairs to Tina's apartment. She got faint for a moment and placed her arm on the wall for a moment.

"*Káła!*" Emily rushed to grab her.

"Hands off!" she responded angrily and pulled herself more erect at the top of the stairs. Brenda Oakley opened the door.

"Get out my way!" Elisi pushed her way past her.

"You can't come in!" Oakley yelled. "This is a state-sanctioned visit, and I'll call the police!"

She pulled out her cell and held it up threateningly in Elisi's face. Leila smacked it out of her hand and onto the floor. Then she jumped on it with both heels.

"That's state property!" Oakley whined. Leila's expression made her suddenly more wary.

"Where are the children?!" Elisi demanded.

"Right here, *káła*," Samuel answered, sitting in the corner of the wooden floor, playing a hand-held video game.

"Where's your sister then??" asked Leila.

"Outside playing," he answered, looking at Tina who sat at a small kitchen table.

"Outside alone??" Emily turned and scrambled down the stairs. She came back in what seemed like seconds.

Ce Ce was gone.

"*Pinátɬ'uyank,tílaaki pyúsh! Ch'ishklá! . . . Wyasaptayákyaw Tamanwilá! Kwyáamtimt niwít!*" Elisi sputtered at Tina.

"I don't understand Indian language," Tina retorted sullenly from where she sat.

The Taurus 85 jumped out of Elisi's sweater pocket and into her right hand. Brenda Oakley's eyes went wide, and she slunk quietly out the door behind us; I decided it might be unwise to try to stop her. Leila came forward and grabbed the back of Tina's hair; Elisi thrust the barrel into the center of her forehead and pulled back the hammer. These things happened as though the two of them were one person. Frank, Emily, Samuel, and I became passive bystanders watching Elisi and Leila with Tina.

"You know exactly what I mean," Elisi said. "*Where's Ce Ce??*"

"She was right here; we come inside for a few while she was out playing in the little playground area!"

Elisi pressed the barrel harder, and Leila pulled Tina's hair back farther. Inexplicably, a small mirror fell off the wall next to us and onto the floor. Everyone, including Tina, jumped. The sound of broken mirror pieces scattering across the floor seemed to bounce off the rear of my cranium. I thought the gun would go off.

Samuel watched his *káɬa* closely, wondering if she might murder his mother. Tina grimaced and closed her eyes, preparing to meet her Maker.

Elisi whispered to her. "You don't care nothing about her. You knew all this was going to happen today. What you don't know is whether I die here, or in prison, makes no difference to me. Now, *where is she??*"

Leila put her face up close to Tina's. "She might really shoot you, sister."

Sweat sprung from Tina's forehead.

"Ruzga . . ." I began.

Tina gaped at both of them, then her eyes peered sideways at me.

"Ruzga, Tina," I said again. "You've wanted to go find his money. Ce Ce's the key. You wanted to see her heel. We know."

A look of terror crossed her face.

"He'll kill me," she whispered.

"No," said Elisi. "I will."

She snapped the trigger on an empty chamber. Tina nearly fell from her chair.

"Misfire," Elisi complained. "Must be old ammo. Next one will work better."

She raised the pistol toward Tina again.

"No!" Tina cried. "You're crazy!! Okay! Okay!!"

Elisi eased the hammer of the revolver back and lowered the pistol. Leila took a step back.

"I need a cigarette," Tina said hoarsely.

Frank fished into deep pockets and pulled out his bag of Bugler. He fashioned a cigarette without even looking at what he was doing. The result was perfectly formed. Tina accepted it tentatively. He reached in another pocket, pulled out a kitchen match, struck it with a flick of his thumbnail, and held it before her, locking eyes with her.

"Seen your dad suffer over you and shed tears for what you done," he said. "Get busy and tell us all you know."

His involuntary look of malice made her shiver slightly.

"He put a gun to my head just like you!" she whined at Elisi, her face rolling up into a falsely tearful expression. "But told me he'd cut me in if I helped. He said he can take care of her himself anyway. After all, he's her daddy!"

"You think he's a daddy?!" Emily sneered.

"There we are," said Elisi, spinning the cylinder of the Taurus. "And we all know who you mean. But you say who,

Tina."

"Jack. Jack Brie."

"Where's he taken her, Tina??" Leila cried bitterly.

"I don't know!" Tina screamed. "I got no idea. Maritza—she knows!" She pointed at me. "Hector and Maritza were supposed to play him for information and keep an eye on him. Jack's been working to make Barlow seem like a problem for Christophe Ruzga too, likely so Ruzga don't understand what Jack's up to."

"Are you saying there was a plan to set me up as a target for Christophe Ruzga? Why?"

"Jack wanted to know what you knew on all of the kids, especially Ce Ce." She pulled on her cigarette. "He was worried you might already know about the tats. He don't like you but thinks you're too smart and nosy."

"The marks on her heel . . ." Frank said. Tina nodded affirmatively and inhaled more smoke.

"What kind of mom tattoos her own baby's foot??" Emily snapped.

Tina glanced around at the rest of us to see if we really wanted an answer. She shook her head and looked at Samuel. He had a sad expression, and shook his head back at her.

"This one here had the croup bad when he's little, and the IHS give me a codeine script for him. Okay, so I give some to Ce Ce to make her sleep when she's a baby." She sensed the disgust around her. "Look! Jack Brie—he beat on me! I did what he said if I wanted to live—that's how it was. I used a needle and some red ink from a BIC pen. I heated 'em up first to be careful and not infect her."

She surveyed our faces again but got little back. "I'm not saying it was right!"

"This is all beside the point," said Frank. "What do the tattoos mean?"

She swept her eyes around and licked her lips nervously.

"I don't know exactly what they mean, but I figure

they say where Ruzga's money is. Ruzga paid Jack a percentage on running guns, but Jack always held some aside. It grew to a whole lot of money—thousands, maybe hundreds of thousands, by the time the ATF bust went down. Jack said anything happened, we'd still have that money."

Elisi spoke: "Tell us where Jack Brie's taken her."

"I don't know," Tina muttered. "I'm telling you the truth! He told me he'd never hurt his own flesh and blood!"

We all walked back downstairs with Samuel and left Tina staring out the window. I noticed 'Wheel of Fortune' on the screen as we walked out. I hadn't noticed the TV..

"Sorry you saw that, brother. Doing violence is no good," Emily told Samuel.

"*Káła* and auntie hate my ma," he responded.

"More pity her, Samuel. Your ma did wrong, and we have to try to find Ce Ce," Leila told him. "She's very mixed up and has been for a long while. If she hadn't done what she did, we'd have stayed peaceful and just prayed for her."

A young native man pushing a custodian's cart met us by the bottom of the stairs.

"This is Michael," Leila announced. "I known him since grade school. He's a regular at Mel's and works in the building here."

We shook hands lightly just as the sound of many cars pulling in erupted in front of the building.

"Nephew," Elisi whispered to him. "I'd appreciate it if you'd hold on to this for me."

"Sure, auntie," he said, placing my Taurus 85 in the pocket of his nearby janitor's cart.

"Hey, that's mine," I protested weakly.

"You want to carry it then?" Frank asked me with a sly grin as car doors opened outside.

"I guess not."

"Is it loaded?" Michael asked.

"Oh, no," Elisi answered. "I don't ever carry round loaded guns. That wouldn't be safe."

"*Nána!*" Frank laughed. "Really? Goddamn!"

She smiled her Cheshire cat grin at him.

Many police cars surrounded Leila's pickup truck. Deputy Anderson had his sidearm drawn and several officers had rifles out. Detective Jacinto was pulling up in her unmarked car.

The handcuffs seemed quite unnecessary.

SIXTEEN

The *wáx̱'push* [rattlesnakes] are moving from their home
Along the mountain below Toppenish . . .
They cannot fight the mowing machine
Killing them in the meadows . . .
Its teeth were swift and sharp,
Tearing them to pieces.
The Chief has ordered his people to move.
They are now on the trail.
—*Louis Mann, 1910*

"I've used my one phone call to get hold of my pregnant wife. Now, let me out of here, detective."

"We're considering detaining you for eluding the police, doctor."

"Garbage. I've committed no crime. I want an attorney."

"Doctor, you were involved in a multiple department, twelve-mile police chase."

"I don't recall doing any driving lately."

"Then tell us where the truck you were riding in might be."

"Back up a bit, Detective," said FBI Special Agent Phil Alston, a well-groomed African-American man in a tailored black suit sitting in the chair next to her. His demeanor invited calm.

"Dr. Barlow," he said, "we believe you may have information pertaining to the recent disappearance of Ce Ce Miyanashatawit as well as several murders around Lower Valley. If you withhold information, you could be seen as obstructing justice. That's a federal crime and more serious than running from the police. We believe the Miyanashatawit family and even you and your family may be in danger, and we're trying to help you."

"Thanks for that. You can't help me. Am I under arrest?"

"Um," he answered cryptically, "you're being detained for questioning. We do have video footage, however, and about nine officers saw you sitting in an extended cab Tundra pickup truck during the chase. I understand local law enforcement is considering charging you."

"With what, huh? Riding in a car that's driving too fast? Don't push me around right now. There's a guy back around here who tried to kill me and Tessa Miyanashatawit five years ago. Local law enforcement assured me he's dead. He's not. His name's Jack Brie. He's your man for kidnapping Ce Ce. And he's been trying to intimidate all of us and get me murdered."

"We understand all that, doctor, and are doing all we can," said Detective Jacinto.

"Great, which isn't much to be relied upon—so do you think I really give a shit what you do to me at this point?"

Alston seemed subtly amused for some reason; Jacinto held a smirk.

"Okay, doctor, what do you want?" asked Alston.

"I want protection for my wife and me."

Alston looked at Jacinto, who held her gaze on me. She eventually sighed.

"We can put a deputy at your house at taxpayer expense for a while. We want you to tell us about connections between Maritza Rios and Christophe Ruzga."

I filled them in on everything I could recall from Maritza's disclosures, including the allegations about Tina, Hector, and Ruzga's hidden money.

"Brie now has Maritza's file. Hector stole it from me so Brie could blackmail Maritza into playing games with me so as to get Ruzga all worried. She's deathly afraid of Ruzga. He's apparently very paranoid and worried she tipped me off about particulars regarding his criminal activities. The guy's a threat and will come after me and my wife."

"And how do you know that?" asked Jacinto.

"Because he already came by my home and manhandled and threatened Ruthie about the file. I figure Hector told him about it before he got murdered."

Alston and Jacinto looked at each other. I kept talking until I'd spilled nearly all the beans.

I didn't say a word about the marks on Ce Ce's heel. I was convinced they'd mishandle the information, jump the gun, try to chase Brie down prematurely, and get Ce Ce killed in the process.

I hadn't developed a lot of confidence in law enforcement over the last six years. At that point, I didn't have any and was just talking enough to get released.

Frank Mathis was leaning against a pillar by the front door of the downtown Yakima police station, smoking a hand-rolled smoke and waiting for me.

"Figured they'd spring you, doctor. I can drive you back in Leila's pickup."

"Geez, Frank! How'd any of you ever get yourselves cut loose after the ride we took?"

"Washington Council of Police and Sheriffs," he answered lazily, winking. "Stickers on both side windows of her truck; didn't you notice? They couldn't think what to charge Leila or Emily or Elisi with anyway. I looked bad, but these folks got bigger fish to catch, and we're all their bait."

"What do you mean?"

"Look at how things lie, doctor. They smell a big case to solve, and they're hungry. Probably the D.A.'s already in on it. They don't want to keep us locked up for our crazy driving while they have to go after Jack Brie and Ce Ce. No, these police want to see what garbage the little mice go gather if we're let go to run around. From the trouble we've attracted so far, it's not a bad idea."

I called Ruthie as we drove back. I was so grateful to hear her voice, I could hardly speak. The need to get back to her was burning a hole right through me.

Elisi, Leila, and Emily were all home already when we got back to Leila's.

"The Deputy asked me a couple of things about Ce Ce," Elisi explained with great anxiety. "They sort of understood my level of upset. There's an Amber Alert on Ce Ce now, but we got no idea what kind of car took her away. The nicer one, Mr. Deputy Anderson, gave Leila, Emily, and me a ride to the impound to get Leila's truck."

"Now don't be fooled," Frank told them. "They cut us loose because they want to watch where we go and what happens to us. That's what this is all about. Otherwise, they'd have us under lock and key for making a scene. They don't like being outfoxed."

"We're under surveillance?" asked Emily.

"Bet on it," said Frank.

"Cool," Franklin said from his place lounging on the couch. We all turned to him. "Maybe ESLs will stay backed off."

After two more nights of solid rest, Ruthie and I decided the Super 8 was plunging us into financial doom. We drove home and found a sheriff's car eased up in front of our house with one wheel hung up over the curbstone. The deputy inside was sound asleep and likely posted to an empty house for the last forty-eight hours. I pounded on his window, and we introduced ourselves. No, he hadn't known we weren't home, he confessed. Ruthie brought out strong coffee for him in an old thermos.

She kept waking me up, wanting me to check that his cruiser was still out there, he was awake, and the front door still locked.

"And how much is this all costing?" she asked, peering

out the lead-filled window at the deputy's car the next morning.

"They won't keep him out there forever, I don't think," I answered.

"Then I want to learn to shoot that Marlin," she insisted.

"You can't. You're pregnant."

"I'm going to check and see if that's true," she insisted. "I'm not going to just lie around here in total fear after that deputy leaves, Ret. Women have babies in war zones, and that's what I feel we're living in right now."

"Dr. Welch isn't going to like it. You have to stand up to learn to shoot. No way. You can't do that."

"I'm not going to live in total fear. I'll just have to sit down a lot between standing up."

"What about the noise, Ruthie? That can't be good for a baby!"

I didn't like the idea at all. Back and forth we went until she called Dr. Welch and simply asked without giving very much information. Unfortunately, Dr. Welch turned out to be an avid hunter and not as unsupportive as I thought she'd be. She said the baby couldn't hear too well yet, and the amniotic fluid would cushion the noise. The lead fumes should be mentioned, she added, but was probably of minimal risk. As to Ruthie's spotting, she knew she was very bored, still wanted her on her back or seated as often as possible, and "moderate sport shooting was fine" provided there wasn't much walking involved, and she shot no more than an hour.

We thought our efforts to train ourselves on Arnold's Marlin would work best at a genuine shooting range. There was a big one out near Rattlesnake Hills, and about thrity-five people were already there blasting away the first time we went there.

After I'd shot a few times and walked down to get my target, the manager met us both at our assigned shooting booth.

"You may have noticed," he said, "that people are shooting guns here, sir."

"Of course," I answered with the same formal tone.

"I, for one, am very glad all of them stopped shooting their guns, so you could go out and get your target. Did you get hold of your target all right, sir?"

I nodded wordlessly. Ruthie raised her eyebrows and turned beet red.

He pointed to a conspicuous yellow rope above our heads. "Up here is a rope attached to a pulley. If you pull on this rope, you can get your target more safely."

"Oh," I noticed.

"Please do us all a favor," he concluded. "Stay off the range!"

With that, he turned and stomped away, shaking his head.

We didn't stay off the range and by our third visit Ruthie was a better shot than me, although I'd gotten to be pretty good. We probably talked about Ce Ce's kidnapping more while we were shooting than sitting down drinking tea.

"What happened to that Brenda Oakley?" she asked me.

"Out of the picture. On paid administrative leave. The state doesn't fire people too easily."

"What about Tessa?"

"Leila got her over Skype and told her the basics. She can't come home. She's in the middle of AIT for military police certification. Her CO might give her some kind of hardship leave if Ce Ce isn't located by the end of the program."

"God, that's awful."

"The military doesn't recognize extended family connections. There's no military policy that gives her any sort of out."

"Ret, what if they deploy her?"

I took a bead on number five in a blue ball at the

bottom center. "Like Lori Piestewa?"

She gently pushed the barrel down before I clicked the safety off.

"Set it down for a second please. It's so *loud*! I don't really like it that much, Ret, even if I'm good at it. Now Lori who?"

"Lori Piestewa. She was a Hopi woman; she came from a beautiful and spiritual people. She left her four-year old son and three-year-old daughter with her folks out in Tuba City, Arizona, because she needed the money. Lori was the first Native American woman to die in U.S. combat and a single mom like Tessa. She was also the first woman to die in combat in Iraq. She almost succeeded in saving her team by racing her Humvee around an ambush but an RPG caught her.

"Most folks remember her teammate more, Jessica Lynch; she got rescued. She happened to be white and also survived the ordeal, so she got the media attention. But Jessica called Lori the real hero."

Ruthie shook her head. "Let's pray Tessa doesn't have to go. I guess I'm glad she's not able to come home—she'd try to chase Jack Brie down herself. Do you believe he's left the state?"

"No, Ruthie. I wish I could say so, but he's not far away. I don't think he'll come near us now, and I also don't think he'd hurt Ce Ce. He may be a sociopath, but he's also a narcissist. Hurting his own little girl would be a blow to his ego. Jack Brie wants Ruzga's money. He'll be single-minded about that."

Ruthie nodded. "Elisi said Tina's the one to watch. She thinks she wants Ruzga's money, too, and knows more than she's saying."

Trusting what Franklin said about Ce Ce's dream, Elisi said, meant going to Signal Peak to see if we could learn anything about Jack Brie or her whereabouts. I knew how devastated she was and hadn't been out that way anyway. She rode along mostly staring out the window of Frank's Tundra FFE while he drove us. We'd already retrieved her car from the orchard hiding place and taken it to her home a few days earlier, but the Tundra had four-wheel drive. We didn't see anyone following us although we knew law enforcement and maybe even other people might be keeping an eye on us. Elisi had been understandably more prickly lately.

"Frank, how'd you afford a fancy truck like this?" she asked. "As far as I know, you got a government pension and your monthly per capita, which can't be more than twelve hundred a month together. There hasn't been much work since the housing crash killed the logging mill. As far as I can tell, there's only seasonal work with Yakama forestry or pulling salmon at the fisheries. I don't know you to play the casino."

"I bought this truck used seven years ago and treat it like a baby," he said. "I had a little bit of money from Aida's life insurance. As to my month-to-month," he glanced sideways at Elisi, "if you think I do anything below boards—"

She waved her hand. "That isn't it, Frank. I know better than most how things were for you back on council— other folks around here do too. I wasn't implying anything."

Frank stared ahead at the road for a moment. "Sorry, sis."

Frank was not related by blood to Elisi but sometimes called her 'sis' or *nána* anyway. "I'm sensitive on that, I suppose. I don't make much more than what you say, maybe some less. I never been afraid to work my garden or take what I need hunting and fishing. I make up a good salmon jerky, and when I can get a cooler full of fish, I drive into Toppenish and set up out in the parking lot at Safeway's."

"Ah," she nodded. "They may not like you bringing in wild caught salmon for two dollars a pound, I take it."

"Not when they figure it out."

Elisi's eyes scanned across the pale green, unfenced range by the road.

"Leila got news last night that Tessa's coming home

on hardship leave this weekend," she said.

"How'd she get permission?" I asked.

"I don't know. She won't talk, won't say much about it. I'm about dead with worry about her," she admitted. "I'll have to keep her away from Tina."

"She's going to try to chase that *chilwit wapsúx*," said Frank.

We were all on edge and didn't talk much while we climbed slowly, moving leisurely back and forth over rising switchbacks. I was grateful for the road's smooth, winding contour given our mood. Small trees and brush gradually gave way to conifers and huge ridges jutting up at every side, hovering over wide meadows filled with tall grasses.

We rounded a sharp curve and stopped to watch two *k'úsi* dance off into the scrub, one dark and ruddy, the other, a paint of brown and white. Soon the whole herd was visible, lounging and grazing in distant grasses.

There hadn't been another car, house, or any sign of human habitation for over an hour.

"Coming on toward Jacob's," Frank said.

"Who's that?" I asked.

"Yakama man working the gate," answered Elisi.

An old yellow dog with matted fur padded toward us from the low porch of a cabin set slightly off the road. A sliding door opened and out bounded a smiling young man with long braids. Elisi, Frank, and Jacob visited; she introduced me, and we exchanged a few platitudes. He moved over to a steel cross beam and swung it away from the road, waving us through.

"You're now in a place not too many outsiders ever been," Frank declared. "At least not since we claimed this land after a surveyor's error turned out in our favor back in the 1960s. This is what we call the 'closed area'—non-tribal members by permit only."

"Do I have a permit?"

"No," Elisi answered more sharply than she likely

meant. "And I don't need some tribal bureaucrat shoving down my throat some inherited federal governmental process for taking my friends where I've been going since I was a baby."

She looked out the window.

"Just don't try coming out here on your own," she added.

"What would happen?" I wondered.

"Wouldn't be good," was all Frank would say.

The road was gravel from there on out.

"Please tell me about this place, *kála*," I requested. I wanted to learn, and I also wanted to try to keep her talking instead of brooding about Ce Ce.

"Well, I told you about *kluní* and *Páchi'analá*," she said. "This place is sacred. Like a lot of Yakama people, Frank and I been coming around here since we were kids. There's a fire lookout way up top, maybe a little snow. Some place at the foot of the mountain along Klickitat River's called 'Parrott Crossing' in the borrowed language. Old mother Parrott used to brag to my *kála* about seeing Indians hung when she was little like that was some great thing."

"How'd your *kála* respond?" asked Frank.

"Oh, she wouldn't say anything. Dying by hanging was thought to mean your spirit couldn't leave your body but would stay trapped inside. If an Indian was to be hung for something, they'd beg the authorities to kill them in any other way they liked. But they'd not get their wish granted, would they? Just another grief our communities carry. Shut down your broken heart and carry it is what I mean. The boarding schools taught the native children of that time not to know their own hearts."

She laughed a little, distracted by worry, perhaps to shake off what she felt.

"We got fire spotters come to live up here when it gets real dry," she said, changing the subject.

"UFO sightings back in the seventies," said Frank.

"Really?" I asked.

"Hundreds of sightings, doctor," Elisi echoed.

"You don't," I looked at them both skeptically, "believe in UFOs, do you?"

"Believe in what I seen?" she answered as we steered around potholes. "I don't know, do you believe in what you've seen?"

"You're saying you've seen UFOs around here . . ."

Both Elisi and Frank nodded.

"Unlimited Family-making Opportunities," said Frank, and they both laughed.

Elisi tried to clarify: "Frank's being polite, doctor. The joke usually goes to Unlimited Fornicating or maybe something more inappropriate."

"But what the doctor likely means is strange lights zippin' around the sky, right?" asked Frank.

"Yeah," I responded, certain I was being teased.

"Plenty of those out here, too."

"And so when you ask me do I believe in those kind of UFOs," Elisi continued more sincerely, "I say I believe in what I see and in what I know in my heart."

"And so are UFOs a modern version of stick people? I've heard talk before about them."

"Stick people don't have anything at all to do with UFOs and flyin' lights. No, they're part of the land here. They've always been here. And, yes, they get spotted sometimes too."

"Come on. You're still teasing me."

The terrain around us became even more remote. Frank's Tundra slogged up and down a couple of times violently in response to rough terrain. The scrub trees were getting larger, punctuated by sage meadows and grass.

"Catch this two-track," Elisi told Frank.

"Looks like a logging trail," I said, trying to sound outdoorsy.

"Hah," she laughed mildly. "This trail's always been

here. Aren't any logging trails for tiny trees like these, doctor."

We hit a big bump so hard I thought we might crack Frank's oil pan.

"Stick people made the trails up here, doctor," Frank added.

I laughed somewhat uncomfortably.

"I wish you'd quit being a dummy, doctor," Elisi chided as Frank hit another smaller bump and jostled the two of us. "You're all skeptical and whatever, think your big degree allows you to say what is and what isn't. Europeans forgot all the kinds of relatives they had. There's been many relatives across thousands of years we humans have been aware and conscious of our surroundings. Consider yourself blind to what we're talking about."

"I'm very sorry," I said.

"Should be. Now shush and listen. Back at the time of Creation, elders tell of two sisters, the *Tat'tat'liya*, who were created as a kind of beginning human being. They had very big appetites. Maybe there's leftovers of them among the disordered society still alive—all stuck in greed and such. These two sisters were in danger of eating all the animals because they couldn't stop feeding themselves. *Spilyáy*, our name for Coyote, come to them and told them to have *tm'áakni*, respect, for the animals they were eating up. He told them other people were coming, and they should stop eating all the animals. Those sisters were scared of *Spilyáy*, so they decided to move down to *Nich'i'wana* to eat fish instead. But they died of starvation on the way there, which is good, because they left our people all the fish!"

Frank and I both laughed.

"Our people made a little shrine of stones to *Tat'tat'liya* back in the forest up there. I been to it when I was little. Anyway, stick people were a kind of people the Creator made before us. They're smaller."

"You've seen them."

"Well, they're very fast and difficult to see, doctor," said Frank.

We hit a big bump.

"Hey, Frank! Hurts my back when you keep doing that," Elisi complained. "Slow down."

He ignored her and spoke to me. "Just because you can't see somebody, doctor, doesn't mean they're not there. You've had some experiences here you didn't expect."

Our ascent became sharper up the two-track, and I really didn't think even Frank's sturdy pickup would make it. A big thunderhead came into view up ahead of us, and I began to think twice about going much further.

"It looks like rain," I said with some trepidation .

"You won't wilt," said Elisi. "This track runs out in just a minute. And there's something up there don't look like mist so much as smoke. Let's pull up here, Frank."

I didn't like where we were very much. There's remote nature and nature and feeling remote.

"Used to pick huckleberries here with my grandma," Frank laughed. "There's bear nearby, so you have to leave some for them."

"I'm fine with them taking all the huckleberries," I said as the rain started.

At her insistence, we helped Elisi hobble about a hundred yards beyond where the two-track dwindled. She became quite winded.

All our exercise began to seem pointless. We were looking for signs of Ce Ce or Brie—but what the signs were, I had no idea.

The grey and black swirl of low clouds above us blended with mist.

"Doesn't seem like there's much here," I told them.

"Not much more than beauty, doctor."

Elisi paused and stared carefully into the distance. I followed her eyes.

"What, sis?" Frank asked and she pointed above where

we stood.

A wisp of smoke floated over several boulders about sixty yards up the slope. "Why don't you two go have a look?"

"Have a look?" I responded.

"Come on, doctor," said Frank. "Let's you and I climb up a little higher. It's too hard for sister to climb."

We struggled further upwards, slipping on wet grass and loose soil. Frank was wearing traditional cowboy boots instead of his usual Caterpillars.

"I can't go much higher, doctor. See if you can make it to where that little spot of smoke is."

It was a hard climb, but I reached some boulders clumped around a stand of short pines. A slight twinge of smoke mingled with the rain. Suddenly, a clap of thunder boomed like a cannon, and I almost fell prone.

"What am I looking for?" I shouted back down.

"Hush!" Elisi hissed loudly, shook her head, and gestured at me. "You don't know but somebody's up and around here!"

I slipped again and grabbed a handful of blackberry thorns, yelping and finally managing to lean over one of the boulders on the slope. There was nothing behind them except for a ring of rocks, and a pile of smoldering ash. I came around the corner and poked at it. Then I peered under the boulders and noticed how the indent in the ground by one of them didn't match the rest of the ground.

I poked at that, too. A rattling sound emerged from it.

That's a weird noise, I thought to myself. I'd never heard anything like it before.

I jumped, fell down backwards onto the slope, and slid down fifteen feet, wrenching my leg. "Ow! Goddamn it!"

"What's the problem, doctor?" Frank cupped his hands over his mouth to try to muffle the sound of his voice.

"Think I heard a rattlesnake."

"Best stay away from him!"

"I think I've got that much figured out!"

"Don't scare off too much! Try to go back up and look some more!" he encouraged.

There's a rattlesnake up there, I thought to myself; are you crazy?

"Just keep well back from the snake and try to get a better look, doctor," Frank said. "Somebody's been up and around here. Don't get within six feet or so—that way he can't reach you if he strikes."

I pulled myself forward, painfully, and got back up near the boulders. I grabbed a stick lying nearby. My heart pounded and bits of acrid smoke seared my eyes. Out of some strange combination of terror and curiosity, I poked the stick at the indent in the ground. I heard the rattle loud and clear but didn't jump so high. I was able to lift up a cover made of woven grass and sticks. The snake struck at the stick, and I jumped back again. Then, he sailed away smoothly underneath one of the boulders.

I looked down into the hole and saw four or five unopened cans of salmon and beer.

"A stash!" I shouted down to Frank and Elisi.

"Hush up, doctor!" Elisi snapped at me.

At that same moment, a gunshot rang out and the left tire of Frank's Tundra started to hiss. Both of us ran full speed, mostly sliding, down the steep side of the ridge. I took a tumble and Frank helped me up as the next shot ricocheted off a tree next to us.

"Aw, hell!" Frank yelled.

We fell more than ran up to Elisi and struggled quickly to get us all back into the truck. Another gunshot echoed around us, and the mirror on Frank's driver's side exploded. It was difficult to see where the shooter was firing from.

"Shit!" Frank shouted again, reaching beneath his seat, and pulling out an old, scratched-up Winchester lever-action rifle. He quickly popped out of the cab, cocking his rifle at the same moment, and then fired three shots in rapid succession towards the tree line. I knew he was firing blind, but he was trying to get the shooter to back off.

He jumped back in, threw his rifle across our laps, and dropped his shifter into reverse. His rear wheels hung up in the mud building up in the growing downpour. Behind where we were stuck was a very sharp drop of perhaps fifty feet.

"*Tamanwilá*, save us!" Elisi shouted, peering through the back window.

"Can you see where he's at?" Frank yelled at us.

"Somewhere near the edge of the ridge!" Elisi started to open the door. "We're stuck!"

"Stay inside!" I had to know. "Is it Brie??"

"No way to see! I can't back up any more!" Frank squinted through the wipers clacking back and forth.

I jumped out and grabbed clumps of grass, sage brush, sticks, and dirt, anything I could lay my hands on. Gunfire rang out, and pieces from branches just above me bounced off the top of my head. I threw the ménage I was holding beneath Frank's tires and started pushing by the rear fender while he rocked back and forth. The steep slope was just behind me, and for a moment, I thought if he succeeded in getting traction backwards, I might very well be pushed over. Suddenly, he cut loose and onto the two-track just as another shot echoed, this time knocking another branch onto the front hood.

"Good work," Frank muttered when I jumped back in, spinning his steering wheel, watching the side mirror that hadn't been shot out.

Elisi rolled down the window as we pulled forward.

"Jack Brie, we're coming back!" she screamed. "We'll never stop coming for her, *chilwit wapsúx*!!"

Frank's voice became very strained and hoarse. "Got to get back down below with a flat. If somebody tries to run us down, even on foot—they might be able to."

I spun around but didn't see anyone. The lurching, revving, and slow progress of the pickup coincided with the surging adrenaline in my veins.

After we finally hit solid pavement, Elisi remained

quiet. I asked her if she was okay, and she just shook her head. We hobbled on, trying not to ride the rim of the flat, for a mile or so to a spot where we could pull over. The sky cleared, and Frank and I stooped down together to get a look at the tire before we changed it.

"Doctor, get a look at her expression," he whispered.

We both gazed up at her. It was as though she was experiencing some sort of rapture. She'd been so sick and short of breath lately, yet she now had a rosy glow, and her eyes were wide with excitement.

"Creator's vengeance on Jack Brie," she said with enormous passion. "What a great gift, *Tamanwilá*! You're taking us right to her!"

"Sis," Frank said, trying to be supportive. "Lots of people growing weed, mixin' meth, or doing other criminal things back in these hills."

"No, Frank, it was him," she said assuredly. "We found him. And we'll get Ce Ce back."

Neither one of us had the heart to challenge her.

SEVENTEEN

Mental deficiency of the moron level
Is definitely more prevalent among children
Originating from the lower socioeconomic classes
Than among the progeny
Of the more favored sections of the community.
Idiots and imbeciles, on the other hand,
Appear to be fairly evenly distributed through all classes.
–*Paul Lemkau, Mental Hygiene in Public Health, 1949*

Early the following morning, I filled Ruthie in on what had happened out at Signal Peak. She was not happy.

"You are not, repeat, not to go out there again!" she said to me with a searing look. "I am tired of you so freely moving toward risk and danger. What are you, some sort of adrenalin junkie?? Stop trying to get yourself killed, Ret! You are *going* to live to be a father, no matter how frightening the prospect may be!"

All she said felt accurate to me, and I had sufficient common sense to not disagree in any case. We were sitting on the front porch drinking herbal tea, she very plump in a recliner, and me in an old wicker chair we bought second hand.

Beyond the weight she'd gained, Ruthie looked physically stronger than I'd ever seen her. The phone extension rang, and she passed it to me. Elisi said Tessa was back home on leave and wanted to stop by our place and talk to us both.

An hour or so later, she jumped out of Leila's pickup in field fatigues with her hair pulled back tight. She looked like a soldier.

"I already know Brie is back around, so don't either one of you try to bullshit me," she said walking up. She hadn't even said hello. "He's got my sis, and I've only got three days to find her."

"What are you planning?" asked Ruthie without hesitation.

"I've got to find her . . ." She bit back tears.

"No, Tessa . . ." Ruthie responded.

"I'm full trained now. I been dealing with Jack Brie since I was seven years old. I can't be off trying to become an MP and do what I'm doing with this thing going on with Ce Ce. I almost went crazy after I heard at AIT. The instructors said I lacked focus. I'll get Ce Ce back before my leave's up, or I'll end up booted out anyway from worry."

"You kill Brie, Tessa, you'll be in military prison, not MP school," I said.

She shook her head. She had no more words. She sat down in a corner chair on our front porch and held a half full Gatorade bottle loosely in both her hands.

"Not if you write a letter for me and say I've gone temporarily mental from the stress."

"Tessa," I tried again, "the Sheriff's done four search and rescue parties across Lower and Upper Valley in the two weeks she's been gone. They focused especially on Signal Peak. They haven't found a trace. Brie knows where to hide. You won't find him either. I don't believe he's going to hurt your sister. He'll get dumb and go looking for his money, and he'll do it soon."

"Yeah, well, that's funny coming from you, Barlow, and what I hear's been going on. And *káła* says you and Frank already found him out somewhere around Signal Peak."

"If we did, he's long gone. We got shot at. There's shady business back there, and the whole area is vast. If you go out looking for him, Tessa, the law is going to notice. We're all being watched, count on it. And we're pretty sure it's not just cops. Don't get picked up while you're on leave."

"Don't do it, Tess," Ruthie repeated. "Please."

"And Tessa," I added, "you know I'm not about to write a letter saying somebody's crazy for being terribly worried about her kidnapped sister . . ."

Tessa stood up quickly and threw her Gatorade bottle against the porch brick wall. Then she sat and put her head in her hands. Her voice was broken with desperation.

"I can't stand it!!"

She began weeping with such anguish that Ruthie struggled to her feet and came and put her arms around her.

"He raped me," Tessa muttered, out of the blue.

"Who?" asked Ruthie, shooting me a concerned look. "Who raped you, Tessa?"

"She's talking about Brie," I said when she didn't answer right away. I really should've known much better than to say anything at all.

"No!" Tessa yelled, then sat upright slowly, looking back and forth between each of us. "Not Brie! That's not who I'm talking about. My squad leader! He raped me. And everybody on my team knows it!!"

With this, she broke free from Ruthie's extended arms, leaped from the porch, and flew off in Leila's pickup.

Leila called a few hours later saying she was stranded and couldn't get to work at Mel's, and wanting to know where Tessa went with her pickup. Chase had only seen her mom for about an hour after Leila picked her up from the bus station and was crying for her. Tessa said she'd only be away while Chase was at Head Start; now she was nowhere to be found.

Three days later, she was officially AWOL—the military police stopped by Larena Lane looking for her. Leila reported her as a missing person to the Yakima County Sheriff and the state police.

Darkness fell more deeply on the family. Tessa was now gone, and there was still no news on Ce Ce.

Ruthie and I shared everyone's general sentiment that

Tessa was going to try to hunt down Jack Brie and rescue her baby sister. We decided to express that concern to Agent Alston and Detective Jacinto, who assured us they sympathized with her motivations, but would have to do their best to try to stop her. They said a four-state manhunt for Brie had intensified, and Maritza Rios had become a suspect in Enrico Astorgia's, aka Hector's, murder for reasons we weren't allowed to know.

Ce Ce's picture and profile was entered into a national database of missing children, offering regular alerts to law enforcement agencies regarding both her and Brie. Officers stopped in and re-interviewed everybody periodically. Ruthie and I got re-interviewed twice.

My psychology practice was dead. I'd either referred clients on or they'd quit in irritation due to my frequent cancellations. You can only get away with 'family emergency' excuses for so long. Frank and I met for coffee from time to time, and I even tried to refer him on to someone else. He said he'd talk to me or nobody. He was still dealing with nightmares about burning houses. I refused to accept money from him and wouldn't let him buy my coffee. My professional role with him was obscured. Even so, I tried to stay helpful.

Ruthie and I were living on savings. I was damned if I'd do anything about finding a job, but I finally went down to the unemployment office and came back gratified to learn I'd qualified for half benefits and food stamps. Let the tea partiers eat cake, I told her. On the plus side, I started losing weight, running three miles nearly every day, and took to pounding the old bag I'd hung up in the garage.

Thinking about all that had happened, one evening I kicked the bag so hard it fell off the rafter.

Two more weeks passed. Ruthie still had to stay on her back on the couch, and I paid short visits to Leila and the kids. Elisi and Frank were stopping in, too. The pain and fear of Ce Ce's kidnapping scabbed over for short durations, became numbness, and then reemerged in quiet tears, especially for all the kids. The entire Myanashatawit family became locked into a kind of abiding despair.

I blamed the state child welfare system, not the people working in it. Even Brenda Oakley was a byproduct of the system's socialized arrogance and rigidity—how many Indian kids had I known to be returned to their abusers, native or non-native? How many had been pulled away from relations who clearly loved them—their siblings, grandparents, aunts, and uncles—floated across multiple placements, repeatedly subjected to new schools, continually rejected by new peers, trying to keep their spirits up, hoping someday to go back home, calling grandmothers in the middle of the night from hundreds of miles away?

"It's the disordered society," said Elisi.

Samuel suffered the most, and I thought I knew why. He carried a kind of 'survivor's guilt' in relation to Ce Ce. Although he was younger than her, he certainly wished he'd gone outside with her and been taken in her place or at least along with her, so he could try to keep her safe.

"I try to get him to talk about how he's feeling; he just says 'auntie, leave me alone' and walks away," Leila announced to us, sitting in our living room. "That's true of all of them. What they're doing right now is exactly what they do at home."

Samuel sat playing a game app on Leila's cell phone by the front window. Franklin had his head leaned back and listened to an ipod, a black patch over his bad eye. Emily read a magazine. Eloise beaded a project Elisi had given her.

No one would talk. Everyone was waiting.

One Wednesday, the mail brought notice that my psychology ethics board hearing was ten days away. This increased my output on the garage punching bag. After we had finished up eating, Ruthie and I took a drive down to Larena Lane.

"Are you sure you should travel at all?"

"Ret, it's twenty-five minutes—five minutes longer than it takes to get to Dr. Welch's. I can lie on Leila's couch just as easily as I lie on ours."

She was now extremely bored with staying at home on her back, and I went along with her wishes.

We'd only been there fifteen minutes. Leila took a cell phone call in her bedroom.

"Tessa's been found," she announced flatly, walking back out. "She's okay. She's in jail."

A sigh of relief moved through the room. Leila shook her head a little, and then her face folded inward as she lifted her hands to cover her eyes. She shook her head again quietly, and we all kind of watched her standing there for a second or two.

"Really?!" Franklin, pulled his ear buds out. "She all right?"

"She'd been camped back near logging trails along Klickitat River. I don't know how she took care of herself. God knows, she might've died of exposure. How'd she even eat?"

"What jail?" Ruthie asked.

"Klickitat County. She's gets handed over to the MPs tomorrow. They let me talk to her for a minute," Leila sat down. "She's got some attorney who's going to help her file assault charges against her squad leader. She says that's the main reason she went AWOL, but then once she made the decision, she made up her mind she was going to find Ce Ce no matter what."

"I want to say thanks," said Eloise, and Elisi seemed to catch her meaning.

"Well then, you go ahead, young one, and lead us in your good words," she answered.

This felt very premature to me—Ce Ce was still gone, Tessa now under arrest. I looked across the room at the patch over Franklin's eye, feeling like nothing had really changed except for finding Tessa.

"It's the first good thing that's happened," said Eloise as if responding to my thoughts.

Nonetheless, the forming of a circle of hands in response to her suggestion was very tentative—Elisi reached for Eloise's hand first and then Ruthie's hand where she lay on the couch. Ruthie's other hand came up into mine where I stood behind the couch, and it was then that I became aware of a kind of quiet longing.

I reached over toward Emily sitting at the end of the couch, and she took her book off her lap and set it down. There were tears in her eyes, and the grip of her hand was very light. Franklin's face mixed false toughness and awkwardness, but he left where he was sitting to sit on a plastic kiddy chair and reach Frank's proffered hand. Samuel was not willing to join us until Franklin raised his hand and nodded knowingly at him. I think Samuel took hold of Frank's other hand out of respect more than anything.

Chase bounded into the room holding Tessa's Pup. Leila coaxed her in with us, the circle closed, all hands were now being held.

"Your mommy's been found, Chase."

"Mommy's found?" Chase gazed questioningly at the rest of us.

"Eloise wants to lead us in giving thanks," Emily explained.

"But what about Ce Ce?" asked Chase.

"We'll pray for her too."

We waited. I became worried for a moment that Eloise might be too intellectually challenged to form a prayer.

"*Tamanwiłá*," she began. "I am a lowly child . . ."

And Ruthie and I caught each other's eyes bearing witness to that.

"I love my big sister, Tessa, *Tamanwiłá*, but she's got herself in trouble again. You kept her safe, and I thank You. I know You're everywhere and keep watch."

There was a pause. I thought she'd lost her train of thought. I glanced up and saw Eloise was surveying this big circle she'd created with her family. She appeared stunned— as if really seeing it for the very first time.

"We're very happy You pulled her away from the darkness and got her safe now. I always knew You would. Thank You, *Tamanwiłá*—because we got nobody to turn to except You now."

"But now . . . now, we still need to find our little Ce Ce. Oh," Eloise's tone fell, "we been looking so long for her but You can see everyone and everything. We can't stand all this no more. We all been so scared all the time. So show us where she is. Please, please keep her safe and help our family."

"I know You will," Eloise became teary. "I just know that already. Thank You, *Tamanwiłá*."

Ruthie was at thirty-eight weeks, and Dr. Welch was encouraging us to induce labor. Linda, her stalwart midwife, opposed this idea out of hand, and Ruthie lay on her back, listening to her verbally bearing down. I haven't mentioned that Linda is a rather huge woman, but Ruthie had become almost as big as her.

"Dr. Welch is always in a hurry. Hell, wait a couple more weeks."

"I'm starting to get all this zapping in my legs."

"That's just baby touching a few nerves."

"I'm so damned big. I can't sleep."

"A little while," Linda looked at me. "Dad you better stay close to home."

I paid the rent in Harrah and snuck out there to get the mail from time to time, which would have infuriated Ruthie. The youth center I'd volunteered at was less than a mile away, and they decided they needed me to do some overflow crisis counseling.

On off days, I went down to Larena Lane to hang out

with Frank and Franklin for no more than an hour or so. I kept to that strictly, given Linda's advice.

"Why don't you want to go hunting?" I asked Franklin point blank.

"I used to go hunt with *tila* every now and then, but I'm not like some kids who done it all their lives. I shot a pistol but never a rifle. Besides, the doctors told me I got no deep field no more."

"Huh?" said Frank.

"Depth of field?" I asked.

"Yeah, that's it. With my one eye, that's what they said."

I was a little irritated. "I love docs who make summary statements like that and don't think about how somebody might interpret it. I'm not saying it isn't true, Franklin, but one-eyed people still drive. Maybe you have less peripheral vision, but that shouldn't affect your ability to aim and shoot."

"I thought I'd just end up following people around if I went along."

"Isn't that way—that's what the doctor's saying, Franklin," Frank reiterated.

"Hmm," Franklin thought for a moment. "I could hunt?"

"Yeah," said Frank. "You could."

"General discharge," Tessa murmured to Elisi, Leila, and me on the drive back from the Yakima Bus Station, where she'd been dropped off by her attorney. "That's the price I have to pay. 'Under honorable conditions' isn't the same as an honorable discharge."

"Well, you avoided a full court martial," I offered gently.

"But I get no GI Bill and no financial support for school. . ."

"Still, you put that squad leader on notice," Leila affirmed. "Maybe he'll think twice from this point on."

"I doubt it," said Tessa.

"Any woman does that," Elisi added, "stands up to some big man trying to force himself on her—is a warrior among our people as far as I'm concerned."

Tessa looked over at her adopted grandmother who stared straight ahead out the front windshield.

"Thanks, *kála.*"

"All I want for you," Elisi responded, "is to get onto healing up. Our women been coping with assault and predation for two hundred years around here, almost all of it from outside our community. Now's a time to purify your spirit and come back home from all you been through."

"I'll be able to heal up, *kála*, when I know Ce Ce is home and safe, and Jack Brie is dead."

"I understand how you feel," said Elisi. "I know the hatred too, but it's not our way. Let the law go after him, *kála*. Leave all that alone."

We pulled into Leila's driveway on Larena Lane to a remarkable sight. Frank and Franklin stood almost at attention next to Frank's truck. Franklin had one foot on the bumper and was resting Frank's rifle across his knee. He saw us coming and was posing. His black patch covered his bad eye, but the other smiled. His face was lit up.

In the back of the truck lay a dead elk.

"Full three-eight," Frank smiled in his grimaced way while we climbed out of the Sunrise. "Full three-eight and first time out from about a hundred yards. Shot him with my old Winchester .308. I could never even have spotted such a bull when I was his age. Seems that good eye's working fine. There's a forty-three inch spread at the beams."

Frank wasn't just trying to build Franklin up.

I had no idea what Frank meant by all the specs he cited, but I knew what it meant to shoot at a moving target, especially with one eye.

"It ain't for sport, Barlow," Franklin declared. There was purpose in his voice. "I got this bull 'cause he looked right at me and said I could take him home."

"That's right," Elisi responded. "That's our way. When the male elk, which we call *wáwyukya* or the deer, which we call *yamesh*, look toward the hunter, they are surrendering their spirit to feed us. We take no delight in killing, but it is very good for you to provide food for those who are in need."

She peered directly into Franklin's eye. "You have come such a long ways, *kála*. I've watched you do that. Now you're a hunter, and you can provide for our community. I think you are a man, and we can count on you. You are no longer a child."

She looked at Frank. "It'd be time to get him a First Kill ceremony."

Her words seemed to resonate through Franklin's entire being. Frank nodded back in agreement.

My ethics hearing came on Thursday, November 3rd at 4 p.m. Normally, I would have had to go to Olympia, but I explained our pregnancy predicament, and it so happened that members of the ethics committee would be at a general licensing board hearing in Yakima that month. They agreed to have my hearing in town in an office building nearby the Superior Court. I was informed my 'accuser,' Dr. Margaret Fitzsimmons, would attend the hearing personally.

At the appointed hour on the designated day, and together with Francis Munoz, JD, I entered the conference room in a pretty bad mood. The room looked like any other I'd ever seen but with a particularly expensive table, long and narrow, custom-built mahogany, and even having a carved edge all the way around it. I was afraid to set my paper latte cup on it. I was sure that would be the first *faux pas* of many I'd soon make.

"That's okay, doctor," said a pleasant young Asian woman at the head of the table as I flinched slightly. "It won't hurt the finish . . ."

Three psychologists, all men, and two lay members of

the board, both women, sat at one end, looking neat and prim. Margaret sat across from us, also looking well-groomed. I'd slept with a very pregnant woman who rolled, groaned, and re-situated herself throughout the prior night, and wore a shirt I hadn't ironed from the day before. Moreover, I'd dripped tiny droplets of espresso in a wide pattern down the front.

The hearing began with a reading of the complaint. The Asian woman took care of this, and it was word-for-word from Margaret's letter to the ethics board. She alleged I'd interfered with another 'mental health provider,' to wit, her, in her efforts to medicate Franklin. At the tail end of her complaint, she said that I'd violated the 'do no harm' clause of my own ethical code by encouraging Franklin to go off his meds.

Munoz earned the $500 he'd milked me for and then some within the first five minutes of his interrogation of Margaret. I'd given him all the research I had on akasthesia and SSRI-induced violence, and he got interested in the topic and did some more investigating of his own.

He pulled out excerpts from the trial transcript in the Wyoming lawsuit and made Margaret read the expert testimony aloud for everyone. I particularly enjoyed it when he then had her read the side effects insert from the medication she'd prescribed from the Physician's Desk Reference.

The Asian woman got a little impatient with all this and said "this isn't a court hearing," but Munoz said he was almost done, and "Dr. Barlow deserves due process in an ethics hearing bearing upon his credibility and reputation."

Margaret picked up the issue of a journal Munoz had handed her.

"Before you begin reading, could you just tell us the name of this particular journal, Dr. Fitzsimmons?"

"The Journal of American Physicians and Surgeons," she answered reluctantly.

"And the title and author please . . ."

"Uh, 'Selective Serotonin Reuptake Inhibitors: More

Risks, than Benefits?' It's by Dr. Joel Kaufman, whoever he is."

"Dr. Kaufman's credentials are listed at the end and highlighted for you. Please do read them to us, doctor, so we can assess whether he seems qualified to render an opinion."

Margaret shuffled through several pages in irritation and found the little blurb.

"Professor emeritus in chemistry at the University of Sciences in Philadelphia."

"Very good. And lastly, the date of this publication."

"Spring, 2009."

"Great. Now could you please read to us the highlighted portion in the discussion section of this review article? Go ahead, then, doctor. Just the highlighted portion please."

Margaret looked as though she'd just been fed vinegar. "Adverse effects, mostly dose-dependent, will appear in up to 75% of patients on normal doses. Of these, studies suggest that suicidality will be observed in an additional two to thirteen percent of patients on normal doses, beyond what is seen on placebo or many non-SSRI antidepressant drugs. This is sufficiently frequent that a typical prescribing physician should observe examples in routine practice."

"Do continue, Dr. Fitzsimmons. "

Margaret now looked as though she'd swallowed a cat. I thought for a moment she was going to spit up a hairball.

"Dr. Fitzsimmons," the Asian woman encouraged. "Please read what's been requested, so we can finish our business here."

Margaret swallowed hard. "Available data suggest that actual murders may be committed at about the rate of 250 per 100,000 SSRI-treated patients beyond what is seen on placebo or many non-SSRI antidepressant drugs, and that many more murders will be attempted on normal doses as well."

"I see," Munoz remarked, "does it seem this review article links the drugs you prescribed to Franklin to a potential for violence, Dr. Fitzsimmons?"

"Perhaps."

"Perhaps, then," Munoz turned to the ethic board members. "it seems by Dr. Fitzsimmons' own admission that my client, Dr. Barlow, was trying to do her a favor in alerting medical staff at Provincial to the possibility that Franklin's violent behavior might be linked to the drugs she'd prescribed."

Margaret seemed to be literally biting her tongue. I was asked to review my approach to working with American Indian clients. At one point, Don Helbert, an academic, chimed in.

"Now Dr. Barlow, how well do these techniques you describe work with an American Indian of borderline IQ?"

Don could get away with a racist question like that although the Asian lady rolled her eyes. I looked at Munoz, who shrugged slightly.

"Well, Dr. Helbert, I did have the finer points of salmon fishing on the Columbia explained to me by an elderly Yakama fisherman after I started working at Yakama Nation. But if you got me out on the river, I'd be pretty helpless to catch a fish. I'm deficient in Indian IQ."

He got red in the face at this and interrupted, "That's not what I mean, Dr. Barlow. I'm trying to . . ."

The young Asian woman looked at her watch and held up her hand. "We are truly out of time and need to move on."

We were all invited to leave the room. I sat across from Margaret in the waiting area with her eyes spitting bullets at me. Dr. Helbert came and brought us back in.

The Asian woman made the call.

"The board has deliberated and finds no grounds for the ethics complaint made by Dr. Margaret Fitzsimmons against Dr. Return Barlow. Our findings are entered into the minutes, and Dr. Barlow, you can be assured there will be no mention of the complaint or this hearing placed upon your licensure record."

I shook Munoz's hand, thanked the board, and got up and left. I didn't even look at Margaret.

The daylight hours were shortening, and the parking lot was as "dark as the inside of a cow," to use a phrase Frank Mathis once shared with me. The two streetlamps nearby did not appear to be working. Margaret popped up next to me while I lit a smoke.

"Lucky, Barlow."

"Margaret!" I jumped, almost tripping over her mukluk boots. "You scared the hell out of me. I thought you were somebody trying to mug me."

A figure immediately jumped from behind the car next to her, grabbed her by the hair, covered her mouth, and pulled her backwards into the shadows. I would've been shocked but somebody grabbed my hair the same way and covered my mouth. I got hold of his collar for a moment and tried to elbow him, but he had me in a choke position. He was way too strong.

A cargo van shot up next to us, my head was slammed into the door before it opened. That hurt a lot and stunned me. I remained aware the two of us were being thrown in together. The zip of duct tape sounded out next to my ear and then pulled tight across my mouth and my eyes. They even wrapped my hair, and I knew it was going to hurt like hell getting that stuff off. I had little time to ponder this before a sock filled with bb's or something similar put a loud, painful ringing in my left ear.

I saw the Milky Way and set my thrusters for Alpha Centauri, which I understand is the closest system to us.

EIGHTEEN

Lightening is the honey of all beings
And all beings are honey for the lightening.
—*Bridadäranyaka Upanishad, IIv:8*

They ripped the duct tape off my mouth, and my lips
and cheeks sang with pain. It was completely dark around me.
I could hear Margaret whimpering.

"Let her go, she's got nothing to do with me," I slurred
into blackness when I could effectively mouth words.

RIP! The duct tape around my head was removed. I
can't really describe the hurt. I tasted blood on my lips. A
hand shot out beneath a really bright light, holding up a tangle
of duct tape covered with my hair, including some from my
eyebrows.

"Where's the money?"

"There's thirty bucks in my wallet."

A fist like a sledge hammer hit my neck and then my
abdomen. I retched and nearly vomited. The glare from the
bright light behind the guy with the fist made any other
features of the room obscure. I was in a lot of pain. His speech
was street-inflected with an edge of sadistic pleasure.

"Dat's black hand, doc. Some fun for me, less for you.
Thirty bucks is not the money I want."

"I don't know about your money, Ruzga." Again, the
black-gloved hand folded up and pummeled me in the same
places.

"Don't ever say my name; it pisses me off, you doin'
that. I jes don't want to do more damage than I gots to do."

"Honest to God, I don't have your money."

"Let's try the lady friend then."

"Talk to me instead!"

"But you talk too slow."

He lifted Margaret to her feet. I sat in a chair looking up at her taped-up face. She squealed in a muffled way through her duct-taped head. He took out a very sharp hunting knife.

"No worries, bro. I'm gonna scare her jes a bit. Then you tell us where de cash is, and the bitch won't get hurt for reals, understand?"

"I don't know where your money is!"

He shoved her around like a sack of potatoes, hoisting her nearer to the table. He cut the duct tape off her wrists, and smacked her hard in the head when she tried to resist. She moaned and squealed while he tugged one of her hands hard and out in front of him.

He was incredibly strong. Margaret became a rag doll. There wasn't much fight in her—she retreated inwardly as most of us must do under such dire circumstances.

He spread her fingers out onto the table I was sitting by and forced her to lean further forward, which was easy given how bound up she was and how passive she'd become.

Then he pulled a small ballpeen hammer from his back pocket and started tapping around her hand with the hammer.

"This is a little game we play . . ." he murmured with a light tap, tap, tap.

"Let me play instead," I said.

He ignored me. "This game's called 'Breaky-Fingers', citizen."

He suddenly started pounding the hammer very hard on the table, just missing her fingers. She could feel the wind of his near-misses, the thud by her vulnerable fingers, and tried to pull her hand back. But she couldn't.

"Where's the money?"

She moaned with her mouth taped shut; the question was obviously for me.

"I don't know! And she doesn't know anything at all!

Let me play instead."

"You say so," he exclaimed, flinging Margaret backwards and onto the floor. She practically bounced. I wasn't sure she remained conscious, he threw her down so hard.

He sliced through the duct tape and freed my wrists. I wrangled with him and became harder for him to deal with. Another figure stepped into the light—I couldn't see who—and grabbed me around the neck from the rear. Together, they pushed me forward, leaning me toward the table.

Bang! Bang! Bang! The hammer sounded around my spread-apart fingers. BANG!

"Where's the money, doc?"

"I don't know about your money!"

THUD! The hammer just missed my thumb.

"I like to just miss. But I get tired at this game, doc. I could have an accident." His sadistic pleasure began to shine.

"Fuck you, Ruzga," I said for no particularly wise reason.

THUD! I could actually feel my index finger crack, shooting unbelievably sharp pain all the way up my arm that exploded out through the top of my head. My head seemed to spring off the top of my neck with the electricity of it. I guess I fainted dead away. I felt hands lower me to the ground.

Cold water splashed my face.

"Wake up, pussy," Ruzga said. "Just your finger. It don't hardly hurt."

I tried to catch my breath but coughed on cigar smoke.

"That's enough," said Jack Brie.

I could see them clearly now, standing above me as I lay on the floor of some kind of barn. There were stable stalls on the other side, farm implements hanging overhead, and a dirt floor.

"Hurts, don't it, Barlow? Really a fucked-up game. We used to do that with tweakers who snitched, but it gets old. Eventually people will tell you anything you want to hear. Not reliable.

"I guess you already figured this here's Mr. Christophe Ruzga."

"Hunh." That was all I could muster.

"Don't say my name, dawg," came the gruff voice in response.

"Sorry . . . dog," said Brie. "He wants his money, Barlow. He keeps thinking I have it, but I've told him you know exactly where it is. You have it in your files, right? You were seen with those Indian folks driving up to Signal Peak. I don't think it right for his man to take potshots at you, but I do think you should at least tell him where his money is."

Christophe Ruzga was broad-shouldered and stocky. I looked at him as I tried to sit up. He'd put his big hands around my wife's neck. He had a tattoo on his neck and a gold front tooth. He might need to shave his face twice a day but definitely hadn't bothered that morning.

"I talked to a shrink like you in prison," he said. "Another pussy, if you ask me. A broke finger ain't shit."

Brie reached into his pants and what I guessed was a Smith and Wesson .44 magnum revolver. It had the big barrel and wide opening at the end. He looked at it for a moment and showed it to Ruzga, who smiled in admiration.

"Nice gun, dawg," he said.

"Thanks for that," Brie answered politely and then held it right up to my head.

"Where is this man's money?"

"What the fuck, Brie? Who do you think you're kidding?" I responded. "I don't know!!"

He pulled the hammer back. My last thoughts were of Ruthie and how she'd make it on her own with our baby. She'd need a better man, and I guess that seemed okay with me.

Brie swung the gun to his right in one motion and up to Ruzga's head, blowing his brains out.

It was god-awful loud. Blood spattered all over me and

Margaret on the floor, and she writhed and moaned as Ruzga's body toppled partially on top of her.

Brie then swung the gun back to my forehead and cocked it again. He appeared pensive and, for me, moments became hours.

"Long fucking time, isn't it?"

He laughed out loud as I kneeled before him with his pistol at my forehead.

I heard a sound and spotted Maritza Rios limping in through the barn door. Ce Ce held her hand, looking dazed and dirty. Maritza nodded slowly at me.

"Bet on the right rooster, huh, Maritza?" I said.

"Jack," she said, "don't kill him. He's got a baby on the way. He's known all around here, so is his wife, and this lady here. It'll just make much more heat for us trying to get free and clear."

He pushed the barrel hard against my head and twisted it—his face contorted in glee and hatred. He lowered the gun to my neck and held it there to try that too. Then he tapped the pistol barrel lightly on my forehead. I didn't move. The ragged scar on his neck made by Tessa's assault six years earlier seemed to bulge out toward me.

With his other hand, he brought up his cigar, took a puff, and exhaled in my face. He shook his head very slightly.

"Goddamn, she's smart!" he exclaimed suddenly. "I'll be goddamned. You know my Maritza here. She shares everything with me, don't you, *gordita*? She's a great piece of ass, and she's saying I got to think this through. Better for us if I don't take your life, she says.

"Shit, with Arnold, I just kicked over a steel drum with burning trash. I wouldn't think twice about my girlfriend here trying to stop me from doing that. But killing you she objects to and, doc, well, she makes a bit of sense; I got to give her that."

He lowered his gun and looked at me long and hard.

"Isn't it amazing what the love of a woman does to a

man? Don't think I couldn't change my mind and just kill you anyway, anytime. But I guess that'd really mix things up right now. Here she is actually helping with my impulse control, don't you think? Taking care of my future mental health. I guess I'll try to be magnaminous. Isn't that the word?"

He fumbled with grabbing my shirt and pushed me lower toward the floor.

"It's the money's really matters, after all. But we had to pick you up, you see, because I got Mr. R here all curious about you. And also for old time's sake, really—I felt I owed you and me a little interview. My point is, I was pretty set on killing you right up until now, doctor. But my woman here seems to be right—I got to let logic prevail, and there's just too much attention on us."

He glanced at Maritza with what might pass as an affectionate look.

"So now you've helped us to take care of Mr. Ruzga in our own way. You and your lady shrink friend, we're going to tie you good and drop you somewhere. This comes with conditions, and here's how it'll be—I want you and yours to know from this day forward, I'm always ready. We'll be moving on; we'll have what we need to get our little family all started. I just needed to distract Mr. Ruzga long enough, so I wouldn't have trouble from him taking back what's mine in the first place. He always did underpay me, you see. Didn't realize what I was worth."

Brie glanced at the corpse. "He's always been a rough customer, but not so much now."

Margaret squirmed from beneath Ruzga's limp, bloody body, and tried to move into a crawl. Maritza moved up closer and kicked her in the ribs, and she fell prostrate.

Ce Ce watched us all and kept holding Maritza's hand even when she kicked Margaret. She was just surviving, stuck in Stockholm syndrome, I thought.

"I know what you think you want to do," Brie chattered. "I know you got law enforcement all excited. Take

my advice and back off, doctor, and from here forward, don't
do shit. I'm going to go and get my money, and that's all there
is to it. Don't make trouble for me. Then, *adios.* We'll leave
the whole situation alone from that moment, *de acuerdo?*
Because you're a family man soon, and you and yours will
know I can come around anytime I like. Leave us alone, I'll
leave you alone. Remember that— because I can always come
and make an impromptu visit, maybe to your cute little wife,
Ruthie, and even your new babe. She's about ready to pop, I
understand."

"Let Ce Ce go, Jack," I said.

"Oh, no. No, I don't think so. That's not the idea. Ce
Ce's my flesh and blood. I don't have any other relations.
'Sides, you know about the marks. I understand that. I can't
have anybody looking those marks on her heel over, can I?"

I realized right then that he didn't know Arnold had
made a copy in his journal. How could he?

He grabbed my hair and pushed the barrel of his gun
back into my forehead.

"Like that, Barlow. You, Ruthie, and baby makes
three. Family men, they bear this kind of thing in mind
because they got people they need to stay around for. Right?"

He shook my head loose and lowered his pistol. I
glanced at Maritza and realized she'd saved my life.

"You tried to stab me," I said to her, confused.

She shrugged. "I would've killed for that file, doctor.
Now it don't matter."

Ce Ce turned her face into Maritza's lap like I'd once
see her do with Arnold. I figured the plan to kidnap Ce Ce was
in place long before Maritza ever came to see me for her first
session.

"You strung Hector along to help Brie's game and then
stabbed him in the throat when he got in the way," I guessed.
She didn't respond.

"There, there. Be respectful, doctor," said Brie.

He knelt and alternated pushing his pistol into the

backs of each of my head and Margaret's while Maritza taped us back up. He checked her as she worked.

"Tight, baby. No bullshit. Real tight. I want them to lie around for a while. Peas in a pod, right? The two shrinks seeing eye-to-eye."

Brie shifted the pistol into his opposite hand and rubbed Maritza's bottom when she put the duct tape back over my eyes. Her pleasant glance toward him had as much conviction as a rabbi in the Vatican. She'd built the cage she now lived in.

"I like a woman who don't talk much," Brie chattered.

Once we were completely trussed and blinded by tape, they pushed us separately onto some sort of wheelbarrow or cart and rolled us into the back of a truck or van, I'm unsure which. Margaret moaned loudly throughout the operation. I didn't know what she thought she had to complain about. My finger was swollen to twice its size, and I thought to myself that the pain emanating from such a small appendage was quite amazing.

As we were being pushed around, hands kept fiddling with my finger, and that made it hurt like hell. I thought Brie was doing this on purpose, wanting a last yelp of anguish from me, so I almost didn't grasp the tiny pocket utility knife. It was the kind you can fit on a key chain. I almost didn't realize what Maritza was trying to do.

The ride was very bumpy, and my finger throbbed. Searing stabs of pain ran up and down my arm. I was unsure how to keep from dropping the little knife.

"Here's good," I heard Brie say after a long while. "Pull up."

I held the small blade as tightly as I could in my mangled fist but I felt it slipping in the sweat of bumbling fingers. He grabbed me from where I was taped at the wrists and ankles, like a roped-up calf. He was certainly stronger than I'd given him credit for. He flung me into a ditch.

Where the little razor went from there, I didn't know,

but my head went underwater. I held my breath as best I could.

Not much longer, I said to myself, blackness all around me.

Not much longer. He must have changed his mind and decided to kill me.

At the last second, he tugged me up.

"Goddamn, that is so weird," he observed inquisitively and without emotion. "And that was even by accident. Maybe you'd make it, maybe not. Wouldn't have been my doing, right? Then you never know these days, the law being what it is. I thought of what Maritza here wants—keep the heat down, get the money, get a new life, all that. And, you know, I couldn't do it. Couldn't let you drown 'cause she don't want me to, and it's bad business around our future together. Love's like that, Barlow. Now Hector, he bought the farm somewhere out nearby here, doctor. She kissed his lips and stuck him in the throat like he was made of butter, all because I asked her to so we could have our life together. She's that in love with me."

"Be sure to tell little Tessa she has to let bygones be bygones. She's got to let her little sis here go with her real daddy. Tell her Ce Ce's still got family, and nobody has more rights to her than me. Don't try anything is what I'm saying to every single one of you. That's better for everyone involved, if you understand my meaning.

"So long."

I thought he'd just leave but, again, heard the swish and smack of bb's inside a sock and lost my bearings completely. It wasn't hard enough to knock me out, but it might have been some another day. He hit Margaret, and I did hear that. After this, they loaded back up, and drove away. I could hear Margaret nearby a few minutes later, moaning again.

Is that all she does? I wondered to myself, on fire with pain in both my head and finger. I rolled around, using my cheeks to feel the ground. This activity brought back very painful memories for me.

I had all the time in the world now, so I found it.

I rolled around, got the razor into my good hand and cut through the tape. I can't describe how little fun it was getting duct tape off the skin on my face for the second time after he'd taken care to have Maritza tamp it down firmly.

I got Margaret all undone and pulled her to her feet. Dawn was rising in the east, and she gazed all around in something of a stupor, blood spatter still on her cheeks, and a big, rising welt on her right temple. We were standing in a ditch on a back road of the reservation.

She started flailing at me, landing a couple of good ones on my neck and shoulders.

"You bastard! Get off me!!"

I had no choice; she'd flipped out completely. I took her down like I'd learned in crisis management class. First, you grab the back of the hair and then lift the chin up and back. The neck muscles in that direction are pretty weak. I spun her onto her tummy and pulled her hands back behind her again. Then I sat down on her back.

"Get off me!"

"Dr. Fitzsimmons," I said as calmly as possible and recalled the time she'd had Tessa forcibly restrained and injected her with halperdol at Provincial Hospital six years earlier.

"Babe, I'm sorry, but you've got to get control. You were hitting me pretty hard, and we can't have that if we're going to get out of this. Can you calm down?"

She struggled and writhed. I was stronger. She settled gradually.

"Let me go, you son of a bitch."

She got up and started stumbling down the road. I was still trying to figure out where we were. She started to cry and fell onto the gravel, sobbing.

What a baby, I thought.

How ironic is this? I appealed to *Tamanwilá* myself, looking up at the sky. I'm supposed to take care of her? That seemed so completely crazy to me. I walked over and helped her up again. She swung and missed.

"Bastard!" she shrieked, spewing hate. "What kind of people do you get mixed up with?"

I tried smiling but stopped because doing that hurt.

"Obviously, those weren't friends of mine, doctor. We're actually very lucky to be alive."

She spun around and started walking. Then, she stopped.

"I don't even know where I am," she sobbed.

"Dr. Fitzsimmons, babe. Let's take a moment so you can get your shit together."

I'd already figured about where we were—somewhere in the back country leading to White Swan. I even saw a water tower I knew in the far distance.

I began walking toward the tower.

"Are you just going to leave me here?"

"Your choice, babe."

"Stop calling me that!" she yelled, pulling herself upright.

"I work a psychosocial approach, doctor. You mentioned it's out of date, but it's the best I've got. You've got to figure your own path in life for good or bad. I don't have time to help with any more insights than that right now."

I kept walking; she kept yelling, but I wasn't listening. My cell phone rang. I had pretty poor reception.

"Ret?!" said Ruthie.

"Hi, darlin'!"

"Where are you? The connection's terrible."

"Uh, I'm out in White Swan."

"Ret, my water broke!"

"Holy shit! I'm on my way!"

I started to sprint and spotted Cougar Den from the top of the ridge line. I ran full speed down the slope and across the range, tumbling several times. I was vaguely aware Margaret was trying to keep up in her heels, falling, bitching, screaming at me from far behind.

By the time I got to the front door of the restaurant, I was totally winded. A slick black pickup truck was about to pull out of the lot, and I picked up a handful of gravel and pitched at it. The driver's side door opened, and an angry expression peered back at me.

"Barlow?! What the hell?" said Charlie Whitcomb, the ex-tribal cop who had handcuffed me and delivered me to Jack Brie six years earlier.

Having it be him made a strange sort of sense to me. I'd been forced by divine intervention into need and acceptance all in one small second.

I hopped in and hurriedly explained my situation.

"Well, let's move!" he responded.

Margaret was just touching pavement when he patched out of the parking lot. She appeared appalled but there was nothing really unethical about my behavior.

I made it to Provincial Medical Center within half an hour and found Ruthie on a gurney already in the delivery staging area.

"Ret!! What's happened?? God, you're a total mess!! You're hurt! Your head!!"

She stroked my forehead.

"Forget it. I had an accident. Oh my God, I'm so glad I got here. Thank *Tamanwilá*."

"Okay. But you're hurt."

"Don't worry, darlin'. I'm here."

"Ret, Dr. Welch had to induce. Linda's waiting. I'm dilated."

She smiled this glowing, beautiful smile at me.

"It won't be long then . . ."

Linda, large and jolly, bounded through the curtain.

"Ready, Mom and Dad? Let's check."

She lifted Ruthie's gown and took out a measuring tape.

"Oh my, we're almost there. Wish we could get you into a room."

I got faint.

"Ret," said Ruthie.

"No, no, I'm here," and I leaned over and stood back up with blood rushing all through my body.

"Don't fade on me."

"I'm here. I'm here."

Linda looked at me. "Oh my God, what's happened to you!?"

"I'm fine."

"We need to get you some medical attention, Ret. Nurse!"

"Shush, Linda! Not now."

"But you're all red and bloody," she reached into her bag and pulled out some gauze pads. "Here, tamp this on your face. Use the sink and wash up. Is that road rash on your forehead? Are you drunk??"

I sort of lost it. "Not now, goddamn it, Linda!"

"Okay. Don't let the doctor see all that. Here put this on."

She handed me a nursing cap, and pulled it down over most of my forehead and eyebrows.

"Really?" asked Ruthie looking at me with the light blue cap on. She began to laugh.

"Ohhhhhh." She went into a contraction.

"We need to get you a room now," said Linda, and we wheeled her away together.

It was party time on the maternity wing. There were five mothers in labor simultaneously and four rooms. We were stuck in the hall, listening to a teen mother screaming at the top of her lungs. Every time that girl screamed, I kept asking Ruthie if she was okay.

"Ret, it's not me," she finally said. "I'm not

screaming."

She writhed. "Ooooohhhh."

"We're really close," said Linda.

"Close," I repeated.

"Ret?"

"Yeah, darlin'."

"I think I do want something for the pain."

Ruthie had refused pain meds all the way through. She assured me she wanted to keep the whole birth natural. But Linda told her several times, "you might change your mind."

"It could be too late for that," said Linda. "Ret, can you find a nurse?"

I'm sure I looked torn.

"It's going to take a little more time still, Ret," she said, "It might help if dad asks. The nurse's station's around the corner."

I hustled. There was nobody there. I found a friendly, matronly-looking nurse standing at a computer portal.

"My wife's waiting for a room. She's asking for something for the pain."

"Sure," she said sweetly and then shoved past me, "Pain meds to the hallway. Back in half a second."

I returned to Ruthie and Linda.

Linda looked anxious. "I'd say fifteen minutes and she'll be crowning, and we'll let her push. What's the status on the meds?"

I shrugged. "She said she'd be here in a second."

I stroked Ruthie's forehead with a cool washcloth. She suddenly bent forward hard. Even her hair seemed filled with muscle, and frizzed out from her head like a Medusa.

"Oooooooh . . . ooooooooh."

"Breathe, darlin'," I coached.

"No pushing yet!" said Linda.

"I need something," Ruthie cried. "Owwwww!"

I shot back from the gurney and stopped a male nurse strolling by at a clip.

"My wife needs pain meds," I asserted.

He stepped in for a moment. "Excuse me, ma'am."

He started to reach under her gown to have a look.

"Um, excuse me. I'm the midwife," said Linda irritably.

"Oh, sorry!" he responded. "Pain meds. Sure! I'll be right back."

Seconds passed. Ruthie wrenched forward like some hydraulic tool.

"RET! Get me something!!"

Her eyes filled with fire and fury.

"Oooooooh!"

"No pushing!" shouted Linda.

"Breathe!" I yelled.

The teen girl screamed shrilly, "OOOOOH MY GOD! FUCK! FUUUCCCKKK! Oooooooooooohhh!!"

A long groan followed, approving murmurs, deeper groans, more approving murmurs, and then total silence for three full seconds. Then I heard a tiny cry.

My mind and heart snapped fully into the reality of the moment, and I jumped up and ran out to the nurse's station. A very young nurse stood reading a clip board. She was chewing gum. For some reason, her gum chewing annoyed the hell out of me.

"Hi," I said in a totally false tone of patience. "Uh, we've been asking for pain meds for my wife in the hall here, and two nurses said they would bring some by . . ."

"Hmmm," she responded, gazing over the clipboard, and not looking at me. A generational gap opened between us.

She set down her clipboard on the counter and squinted slightly. "Umm, we just had shift change, and I don't see any note. It's been really busy today."

"Could you come with me please?"

She followed me around the corner and into the hallway. She lifted Ruthie's gown.

"Umm. I'm the midwife," said Linda, even more

irritably.

"Oh," said the young nurse, continuing to look and pretty much ignoring her. Then she spoke to Ruthie, "I'll go ask the doctor if we can give you something for pain."

"Thank you!!" Ruthie exclaimed with unusual cheer.

Young nurse disappeared. More weighty seconds passed; another powerful contracture, eyes of fire.

I rounded the corner and saw young nurse standing at the station still looking at her clipboard. I suppose I had a smile on my face, but let's face it, I wasn't at my best.

"Uh, hey there. Were you able to talk to the doctor?"

She looked up. "Oh, sorry! Yes. Dr. Welch is in room Four. She said she'd join you in just a minute. She's having some minor issues with another mother's situation."

Her left hand went absently to the pocket of her scrubs. I watched in astonishment as she slowly pulled her iphone out, chewing her gum.

"GODDAMN IT!!" I roared. "Goddamn it! I want pain medication for my wife, and I WANT IT NOW!!"

I slammed my fist down on the counter in front of her, and her clipboard flipped onto the floor. Young nurse dropped her iphone and bent to pick it up.

"STAT!!" I yelled.

She ran back up the hallway, and Dr. Welch came around the corner.

"Ah, Ret," she smiled, talking smoothly. "I guess Ruthie wants something for the pain." She had a hypodermic in hand and followed her back to Linda and Ruthie. "And, congratulations, you're about to be a new dad. I've got what she needs right here."

She smiled soothingly at Ruthie.

"Ruthie, this is propoxyphene. I can't really give you more at this point, but it will help relax you and take the edge off."

"Great. I don't usually take drugs."

"I know that."

As the medication took hold, Ruthie, who I'd forgotten is very sensitive to any consciousness-altering substances started to gaze at me, even laughing a little during the next contraction.

"Oooo ooooh. Ha-ha-ha. Blue head, red face."

"Darling," I said, hoping she wouldn't draw attention to me. "Try to breathe properly."

Dr. Welch took a glimpse down below.

"She's crowned," she looked at Linda. "Can you solo? I've got a breach birth I'm trying to turn in Four. We just cleared and disinfected Three."

"Of course," said Linda, kicking off the gurney brakes and wheeling us in. Ruthie looked up at me, and I held her hand.

"I love you," I said.

"Me too," she whispered with a slight slur. "Ret?"

"Yeah."

"Do you remember? Oooooooh. Ha-ha-ha. Do you remember? Your blue head. Ooooooh. Ha-ha."

"Okay, Ruthie. Okay, Ret," Linda coached. "Next time. I want you to push."

The contraction came.

"Push!" I said.

"Go, harder!"

"Push, darlin'!" I dabbed her forehead as sweat broke out. "Breathe, sweetie. Ha-ha-ha."

"Oooooooooooooooooooooh."

"Push! Harder! You can do it!" said Linda. "Look, Ret, see?"

The head was almost out. Fluid, blood, shoulder.

"Push!" Ruthie's hair was soaked, her face bright red, Linda lifting, Ruthie finally settling backwards in utter exhaustion.

A girl, a baby girl. Linda lay her Ruthie's belly and reached behind her to grab a pair of surgical scissors. She pushed them toward me.

"Huh?"

"Cut the cord, dad."

And I did.

NINETEEN

The drum is life.
It is the sound of life within you.
It is the sound of life in the world.
When the world ends,
It will sound just once for you . . .
It will ask you if you have been bad or good;
And you can answer only one way
Because Nami Piap is listening.
—*Smohala*

Brie's threats still rang loud and clear through my mind—I'd watched him kill Ruzga in cold blood. Yet somehow I knew that with silence, we need not feel threatened in our home any more. I wasn't about to cross him. Although I'd seen him and Maritza with Ce Ce, not going to the police felt safer for now. It didn't feel right, but it felt safer, and there was no getting around that.

Margaret remained the wild card, however, and after I told Ruthie about all that had happened, we were both very afraid of her big mouth.

We both decided it was time to deal very directly with Margaret.

My first task after we got home was to get hold of her and this proved quite daunting. She'd erected many professional barriers, but I was able to convince a nurse "this is a psychiatric emergency" and finally finagled her cell number.

Of course, she was enraged. She'd paid a Yakima taxi to pick her up in White Swan. She was still irrational, traumatized, terrified, and I was also glad to hear, afraid to call the police. Even if she had called, she didn't know her captors or what they even looked like. She didn't even know where she'd been taken.

However, she'd overheard the names 'Jack' and 'Maritza,' and I didn't like that much at all.

"I didn't know taxis went out there," I began our conversation.

"Barlow, I am going to sue you for reckless endangerment."

"How will you go about that? Look, I'm very happy right now. We just had a baby, Margaret."

"My God, what the hell are you talking about? You ought to be committed. You and me have a baby? You must be psychotic."

"Speaking of lawsuits, there's a lot at stake here. My attorney, who you've already met, is interested in the akisthesia issue you failed to detect providing Franklin's medications."

"That's ridiculous. Utterly ludicrous."

"What's not ridiculous, however," I said. "Is when you really think about it, you don't know the people who nearly took our lives, and you don't really know me or what I might be capable of."

She didn't respond, but I knew she was still there. "And I'm the one who ended up with the broken finger, after all."

"And why did you do that?!" she exclaimed suddenly.

"Do what? Get my finger broken instead of you? That's neither here nor there."

"I want to know why . . ."

"Why I stepped up for you after you put me down and tried to ruin me? Hell if I know—I doubt you'd do the same. But maybe we make a better world if we show some *tmá'aakni* for others, even if we don't like their ideology."

"I didn't catch what you said."

"No matter. I'm asking you to keep this whole thing, all that happened, on the hush hush."

"Or?"

"Remember, I took a shot for you. I'm not saying you owe me, I'm just advising you that these are very dangerous people. You currently have a successful professional position. I'm asking you to forget what we went through for sake of our own safety. There's a young life still at stake in this."

"Ce Ce. The kidnapped sister. The police should know what these people are doing to that little girl, Barlow."

"Do you really believe the police can keep her safe from the people we just met up with? At least what Brie has planned doesn't seem to involve killing her. One thing at a time—we've got a lot of people trying to work on getting her back, the police among them. If you say anything about all this right now, I'm afraid they'll go after Brie, he'll see them coming, and if he dies, you can be sure he'll take Ce Ce with him."

There were a few moments of hesitation.

"Oh, all right."

I clicked off without a goodbye and went back to my wife.

"Hannah," said Ruthie. "Hannah Lillian Barlow."

"It will roll off the tongue when she's formally introduced," I added.

We were lying on our couch with little Hannah swaddled between us. She had blonde hair, which we'd been assured she'd lose. She was now two weeks old, and we'd all been for a walk around the neighborhood.

Lillian, Ruthie's mother, would be visiting from Nova Scotia on Saturday. For now, we hunkered down and snuggled with Hannah.

Leila's pickup pulled in at 6 p.m., and she almost lifted Elisi with the support she gave her up the stairs to our door. Elisi looked very sick. I helped ease her into an overstuffed chair while Leila went back to her pickup to hoist a large wrapped item onto the top of her head.

"What's this?" Ruthie asked. "What's this? You didn't need to bring us anything."

"Oh yes . . ." said Elisi, really struggling for breath, "for little Hannah."

Hannah lay in an antique cradle we'd grabbed at the thrift shop. Leila lowered the package and cooed at her, smiling close-lipped. Then she put the package on Ruthie's lap. Ruthie tore it open from one end and slid a small, navy blue, Pendleton blanket out. These are very expensive.

"It's beautiful," she said, looking it over carefully.

She pulled the rest of the wrapping off, and a handmade, traditional Yakama cradleboard emerged.

"We call it *sk'ín*," said Leila.

"Well, it looks like it will fit Hannah like skin, so I'll remember the Yakama word," Ruthie declared.

"Rim out in the front . . ." Elisi mumbled and coughed, "keeps her from being hurt . . . if the board falls. Rose hips dangling . . . keep her in good health."

"Let's put you in it, little poot," Ruthie said, filled with wonder at the excellence of the craftsmanship. Hannah soon leaned up against the couch, watching all of us as best she could with her newborn gaze.

"Hi, little baby," Leila chimed sweetly.

I noticed aloud how much we missed Tessa.

"She's not up for visiting," said Leila. "She's still dealing with the rape. She wants her sister back like we all do and keeps threatening to go hunt Jack Brie down by herself. Just the other day, she told me, 'I've got unfinished business.' I told her to keep a clamp on it. She's closed to us."

I could see they both wanted to talk more openly. Ruthie looked back and forth between them.

"Don't try to protect me," she said. "Protect every one of us instead. Don't leave me out—I'm warning all of you. I value your friendship, but don't keep secrets from me anymore. Spill it."

Elisi nodded toward her apologetically. *"Tma'áakni,* Ruthie . . . won't happen again . . . it's about those marks. We need to figure more on them once and for all."

She pulled Arnold's journal out of her purse and handed it to me.

"Yeah, Morse," I remembered.

"Let me look at those," said Ruthie, and I handed it to her.

"46.2262334, -121.1364626," repeated Ruthie.

"How the hell??" exclaimed Leila.

"Should have asked me," she said as I gaped at her. "My Jewish *zayde* who taught me how to shoot was a Gideonite. He taught me all about Morse. It's like riding a bike. I see it, and I read it."

I could only laugh loudly.

"Well, we've been together a long time and I've heard stories about your grandpa, but I never knew you knew Morse, Ruthie," I said and tried to explain to Elisi and Leila. "Gideonites were ham radio operators helping Jews immigrate to Palestine before Israel was founded, correct? Her grandpa, her *zayde*, was a Lithuanian Jew."

"Yes, that's my tribe," Ruthie confirmed, and they smiled at her. She pondered the code a bit more. "These are probably global positioning coordinates. Plug them into a GPS, even a smart phone with an app, and it'll take you to an exact spot."

We all gaped at her.

"Well, it's old technology now; didn't you think of that already?" she asked sheepishly. "We used to have GPS treasure hunts at school to help the kids learn local geography before funding cuts. . ."

"Ce Ce," Elisi's eyes went wide.

"Yes," Leila said. "Do go now? Do we call the cops?"

"I don't know," I answered.

"Tina hasn't made a move yet," Leila said.

"We wait," Elisi concluded. "Brie will bait Tina until she tries for the loot. That's what I believe. Then try to eliminate her like he did Ruzga. Leila's friend Michael has been watching all her comings and goings. We wait."

"This is a celebration, this sweatlodge today because our mixed-blood brother and his *áyat* made a baby," said Trick, pouring cold water on red hot rocks before us as Frank and Franklin sat in the dark with us.

It was an 'honor round' and his turn to speak. He was also leading the lodge, so he poured. Trick likes to pour lots of water when I sweat with him as he enjoys hearing me moan. I don't moan at a broken finger, but apparently I do when Trick pours.

"Our *xáy* just donated a tiny speck of himself, his *inásh*, and his *áyat* did all the hard work. It was a hard pregnancy for her being on her back. So think on how women carry us into this world and give everything to their children, you know? The man—he's only got his testicles and a little bit of fun to make babies. The mother, she can have a rough time and have to lay on her back like that to give life to her little one. The mother's carrying her heavy child around, maybe singing or cooing to her belly, caring for it from the start until the time to bring baby outside arrives."

Frank and Franklin both shouted 'ee-ahh', signifying assent.

"His *áyat* grew that little life. And after baby gets born, she feeds and nurtures their new little girl, hugs and cuddles her, getting up all through the night, changing more of the diapers 'cause the man can't do it without losing his cookies."

Laughter ascended, followed by a silent period with more water pouring.

"And then she teaches that little baby about the world. She's little Hannah's first teacher; the father, most times he has to wait until later."

Cascades of hot steam shot up to the roof of the lodge

and down onto our backs.

"So we got to remember our mothers, and we do that in the sweatlodge in the dark here. The old people say this place here is the womb of the mother of all of us, so we need to remember that. We should honor our mothers as much as we can, even if they may not always do right by us. Whoever you call mother, you have to respect who cared for you, who raised you."

He poured two more scoops onto the rocks, and the steam was blisteringly hot on my shoulders. I moaned again.

"There we go. We boil up some of that mixed-in English blood and remember the mother carries all this pain for sake of her child. She can't stand for her children to suffer. Remember that, being a father, my brother Ret. Be thinking on that always, and always do right by your wife and your children."

"At this point," Frank spoke as it was his turn. "I have so much to be grateful for. I'm back here to sweat after so many years. I found family to connect with and help out with, which gives meaning to my life. I'm proud of my new nephew being in here with us, and I know his *tila* would be proud, too. I want to honor this occasion for my brother, Dr. Barlow, and sing a traditional song we have to welcome little ones into the world."

In the dark, he lifted his hand drum and began to beat lightly. The song entered my being alongside his rhythm. I tried to sing with it as others did, but I could only mouth the syllables, not knowing what they actually meant. Still, I felt glad to try to sing for Hannah. I felt stronger. I know everyone there felt stronger .

"Open up!" Trick shouted and the blankets were pulled back. I crawled out with everybody else. I thought he'd stay inside like he sometimes did but he came out, and lay on the ground next to us.

Stars hovered above us, and endorphins rushed all through me. It's a strange and wonderful sensation to be piping hot in cool night air, steam floating up from your naked body. I heard the hoot of an owl nearby.

"Hoot, hoot. _Kɨ'ɨp'ká_. Barn owl," Trick said in the dark.

The bonfire used to heat rocks burned low next to us, heating my left side, while my right side started to chill.

"What's it mean?" I asked.

"Means—I'm hungry!" Franklin answered, also on his back and looking up.

"Doctor's asking if it's a sign of something, right?" asked Trick.

"Okay, okay," I tried to back out of his teasing.

"It's a sign the owl is hungry," Frank laughed.

We held quiet for a long while. Then a coyote howled.

"Now, there's a sign," said Trick. "That means something."

"What?" I asked.

"Owwww," Franklin mimicked. "Means 'I'm hungry too.'"

"I'm all done," Trick laughed, getting up to shower himself off with a garden hose. He dried off and started dressing.

"Hey, what's up with the girl there?" he asked me.

"Ruthie?" I asked.

"No, Tessa."

"What do you mean, uncle?" Franklin asked. "Sis has just been through a lot and got out of the military sideways— not the best way, you know."

"Yeah, I know all that, but she's still pretty mixed up, eh?"

He lit a cigarette. I started drying off and getting dressed.

"What do you mean?" Frank paused as he turned over.

"Oh, my buddy Alfie works at the Feed and Sow in Yakima yesterday. She wouldn't talk to him."

"She's been that way," Franklin explained. "Leila and

Elisi wants to get her brushed off Shaker way."

"Yeah," Trick pulled again on his cigarette. "Well, she seemed all angry. She was looking an M-4 over."

"What's that?" I asked.

Alarm had already crossed Frank and Franklin's faces, and they looked at Trick pensively in the glow of the dying fire.

"Commando gun," he told me. "That's what they call it. Colt M-4 Commando. Civilian issue AR-15, no automatic fire. It's probably what she carried in MP school. I mean some folks hunt deer with a gun like that. People do."

Frank tossed his own smoke into the embers. "Just not usually."

"Tina's on the move," Elisi whispered weakly through the speaker on my cell phone. "I'm too sick. . . that young man, Michael, he called Leila. He said Tina was pulling on some girl from her recovery group named Amy to drive her out to White Swan."

"When?"

"This morning."

"And there's something else . . ."

I waited.

"Tessa got those numbers from Leila. Darn Leila for leaving out what she wrote down from what Ruthie said. She's gone."

Her voice became guttural, juxtaposed by both the weakness of illness and the emphasis of worry. "She's going to try to kill that devil . . . I know it . . . she's got herself a rifle, doctor. Franklin got caught trying to take it from her room and she whooped on him."

"We have to stop her," I said.

"I'm too sick. . . please. . . follow those numbers, doctor."

"The police are watching all of us."

"Don't matter now. . . she'll get herself shot dead. . .

please stop her."

I explained to Ruthie the moment I got off the phone.

"Call the police, Ret. Even if they can't do anything."

I got hold of Agent Alston first because I had his cell number. I told him about the coordinates.

"I should arrest you for obstruction of justice."

"Fuck that, Agent. Do it later."

"Stay home where we can contact you. I've got a lot to do." He hung up.

I walked over to the corner by the front door and picked up the Marlin where it stood. I went into the bedroom, affixed the sight, and grabbed two boxes of ammunition.

When I came back out, Ruthie was nursing Hannah on the couch. She looked at me with very sad eyes.

"Ruthie . . ."

"Don't, Ret. I know."

"I can't let Tessa . . ."

She put her fingers to her lips. "Die. Shh. Hannah's asleep."

I bent down and kissed her and Hannah. I'm no soldier, I thought to myself. I just couldn't let Tessa get killed.

"Come back home, Ret," Ruthie said, looking up, lips trembling.

I nodded and finding no more words, I left.

I didn't have a GPS application and wasn't smart enough to know how to use my smart phone like that anyway. The Radio Shack clerk must have thought me crazy purchasing the last, beat-up demo he had in portable GPS devices and asking him to plug in coordinates for me. I didn't have time to read the manual. He explained the general principles, and I ran out of the store.

"Treasure hunt?"

"No!" I shouted behind me. "Well, sort of . . ."

I was being directed toward Signal Peak, which was no surprise, but I wasted precious time driving in various directions thinking otherwise. It was 3:30 p.m., and the air was crisp with late fall; the sun would set near just after five o'clock. I had very little time left.

Past White Swan, I saw two sheriff's cruisers including Deputy Anderson's and felt very lucky they were talking to each other while looking in the other direction. A state trooper with his flashers on suddenly sailed up behind me but then passed. At least he didn't know who I was. I didn't want Alston to know I'd disobeyed him.

About a half mile distance ahead, I could barely make out somebody on horseback cantering across the road. For the first time, I thought of Ámashitum and wondered where she might be. I passed a herd of *k'úsi* on the left along Signal Peak Road and sped up.

As I approached the guardhouse for the closed area, I realized I hadn't any way to get through. There was no time. Jacob's yellow retriever came into view and barked loudly as I pulled up. They both recognized me and came bounding up.

"I gotta go in!" I shouted, rolling my window down.

"Not without a permit, doc, and a tribal member along."

"Sorry! There's lives in danger."

He leaned up against the window and paused.

"What do you mean?"

"Tessa Miyanashatawit been by?"

"Maybe ten minutes ago in her auntie's truck."

"She's in danger. So's her sis."

Flashing lights came up in the distance, and he looked up at them. No sirens.

"Say, what the hell's going on?"

"No time. Jacob, you've got to let me pass."

Just then, a helicopter lifted over the pines on top of the ridge at our left. The sun was setting, and his searchlight was already lit.

"Damn," he said.

"Jacob . . ."

I patched out and away from him, skidding my car between the gate and a nearby tree. My left mirror flew off as I sideswiped the tree. State cops, county cruisers, and two unmarked black Ford Expeditions came into my rear view mirror pulling up on Jacob where he stood now pointing at me. I shot forward, and my Gran Fury's ancient engine knocked loudly. I was asking way too much.

"Come on, dear . . ."

There was a bend in the road. I glanced at the GPS, and the battery was fading.

"Fucking cheap . . ."

I used one hand to zoom out, and saw the arrow pointing at my destination straight ahead about a mile as the crow flies, while the road route was about three miles more. A two-track presented itself to my left, and I took it. The Gran Fury took the heat I poured on until I got about a quarter mile in and the road ran out. I slammed so hard into a dip in the road that she stalled out. I tried a couple of times to restart her until the steam began to rise. Cracked radiator. At least no one was behind me.

There was still daylight on that side of the ridge. Signal Peak stood above me and on my left, and I could even see the top of the lookout tower. The pine forest ahead was dense, but the top was quite bald, just as Elisi had described. It was starting to snow a little, and the ground was slick and wet. I grabbed the GPS, took one more glance, clicked the menu button, and noted there was a selection for 'Last Destination.'

I turned it off, picked up my rifle, loaded it, and tossed extra shells in my pockets.

I walked straight ahead to where my mind's image of the last screen pointed to on the GPS. At about 400 yards, I heard movement and crouched low. Voices sounded close below me. Slowly, I crept forward, flicking the GPS on as quietly as I could. It pointed to where I heard the voices. I fell prone, and began to ease myself forward along soft ground in toward a stand of virgin pine.

Every nerve in my body was alive. My hands trembled, my heart surged, my mouth tasted like burnt paper. I had no idea how close or far away they were. It took me ten minutes just to go thirty feet. I finally made the tree and eased up into a crouch. I leaned my head to peer around and heard Brie talking.

He was no more than fifty yards away in a clearing, surrounded by small brush and briars. It was a perfect locale, hard for anyone to close in on and not be seen unless you were able to get through the blackberry thorns directly below. Maritza was standing and watching him near a small group of short pines.

Ce Ce stood in front of her.

Brie was taking apart a large stack of stones. Most of them had sharp, flat edges; they weren't round and smooth like the river stone that gets heated and used in sweatlodge. I assumed those stones had been piled there by human beings, likely Yakama and other native people, at times of retreat or vision questing. I guessed most of them were andesite.

He looked up suddenly, peering around for danger, and then poked back into the pile like an old raven after something that glittered. Jack Brie was about to finally get Ruzga's money.

There was no sign of Tessa or Tina, but I knew they were both likely there somewhere.

Tessa had the GPS numbers, and she was now a trained soldier.

I could only surmise she already had Brie sighted. If she shot first, she'd go to prison. If I shot first, I would. I had no idea if I could kill a human being, but I believed I could kill Jack Brie.

The noise of the chopper took me completely by surprise. When one floats up from behind a ridge like that, they can tip the props so that sound waves mostly bounce down and backwards.

The chopper dropped down like a hawk on prey,

focusing landing on the camp, blinding anybody looking up. At that same moment, an armored SWAT vehicle charged through small brush to my right. Brie was across the span between him and Maritza and Ce Ce. He grabbed Ce Ce as he pulled his Smith & Wesson from the back of his waistband and shoved it up against her head.

So much for father and daughter bonding; my greatest fear was being realized.

I now had a reason to do what I had to do. I shouldered Arnold's Marlin and centered him in the scope. All movement slowed down. The helicopter landed, and men jumped out in black tactical gear; they were quickly signaled into a crouch and wait posture. The armored vehicle stopped. Everything went still. I chambered a round and eased my eye forward while I pointed. My finger was on the trigger, I was watching the movement of his finger on that pistol. He kept waving it around and then pointing it at her head. I couldn't make out what he shouted at them.

On his very next wave, I'll do it, I said to myself.

His arm went upwards, and my finger tightened on the trigger.

"Drop your weapon!! Now!!"

I heard two loud gunshots. That was all.

"Drop your rifle, Barlow!!"

Did I shoot? I did. I was full of adrenalin; it was totally surreal. I looked ahead—Jack Brie lay on the ground, making seizure movements. I'd hit him with the first shot.

He was dead.

Ce Ce stood completely still. Maritza was running back into the woods behind her.

Only then did I turn to look behind me.

Detective Dolynda Jacinto and Deputy Almont Anderson were pointing shotguns at me from about fifteen feet back. I dropped the Marlin as they demanded, went completely prone, and pushed my hands out in front of me.

They took me into custody.

"I killed him," I confessed. "I heard two shots, but I only pulled the trigger once."

Jacinto and Anderson looked at each other, and then shook their heads.

"No, doctor, you didn't pull the trigger at all," said Jacinto. "It wasn't you."

Anderson acted bemused while escorting me down a path and into the camp. He listened to his shoulder radio for a moment which was all gibberish to me. I felt very odd—like I was staring down a tunnel trying to see toward the other end.

"Tessa pulled the trigger, doc," said Anderson.

"She killed him?" I asked, perplexed and then horrified. I didn't want her to do it. I didn't want her to go to prison. "But didn't I shoot?"

"No, doc, you didn't shoot. You really didn't. You were about to, but it was Tessa."

"Where is she?"

"Right over there. SWAT's taking her into custody, but they're being uncharacteristically loose about it right now. She apparently tackled Brie's girlfriend before their team got to her."

"Ah." I was in a fog. "Tackled Maritza?"

Tessa was hugging Ce Ce; they were both crying. Two tactical officers stood nearby, watching the woods, pointing their rifles at the ground. Anderson walked me past the body.

Jack Brie's eyes were empty saucers, much like Jamie Jamison's. He was flat on his back and looked totally relaxed. It occurred to me that he may never have been so relaxed in his life until that moment. Whatever sordid life details populated his brain, making him who he was, prompting him to rape, maim, steal, or kill, he only stared at the sky completely empty of thoughts or desires.

If Jack Brie had a spirit, it had fled. He'd been released from the prison of self and the struggles of life.

The police let me go mostly out of expediency, rather

than because they wanted to do so. There were various things they were really mad about—obstruction of justice, interfering with law enforcement, criminal trespass, even possession of an unregistered weapon.

I think it was hard on them that I readily admitted to everything they said. I figured Tessa and Ce Ce were alive, Ruthie and Hannah were safe; everybody was now okay. I wasn't even dead. My mildly euphoric attitude shook them up. Prosecuting me for crimes that would make them look incompetent would end up making me look better than they thought I deserved. I don't think Detective Jacinto had to work too hard to talk the prosecutor out of the idea. Even so, she wanted to read me the riot act.

". . . and we'd love locking you up in Yakima County jail because some of these charges would be felonies, and you could do time, which is what you deserve for being so unbelievably stupid as to take the law into your own hands."

I tried to appear chastised. "Sorry about all that, Detective."

"The county prosecutor, however, is up for reelection and doesn't seem to value having you on her hit parade. From my end, I can even understand *some* of what you did. Maybe you got between a rock and a hard place. But we know very well how you held out on us, and my professional policy says that's unforgiveable. I can't do my job with people like you around."

I just gazed at her. I was so tired, and she seemed to have so much energy.

"Get out of here. Go home to your family, and think about what I'm saying. You were willing to shoot down Jack Brie to protect Ce Ce. If you'd really used your rifle, missed, and hit that little girl, you'd be seeing your wife and new baby every couple of weeks for a half hour over the next ten to twenty years. You'd also find it very hard to live with yourself. Think about all that, Dr. Barlow."

I said thank you for some reason and started to leave.

"Um, speaking of rocks and hard places," said Special Agent Alston, who'd been listening with his overly casual expression. He reached into his briefcase. "Deputy Anderson wanted me to pass along a souvenir."

He handed me a small rock, and I looked it over, hefting it in my palm.

"Andesite?"

"Yeah," he nodded. "It's not the same one, of course. But he said tell you it's all over the place up there."

The next morning, Tessa was charged with the murder of Jack Brie. Ruthie nursed Hannah, and I held the newspaper. We read with quiet, embittered faces, not knowing what to do.

Several hundred demonstrators surrounded the Yakima County Jail—from old to very young—many dressed in full regalia, standing side to side and holding signs and placards: 'No Justice, No Peace. Know Justice, Know Peace', 'Thank You, Tessa', 'Our Land, Our People, Our Children,' or even more simply, 'Free Tess, Bury Brie.'

The prosecutor remained adamant, issuing a statement that "vigilantism will not be tolerated," and "Tessa Miyanashatawit took the law into her own hands and will be held to full account for the murder of Jack Brie.'

Elisi, Frank, Leila, Ruthie, and I plugged into several brief visitation slots held separately at different times of day. I was the last, and they brought her in cuffed and shackled. She was the second Miyanashatawit I'd seen held in bondage by the police in the last month. *Walak̲'ikláama.*

I hoped she'd speak, but instead, she stared at the floor. I had seen her that way at the tribal jail nearly six years earlier when she was only fifteen years old. I felt I'd failed her somehow. I thought about Arnold. He thought so much of her and tried to guide all his grandchildren as best he could—he had lived his life to avoid an outcome like this.

"I didn't do it," she declared to the table she gazed upon.

"Wha . . .?"

"I didn't kill him, Barlow. My aim was wide, and the cops were closing in. I got nervous and shifted when they charged up."

"But you fired your rifle."

"And I didn't hit him."

"So that means that I?!" I stammered.

"Barlow. Not even if you wanted to. You never fired. You have to get over that. I appreciate you trying to protect Ce Ce and me, but Jacinto was clear. You can even go by and pickup *tila*'s old Marlin at the evidence room as long as you get it registered in the next few days. Jacinto said that, too. They already looked it over; your barrel's totally clean."

"They say you killed him."

"But they're wrong, Barlow," she looked directly at me then. "I know what I did and didn't do. I fired—once. It went wide!! I saw brush jump behind him. I wish I hadn't, but I missed."

"Time's up," said the guard, who'd been listening to us with a pronounced smirk. Her face pleaded with me as he pulled her out through the doorway.

She wanted me to believe her.

Two days later, Frank Munoz called. We'd given him two hundred dollars out of the twelve hundred remaining in our entire bank account as a retainer to represent Tessa. I'd spoken to Frank immediately after I'd seen her about what she'd claimed. He talked to the prosecutor directly and, not surprisingly, was met with unbridled skepticism.

Everyone knew Tessa had lots of reasons to go after Jack Brie. The prosecutor considered Frank's challenge to be defense counsel posturing and suggested some negotiable room to bring the charges down to voluntary manslaughter on a plea because she was clearly provoked by Brie's years of assaults and intimidations of her and her family. The prosecutor even mentioned an insanity plea might be agreeable.

"Ret, the whole situation started to make me very curious, and I decided to send my paralegal and another young woman who works for me out there. That wasn't easy—I pulled a few strings and got a bondsman named Charlie Whitcomb who used to be a tribal cop to take them there. He told us he owed you and Tessa a favor."

"They still had the place taped off, but not around where we wanted to look. Anyway, we estimated about where Tessa had situated herself and taken that shot at Brie. Then they used a metal detector Whitcomb brought and damn if they didn't find a .223 round matching an AR-15 along the ridge directly behind where Brie was standing. They photographed the spot, the likely shooting area where Tessa had been, and the round before turning it in to FBI ballistics to match the gun. We were not met with big smiles at the prosecutor's office when we notified her."

"It's pretty certain we can prove she missed," he answered. "That all came down late yesterday. Here's the twist: I got a call just ten minutes ago from the coroner. He just finished the autopsy. The round they found in Jack Brie's brain was a .32."

"A .32?!"

"Yeah, a pistol round."

"How??" I responded, but a distant awareness nudged at me. "Well, what do they make of that?"

"Well, there's a bunch of folks back up there looking for a pistol at this point," said Munoz. "Clearly, there was another shooter. At first, we thought it was Tina, but she never even made it out there. And Charlie Whitcomb said he found some fresh horse tracks behind that stand of pines."

"Did he tell them that?"

"He told me . . ."

"Are you going to tell?"

"Hell, Ret, I'm sure many native people ride around up there all the time. I'll leave it to the prosecutor to determine what's circumstantially relevant to her case. I'm not in the business of doing forensics work for my clients unless it's going to help them."

Tessa was out of jail with all charges dropped the next afternoon. Frank Munoz, JD, tireless in his efforts to make a living, proposed to her that she consider suing for false arrest.

The county prosecutor was terribly irritated and, having a sense of Frank's style, vowed that any such idea could encourage her to look into charging Tessa with interfering with police operations. A legal stand-off ensued, and Tessa was allowed to walk away free from further scrutiny.

TWENTY

Though darkness produces this sleep and quiet,
Is not the water of life in the darkness?
Are not spirits refreshed in that very darkness?
Is not that silence the season of heavenly voices?
For from contraries, contraries are brought forth.
Out of darkness was created light.
                                    —*Rumi*

Several days prior to Brie's demise, Ámashitum had been discovered running around open range behind Adams View housing project. A family by the name of Brandon recognized her and got her corralled using a couple of apples and some sweet talk. Emily took their call at Leila's, her plan being to surprise her moody and alienated sister with the news. But Tessa had already bought the Colt rifle, and Franklin had just fought unsuccessfully to get it away from her before she stormed out of Leila's. So Emily didn't tell her.

Leon Kusitway explained this to me while Ruthie, Hannah, and I sat on cedar timber benches filled with Miyanashatawit kids, Frank, Trick, his girlfriend, Florence, Edward Kusitway, and Leonora Waldrup in the dining area of the Seven Drums Longhouse. I was surprised to also see Dr. Arundhati and Alice and Warren Neir join us.

Elisi entered in a wheelchair pushed by Emily, and they began an animated conversation with Leila by the kitchen. Tessa held Chase in her lap. Ce Ce leaned on her arm. They both looked very loved.

"I still qualify for law enforcement," she told Ruthie and me.

"I'm really glad," I said.

"General discharge is no big deal for tribal law enforcement. From there, I can at least get some experience."

"That's great, Tessa," Ruthie said. "Will you be able to go to school?"

Tessa looked at Chase. "Yeah, but with all that's happened, my dream is changing. I'm looking to scholarships. I'm staying away from the money-maker college."

Then she glanced at Elisi talking with Leila and caught my eye.

"Barlow, you knew *kála* was sick when I headed off to the Guard. You and Leila both knew—*kála* wouldn't tell me. I wish you you'd let me know."

I shrugged. "I can't violate a confidence, Tessa."

"I never would've left Chase with her if I knew how sick she's been. I should never have gone."

Emily was rolling Elisi over toward us.

"Doesn't matter, Tess," said Ruthie. "Don't feel guilty. It's how Elisi wanted it."

"I meant what I said not just about *kála*, Ruthie," answered Tessa, " but also 'cause of my daughter's needs. I want to do what I been put in this world to do, and that's take care of her and help her grow. I can become a cop at the same time. I get that now. I just can't get over that *kála* would let me get away with all I did and not say anything about being sick."

Chase leaned into her mother and wrapped her arms around her neck.

"How's my Ce Ce?" asked Elisi when Emily had her nearer to us.

"I'm okay, *kála*," Ce Ce answered. "My bad dream is all over now, and I been waking up to better days."

"No nightmares?" I asked.

"A couple," she confessed. "But I'm back home with everybody and glad my mom's locked up again on parole violation. That man is dead, and nobody can hurt us now."

"We'll need to get you brushed off Shaker way, I think, and also maybe your first time to the sweatlodge has come," said Elisi. "That should start you moving away from the ordeal you gone through."

"How are you feeling, Elisi?" Leonora Waldrup chimed in.

"Better today—my breath is better when I'm getting carted around this way. Good and bad overall. I'm all ready to meet my Maker," she smiled passively at the judge.

"*Kála*, hush," said Emily. "Please don't talk like that."

I don't think Elisi was annoyed, but she became stern. She started speaking loud enough for everyone to hear.

"You may've learned nobody hushes me easy, dear. Now don't worry so much. Looking around here at all my family today, I'm just saying I know I'm all ready to move on. I've had a long life."

An awkward silence ensued with so many close people facing the truth of her decline. She seemed to find this mildly amusing.

"You all look pretty confused. The disordered society, which I sometimes call the dominant society, but that's what it really is—disordered—they want to hide away death from you and me. But the Yakama people, we often see it much closer than most. So let me speak to that because I feel much better today, and I have my *breath*, which I know won't be with me much longer.

"Children," she looked at Chase and Ce Ce specifically. "What you need to understand is I *am* going to die, and I won't be around you no more. I know you might think on me and miss me, but I've had a very good life. Let me walk on. Let me go where I want. That's how I've always lived. Now, on this day here, when we're all come together to celebrate Franklin here," she gazed at him lovingly, "I get to witness everything made right and that includes him getting onto the right road. *Pinana'nak'núuwit*, Franklin—you have turned yourself around, and you finally know who you are and the strong family you come from—like your older sister learned some time back. We're come together to celebrate you becoming a new provider for your people."

I glanced up and noticed many more people were beginning to hover nearby, some having just arrived for the First Kill ceremony, others having been there for a while. They wanted to listen without intruding. Several stopped and crowded in near the tables. They'd formed a broad circle around the entire Miyanashatawit family, and their larger circle surrounded a smaller circle.

"*Pina ch'achanwit wawnak'sash*, all you girls and boys," Elisi addressed the children, but her words weren't just for them. "What I'm saying is you *must* take care of your body and follow our unwritten laws by not polluting yourself with alcohol or drugs. Save your sexual feelings for someone you love and marry."

Eloise giggled.

"Oh, I know what you feel and how that is; I was young once. Just remember the disordered society all around us wants you to act otherwise. They want you to believe you don't amount to much. Your body is a sacred gift to the one you love. I'm a very old woman with nothing to lose in what I have to say; I don't care who's listening except *Tamanwiłá*. I'm telling you none of what the disordered society says about you is true. Don't believe it.

"*Tamanwiłá* give you your sacred life, and your self-awareness, and put a strong spirit in every one of you. *Átaw pxwin* is two words I'll share with you from our Yakama language. Don't worry if you don't know it, because our language was taken away from us. We just have to take it back. What these words express is what the borrowed language can hardly say—and that is to practice looking closely at yourself and this great and beautiful world all around you every single day, always be aware of your thoughts and feelings, pray with gratitude for the life you have, and use your mind to learn, which includes taking your schooling very seriously.

"*Pinana'nak'núuwit* is another word I'll teach referring to the self-care you need so as not to put yourself down if you make mistakes or get on a bad road for a time; just remember to go back on the good one," she looked at Franklin and Tessa, "don't give in to hopelessness. Be brave. *Yáych'unal!*"

Frank smiled, although you'd have to know him to be able to tell.

"Your heart knows where the best path is, just like *k'úsi* always knows how to get back home. Stay healthy in your body and mind. Doing this for yourself is balanced with *wapítat ttáwaxt* which means to do all we can to help our community here, help our families live, heal, grow, and this means always trying to serve others in whatever way you can think of—chopping wood for the old folks in the winter or bringing food you've gathered to others.

"Don't be backbiting or gossiping," Elisi glanced at Alice Neir, who blushed. "Oh, I know it goes on around here, but our unwritten laws forbid it, and you already know how wrong it is to carry on about others when you should be looking to grow your own heart and spirit. Bad words and stories carry the hurt of others forward for many years, even generations.

"We have to keep up with this good way, our Yakama ways, because the disordered world around us is a very harsh place right now. It's the human beings stuck there who've made it that way for the most part, and it's the humans who will also make it better. That's why *Tamanwiłá* lets us choose how we'll go—because we make our world for better or worse.

"*Timnák'nik* is our word for being compassionate and always extending everything you do in this world right from your loving heart. That is what I'm trying to tell you kids today as to how to live. We humans are leaves of one tree, and *Tamanwiłá* tells us as indigenous people of this land that *because* of all we've lived through across generations, we can help heal our fellow humans. What we have in these ways has been preserved since time immemorial and against every form of hardship, war, poverty, and oppression you can think of. We've got to heal ourselves first, and you children are the key to all that.

"Life moves very fast, I can tell you. I been getting old, and I'm tired and not very well. I am nearly done, but I'm not sad at all about that. I can only really talk to you about what you need to do from this point forward."

I heard a quiet choking noise emerge amid what was otherwise utter silence. Leon Kusitway was shaking his head slightly, dabbing his eyes with a dirty bandana.

"What I'm laying out is not the easy road, I'll say that, but it's what I've tried to follow, and the same way both your *tila* and *ála* took to while they were still alive. You'll find others, especially in the disordered world, living easier, taking advantage, acting selfish, hurting others, talking trash about anybody who's fallen or failed, just to make themselves feel better. Some of this has infected our own Yakama people. Only you and some sort of close relationship with *Tamanwiłá*, the Universal Voice," she looked at Dr. Arundhati, "Brahma, Allah, or whatever name somebody happens to know, whatever you need to make you a *real* human being, what brings us here to this time and place to try to live our lives fully and lovingly; I'm just saying always be listening, looking, and noticing *what* speaks to you and through you *in a good way.*

"Way I see it," Elisi glanced at Chase and then at Ruthie and Hannah, "None of us are too different than this cedar log here," she tapped the bench I was sitting on.

"I was a little baby like this pretty white one over here only I come in the red model," several people laughed out loud. "Like the cedar tree made this log, I grew from a very tiny seed. But I got movement, sense, and my voice. That don't mean the wind and trees don't talk if we listen. All these things that make me and you alive in this life are temporary and come on loan to us from Mother Earth. We must never forget that. And like that tree made this bench, we get to become useful. I get to sing my own song, and so do you.

"That's no different than you," she spotted Samuel, "you," she spoke directly to Leonora Waldrup, "or you," she settled her eyes on Ce Ce and finally on Eloise.

"Today there will be songs for Franklin, and that's very good. I want to ask you how after we all leave here, how are you going to keep up singing your own life? After all, a song and a drum is all we are."

Eloise looked back at her intensely for a long moment, and you could have heard a pin drop.

"If all you say is true, kála, I am going to sing very loud."

"You do that, dear," Elisi answered her. "You do that. And you go ahead and test out the truth of my words."

Frank chuckled at this. Eloise continued to gaze at her with great seriousness.

"Well, let's go in, Franklin," she continued. "Emily, thank you for rolling me around. Gravity's tugging too hard lately, and it's harder to stand. If it's all right, I'd like Franklin to push me inside for ceremony, this being his day."

We entered together—hands over hearts, spinning counterclockwise before entering the cavernous longhouse with its great span of cedar beams, planked on either side for separating women and men.

Apparently, during a celebration such as this, we were to sit in more of an audience style facing the front on the cedar benches. We faced the east together, the land of the dead— I glanced at Ruthie, who handed me Hannah, drunk on breast milk—and I nuzzled our baby, aware of the great symbolic contrast laid out in the direction we faced.

With some difficulty, Franklin wheeled Elisi over a small ramp and across the longhouse dirt floor, closest to the front. Seven drummers stepped forward along with the longhouse leader. Franklin came up onto the planking next to him. He stood straight and tall in a black tear shirt with blue ribbons, the black patch covering his right eye socket. I'd loaned him the shirt, the only regalia I owned, because he didn't have anything to wear for the occasion.

The leader gave the signal, and the drums held the rhythm of the human heart, the voice of the singer echoing across wooden walls. I'd been to enough reservation events to recognize an honor song.

Several young men carried out a table from the longhouse kitchen stacked with frozen elk meat, cut up into innumerable portions, and wrapped in butcher paper. As the drumming continued, they began distributing this abundance of packages to everyone present. The longhouse leader gently moved Franklin forward to stand in front of the drummers and singer while they continued, picking up an old microphone, and calling out over the music:

"This *wawúkya*, this elk, being Franklin Miyanashatawit's first kill, in bringing it to us, he can now no longer be thought of as *áswan*, a boy. He is now a man, *ináaw*, and a provider. He used his uncle's rifle, spotted this animal, asked for his help, and took him with but one shot and one eye to target. Franklin would like to give these portions to you and your family in memory of his *káła*, Georgina Miyanashatawit."

The prohibition against saying the name of the deceased therein found exception as Georgina's spirit was invited back to witness her grandson's accomplishment. A young man moved through the rows, handing Ruthie four huge, wrapped elk steaks, which she struggled to fit in her lap while I held Hannah.

I looked up, and Franklin was being handed Frank's Winchester .308. Frank rose up from his seat near us and came onto the planking to stand next to him.

The song ceased, and the longhouse leader spoke:

"The hide of Franklin's first kill is being cured and

tanned. When it's ready, the hide, hooves, and teeth will be donated to our longhouse for those without adequate means wishing to make regalia."

He paused before holding up the rifle.

"The rifle used in this first kill is now gifted to uncle Trick in honor of the memory of Franklin's *tila*, Arnold Miyanashatawit."

Trick moved carefully to the front and stood on the other side of Franklin, accepting the .308 with a smile. I knew this was my cue. Leila shifted to make a little room, Ruthie stacked the elk meat in the space between them, took Hannah from my arms, and I got up.

As instructed by Frank, I climbed onto the planking and went over to the table the young men had brought in. I picked up the last item and carried it to the leader.

He held Arnold's Marlin 30-odd-6 up high for everyone to see and waited a few moments before lowering it and looking it over himself.

"This is a very good rifle your uncle Ret and auntie Ruthie are gifting back to you, Franklin. I've known and shot this rifle when it was your *tila*'s and am very glad it will stay in your family. You should use it to feed your family and provide for our people."

He handed the Marlin to Franklin, who held it with reverence.

"*Kw'áała*," he said very quietly, glancing up at me and then nodding at Ruthie.

"*Kw'áała*," I responded, returning thanks and congratulations.

The drumming and song came up again behind us, continuing for a few more minutes.

From where I stood, I could see everyone, and I surveyed the faces. Leon Kusitway's eyes smiled at me. Leila beamed at Franklin. Tessa tickled Chase, who sat in her lap. Leonora Waldrup whispered to Edward Kusitway; Ce Ce had her arm around Samuel. Ruthie held Hannah and nodded at me knowingly.

I stood facing all this human life, my back turned to the land of the dead.

Elisi appeared before me in her wheelchair and for just a second, I saw only her, grey hair thinning but still very long, twisted into tight, uneven braids. The skin sagged over her high cheekbones. She was quite stooped in her seat, leaning her elbows on the rails. Her mouth was firm and as resolved as ever I'd seen.

From where she sat, she stared head on toward the land of the dead. Very slowly, she winked at me, and then her lips shifted into her Cheshire cat grin.

I hung up my cell as Ruthie, and I walked out to get the car.

"That was one of the Yakama Nation Firefighters," I told Ruthie. "He said I could use his name, and he'd get me a permit to camp out at Signal Peak lookout now that fire season's over. He said I could spend a night out there if I want."

She caught the suppressed excitement in my voice and teased: "Hmm. And is that something you want to do, Ret?"

"You already know."

"Because you want to convince yourself there's no such thing as Sasquatch or UFOs."

"Or stick people."

"What in the world?" she asked, but I only smiled.

Maritza took the easy road out although I was sorry she did it. She hung herself in Yakima County jail cell number six the Friday night before I left to camp at Signal Peak. She was Tessa Miyanashatawit's first arrest and was awaiting trial for murder, attempted murder, kidnapping, fraud, and a host of other things.

Her real name was Adelaita Ramone, and she was from Michoacán. Her father was a Kusitway, according to Leon, who once knew him. Nothing more was known about

SIGNAL PEAK

her history or her family or whether they were still alive. Leila said she didn't want Ce Ce to ever know what happened to her. Ce Ce had told Leila that Maritza was a nice person and treated her well while she was held by Jack Brie.

Tina was adjudicated, back in jail, and up for prison time. No one expected to see her again for a while.

Jack Brie's ashes were placed in a plastic urn and are still in storage at a cemetery building up in Yakima city somewhere. No one ever came to claim his remains.

Ruzga's money was eventually found. It had deteriorated in its plastic ziplock bags to such an extent as to make the bulk of it unredeemable. I understand law enforcement and the county prosecutor donated what was still legal tender to a substance addiction center for pregnant women. There was about two thousand dollars when they got it all cleaned up. Three bad guys—Jack, Christophe, and Hector—gave their lives to help soon-to-be mothers recover from drug and alcohol addiction, a fitting form of restitution it seemed to me.

I never saw Margaret Fitzsimmons again. She quit her position at Provincial Medical Center and left the area. I heard she was out in Boston practicing with the Harvard zealots, diagnosing childhood bipolar disorder right and left. I ended up wishing I could've helped her more. She was quite a troubled person, in my professional opinion.

Elisi died on the Sunday after Maritza took her life and was buried on the Tuesday before I went out on my own to Signal Peak. She died in her sleep which was surprising because pancreatic cancer usually has a longer demise. I think she willed her own death. She had that kind of strength to choose when she wanted to go. Yakama Nation shut down to observe her funeral, and we felt fortunate to be able to come to say goodbye.

She was too wise and too good to mourn in a manner unbefitting to her wishes. By way of doing our part to honor

her and because I called her *kála,* we put away all pictures of
her the day of her funeral until we could participate in the
memorial and giveaway to honor her a year later.

While we weren't a part of her dressing, Ruthie,
Hannah, and I were asked to stop in at the longhouse toward
the middle of the overnight prayer vigil. I was permitted to lay
her *ititamatpamá* with her inside her casket before the
morning service.

I really had no idea what this item even was until Tessa
explained the *ititamatpamá* was Elisi's "time ball," a kind of
personal calculator. It was made by weaving strands of nettle
grass into a very long rope of twine, which she added to again
and again over most of her near eighty years. In various
sections, she'd tie knots, bows, or other patterns so as to
remind herself of all the important events and critical lessons
of her life. In a matter of speaking, Elisi's *ititamatpamá* held
all her important memories.

I gazed down at her form. She'd been dressed in her
best cotton dress and handmade moccasins with complex
beadwork seldom seen outside the art of the Yakama. Her
hair was adorned in beautiful otter fur and feathers, her face
colored with rouge, and her hands laid carefully across her
abdomen. She looked very calm, and I thought of the times I'd
seen her praying and meditating.

I swallowed back tears, knowing it wasn't correct for
me to cry then. Tessa handed Elisi's *ititamatpamá* to Ruthie
first, wound into a tight ball.   Ruthie held it up to Hannah,
balanced in her arms. Hannah immediately tried to pull it in
her mouth. Ruthie pulled it away from her, and Hannah
sulked, but not before she'd kissed it.

We'd all touched this *ititamatpamá*—Tessa, Leila, the
kids, even Frank, Ruthie, Hannah, and now me.

It was very important for me to transcend my own
culture's revulsion for death and be as deeply present as I
could to say goodbye. I eased forward, reached out, and gently
lifted her cold hands, sliding the *ititamatpamá* into her grasp,

so she could take it with her to the spirit land.

In this way, we would all be with her—our memories and hers, our touch and hers.

I'd set up camp not too far from where the final confrontation with Jack Brie occurred. Maybe I seemed crazy to do so, but that's how I wanted it. Fire spotting season was over, and it was getting pretty cold. There was snow on the ground. The fire chief thought it strange I didn't want to take the cabin he offered, but after he gave me the full tour, he accepted my explanation that I had many feelings to process, given what I'd been through. This must have seemed like something a shrink would say.

I sat and waited for the light to dim on Wednesday, bundled up warm but shivering some near an open fire inside a little fire pit.

Snow was falling harder when I heard them. They were astride Ámashitum who puffed a bit of vapor out her nostrils as she came through the pines. Her winter coat was coming in. They both wore heavy Pendleton jackets.

"*Shix klowat*, Emily," I said. "Hello, Tessa. Owl Child, hey there, good horse."

"Hey, Barlow," Tessa said easily. "It seems you figured something out. We thought we might run into you."

"I'm not as dumb as I look," I smiled at them both. "I heard you tell Trick you planned to ride back to the scene of the crime this week. I figured out why. I bet you'd pick Wednesday. "

I looked hard at Emily. "How did you . . .?"

Emily looked hard back at me from atop Ámashitum.

"I may have told you, doctor," she reached back to Tessa and grabbed a tuft of hair and pulled. "Yakama sisters got each other's backs."

"Ow!" Tessa responded playfully.

"I been riding Ámashitum so much before she ran off," Emily continued. "I'm pretty good at it. Tessa started going the wrong way and was set to get herself in big trouble. I promised myself a long time ago I'd look out for her like she done for me back when we were little."

"How'd you even know where to go?" I challenged her. This question had stumped me.

"Doctor, I was the one discovered that code in *tila*'s book. You think I didn't write it down for myself before you all got your hands on it? I set my mind to figuring it out like everybody did. Once I had the meaning, I googled over the internet and hitched a ride out to Adams View just as soon as Tessa run out of Leila's house with her new rifle to try to go after Brie."

"I knew it was all on with her at that point because she took her fancy new rifle with her. Well, Brandon family's got a horse trailer, and Mr. Brandon loaded us up. He dropped me and Ámashitum out this way, and I saddled her up as soon as I got her unloaded. There were cop cars flying all around, but I took to the old trails."

"I might've caught a glimpse of you riding across the road on my way out," I surmised.

"It's easier getting back this way on horseback than by car. I told Mr. Brandon he'd better get on back to White Swan quick before the law saw either of us."

"You killed Jack Brie. You killed him with a .32—my pistol. Where were you hiding? I didn't see you anywhere."

Emily just stared at me. Tessa reached around and held her hand up in front of her mouth, which Emily shooed away.

"Nothing more needs answering, Barlow," said Tessa. "I don't want to know, and you don't really want to know either. You can still come down to the river with us if you want. Just don't ask no more questions."

"How far?"

"About a mile," answered Emily.

"You both know this area?"

"Like the back of our hands. *Tila* used to take us 'round here often," Tessa answered.

"Can I walk it?"

"Sure, but we're going the easy way, and that's on Ámashitum." Tessa reached around her sister to scratch her wild horse's mane.

With difficulty, I climbed down with them to the banks of the Klickitat River below Signal Peak. The brush and brambles were nearly impenetrable, but somehow we found our way. I heard water rushing furiously through the shallows. *Kluní*, the bald peak, soon loomed far above us.

They both dismounted and Emily reached into her jacket pocket, pulling out the Taurus 85, a pistol I'd never even fired. It still looked in good shape. She handed it over and asked me how to take it apart as if I knew. I tugged a utility tool out of my pocket and gradually sorted out how to tear the pistol down to parts and pieces.

"Still the Eagle scout, huh, Barlow?" Tessa teased.

We took turns tossing the parts as far out as we could get them into the deep sections of the current.

I suppose if you work hard with a metal detector, you might find a few pieces downstream somewhere south of Parrot's Crossing. Then again, you may just find some old nails and junk from the settler days.

I doubt it'd be worth the effort even if you happen to work for law enforcement.

Emily and Tessa were confident they could make it back to the front gate on Ámashitum to meet up with Mr. Brandon.

Before they mounted back up, I turned to Tessa.

"I've got something of yours that I keep forgetting . . ."

"Oh yeah," said Emily in recognition.

I reached deep in my pocket and handed Tessa the Navaja knife given to her by Parker Heslah.

She backed up in shock. "How did you ever get hold of that?!"

I explained what I knew of Jack Brie stalking her and the family for the last two years. I described the fight with

Maritza, and how the knife had come full circle back home.

She held it in the palm of her hand like a talisman. She opened and inspected it. There is no other knife quite like it— it's very sharp and dagger-like for a folding knife. She'd once used it to stab Jack Brie in the neck. Parker had given it to her before he lost his life, and it was likely the only object he possessed relating to his own father.

Tessa hefted the knife a little and gazed out at the Klickitat River. She lifted her arm to throw, but then stopped herself.

"Nah," she said and shook her head, smiling at me, then at Emily.

She slipped the knife into her jean pocket, and she and Emily mounted back up on Ámashitum's back. She turned to wave at me as they began the climb back up the trail.

She looked kind of shy to me—like she did when I first met her.

I found myself alone, frying a small frozen river salmon I'd bought from a stand near *Nch'i-Wàna*. I was in no way competent to catch salmon myself, but I still wanted an authentic meal. I only had the one night before getting back to my wife and child.

I used lots of butter and salt and pepper. I mixed in sage plucked nearby and even had some wild potatoes the fire marshal gave to me. My non-alcoholic beer was ice cold. I folded up my blankets and set them in the indent of a low boulder.

It was cold as hell by nightfall, and the fire had died down. There are no words for the stars that emerged; no city or even country lights could drown their glory. I pulled my sleeping bag outside and lay beneath the Orionid meteor shower. The universe stretched out above me; my body, gripped by earth's gravity, compelled me to pay attention to the vastness overhead.

I saw nebulae, galaxies, and an infinite number of

worlds, even the black hole towards which the Lakota point the doors of their sweatlodges was somewhere out there.

I became just one more spinner of atoms and electrons, quanta and empty space merging with coyote's call and the sound of owls, poorwills, even the subtle surge of a fluttering bat.

I was about to crawl inside my tent, nearly dead with sleep when I sensed movement in the sky and turned, thinking I might spot another meteor.

Strange lights flew along the southwest horizon, stationary at first but then soaring up high over Pahto, the mountain goddess. They made no sound. They flicked rapidly back and forth.

They weren't meteors, or aircraft, or swamp gas, I'm sure of it.

I accidentally left my salmon bones on a rock by the fire embers, not a smart thing to do when you're in bear country. In the morning, the bones were gone and not a grease stain or a trace was left on the rock. It was as though I'd never set them there.

I didn't encounter this puzzle for quite a while. The flaps to my tent had been tied in knots—from the outside— and I had to cut through them with my Swiss Army knife in order to escape.

It was probably just some kind of fire spotter prank.

GLOSSARY

ála: paternal grandmother; paternal grandchild

áswan: boy

at'aw pina shuukt: 'recognize who you are with love'

átaw mí̲xa: important or valuable uncle

áyat: woman, wife

chilwit wapsú̲x: devil

Cualquiera que sea, esta es una mierda que tengo que vivir con (Spanish): 'Whatever, this is shit I have to live with.'

ináaw: young man of marriageable age

inásh: seed or sperm

ínk átawi mash: 'I love you dearly'

ititamatpamá: time ball, traditional technology for maintaining memories

i̵tút: 'your father'

kála: maternal grandmother; maternal grandchild

k̲i̵'i̵p'ká: barn owl

kluní: bald head

k'úsi: horse

kw'áała: thank you

k̲w'shím: disruptive, unruly, mischievous, stubborn

náktkwanin ttáwaxt: act responsibly for sake of family

Nami Piyap, Tamánwi̵łá, x̲ni x̲tuyt ku Tamánwash, Nami Piyap, Tamánwit: 'Elder Brother, Creator, dig down deep for Spiritual Power, Elder Brother, Maker of Laws'

nána: man's older sister or man's older female cousin

nápayu'nash ttáwaxt: 'protect my family'

Nich'i'wana: Columbia River

núsu̲x: salmon

Páchi'analá: 'Mean Bird'- a huge monster bird of Yakama legend

piná'i̵waat ku kw'ałáni: 'gives it all away,' self-denial, humility, and gratitude combined *pinana'nak'núuwit:* taking care of oneself; maintaining good health

pina ch'achanwit wawnak'sash: personal dignity, self-preservation, purity, chastity

Pinátł'uyank, tílaaki pyúsh! Ch'ishklá!
Wyasaptayákyaw Tamanwilá! Kwyáamtimt niwít!:
 'Shame on you, daughter of a snake! Liar! Swindler toward the Creator! Honesty, now!'

shix klowat: good evening

shix pawchway: good afternoon

shuyápu k'usik k'úsi: 'white female dog'

Spilyáy: Coyote-trickster of Yakama legend

Tamanwilá: Creator in Waashat longhouse religion

Tát savitúr várenyam bhárgo devásya dhīmahi dhíyo yó nah pracodáyāt (Hindi): 'Source of all, deserving all worship, radiant Divine One; we meditate upon you. Propel our intellect towards liberation.'

Tat'tat'liya: Twin sisters from Yakama creation legend

tila: maternal grandfather

tiskáy: skunk

tm'áakni: respect

timnák'nik: 'extending from the heart', compassion

túktu: hurry

túta: father

twáti: medicine man or woman, Indian doctor

walak̲'ikláama: 'one who ties another in bondage', police

wáwyukya: bull elk

xáy: man's male friend, 'friend-brother'

yamesh: deer

yáych'unal: courage

Unless otherwise noted all words are from Yakama language. For more information on Yakama definitions, grammar, and pronunciation practice the reader is referred to the excellent resource, *Ichishkíin Sínwit Yakama/Yakima Sahaptin Dictionary*, by Virginia Beavert and Sharon Hargus (2009) from University of Washington Press.